LONG STORY SHORT

A MERRYMOUNT SERIES

ILA SIKORSKI

9¢
welcome to
22¢
a merrymount series
Long Story Short
6¢
13¢
87¢
ila sikorski

To the survivors.

AUTHOR'S NOTE

Dear Reader,

As a writer, I think (okay, really *hope*) all of my stories are special in their own kind of way. I write with that same hope that a little something will stick with at least one person with every word, chapter, and book I write.

I always knew *Long Story Short* was going to feel different.

This story is for me, because it is partly my own. It's heavy and hard, and I spent a long time with a lot of these thoughts and feelings locked away, terrified of the ugly being given any sort of light.

I didn't want to be scared and hiding in shame anymore. Daisy Stiles didn't deserve to sit with it all either.

I lit those nasty thoughts on fire and in the ashes, found…this.

If you or someone you know experienced sexual assault or harassment, you are not alone. There are resources that can help you heal and offer support for both survivors and people close to them.

The Rape, Abuse, and Incest Network (RAINN) has a 24 hour, 7 days a week support line you can reach over the phone or by online chat.

The following page contains a content note and a list of trigger warnings.

CONTENT NOTE

Long Story Short is an adult romance novel.

It addresses the FMC's past sexual abuse (recounting events to a character on page) and the MMC's childhood abuse. There is verbal and emotional abuse, drinking/alcohol, explicit language, accidental and planned pregnancy, open door intimacy, childbirth, self-sabotage, anxiety, and depression. Readers who may be sensitive to these subjects, please take note.

A spice guide has been included in the back matter of the book outlining the chapters that contain explicit sexual content for readers who wish to find or avoid them.

THE PLAYLIST

long story short by Taylor Swift
Dial Drunk by Noah Kahan (with Post Malone)
Big Boy (SZA) - Sped Up Remix by Virality
us. (feat. Taylor Swift) by Gracie Abrams
Nosedive (feat. Lainey Wilson) by Post Malone
You Might Not Like Her by Maddie Zahm
The Bolter by Taylor Swift
Sailor Song by Gigi Perez
Peter by Taylor Swift
Messy by Lola Young
Afterglow by Taylor Swift
waiting room x fix you by get lost stranger
Funeral by Phoebe Bridgers
Cinderella Man by Eminem
All I Ever Wanted by Dean Lewis
18 by One Direction
I Lied, I'm Sorry by Chloe Qisha
Praying by Kesha

RECAP O'CLOCK

To catch you up to speed…

Gwen finally accepted the love she always deserved and made a home with Miller and their daughter, Penelope. Oh, and the cat. Ladybug.

Margot and Sawyer are expecting surprise twins and have asked Gwen and Miller to be the godparents to one, while the town's favorite archnemeses, August and Daisy, are godparents to the other.

So, now August and Daisy have to either put aside their differences or ditch altogether.

They hate each other.

Absolutely nothing could go wrong.

Aaaaaand that's what you missed in Merrymount.

PROLOGUE: AUGUST - THE BLUEBERRY FESTIVAL

J'm telling you right now, I'm not letting Daisy Stiles
fuck this up for me.

And I'll tell *her* just as much as soon as we get out of earshot
from the only people on the planet who've ever given a shit
about me.

Margot's words hang in the air, and I realize neither Daisy
nor I have responded. I glance at Daisy beside me, and for half a
second, I see the teenage girl who listened to me when I thought
no one cared about what I had to say. But in the other half of that
second, I see who I'm actually up against, and I feel my face form
a scowl I try like hell to suppress.

Her mean mug I'm sure matches my own, but we agree
silently to drop it. For now.

"We can manage," I say after clearing my throat.

Margot and Sawyer just asked me and Daisy to be godparents
to one of their twins Margot is currently growing. And we
agreed.

The café bursts into celebrations of cheering and hugs and
kisses among everyone I care about in this small town. I've come
to learn they'll always accept me for exactly who I am, and I'm

not the guy who's hooting and hollering in a setting like this. So I take my rightful place by backing out of the crowd to watch from the outskirts.

Once again, Red's Place is home to the grandest of announcements and celebrations. In the past couple years, the café has been host to secret half-siblings uniting for the first time (hello, Margot and Miller), a joint surprise birthday party (Miller and P, I'm looking at you), a Thanksgiving that thankfully did not end in WWIII, but came pretty damn close to it (apologies from both Daisy and me), and now a pregnancy announcement times two for Margot and Sawyer.

Damn. Sawyer's gonna be a dad. My best fucking friend. Although now I think his title leans more toward brother. One minute we were messing around after school, getting into trouble and trying like hell to not get caught by his grandmother, Beth, and now we're here. Getting married and having babies.

Well, he's there. I'm just kinda on the sidelines.

I don't hate that part, though. I wasn't destined for the family man life. Didn't have it growing up, can't expect to be able to manage it as an adult.

When Sawyer woke me up this morning telling me he needed to take a drive, I somehow knew right away that something was going on. Whenever Sawyer says he wants to take a ride, he means he wants to go to his parents' gravesite, and I've considered it a privilege to be included every time he's invited me.

I held back as we approached the stone markers that sit side by side, letting Sawyer have his private moment first. I tried really hard to not eavesdrop, but it was next to impossible given the fact that we were the only two living people in the whole lot.

"Margot's pregnant. I'm gonna be a dad, guys," Sawyer whispered. I watched my best friend-turned-brother place his hand at the top of his mom's headstone and let his body drop forward. I could tell the rise and fall of his back was from crying. No shame in that, but I know he didn't want a show.

I didn't know about the twin or godparent thing until five minutes ago though. Kind of wish he thought to clue me in on that, so I wasn't standing here feeling like I just had a pie thrown in my face.

Why do Daisy and I need to be roped together for all of this anyway? Can't we love the rugrats on our own like we do with everyone in this room already?

They're probably sick of you starting fights and ruining things, I think to myself. Smells like meddling. I'm ashamed and angry that it's probably valid at this point.

Sawyer claps me on the back, breaking me out of my silent stupor. "Sorry I didn't tell you sooner. Margot wanted it to be a surprise for everyone. I know you heard me earlier though."

"Well, Mr. and Mrs. Hale weren't exactly chatty this morning. Woulda been hard for me to not overhear. I'm happy for you, man. This is huge."

Sawyer chuckles; dark humor has always been his thing to cope with loss. "So I gotta ask, do you really think you and Daze might have a shot at working it out?"

I sputter, "There's nothing to work out. Me and Daze don't belong in the same fucking sentence. But I'll do better. You have my word."

"And your word means…" The voice is the sound of nails on a fucking chalkboard.

I turn my head to see the devil herself leaning against the doorway, a lollipop sticking out of that loud ass mouth of hers. She's in one of those frilly white sundresses that flounces out because of the way her hips curve. The top is tied around her neck into a giant obnoxious bow. Her curls, that are in fact as black as her goddamn soul, sit picture-perfect flowing over her shoulders. I don't watch her tongue swirl around the bright red candy.

I don't watch her eyes track mine as I do either.

"You know what?" Sawyer looks between the two of us. "Duke

this one out. Get it out of your system." He throws his hands up and walks away, back to Margot. Daisy and I both watch him immediately wrap his arms around her. I don't think we'll be seeing much of them separated over the next eight or so months.

Snapping out of it, I gear up for yet another verbal battle with Daisy Stiles despite the promise I just threw at Sawyer. I'll vow to be good after this. "Save it. If you feel like you can't be an adult, let Sawyer and Margot know now. I promise I won't miss you when you go."

She rolls those piercing blue eyes, and I hold myself back from throwing another insult at her. Daisy straightens from her lean on the doorframe, bringing her to the remarkable height of barely 5'4". Terrifying. As you can tell, I'm shaking in my boots.

"I don't trust you, August. Never will. But I know *I* can manage not royally fucking this up. Can you?"

I step into her bubble. It's infuriating how she's always been the only person who doesn't back away or cower when I crowd her space. My irritation intensifies when I inhale and get hit with her scent. Always an overpowering floral that gets stuck in my nose for days.

"Yes," I say on the exhale. "For them. I don't give a fuck what you think about me."

"Yeah, you've had no issue making that abundantly clear."

"I'm afraid I haven't because you're still fucking *here*."

"And where would I go?"

As far as the wind will take you is what I want to say. But I don't. I have an unspoken line with Daisy that I never cross. From the outside, others think it looks like we always take it too far, and don't get me wrong, we do. But I'll never throw her words in her face. Words and secrets and admissions that were never meant for me.

"Forget it. Let's just—" I heave a deep sigh. I don't think I'm a bad guy, but I don't think I'm one of the good ones either, so this is taking a lot out of me. "Look, Daze." My first mistake is making eye contact with her. My second is every word that falls out of my mouth from here on out. "You hate me. I'm never going to be your biggest fan." She scoffs. *Typical.* "But for some reason everyone here still gives a shit about us. We need to drop it. For them. For the babies."

Daisy shakes her head, clearing whatever emotion was trying to break out of her. I watch the metaphorical light bulb turn on above her head. "Want to make it a competition?"

"Huh?"

"The twins have some time to cook, right? We agree to put our differences aside for as long as Margot's pregnant, and when you break the truce—"

I bark out a laugh. "Don't go assuming it'll be me."

"Whatever. *If* one of us breaks the truce, the loser walks away. Not like, entirely. I'm not evil, asking you to hightail it out of Merrymount or anything, although I wouldn't hate that…" She mutters the last part to herself. "But the winner gets first dibs on all family get-togethers and events going forward."

"That's insane."

"No, it's not. If we can't coexist for the most innocent forms of life, then there's just no use in trying. Frankly, they"—Daisy motions to our crowd of people—"don't deserve us at our worst anymore."

If it was coming out of anyone else's mouth, I would have instantly agreed. It's actually kind of genius. I'm not telling *her* all of that though. "Hmm," I start non-committedly.

"I know you're only not saying it's a good idea because I came up with it. Don't be fucking dense, August. For once."

"Ah! There it is." I wag a finger at her. "You'll never survive this. You'll be out before we find out the genders. You know what? Sure, Daze. Let's shake on it. Nine months, me and you, buddy-buddy." I hold out my hand.

When her tiny fingers attempt to wrap around mine, I almost pull back at the shock. Static electricity must be weird today. I don't know. For how small her hand is, the grip is tighter than I expected. It'd feel fucking amazing wrapped around something else.

And that's the intrusive thought that tells me I haven't been laid in a while, if I'm thinking about Daisy Stiles anywhere near my dick from a simple handshake. Nothing a quick night out can't fix. Nothing to cause alarm.

"As much as this pains me to say...deal," Daisy agrees. She snatches her hand back in the next second and takes a step towards where Margot and Red are gushing over ultrasound pictures. "For the record, Gus, I don't...I don't hate you."

For some reason the only thing my brain can come up with is a one-word answer. "Okay." With that, she turns her back to me.

It wasn't a compliment, it wasn't an admission of affection or close to anything you'd write home about. But for the first time in ten years, Daisy Stiles said one singular sentence to me that wasn't an insult or jab. It was just a simple fact she felt the need to drop on me.

And I have no fucking clue what to do with that kind of world-shattering information.

Because Daisy Stiles hates me. It's one of the few things I've known with complete sureness.

And if she doesn't, then...

Well, if she doesn't, then it changes nothing. She's still the most insufferable, stuck up, bitchy, unreliable, messy woman I've ever come in contact with. We still mutually can't stand the sight of each other, and when she loses the dumbest kind of bet she could have come up with, I'll get to enjoy this makeshift family I'm somehow included in without her breathing down my neck.

CHAPTER 1: AUGUST - GODPARENT TO GODPARENT

One Month Later

*A*nother day, another dollar.

I couldn't tell you why my piece of shit stepdad's dumbass saying is the first thing that pops into my head every single morning when I wake up. But here I am, slamming my fist down on the old digital clock I have on my nightstand to snooze the fuck out of the alarm, repeating those four words for no reason.

Sometimes I wish those memory wipers from *Men in Black* existed. Can't say I haven't thought about using one a time or two. Can't imagine how nice it'd feel to wake up and not be bogged down by years worth of bad memories.

Things aren't so bad now, I remind myself.

I rub my hands over my face, forcing myself to fully wake up. When I finally open my eyes, I'm faced with the remnants of the mistakes of the night before. There are empty beer bottles lined up next to the bed, clothes discarded around my room, and a pale blonde woman has made herself comfy on the other side of my mattress. She's passed out with her bare ass up in the air. The only thing covering her is a shirt of mine I doubt I offered, given the fact that every single drawer of mine is hanging open like a raccoon was rummaging through them.

Shit.

Don't remember inviting her in here. Don't really know how I'm supposed to get her out either. This is, uh—this is a first.

Not my first time with a woman, fucking *obviously*. But it's the first time I've let myself go too far and not get her out the door, safely in a ride home from literally anyone besides myself before passing out.

I blame Daisy Stiles for this.

If she didn't get me all riled up last night, I wouldn't have been looking to blow off steam any way I could, after she pushed every fucking button I have trying to get me to crack on this insane bet we agreed on. I would have known better. I do know better.

"Hey." I poke the blonde. She doesn't budge. I sigh deeply and try again. "Hey, uh, it's check out time, honey." I internally cringe at the pet name, but fuck if I know what else to call her.

She groans into the pillow and starts to wiggle, trying to get closer to me. I throw my legs over the side of the bed and push myself up.

"Wait, where are you going?" she asks. "It's so early. Let's go back to bed and pick up where we left off."

"Let's not," I say, standing with my hands on my hips, surveying for any further damage. I spin to face her again. When I get a good look at her, not a single familiar thing pops into my head. I couldn't pick this woman out of a line up. I sort of feel bad. "Wait, where'd we leave off?"

I normally sleep naked because I normally sleep alone, and I just realized I'm still in the same clothes I left the house in last night, jeans and all.

"Well, you weren't exactly in the *mood* for fun last night. Going on and on about flowers and how much you hate them because all they do is eventually cause a mess or *whatever*. It was annoying. But like, in a cute way, y'know? It's okay, August. Like I said, we have time now…" Nameless Barbie rubs her palm on my sheets, seemingly inviting me back into my own damn bed. Alright, I'm irritated.

"It's Gus. Only family can call me August. And thanks for the offer, but I'm passing. And you should be on your way. I'll leave you to get dressed." I turn to stalk out of the room when I hear her whine.

"Are you always this grumpy?"

Christ. Why is she still *here?* "Yeah. Best leave so you don't have to deal with it."

"Come on, Gus, don't you want to play?"

"No." The one word answer will have to suffice because I'm shutting the door behind me before she can say anything more. I do hear something solid slam against the door though.

* * *

"I'm telling you, I've never seen this chick in my life," I say with my head cradled in my hands. I'm sitting in a chair at Red's, hunched over, elbows on my knees, nursing a migraine. Serves me right for my stupidity. "And she moped around the house for a whole fucking hour after I told her to leave."

The unidentified woman wouldn't shut up, bitching and moaning the whole time about how she thought I'd exceed my reputation and instead, I disappointed her with my lack of enthusiasm in the bedroom. I couldn't give less of a fuck. I just wanted my silence back.

"Did you even get her name?" Miller questions.

"Why the hell would I do that?" I ask incredulously.

Miller shakes his shaggy head of hair while laughing. "Yeah, guess you got a point there. But, what happened last night? Everything was cool and then you kind of took off."

With my best friend Sawyer being preoccupied with the

imminent arrival of his two children and taking care of his pregnant fiancée, Margot, I haven't really wanted to burden him with bitching about Daisy. I mean, the both of us bitching to and about each other is the whole reason we're in this mess right now, trying to keep our shit together and make things work for everyone we love around us.

Well, I'm trying. She's just insufferable.

I think I can talk to Miller. He's a cool guy. He and that little girl of his fit right in here in Merrymount. We've gotten to hang out a lot over the past year or so, and while I'm not usually in the habit of expanding my circle, they're the kind of people I make exceptions for.

I look up and do a quick scan of the café, assuring no one important is eavesdropping. Red and Penelope are yapping at each other while Red chaperones Penelope filling the pastry case with cinnamon buns. Chris, the town weirdo, is working the cash register. Not really sure how he scored a job here, to be honest. There's a few Merrymounters scattered around tables and sitting in booths. No one I think would give a shit, but I lower my voice anyway. "Can I tell you something, godparent to godparent?"

"Is that…is that a thing?" Miller asks earnestly.

"I'm making it a thing. Look, we all know Daisy and I—"

"Have weird beef that you refuse to talk about but make everyone suffer through repeatedly? Yeah. Yep. Mm-hmm." Miller leans back against his chair and throws his hands up behind his head.

"Alright, I don't think it's that bad."

Miller raises an eyebrow.

"Okay, it's pretty fucking bad. We're working on it."

This gets Miller's eyes to widen. "*We?* As in you and Daisy…together?"

"Yeah." I shake my head. "No. Not together. Just—Okay, listen, we made a bet. We can't be outwardly nasty to each other. First person to crack loses."

"Loses what?"

"Don't worry about it." I'm giving him enough information. He doesn't need to know the stakes. No one needs to know our personal business or details.

"Ooookay. So, what? You're just like, trying extra hard to not knock each other out?"

"Basically." It sounds really fucking dumb when he says it out loud. We should have been able to do this without some ridiculous ultimatum. But our foggy logic and reason doesn't help us too much when years of deep-seated loathing sits on the forefront of both of our minds.

"Can I ask how you guys got to this point?" Miller questions.

No. I instinctively want to snap, but I don't. "I'm trash, she's not. There really isn't more to it. But anyway, she's not holding up her end of the deal. It's like every time we have to see each other, she does everything in her power to get a rise out of me. I'm struggling."

"At the risk of you squashing me—"

Red slides her arm around Miller's shoulders and plants herself right on his lap. "You're just as much trouble as she is," Red finishes Miller's sentence.

"What the hell? When did you start listening in?"

"Eyes and ears everywhere, August. You should know that by now. Come on, you know just as well as the rest of us you started that little squabble last night."

"I did not," I argue. Although my memory is hazy, and I'm defending something I don't have a lot to go off.

Red and Margot have insisted on these weekly dinners with everyone for the past couple months. It's usually all fine and good, I even look forward to it. But last night, Beth suggested we all go out, and she'd hang back with Penelope. Again, cool. Sounds like a blast in theory. But Daisy, without a buffer like Mel or Beth, is a damn nightmare.

She's just *everywhere.* Bumping into me while I'm waiting to get a drink, cutting in front of me in line for the bathroom, interrupting me when I'm talking to someone we both know. She's a gnat that won't go away no matter how much you swat it.

"You know I really don't care to get involved in your bullshit," Red starts and I nod. I do appreciate she's one of the few who chooses to ignore the ongoing battle. "But you're stressing Margot out, and I can't let that happen." I stop nodding. I'm about to get a Red Bozelli beatdown.

"You were an absolute animal last night, and *not* in a good way." She adds the last part quickly with a stern face and a wag of her pointer finger. "I watched the whole thing, and I was stone-cold sober so don't even try to argue with my replay because you were sloshed. Daisy wasn't bothering you. She was minding her own business on the opposite side of the bar. She was having *fun* when you smashed the glass you were holding."

"I...what?" I look down at my hands and see the new small scratches on my left palm quickly scabbing over calluses and other healing scars from work. It's something I never would have noticed; I've never had soft, clean-cut hands.

"You yelled at her. For asking if you were okay. A new low, even for you."

The black spots in my memory start to fade slightly, and I remember concerned blue eyes looking up at me, small fingers frantically plucking little shards of glass out of my palm, a high-pitched voice that's never matched the dark and stormy features of her face asking me what happened. And then I recall the booming of my slurred words telling her to back the hell up and go back to...

Go back to chatting it up with Ben Caponi. One of Dean Fitzgerald's cronies who I can't fucking stand. That's what I saw that caused me to squeeze too tight on the glass that was holding my whiskey. I don't know why, but it pissed me the hell off that Daisy was giving him the time of day. We don't associate with that group of assholes. She knows that.

"The bright side is Margot and Sawyer had already left!" Miller tries to lighten the mood. Of course he's Mr. Positivity now, seeing as how he landed Red.

I'm happy for him, for both of them. Sawyer and Margot, too. But damn, it kind of sucks to be one of the last ones standing. I thought there was more time before everyone around me was ready to settle down. Everything's changing.

"Why was she talking to Ben anyway? C'mon, Red. You know he's bad news." I'm trying to change the course of the blame here, but with the way Red's staring me down, I don't feel like I have a prayer.

"What're you talking about? It wasn't Ben. It was his younger brother, Derek."

"Derek's—" I start.

"Home from his deployment. That's what she was doing. Welcoming him home, you ass," Red snarls. She's feisty as hell today.

Miller looks between the two of us and chuckles. "Oh, shit. You thought wrong, bud."

"Watch it, Caswell. I'm not in the fucking mood," I threaten.

The truth is, I know I'm the asshole here, and I don't want to admit it. If I really wanted to be honest, I'd say I was looking for any reason to get into it with Daisy last night. I wanted her to be just as bent about this whole ordeal as I am.

Daisy doesn't seem flustered at all, and it's annoying the hell out of me. She keeps pestering and poking, making me see red every time I turn and look at her. Her witch cackle haunts my nightmares.

I don't want to be the one who cares.

"Gus, aren't you over it? Can't the war just...be done?" Red asks, and it hurts to hear how hard it sounds for her to say.

But then she doesn't wait for my answer. She keeps going, clearly set on airing out a few grievances now that she has my attention. "We're older now. No one's asking you to settle down.

We all know you like your distance and your freedom." Red chuckles, but I don't join her. She's right, but that doesn't make it sting less when I hear that no one expects me to do more with my life. Or want more, for that matter.

"We're just asking you and Daisy to put aside the drama. It's a waste when you're both individually amazing people who we love so much. Because we do love you. Both of you."

"Didn't I just tell you I'm trying?" I huff.

"Not hard enough, Gus. Something tells me that even if the Ben/Derek mix-up didn't happen last night, something else would have set you off. You were itching for a fight and for once, Daisy wasn't looking to meet you in the middle."

Red's wrong. They all are. They just don't know Daisy the way I unfortunately do. She's always down to go a round or two with me. Hell, she's the one firing first most of the time. I messed up last night, but that's one time out of a thousand.

This was stupid. Looking for advice from a bunch of people who wouldn't get it if it hit them on the head was a dumbass plan. I'm better alone. I'm more than fine with the silence.

And there's not a thing in this world that would convince me to wave the white flag of surrender with Daisy fucking Stiles.

CHAPTER 2: DAISY - INTRODUCING THE STILES FAMILY

The Journal of Daisy D. Stiles - Thirteen years ago

*H*ey.

I feel stupid starting every one of these with some sort of greeting. You're just a diary. Or a journal—diary feels too much like something I'd cry over in middle school. That's not what this is. It's just a place for me to put the extra thoughts. The ones that would get me into trouble if I let them fester too long in my brain. At least, that's what Dr. Saltore says.

Anywho, a new kid enrolled today. He's actually standing across the guidance counselor's office, his broad back facing me, leaning over the counter. He's waiting for his class schedule to be printed. He's large. I know I say that about everyone since I'm constantly looking up at heads towering above my short height, but I mean it this time.

He takes up a lot of space and his voice sounds like thunder rolling in on a summer afternoon. It gave me goosies, journal.

I shouldn't address you by name. That's weird.

Back to the giant. I didn't catch his name. For as booming as his voice was, I caught nothing of what he said. My brain turned to mush when I watched him enter the doorway, and then that mush melted away to nothing when I clocked the tattoo that looks like it climbs the length of his torso peeking out from under the worn and torn T-shirt that stretched upwards when he hiked his JanSport up on one shoulder. I didn't know kids our age could have tattoos. Maybe they can't. Maybe he's not my age after all.

I want to know everything about him, and I'm also scared shitless of ever having to hold a conversation with him. I want the answers with none of the risk that comes with communication. I'm hunched over Ms. Riccardine's desk, pretending to be fully immersed in this entry to avoid the off chance of him turning around and making eye contact with me.

There are two things I know for certain. I'll add to this list as new facts come to light.

1. My heart started racing in a way that would be concerning to a doctor when he walked in the room. It felt like the universe's way of telling me to pay attention.

2. My mother would strike me dead for having a thought like that about a boy like this.

THERE WAS a time when I knew next to every solid fact proclaimed in the universe that August Burton was going to irrevocably change my life. My heart of hearts told me he was going to be the one to dismantle it all and rebuild the foundation of my time on this earth to be one of great love and purpose. August was going to be my escape, my haven, my new home. The place to lay my head and pour out the evil false truths that plagued me. He was everything painfully good and safe.

And then I learned about frontal lobes developing.

While there was some truth to August Burton showing up and altering the course of my life, I also discovered it was only to wreak havoc and be the bane of my fucking existence.

I curse myself for giving into my weaknesses and look down

at my phone to read Red's response to the text I never should have sent.

I sigh and put my phone face down on my kitchen table. It vibrates with another text coming through. I begrudgingly pick it back up because apparently, I'm a masochist.

I scoff to no one but myself. Of course he's okay. It's not like one shattered glass in his hand could take down the giant. He's a big boy who can handle himself perfectly fine.

It was a fluke that he seemed so off last night. He must have been caught up in his head or something.

But there was that one split second where it was pure undiluted pain on his face, directed completely and totally at me. Different from the seething anger I'm used to basking in. It startled me, knocking me off kilter in a way that felt dangerous.

The sound of a stampede rattles the staircase to my left. My younger twin brothers burst full force into the kitchen, not a care in the world for who they're disrupting. I envy the freedom they have thanks to the brick wall I've built around their innocence, blocking them from the view of the shitshow we live in. For the most part.

"Hunter, slow down before you smash your skull," I say, throwing out my arm to stop the first twin from crashing into the table.

"Thing's solid, Daisy." Hunter raps his knuckles on the top of his head before scooping up one of the bowls I already laid out for them for breakfast.

Chase, the sweet and quiet second twin, silently greets me with one of his famous one-armed hugs and a sigh. I catch the quick roll of his eyes at our brother before he grabs the second bowl. Chase waits patiently for Hunter to finish compiling his mash-up of about four different cereals and then pours himself a bowl of safe and trusted Honey Nut Cheerios.

Hunter and Chase are the eleven—almost twelve—year-old products of our father's failed vasectomy. The one he said he went to the follow-up appointment for, to confirm everything was all set. He did not do that.

We listen and we don't judge.

(That's a lie.)

I love my little brothers more than anything on this planet, including myself. I had a plan to get the hell out of here, but everything halted the day they were born. And it really did take looking at them with my own eyes to make the decision, but it was finite the second they were earthside. I don't regret it. Giving them pieces of a childhood that I dreamed of having is worth it all to me. But that doesn't mean I don't feel a sting at all of the thoughts of what could have been.

So much of my life feels like the *could-have-beens*.

"What's the plan for today, my dudes?"

Hunter tilts his head to the right, an antagonizing smirk on his face. "Chase, you wanna go first?" There's half a pause before he continues. "No? Thought so. So—"

"Apologize," I cut him off.

Hunter has the audacity to bristle as if we don't have this same argument at least four times a week.

"*Now,*" I add.

With a harumph and a scoff, Hunter finally again turns to our brother. "Sorry for trying to include you!"

I take a deep breath, channeling every bit of patience I can muster to not slam my fist on the table and scream at the top of my lungs. A very practiced art in this household. I need to remain level-headed. "Chase," I say through clenched teeth. "Go eat your cereal in the living room. Please."

Chase nods, silently grabbing his bowl while getting up. He squeezes my shoulder as he passes me so I can knock dumbass Hunter down some pegs. I hate how much he reminds me of our mom. I hate that no matter what I pour into him, it feels like it just drains right out.

I wait until I hear the sounds of *Big City Greens* playing on the TV to address Hunter. "I'm fucking sick of it, Hunter."

"Yeah, me too. When's he gonna talk again?"

"I meant how you treat him, how you treat *everyone.* You don't just get to bulldoze through people, expecting them to follow your lead. You don't get to act like you're better than everyone else. It's wrong."

Every time this kind of argument comes up, Gus's voice pounds through my outer defenses. His reminders of my snobbery and stuck up-ness that he knows nothing about but insists on commenting on regardless. He's wrong. He's so fucking wrong, I just don't bother to correct him. I have to reserve my energy for this.

Hunter grumbles, and I can't make out what he says. I don't try hard enough to decipher it, knowing I probably wouldn't appreciate the response.

I lower my voice. "And as for Chase…The answer is maybe never. We've been over this. I know it's hard to grasp. I'm sorry, I wish we had better answers. But he's still the Chase we know and love."

"No, he's not. And I'm sick of you saying that. Mom and Dad think he's a freak too!" Before I can comment further, Hunter pushes himself from the kitchen table, abandons his breakfast, and throws himself back up the stairs.

I sink into my chair, already exhausted, and it's barely seven a.m. I can't even pretend to be surprised that Hunter has been eavesdropping on our parents' conversations and that our parents' conversations include how messed up they think Chase is. No care for who might be listening in while they're in the safety of their own home. They don't bother with thinking about how words like that could affect their children, only if they were to run and spill their secrets. Which we wouldn't. We're trained not to.

One day, Chase was on the cusp of his tenth birthday, a blabbermouth kid without a care in the world, not willing to leave a second of silence hanging. And the next, everything went quiet.

Tests, counseling, group and private therapy, programs, day camps—you name it, our parents tried it. Chase stopped talking, and there's not a single verified reason why.

Of course, Mom and Dad worried for different reasons than I did, or why any normal parent might worry: Was there trauma undetected? Some lingering irregularity within his DNA? Could other symptoms for some underlying issue start to present themselves?

No, no. Mary Jane and Ronald Stiles only cared about the optics of the situation. What would the people in their circle say if they knew their son was mute?

I hear the shuffling of socked feet to see Chase coming back into the kitchen, checking to see if the coast is clear. He has a soft smile on his face when he leans in to rest his chin on my shoulder for a second.

Chase communicates perfectly fine. You just have to pay attention.

I ruffle his dark hair. "It's not you, buddy. You never need to change a thing. You know that, right?" He nods before placing his empty bowl in the sink. He turns and grabs Hunter's to clean out and place in the sink as well. God, he's such a good kid.

"You shouldn't be cleaning up after him. It only rewards his tantrums," I remind Chase.

Chase shrugs his shoulders and gives me the *whaddya gonna do?* face before retreating back upstairs to his room. He must be fist pumping on the top landing when he realizes he narrowly missed our parents emerging from their bedroom here on the first floor. Their conversation is floating through the house now that their door is open.

"...and the McIntyre funeral, do we have that one ready to be delivered? The mass starts at eleven a.m. Good morning, Daisy." My mother greets me with a tight-lipped smile. I should have escaped with Chase.

I should have broken out of here years ago, seeing as how I'm about to turn thirty and still take up residence in my childhood bedroom.

"McIntyre should be good to go. I'll drop it off myself. I'll meet you at the car." My dad kisses my mom on her temple and gives me a half wave before leaving out the back door. It's the most acknowledgment I've come to expect from him.

It wasn't always like this. Before everything went to shit, I assumed my dad loved me in the way every daughter would hope for. He'd take me to the movies and fishing with his friends. I was like his little sidekick. And then I wasn't.

"Morning, Mom," I reply before making myself look busy shuffling through my print outs on the table.

A mistake. I snap the hair tie around my wrist in punishment when Mary Jane's eyes dart to the papers. She snatches the top two in her hands to inspect while she prepares her morning coffee. I roll my eyes when I watch her pour at least two shot glasses worth of vodka into the travel mug. She thinks no one notices. It's a fucking joke.

"This is for Hale's illegitimate children, yes?" she asks, holding up the papers.

She's referring to the designs and inspiration pictures for the bouquets Margot asked me to make for the gender reveal. Margot wanted to do something special and unique, without the risk of blowing anyone up with pyrotechnics. She said simple cupcakes just wouldn't do, and I'm downright honored to have been asked to take on the task.

I want it to be perfect, and it will be. But Mary Jane Stiles's and my versions of perfect are two very different things. And she's the definition of throwing stones in a glass house, so she's the real judgmental bitch who hates everyone. But that's beside the point.

"These are my starting points for the gender reveal bouquets I'm doing for Sawyer Hale and his fiancée, Margot, yes."

"They're paying for this, correct?"

They are not. This is a gift. She doesn't need to know that though. "Deposit is in the account and documented in the Excel sheet." Two truths. She'll never dig to find out that the money came from my own personal account. Hell, she'll probably forget this entire conversation in a few hours' time.

The thing with starting your day with spiked coffee is you leave the window of hazy memories open for far too long. Things get jumbled and contorted in your brain.

"Well, good. Can't say I see whatever vision you're going for but..." She tosses the papers back in front of me. "Make it presentable. We have a reputation to uphold. Please ensure your brothers find their way to camp today before coming into the shop. Oh, and Daisy—"

I finally look up. My mother was beautiful once. A complete knock-out who I dreamed every day I'd grow up to be exactly like. She used to remind me of Morticia Addams and my dad, Gomez, fawning over her in a way that made my mom the center of every room she walked into. The lines on her face at the time were only from smiles. Now, she's weathered. Tired. Sunken in and hollow eyes that hold too many bad memories and mistakes.

She tries to hide the aging and flaws. Her bathroom counter and medicine cabinet are filled to the brim with products. Her closet is stocked with pieces picked out by a department store stylist. To me though, none of it matters. I see the reality.

Today, she has on a black cotton maxi dress that brushes along the floor as she walks. Her dry, dyed black hair is collected and clipped into a barrette in the shape of a leaf. A gift from my dad years ago. The only person in the world she has a soft spot left for.

"Yeah, Mom?"

"Your hair looks like shit. Fix it before you leave this house. You're a Stiles, act like it." The door slams behind her.

"Fuck you too!" I call. No one hears me. No one would care anyway. This whole family is so fucked.

CHAPTER 3: AUGUST - NORTHERN ATTITUDE

"You seem off today," Sawyer says, breaking the silence we've been sitting in just fine for the past few hours while we start the riverside's end of season prep.

I grunt, lugging one of the last fallen tree logs up the path towards my cottage. I have plans to get this thing and the three logs we've already marched up here chopped up and in a fire before the weekend's over. A fire I intend to sit by *alone*. To avoid bullshit conversations like this.

"Since when do you feel like you need to comment on how I seem?"

"That's kind of always been my thing, Gus. Remember how you ended up roped into this family?"

"Guess you got a point," I huff. Still evading actually addressing his accurate observation.

The truth is, yeah, I do. I remember it like it was yesterday. Sawyer spent the better part of our sophomore year of high school following me around, not getting the direct and indirect hints that I wanted nothing to do with him. Or anyone. He ignored my every attempt to tell him to fuck off.

I never experienced someone caring so much about a stranger in my life. It felt weird and wrong. And as much as there was a part of me that felt like Sawyer was the kind of guy I could see myself getting along with, I didn't want to risk bringing anyone into the shit show I dealt with on the daily.

Because while a friend at school seems harmless, if my step dad had ever caught wind of me finding any sort of joy…Well, he'd waste no time wiping that someone or something off the planet. It was, and probably still is, his specialty.

Until that one day where everything changed for me. Sawyer, because he was insufferably determined, showed up at my house. He brushed off my last attempt to evade him, and then he pulled every dark truth out of me.

I lived for years in the shadows of my stepdad's abuse and my mother's ability to turn a blind eye to it all. I grew up knowing I'd only ever be good for heavy lifting and being a punching bag when needed. I accepted it. For a while, I felt like I deserved it.

And then I didn't. I try to not think about it much anymore. I don't like to dwell on the past because nothing good has ever come out of it. I don't have anything to work through. Sometimes you get a shitty upbringing, and sometimes you find people who care somewhere along the way. I'm lucky.

I like my life now. I'm happy most days. I have people I can trust, ones who have my back through anything, just like I do for them. And that feels damn good.

But Sawyer's right…I guess. I have been off. Couldn't tell you what it is. I don't feel like hashing it out right now, though.

We reach the fire pit and dump the log next to the others. Sawyer claps me on the back. "Come on, man. What gives? You're like, mopey or something."

"I'm not fucking mopey or any of the other dwarves. I'm fine. Business as usual."

"Plans for the weekend?" Sawyer segues.

"Nope." I regret the honesty as soon as it's out of my mouth because Sawyer's golden retriever face lights up. You know, he wasn't always like this. It's better, seeing as he's actually happy, but shit, it's exhausting. I blame Margot. I love her. She's great. But why'd she have to go and make my best friend some softy?

"You wanna come by my place? I'm thinking it's time I get started on the build out. Got the construction permits approved and everything."

I want to say yes. I probably will say yes. I like helping wherever I can. But I know these kinds of plans now always have to include family time and meals and conversations when all I really want to do is hang out around a fire, maybe play a game of cards, drink some beers, and just enjoy the quiet. There's not much quiet anymore unless I lock myself away in my house.

And that sounds less appealing by the day. I find myself contradicting myself a lot, and it makes no sense, and I hate it.

"Yeah, sounds good. How's Margot doing with everything?" I don't want to talk about my feelings, so maybe I'll be successful in pushing the conversation towards Margot's seeing as how she has a fuck ton of feelings lately.

Sawyer blows out a breath that ends in a sigh. "She's…She's feeling it all, man. I'm carrying a lot of guilt. I mean, this is great. We're excited as hell. But I can't help but feel like I did something wrong. One minute she's crying, in pain emotionally—or physically—and the next she's laughing without a care in the world. I have whiplash. I can't imagine what it's like for her."

I'm gonna be honest, I'm exhausted just hearing about it, let alone living it.

"But the way she loves them already…it's the coolest thing to see. I didn't know how bad I wanted this until we went to that first ultrasound appointment. I'm gonna be a *dad*."

Sawyer's emphasis on the word dad really does show me how much he was made to do this, in a way I know I'll never be. These babies aren't even born yet, and he's talking about how the mention of their existence changed his entire life.

"You're gonna be a great dad, man," I assure him, because it's true.

"I'm scared, though. I know it's lame to say, but I don't wanna fuck this up, you know? My dad always knew what to do. But I didn't get the chance to ask him about all of this."

"You could talk to Miller?" I suggest. He's the only decent father I know. For as much good this town contains, the parental figures really are sometimes lacking.

Contrary to how I reacted to Sawyer asking about how I seem, he and I aren't strangers to deep talks about emotions. He's actually the only guy on the planet that I trust to be that kind of vulnerable with. He has been since the day he brought me into his home and told me it was mine now too. But I got nothing when it comes to this.

He ignores my suggestion, lost in his own thoughts. "Can I just say something?"

"Yeah, obviously," I confirm.

He's quiet and slow to get it all out when he finally does speak. "I'm scared as hell something's going to happen to me or Margot. I feel like I can't enjoy any part of this without that thought in the back of my head screaming at me that I could leave this planet, and my kids will be left alone."

Shit. That's dark. But I guess when you lose both of your parents to a freak car accident at the age of twelve, it's not a far-fetched thought to have.

"That's…" I sigh. "Yeah, I can see why your head would go there. But, it's not gonna happen. And your kids are never going to be left alone. They have a fucking army behind them."

"You're right. I know you're right. I need to figure out how to believe that. But speaking of that army," Sawyer starts. "Not to switch this conversation around again, but Melanie's moving."

"To Merrymount?" I ask, probably pointlessly. If Margot's mom is moving, this little town is the only option.

"Yep. Above the café. Red practically threw the keys at Margot when she brought it up."

"But what about her swim school?" Can't say I didn't see this coming. If you know Melanie LeClair, you know it would be next to impossible for her to miss a second of her grandchildren's lives. She's spent the past year and a half missing Margot too hard. She was begging for a reason to move here without possibly feeling like she was smothering Margot.

"She's wrapping up her last week training her friend Jackie to take over. She was already doing a lot of the backend stuff. But she'll be officially moved in before the gender reveal party next weekend."

A party to tell the world what gender your kid is going to be sounds weird as fuck, but I keep that opinion to myself. "Shit, that's awesome. I bet Margot's ecstatic."

Sawyer laughs, wiping sweat from his forehead. "An understatement. She's happy here. I think she will be forever, just like us. But she misses her mom, and having her closer will be cool. Gran's pretty pumped too."

"Those two will be causing chaos around town in record time. I can guarantee that," I joke. But I'm also pretty sure it's true.

"No doubt." Sawyer claps his hands together like he's a scout leader. "Well, I'm gonna take off. Uh, about next weekend..." he trails off.

"What about it?" I have a feeling I know where this is headed. I hate myself for it. I hate that it's gotten this bad.

He lets out an uncomfortable, almost disappointed sigh. "Keep things clean next weekend with Daisy?" I open my mouth, but he holds a hand up. "I know, I know. You tell me it's easier said than done. It's her. It's not you. There's no fixing what's broken. Just... for me. But for Margot, too now. Please?"

"You rehearse that?"

Sawyer punches me in the arm. "Fuck off."

"So you did." I punch him back.

He walks away, but before he's too far away to be heard, he looks over his shoulder. "Yeah, ran it by Margot last night."

"You're a bitch, Hale!" I yell as I watch Sawyer get into his Jeep. He waves goodbye without another word, knowing I deserved the warning.

CHAPTER 4: DAISY - ONE TIME THING. NEVER GONNA HAPPEN AGAIN.

The Journal of Daisy D. Stiles - Thirteen years ago

That boy from the other day? His name is August.

Not that he told me.

Every time he steps foot in this office—which is daily, by the way— it's like he's purposely doing everything in his power to not look in my direction. I want to be insulted. I want to stomp my foot and yell in his face that I'm a person who deserves to be acknowledged.

But I don't because that would be wild behavior. And the Stileses do not partake in wild behavior.

Anyway, turns out August is my age. Well, he's in the same grade as me. His actual age is still up for debate, given his size and the tattoos and all. I can't imagine being a sophomore and starting at a new school where I know absolutely no one. That's brave.

I don't have much else to say.

Oh. My mom's pregnant with twins. Boys. Exactly what my parents hoped for the first time around, so I'm sure they're elated. I wouldn't know, given the fact that they don't particularly enjoy speaking to me.

It's fine, though. It's better this way.

* * *

Nothing looks right. The arrangements are a mess, and I can't find a single angle, no matter which way I turn the vases, to jump in and fix things. This isn't like me. I'm a professional when it comes to my floral work. Everything is practically perfect in every fucking way, damn it. Why is this the one time it's not?

Because it matters to you and everything that matters to you turns to dust in your hands, I remind myself. My mother's voice rings in my ears about years of disappointment and her inability to understand where she went wrong.

Margot and Sawyer are about to find out they're bringing two perfect little girls into this world, and I want their first impression to be equally as perfect. But with the way the blush peonies are drooping because it's not exactly their season has me questioning every move that led me here.

I let out a frustrated sigh and run my fingers through my hair for the eighty-seventh time today. I jump when I hear the clearing of a throat behind me. I turn and see Gus in all of his annoying-ass, large glory leaning against the doorway that leads into Red's kitchen, where I'm standing.

I've been holed up at the flower shop all week with an influx of orders, chauffeuring my brothers to and from summer camp, and trying to make these two giant vases look more than just presentable for Margot and Sawyer. I haven't seen a lick of August in that time. I guess my luck has run out.

"*What?*" I bark. For once, even I can admit he doesn't deserve what I'm throwing his way, but I can't exactly take out my anger on the two bundles of pink flowers in front of me.

"You good?"

"Can you use a full sentence, Gus? Or did your pea-shaped brain stop developing in the first grade?"

"You know what? Fuck off." Gus pushes off the doorway and storms past me towards the French doors that lead out the backyard where everyone is waiting. He opens the fridge on his way out and grabs a beer from the shelf on the door. I say nothing as his arm brushes my own when he reaches across the kitchen island to grab the bottle opener.

For some reason, I then decide I need to break my silence. "I'm having a bad day."

"What do you want me to do about it?" Gus grumbles in between swallowing the handfuls of blueberries he's grabbing out of the fruit platter.

"Ugh! Nothing!"

"Jesus, you're testy today."

"Yeah, well, it must be nice to not have a single responsibility, therefore never worrying about a goddamn thing except where to stick your limp dick later."

"My dick gets rave reviews, I'll have you know."

"I don't *want* to know."

"You're the one who brought it up."

I smack my hands down on the island. Gus is making everything worse. I need him out of this kitchen so I can continue flipping out about ruining my closest friends' gender reveals in peace. "I didn't mean—I don't—Can you just go? I'll even throw a please in there."

"Daisy Stiles remembering the magic word? What manners you've developed."

"You're still here. Why're you still here?" I ask the ceiling.

"Because despite my body telling me to run for the hills, I don't trust you in here alone with the knives." I think he's joking, but it also feels like there's a little truth in there, and I hate it. I don't need his pity, or anyone's for that matter.

"I'm fine. I'm just frustrated—"

"Sexually?"

I let the truth fall out. "Sexually, mentally—you name it, the frustration is there."

A beat of stunned silence passes and my brain catches up with the rest of me to realize I just told Gus I was sexually frustrated. I'm gonna hope with all that I am that this is a nightmare.

Gus pretends to cough on the last few blueberries, giving me another moment to somehow recover. I come up with nothing.

"That's uh, well. I get that. That...sucks," is what he manages to land on.

But out of the corner of my eye, I see his hand move to adjust his jeans and the dumbest idea on the planet—no, *in the universe* —pops into my head, and I don't think better of it before I'm confessing this plan to the last person—again, in the universe—I should be cluing in. "When's the last time you were tested?"

This is clinically insane of me.

"Probably finals? High school? The year we graduated?"

I can't even lob out an insult about his intelligence because what I've come up with is even stupider. "No, Gus. STDs. Sexually transmitted diseases. You do get tested, right?"

He looks insulted that I would even have to ask, but answers nonetheless, "Obviously. After any time someone new gets a ride on the Magic Carpet."

"Please don't tell me you named your dick."

Looking insulted again, Gus says, "Every guy names their dick. If they say they don't, they're lying. Mine just happens to be accurate as fuck."

"I don't get it," I admit.

"The carpet. Most magical ride of your life. Come on, Daisy, even someone as heartless as you must have seen the movie a time or two."

I scrunch my face in disgust to hide the hurt. *Heartless.* It stings, but it's not unexpected. It's better that everyone thinks that instead of knowing the truth. There's no room in my heart for anything else. I brush it off. "Yeah, yeah, I've seen it. Whatever, okay so your test...the results...the last time was...?"

Gus bristles. "None of your business."

I'm regretting this already. There's no point. I need to just back out now and cut my losses because this is so painful. I'd rather die from celibacy than this. "Never mind."

"No, wait. Now I'm curious. Why do you care so much about what I got going on down there?"

"Because I want you to fuck me, Gus." I press my forehead into the island with the admission.

Gus laughs, a disbelieving kind of laugh that sounds a whole lot nervous. "You wanna run that by me again?"

"Sex. No strings attached. One time. Just one good, old-fashioned fuck to clear my head that means absolutely nothing so I can continue on with my life."

"Why me?"

"Will you be mad if I said it's because you're standing there, and you're not the worst thing I've ever had to look at?"

I'm absolutely not thinking this through and there are probably—*definitely*—about thirteen thousand reasons this is a bad idea, but I'm committed now. It's been…too long since I've spent any sort of intimate time with anyone. I think my last hook up was with some guy who tried to get me off in a club bathroom by saying weird shit in my ear about the way my hair smelled while finger-fucking me with no rhythm. It left…just about everything to be desired.

Some people keep others at arm's length. The distance I keep with others is more along the lines of an entire football field.

I use this rule of thumb for every piece of my life, including sex. When I want to get off, I either handle it myself or find a man to use. It sounds bad, but I know they're using me for the same thing: a good time. And I'm okay with that—more than okay, actually. I get to be in control and call the shots and make the final decisions. When I think my next playing partner isn't someone who will follow the rules, I leave them high and dry without a second thought.

It works.

"Careful, Daze. That almost sounded like a compliment." He

brushes his knuckles against my arm, and I don't shy away at the touch. It's old and familiar in a way only two people with too much history have.

"Yeah, well, don't get used to it."

"I'm in."

"What?" I ask. Even though I obviously very well know what he means.

"I mean, this is ideal for me. I get off and don't have to worry about kicking you out of my bed after."

"I'm not going *near* your bed," I add.

Gus laughs in a low tone. It practically vibrates, and I feel my pussy hum with anticipation. The dry spell I'm in has me acting dumber than rocks.

"Where does a princess like you let this type of thing happen? Do you need sweet nothings whispered in your ear? Rose petals laid out in the shape of a heart?" He leans into me, invading all of my space, and I suck in a breath.

Just when his lips are about to connect with mine, I swerve and duck out of the way. "Rules," I state. "We need rules. We need to establish parameters if this ever has a chance of working. Number one, no kissing."

He doesn't hide the surprise on his face and backs up half a step. "No...kissing?"

"No. That's entirely too personal."

Gus takes a moment before responding. "Alright. I can do that."

"Two, this is a one-time thing. A break from the current Sahara Desert status of my sex life to snap me back into Daisy Stiles normalcy."

"You'll be back for more. Most are," he chimes in.

I turn up my nose and choose to ignore that remark. "Finally, number three, absolutely not a soul is to ever know about this."

Gus nods once. "More than amenable to that one. So...later?"

I grab a fistful of Gus's T-shirt and yank him in the direction of the laundry room just off the kitchen. Despite the fact that it would probably take two and a half of me to equal one of him, he follows without objection.

"Oh, so now? We're doing this now?" he sounds eager as he unbuckles his belt behind me.

I slam the door shut. I don't bother looking back as I hike my denim shorts down my legs and kick them aside. "I assume you have and know how a condom works?"

The sound of a wrapper tearing answers my question, but that doesn't stop Gus from filling this small laundry room with his irritating voice. "I'm gonna fuck the attitude right out of you, Daisy. Mark my goddamn words."

"I'd love to see you try," I quip.

Gus's palm smoothes over the curve of my ass. "How do you wanna do this, darling? Are you true to your name, soft and sweet? A delicate little—"

I twist my neck. "Call me a flower right now, and I'll bite your dick off."

"*Fuck*, that gets me goin', Daze." His voice is rough. It almost knocks me off kilter.

"I like it hard," I inform him with no shame. "I don't want you to be gentle. And I'd preferably like to at least attempt to finish before, oh I don't know, the *party's over*."

"I can do that."

I feel the head of his cock line with my entrance, and I chastise myself knowing I'm already wet. Have been for a little bit now. For some reason Gus's attempts to rile me up are working in more ways than one today, and it's pissing me off that I don't understand why. There has never been a time where I don't need copious amounts of foreplay.

All I know is that I need this so badly right now.

"Daze?" His gentle tone startles me. It throws me off so much that I whip my head over my shoulder to see his eyes already boring into my own. I make it a point to not look down. I see his shoulder moving in a way that tells me he's fisting himself, and I just know that if I was faced with the true size of Gus's cock at this moment, I'd probably back out of this mad idea. And I'm too desperate to change my mind now.

"What?"

"You're sure about this?" he asks.

I blow my bangs out of my face and let out a breathy laugh before turning back around. "Yes, Gus. Against all of my better judgments, I'm more than sure I want you to fuck me. Now prefer—"

He buries himself deep inside me without further question, and though he's gripping my hips in a way that should probably hurt more than it's adding to the fire in my belly, I still rock into the washing machine I've braced myself on.

I'm full, *so* full. *Too* full. "Fuck," I breathe while trying to adjust to the feeling.

I feel Gus's chest cover my back through the shirts that neither of us bothered to even take off and his lips near my ear. "You feel like fucking *heaven*. And I can't understand it, because you've always been the devil."

Without my prompting, I feel my muscles squeeze around him, and he shudders out a hot breath that journeys down my neck, leaving goosebumps in its wake.

Finally and torturously, Gus pulls his length almost completely out, until only the tip is left inside me. And then he pistons his cock back in with little to no remorse. His thick fingers dig into my skin, and I find myself jutting an arm back to capture the top of his hand with mine.

"God, this is—"

"It's August," he interrupts.

I huff.

The hand that was under mine slips out to grip my jaw with the perfect amount of pressure. He turns my head slightly so I have to look at him. "When I have my cock deeper than any fuckboy has been inside you, it's August. I wanna hear it, Daisy."

Now is a good time to admit I've severely underestimated this little arrangement and oversold my ability to keep my shit together. When Gus releases his fingers from my jaw, I throw my head back with a moan. The ends of my hair tickle my lower back as my shirt rides up with every thrust. I swear, every single point of physical contact is lighting me on fire. But I need more.

"G—August," I pant. I muster up all of the attitude I usually have reserved for the man plowing into me, mentally brushing aside the lust-filled fog he's put me in. "Harder."

He slows his pace, and I hear myself whimper before I can think far enough ahead to stop myself. "C'mon, Daisy darling. I know you have more words than that. What's the one I'm looking for?"

His fingers graze my spine through my shirt, from the bottom of my neck, all the way down to my ass. I jolt when his palm slaps my right cheek. When Gus smooths the sting, I try to rock back into him. But the one hand he still has dug into my hip keeps me perfectly in place. I don't budge. "Nuh-uh, darling. You want harder? Lemme hear the pretty—"

"*Please*," I beg. "Please fuck me, August. You're *insufferable*."

"Oh, yeah. You sound like you're suffering, alright." He drives into me again and my pussy is more than thankful he didn't lean into my goading. The machine under me moves an inch, but I don't think Gus even notices. "Fuck, I feel like I'm drowning in you, Daze. You always soaked like this, or is it just for me?"

His words sound like he's falling apart, but the way he's fucking me with just the right pace and pressure, he doesn't let his control slip for a second. I attempt to respond with some witty retort, but all that leaves my mouth are moans of a pleasure I haven't felt in…

Well, I don't know if I've ever felt something this good. But that's not something I'm going to admit to August fucking

Burton, no matter how talented he and that massive cock of his are.

"Who knew all I had to do to shut you up was fill you up, huh?" he teases me.

"Fuck you," I spit.

"No, Daisy darling, I'm fucking *you*."

His voice drops even lower, and it triggers something deep inside me. "I wanna feel you come around my cock, Daze. Give it to me." His arm wraps around my waist, and two of his fingers find my clit. He pinches, and whatever was triggered inside me detonates. I scream, and I hope with everything in me that no one outside this laundry room hears.

"Fucking...perfect," Gus grunts out until his orgasm catches up to the tail end of mine.

A minute passes by—maybe two—where all I hear are the sounds of our labored breathing and bits and pieces of conversation flowing in the backyard, only feet from where we've committed what feels like the ultimate crime.

What the hell did we just do?

I lift my head from the hanging position it was in while I was catching my breath and reeling about the events of the past twenty or so minutes. "Get the hell off me, Burton."

"Way ahead of you," Gus answers, pulling out. I don't move, still bent over Red's washing machine. She can never know this happened. No one can.

I turn to see Gus discarding the condom in the small waste basket next to the door, the door I notice we didn't even bother locking. What kind of stupid spell just came over us?

"You can't throw a used condom away in the open like that. You don't think Red is going to wonder how that got there?"

Gus is already busy adjusting his jeans and weaving his belt back on when he looks up at me with a shrug. "Wouldn't she just assume it's Miller's? You think they don't use this laundry room the same way we just did?"

"Red and Miller aren't using condoms, *Gus*." I hike my shorts over my hips and start buttoning up the front. I walk over to the trash and tie up the plastic bag that was in it to toss before anyone notices.

The way his face contorts into a look of disgust causes me to snort, and I throw my hand over my mouth just a little too late.

"Why the hell wouldn't they?" He sounds scandalized.

"Some people are in the business of making babies. Remember why we're here today?" I laugh, reminding him of the baby shower we're supposed to be taking part in outside.

He shakes his head. "Gross."

"You don't want kids?" I don't remember the last time I asked Gus anything with any real care for the answer. But for some reason, this time I do.

His response is quick. "Uh, no. Not in the cards for me."

I guess I'm not shocked. He's never really been a family guy. But the way he loves Penelope and the way he just worded that makes me pause enough to wonder if he really doesn't *want* kids. Or if he thinks he can't. Or rather, he shouldn't. It's a feeling I know all too well. But it's also not something I'm trying to hash out right here, right now. Especially not with August.

Instead, I go for the more expected response, the one that will take us right back to where and who we're supposed to be to each other. "For the best."

He rolls his eyes while I tuck the front of my shirt into my shorts and attempt to fluff my hair in the little mirror on the wall in a way that doesn't say *freshly fucked by Gus Burton.*

"You smell like stale beer," I say when I catch Gus looking at my reflection.

"And you look like you just got railed."

"Get out," I snap. But he's unfortunately right.

"This was, uh—" he starts.

"No." I throw my hand in his face. "We're not doing this. We're not talking about it. This was a lapse in rational thought and won't ever be happening again."

I swear I see disappointment flash across Gus's face, but he makes no moves to object. Instead, he wordlessly grabs the plastic bag and nods once after looking me up and down in a way that feels more personal than the sex we just shared before leaving me standing here alone.

CHAPTER 5: AUGUST - BUT WHAT IF IT DID HAPPEN AGAIN?

*W*hat the hell just happened?

You fucked Daisy Stiles against Red Bozelli's washing machine, that's what.

I'm not a religious man by any means, but as I'm throwing cold water on my face in the bathroom before facing everyone outside, I'm starting to understand the appeal of a Catholic confession.

What's even worse is how sex with Daisy did nothing to shake the insatiable need for more. If anything, it unlocked a dark box I've stowed away for too long. A desire so instinctual that now that it's been fed a kernel of what could be, I'm desperate to make it happen again.

I can't tell her that, though. I can't tell anyone that. And I especially can't act on that kind of wish. I've already been stupid enough for a lifetime. I need to wipe the memory from my brain.

She just felt so fucking good.

How do I never go back to that?

I can't.

But what if...

"Gus?" I hear Miller call from the kitchen. Shit. I was only supposed to be in here for a couple of minutes to grab another beer from the fridge, and now I'm somehow gonna have to explain my disappearance.

I turn the faucet off and quickly dry my hands on the towel before exiting the bathroom. "I'm here. Sorry, uh, bathroom." I gesture back, and Miller looks at me funny. He knows something's up.

"I mean, I figured. Since I just watched you leave said bathroom."

"Oh. Yeah. Well, party time?" I move past him, reclaiming my abandoned beer from the kitchen table. I take a sip and try not to gag at the flat, almost room temperature taste.

"Yeah, we're waiting on you. And have you seen Daisy?" Miller asks.

I whip my head around. "No. Why the fuck would I be looking for her?"

"Yeah, that's true." Miller nods his head to the two giant bouquets of flowers taking up the majority of the table. So many different kinds of pink flowers are jumping out of the vases in a funky kind of way. If you tried to explain it, it wouldn't make sense. But somehow Daisy always knows how to transform petals, leaves, and twigs into the most beautiful displays.

Back when…Before…*Anyway*, like I said, I don't really linger on the past. But if I take some time to really think back, there was once a time when Daisy let me in. At least a little. I'd sit in the work room of her parents' flower shop when we knew they wouldn't be around and watch her create these big pieces out of visions she put together herself, just based on a few points customers would make note of when ordering.

It's a talent that even I can admit few have.

"Hey, actually before we head out there," Miller snaps me out of my memory fog. "Pink or blue flowers?"

Miller's colorblind. He just finally told all of us a little while ago, as if it needed to be some secret. Or he thought we'd judge him for something he couldn't control. Dumb. I clap him on the shoulder. "P's got two little girlie cousins on the way."

His face instantly lights up at the news. There's no one on the planet who was meant to be a girl dad more than Miller Caswell. He gives the rest of us with shitty upbringings that small sliver of hope that things can be turned around.

It's not for me, but I appreciate it all the same.

Daisy comes around the corner, still fixing that wild head of hair of hers, and stops dead in her tracks like a doe in headlights when she sees Miller. "You're not supposed to be in here!" she shrieks.

"You're supposed to be *out there!* I'm trying to find *you!*" Miller counters. Good point.

"I just—I needed—" Daisy is so flustered as she flies around the kitchen, fussing with the greenery of the arrangements and avoiding eye contact with both me and Miller. She tries to pick both behemoths of flowers up at the same time, and I watch the one on her right wobble a little too much.

Before I can think better of it, I'm coming up behind her, and grabbing the vase before more than a couple drops of water fall to the floor. I reach my other hand around her left and take the second vase, swooping them both above her head and out of her grasp.

"I had it under control, Gus," Daisy argues.

"Say thank you and keep it moving," I grumble.

"Thank you," she huffs. Not sure when she started listening to directions. But I'll chalk it up to nerves.

Miller ignores us, silently following behind. He's probably grateful as hell he didn't have to wade through a blood bath to get us outside.

Daisy halts me at the door with a palm raised. "Let me make sure Margot and Sawyer are ready. We can't spoil the surprise at the last second." She steps onto the back deck, and I wait in her lingering scent. It feels like it's everywhere now.

Only seconds tick by before she reappears, telling me we're good to go. When I grabbed the vases from her, it was a split-second decision. I didn't realize I was signing myself up to be a part of the reveal. But for some reason, the idea of Daisy dropping one of these things makes me twitchy, so I don't object and simply follow. I place both arrangements on the folding table set up with cupcakes and gifts.

I look out to the small crowd in the backyard. Margot and Sawyer have their backs turned to us, standing under the string of twinkle lights Red has hung above the backyard. They're standing in front of a giant vinyl backdrop that reads *PINK or BLUE, either will do. All we know is there are two!*

I want to laugh. If it wasn't Sawyer standing there, if it was anyone else on the planet, I would have. But someone like Sawyer deserves every bit of cheesy happiness that comes his way. He's endured enough.

Everyone else is turned around too. Beth peeks over her shoulder first. We all should've known she would never have been able to help herself. She holds back a yelp with her hand slapped over her mouth. She's shaking with anticipation and nudging Melanie beside her.

Red attempts to hold Penelope, but she can't stay still to save her life. Miller jogs over to them, wrapping his arm around both Red and lil P. I watch him whisper something in Red's ear.

I give myself one last chance to peek over at Daisy beside me. She's fidgeting with two stems that look perfectly fine where they are. I don't think before I place my hand on top of hers to get her to stop. My hand swallows hers. You can't even see Daze's hand under mine, and I'm stuck staring at the scars and scratches that block the perfect, soft skin that is hers. I hear her suck in a breath, but honestly, I *feel* it. It's that…that weird fucking connection we've always seemed to have that goes haywire if we get too close.

Daisy retracts her hand, and I watch her rearrange her face

into one of almost cold professionalism. She raises her voice, ignoring me, "Okay, on the count of three. One…two…three…"

Margot turns around first. The build up of it all must be too much. When Sawyer turns, he snatches Margot up in his arms so fast, it's almost like they blur. They're screaming, and Margot's holding onto the sides of Sawyer's face for dear life, their foreheads pressed together.

It's hard to make out what they're saying amidst all of the tears. Everyone celebrates around the happy couple that's about to become a damn quad, while still giving them that much-needed space to take in the news on their own terms, together.

Everyone swarms around the table, fawning over the flowers Daisy brought to life. I notice Daisy takes several steps back and seems to be having a hard time accepting every deserved compliment coming her way for these arrangements.

She's still every kind of flustered. My male pride definitely fucking likes the sight of that.

I back up a few paces, removing myself from the scene of bliss and love unfolding. I'm good over…here. Here, slightly away from everyone, comfortably on the outskirts—but not forgotten—is just fine for me.

My solitude doesn't last long though. "Where were you, my boy?" Beth's voice comes from my right. I look down to the sixty-something-year-old pseudo-grandmother I've been lucky enough to know for the past twelve or so years.

"Bathroom," I quickly respond before she gets suspicious.

Unlucky for me, it seems like she might already have those nosy fucking gears in her head turning. "Uh-huh. Funny. Daisy said the same thing a second ago."

"Red and Miller have more than one bathroom, you know."

"Not a denial. Interesting…" Her voice trails off, and she looks to Sawyer. She holds space to take him in. "He's happy," Beth breathes.

Sawyer has his hand on Margot's belly. She's a little thing, so those two spawns she's cooking are already taking up a lot of room, and you can see the smallest bump forming. The parents-to-be are both chatting away with George and John, Merrymount's favorite pizza shop and locksmith owners.

"He's happy, Beth." I loop my arm around her shoulders, pulling her in.

Beth Rivers took on the responsibility of raising a storm cloud of a grandson only a couple years after losing her husband, Dale. It was the same day she lost her only daughter and son-in-law. A handful of years after that, she took me in without question. This isn't even mentioning everything she's done for other kids; Red, Daisy, and the town of Merrymount itself. She's spent the better part of her older years taking care of everyone around her without asking for anything in return.

Beth has always just wanted one thing for all of us: happiness.

Today, I think she's watching one of her dreams come true.

"Now, back to what we were talking about," she starts.

"Hold up, no. We weren't talking about shit, and you need to take this moment to let it soak in."

I feel Beth laugh underneath my arm, and she reaches up to pat my chest. "Oh, August, my boy. You can't hide from me. You should know this by now. But, fine. *Fine.* Consider the subject dropped. For now." She shoots me a pointed look before showing me mercy and stepping away back towards the party.

Relief floods through me that I got through that little interaction unscathed. My moment of victory is short lived of course because it seems as though as soon as Melanie is done suffocating Margot and Sawyer with congratulatory hugs and kisses, she decides to set her sights on me.

I don't move from where I'm standing, accepting defeat in the form of yet another adopted maternal figure in my life. Like Margot, Melanie's new to Merrymount. Actually, she very well might be the newest resident, seeing as how she officially moved into the apartment above Red's Place yesterday. But she latched onto all of us so easily, it's hard to remember what things were like before Margot and her found our little town.

"Hey, Mel," I greet her. We clink our bottles together.

"Isn't this such a beautiful day?" she answers. "Two girls! How lucky are we?"

"The luckiest," I offer. I don't have an opinion either way. As long as they're healthy. "So, you come up with a name yet? Granny Mel?"

Melanie scrunches her face the same way Margot does. They're funny together, and it's going to be nice to have them both so close now. "Granny? No. I'm still hip and cool. I'm with it. I'm down with the times." She does this weird wave thing with her hand to, I *think*, emphasize her…cool and hipness? I'm really not sure.

I laugh on an exhale. "My bad."

"I was thinking *Glamma.*"

I almost choke on my beer as I take a sip.

"And we told her absolutely not," Margot says while approaching us. I lean down to give her a proper hug while still chuckling.

"Congrats, lil mama," I whisper in her ear.

"Thanks, Uncle Gus. But there's nothing little about me now," Margot says, rubbing her hand over the extremely small bump.

"Hate to break it to you, my girl, but you're about to get a hell of a lot bigger," Melanie chimes in.

"Who told you that you could talk to a pregnant girl like that? God, Mom, where is your decorum?"

"What she means is, you're cooking two miracles in there, and you're perfect no matter what size you are, Pix." Sawyer comes up from behind Margot and kisses the top of her head. She immediately softens and leans back into him.

"Pfft. Whatever, you have to say shit like that. Anyway, Gus, it was awfully nice of you to help Daisy bring out the flowers. They're beautiful, and everything has been amazing."

"Uh, happy to help." I take another swig of my beer. I need a new crutch because this is fucking nasty. I try not to grimace at the taste and the mention of Daisy.

"I'm glad you two seem to be getting along! We're like one big, happy family now!" Margot continues.

"Ookay, baby. Let's go make the rounds." Sawyer laughs and gives me a knowing look, one that tells me he's appreciative of my effort.

If only he knew the fucking half of it.

CHAPTER 6: DAISY - DON'T ARGUE
WITH THE PREGNANT CHICK

The Journal of Daisy D. Stiles - Thirteen years ago

I'm writing this all down as fast as I possibly can so I don't forget a single detail.

I talked to him today. August. And he talked to me! Like, we had an entire conversation. Well, okay, maybe you wouldn't call it a conversation. But words were exchanged. I feel like I'm high on life right now.

Wait, I need to back up. Mom was in (not so) rare form last night. There aren't many happy days anymore. When she could drink, she was angry. And now that she can't drink because she's pregnant, she's still angry. She threw a clock at my dad.

Shocker to no one, my dad blamed me. I barely slept, and decided I couldn't handle most other parts of life today. So I've been hiding out in the guidance office.

Apparently August got into a fight at lunch. He was sent here after his meeting with the principal. It seems like maybe he has some secrets too if he gets a free pass to cool down here.

I told myself to mind my business. I lasted a total of seven minutes and twenty-nine seconds. Yes, I counted. This is what transpired after the fact:

Me- "Hi."

Him-

Me- "My name is Daisy Stiles. You're August, right?"

Him- "Gus."

Me- "Oh, you prefer Gus? I'm sorry. Gus it is then."

Him-

Me- "I like to hide out here on bad days. It's a good place to be."

Him- "They're all bad days."

Me- "Relatable, Gus."

Ms. Riccardine called him into her office after that. But before he closed the door, he looked back at me, and I swear to christ I'll never forget this. He said: "I'm actually good with you calling me August, Daisy Stiles."

* * *

WITH BETH and Mel most likely a bottle of wine or two deep back at Beth's house for the night, and Penelope snoozing peacefully inside, the monitor sitting on a little table next to Red so she can keep an eye on her, the gender reveal party is officially over.

I think—despite my doubts—Gus and I have successfully managed to keep our little mishap from earlier today a secret. It appears no one suspects a thing, thank *freaking* God.

And even though I'll never think anything I create could be good enough for people as good as Margot and Sawyer, they're over the moon about the reveal. That's partly because who couldn't be excited about welcoming two precious girls into the world? And Margot also says because the arrangements are the most magical things she's ever seen.

Bets on if she's lying to my face to make me feel better?

Or Margot was buttering me up for whatever she's about to present to our group while we're all sitting around the fire Miller and Sawyer got going once the sun started to set. Her eyes and that creepy smile she plasters on her face when she has a plan she hasn't run by anyone are the tell-alls. She not-so-gracefully attempts to lean out of her Adirondack chair. Sawyer jumps to help her perch herself on the end.

"*So,*" Margot starts.

"Here we go," Miller mutters.

"Shut your trap, Milly Vanilly." Margot whips her head to her half brother and shoots daggers with her eyes.

"That's a terrible nickname. I'm not accepting it on the roster, Marge Barge."

Margot gasps, and Miller clocks his detrimental mistake in the next second. The skin over Margot's cheeks and the bridge of her nose flushes to a dark red. "Are you insinuating I'm the size of a *barge?*"

The rest of us attempt to stifle giggles, Red failing miserably, as Miller flounders for a way out of the mess he created.

"*No!*" he yells. "Don't do this. You cannot seriously do this for the next nine months."

"I'm already three months pregnant, you moron! I only have six left to go! You should know this!"

Sawyer tries to diffuse the situation, rubbing his hand on Margot's thigh.

"Hey, hey. No sibling squabbles. What's up? Tell everyone your plans, I'm sure they're all gonna be excited." Sawyer then shoots us all a pointed look that tells us we're about to act excited whether we truly are or not.

Margot takes a second to breathe in through her nose and out through her mouth while Sawyer leans over and whispers something I can't pick up.

"I think we should all go camping," Margot declares.

And the crowd goes...silent. None of us say a single word. I think half of us assume she's joking, and the other half is attempting to avoid a fight with Margot—or Sawyer.

To my shock, it's Gus who finally speaks up. "You wanna

camp, Margot?" The tone of his voice reminds me of how someone would approach a stray, borderline feral cat.

"Didn't I just say that?" she asks.

I decide I can handle whatever the pregnant woman throws at me. "I think we all might just be a little confused. Seeing as how you sort of…barely tolerate the outdoors."

"No, I don't!" Margot argues. "My fiancé here runs a whole business based around the outdoors." She dramatically throws her hand in Sawyer's direction, who slowly nods his head in reluctant agreement. "I love dirt and trees and animals! Even bugs! Come on! I suggested this before, and you all ignored me. You can't ignore me now."

"Absolutely, you're actually so right," Red flat out lies. "I think what Gus and Daisy are trying to say is, umm, it's the end of summer. And you're…"

"Pregnant?" Margot finishes Red's sentence. She's glaring at Red in a way I would imagine an angry dragon might. "Well aware, *Gwendolyn.* I'm not dead. I'm growing some humans. So what? And I want to celebrate and hoorah the end of summer in a tent surrounded by my favorite people. *So what?*"

"Okay, okay," I attempt to settle things. "When and where?"

Margot perks up. "That place you guys used to go! Sockless Pond or whatever!"

"Barefoot Lake," Gus corrects. I notice the hint of excitement in the way he says it. He's already signed on for this trip no matter what anyone else says, and I'm not surprised. Camping at Barefoot has always been one of Gus's favorite pastimes.

"Yeah, there. I was thinking the last weekend of September. It'll be a little chilly, sure. But it's not like we can't all bundle up, right?"

A chorus of resounding *rights* echoes around the fire pit.

Don't argue with the pregnant chick.

The sun has completely set by the time we agree on the date and plan out what we need to pack for meals. Miller mildly panics about leaving Penelope for two nights until Red calms him down. Margot passes out in her chair practically mid-conversation from exhaustion.

An unfamiliar feeling takes over me when Gus wordlessly places a handwoven throw on the arm of my chair about two hours later. When conversation settled and the air began to chill, he went inside and collected blankets for all of us. I assumed he'd skip me because, well, it's Gus.

But he doesn't, and I'm too shocked to thank him so now guilt is worming its way inside me.

Sawyer moves Margot so she's now snoozing peacefully on his lap, wrapped in a plaid blanket, while Sawyer rests with his head tilted up at the sky, playing with the ends of Margot's hair.

Red repositions her chair so she can drape her legs over Miller's, and he's busy massaging her socked feet while they giggle to themselves about God knows what.

I look over the fire to Gus. I practically jump in my seat when I see his eyes are already fixed on me. I need to peel my line of sight away from him. Focus on anything else. But, I can't. And it sort of seems like neither can he.

Seconds tick by that turn into minutes, and I can't tell you a single thing that transpires over that period of time other than Gus staring at me, and me watching him.

Finally, mercifully, Sawyer announces that he and Margot are calling it a night, breaking up our little after party.

Gus avoids me, or maybe I avoid him, as everyone says their sleepy goodbyes.

CHAPTER 7: DAISY - SOMETIMES HOME ISN'T WHERE THE HEART IS

The Journal of Daisy D. Stiles - Thirteen years ago

Today fucking sucked.

I guess now is a good time to admit that I have been measuring the mood of my days on if I see August, or if I talk to August. The results have varied between terrible, no good, rotten, and good-ish. Seeing as how a few times I've mustered up the courage for conversation, his replies have been short.

And by short, I mean usually it's a noncommittal grunt or a shrug. But I take what I can get.

I don't know what draws me to him. Normally I'm trying to avoid contact with the male population in its entirety. Why is he different? A question I might never have the answer to.

I couldn't go to school today because I have an ear infection. Who even gets those anymore? So not only did I not get my hit of August Burton, I was locked in the prison cell that is my house. The only plus side is neither of my parents felt the need to stay home with me, citing the fact that I'm too old for babysitting requirements.

* * *

I DUMP about fifty pounds of my clothes on top of Red's (and I guess now also Miller's...) bed.

"Jesus H. Christ, woman. Did you clean out your entire closet?" Red jokes. Well, at least she I think she's joking.

"I don't know what the weather's going to be like! I needed options!" I try to defend myself.

We're packing for our camping trip that we're supposed to leave for tomorrow. I say supposed to because I'm not entirely sold on the idea of actually committing to going. Everything about this whole ordeal has *bad news* written all over it.

Now would be a good time to bring up my little...*interaction*... with Gus. I really could use some advice as to why not a single second of him and me together in that way has left my brain. The faint bruises in the shape of his fingers on my hips served as an unnecessary reminder of my transgressions. They faded, and I *still* can't get it all out of my head.

For some reason, it only leaves me wanting more. I need that to stop. Immediately.

But by cluing Red in, who would somehow convince me to clue Margot in, I'd be breaking the rule I created about not telling a soul.

And I'm not about to be the one to break said rule. Not when I know the satisfaction on Gus's face if he were to ever find out might actually end me.

"Well, seeing as how it's the end of September, I'm guessing the temp is going to drop at night. But we all have good, insulated sleeping bags, and I'm planning on bringing every comforter I can find throughout this house. We can share! And layer up!" Red throws out suggestion after suggestion.

"Or we could tell Margot this is a dumb idea and kick the plan to oh, I don't know, next summer when it's more reasonable?" I offer.

"I tried," Red huffs.

I narrow my eyes.

She doesn't back down. "I mean it, I really tried to talk some sense into her, but she has it in her head that she's about to become a mom with no other life outside of that because there's two babies coming. And for some reason, camping is at the top of her pre-babies bucket list."

"I think I'm scared to ask what else is on that list."

"I had to cross off skydiving the other day."

Yikes. "Is she…" I start.

"Losing it?" Red correctly finishes. "Yes. I love her, but she's actually going insane, and as her best friends, we have to go insane with her." Red starts picking apart my pile of clothes, sorting them into sections. She holds up a hot pink bikini top I don't remember packing. Her eyes are already rolling.

"That was an accident," I defend myself.

Red ignores me, sifting through each article of clothing. "It's two nights. You need some fleece-lined leggings, sweatpants, thermal tops, and hoodies. Maybe a hat or two, and some gloves. Extra socks and fine—I'll agree with you on bringing all of your underwear. That's more than fair."

She has all of my shit folded and tucked into packing cubes within ten minutes while I sit off to the side on her bed watching her fly through this project without a pause for thought.

Red was always meant to be the mom in charge of things, like packing for trips and pep talks that wouldn't hold the same amount of weight if they came from anyone else.

When Penelope sprints into the room and dives onto the discarded pile of clothes chanting *"Mom, Mom, Mom!"* Red doesn't miss a beat, chanting right back in her face, *"P, P, P!"* She has the biggest smile on her face, and it's even more obvious she's exactly where she's supposed to be in life.

I wish I knew what that felt like.

"What's up, tiny human?" Red asks Penelope.

"Daddy says LB is staying home when I go to Grandma Beth's tomorrow," P huffs. She makes herself comfy right next to me, criss-crossing her legs. LB—full name Ladybug—is the stray kitten who won the lottery by loitering in the back alley of Red's Place earlier this year and landed a spot in the Caswell family tree.

Red makes a face that tells us she's every bit offended. "Excuse me? He thinks we're leaving a baby *alone* for two nights? No, Penelope. Go tell Daddy he's cracked, and I'm putting together Ladybug's overnight bag right after I finish yours. Actually—" She whips her body around and marches to the doorway. "Miller Caswell!" she yells down the hallway. I'm sure her voice carries down the stairs. Probably down the whole damn street.

"Yes, Gwendolyn, love of my life?" Miller's voice comes from one of the rooms that also occupy the second floor of their bungalow. He sheepishly steps into the hallway and bravely plants himself in front of Red. He runs one hand through his hair.

"Don't even try that shit with me. Did you just tell our daughter that our precious boy is being *Kevin McCallistered* this weekend?"

I have to give Miller credit when it's due. He doesn't back away like most men with self-preservation skills might. He cups each of Red's shoulders with his hands, holding her at arm's length and tilts his head with a puppy dog look.

"Gwennie girl, Ladybug is a cat. He will be more than fine to stay at home—the home he is very comfortably taken care of in—for two nights by himself."

Red shakes Miller off, one upping Miller's baby face by picking Penelope up. Penelope wraps her arms around Red's neck and leans in to smush her pouty face with Red's. This is clearly a well-rehearsed song and dance for the two of them, and I have to hide my snicker behind my hand.

"Under no circumstance is that plan being executed. He's a baby, and he'll be going with Penelope to Beth's. Argue with the damn wall, Miller." Red reaches out and slams the bedroom door in Miller's face.

"*Gwen—*" Miller whines from the other side.

"Girls rule, boys drool. Get bent, Caswell!" Red yells.

We hear Miller's footsteps retreat down the hallway over our giggles.

She plants Penelope back on the floor.

"There. That's settled. Now, P, did you pick out the books and toys you want to bring to Grandma Beth's?"

"Sort of," Penelope admits sheepishly. "I got a little distracted."

Red ruffles P's hair. "No biggie. You can hang with me and Daisy for a little to let the door slam have its time to shine for dramatic effect on Daddy. Then we'll finish up your stuff. Sound good?"

Penelope nods and jumps back on the bed, crawling over to sit comfortably against me.

We hear Miller's voice float from the bottom of the stairs. "You can ignore me all you want, but dinner's in twenty! Daisy, we have a place set for you already!"

I keep my eye-rolling at bay. I'm sure Red has passed on the fact that if dinner was phrased as a question, I would have declined. But now she knows I can't rudely balk at the idea with Penelope sitting right here.

"Daddy's making salmon and rice pilaf. That's fancy rice. Because it's my favorite!" Penelope tells me.

So twenty minutes later, I join them. I laugh with Red and the little family that was made to be hers.

I almost choke on my salmon when Miller starts a new seemingly harmless topic. "Oh! I finally figured out the washing machine. It was so weird, it was like it was thrown off balance."

"Huh?" Red asks in between bites. "Well, that's a relief. I thought we were going to have to replace it."

"Uh, what was wrong with your washing machine?" I know

damn well what was wrong with that thing. It had a couple hundred pounds slammed into it.

"I didn't tell you? It was bizarre. Right after the party, I went to put in a load of laundry, and the thing wouldn't drain. It's literally never done that. I've been bringing our clothes to Mel's apartment while I'm working."

"But, hey! Look who figured it out. Handyman Miller!" Miller interjects, directing his own two thumbs at himself proudly.

Red reaches over and squeezes Miller's arm. "That's my man!" They're two dorks who couldn't be anymore in love if they tried. I think the term *lovesick idiots* that used to be reserved just for Sawyer and Margot now applies to them.

Penelope eyes me from across the table and directs her index finger into her open mouth with a fake gag. I don't bother to hide my snort.

God, this place is a version of peace I've longed for as long as I can remember.

It's just what I need before heading back to a house void of any joy that could even come close to the kind of love that pours out of the bungalow.

It's always been that way, though. Red's home has always felt like an escape, a place where I can really be myself, unabashed and free. The only part that sucks is the come down, when I realize it's all temporary and only possible within those walls.

The sound of a TV with the volume way too high greets me as I enter the back door of my childhood house of horrors. Shitty conservative news pours out of the speakers, drowning out any hint of positivity I had just a second ago.

I pretend I don't see the row of dirty dishes lining the counter as I make my way to the fridge. I open it and find empty containers that don't belong, take-out boxes filled with food that probably expired days ago, and half of a thirty-rack still sitting in the torn cardboard box it was carried home in.

Even though I just ate with the Caswells—Red's included in

that now since we all know the wedding is inevitable—I'm still hungry.

Pushing all of the junk out of the way, I find my Tupperware of salad I stashed before I left the house this morning and grab the bottle of Italian dressing on the top rack of the door. I shut the fridge with my foot and begin to assemble my meal on the small bit of free counter space. I try to do this as quietly as possible, attempting not to bring any attention to myself, to avoid a conversation—*or argument*—with anyone.

It's not late enough for my mother to have passed out yet, or for Hunter to be too tired to fight. So naturally, my guard is up. I don't bother to check the living room. There won't be a sight there I haven't seen.

I don't care. I do not care. *I don't fucking care.*

If I say it enough times, maybe I'll finally believe it, and it won't be considered lying. *No one likes a liar*, as my loving, devoted father reminds me of any chance he can.

I put the bottle of dressing back in the fridge and tip-toe my way up the stairs to retreat to the safety of my bedroom. The twins' bedroom door is cracked open, and I chance a quick peek in to see Hunter fully immersed in some violent, war-ridden video game. He's sitting entirely too close to the TV, and Chase, sweet Chase, lying on top of his bed, sheets still perfectly made under him, is reading a book.

Hunter mercifully doesn't hear me over his headset that I'm sure is only omitting sounds of preteens swearing into their microphones and blasts of grenades or whatever. But Chase can hear a leaf blow by, so when his eyes find mine over the top of his book, I shoot him a smile and small wave with my free hand, a silent greeting to let him know my door is always open for him if he needs it. He shoots me a quick peace sign before diving back into whatever story he's finding joy in.

He doesn't take me up on the wordless offer often. Only sometimes, in the middle of the night, do I feel him crawl onto the side of my bed that hugs the wall. He's usually gone by the morning.

I could have slept over Red's. We're all carpooling for the drive up to Barefoot Lake anyway. She offered, with Miller backing her up on it. They have a spare room. I wouldn't have been imposing. I'm told this repeatedly, but I never say yes. I don't do sleepovers.

I'm down for a weekend of camping so long as I get my own tent to call home at the end of the night, but other than that— Yeah, no sleepovers.

The fact of the matter is, I'm an outsider. I manufactured it this way, completely my doing, to no one's fault but my own. I have my reasons to keep the distance. Straying from my regular routine is something that just doesn't happen with me.

I do it for the twins, to make sure they have a responsible, sober adult home who will always care and love them unconditionally.

For my friends, to make sure they never know. Never know…everything.

I hang my tote bag from my chair and place my second dinner on the desk in front of it. I grab my headphones to throw on as I find my phone, waiting for the Bluetooth to connect. I bring up my audiobook and hit play. The heavy tone of the male narrator's voice always makes me jump at first. But once my body recognizes we're not in any actual danger, I can lean into the romance for my form of escape as I eat.

I've never been someone who can focus on words on paper, unless they're my own. My brain doesn't work like that, and I used to feel less than because of it. Was I not smart enough? Not focused? But Dr. Saltore, the trauma therapist my parents threw at me to get me to shut up all those years ago, suggested audiobooks some time ago, and it stuck.

It was like a whole new world was discovered, just for me. I get to transport myself into places I couldn't dream of, learn about people who I would never cross paths with while walking the streets of a small town like Merrymount. The narrators block out the sounds of my dismal reality, for even just a little.

And above all, I get to experience love between people in a way I'm not sure I'll ever find for myself, both platonic and romantic. Because to reach that level of devotion to someone else requires trust and vulnerability that I've never been willing to experience.

I check messages and comments on the riverside's social media channels. I've been running that side of Beth's business for about a year now, and it's something I'm so damn proud of. Seeing the organic growth of customer relationships and engagement online with people who would have otherwise never discovered the gem that is Rivers River is hands down one of the best parts of my days.

Of course, there's the shitty part of this job. I have to get past the dozens of comments and emojis from women who are big fans of Gus—the "giant mountain man"—who somehow makes his way into a few of the videos and pictures I post.

I scoff at the latest.

*Wish he'd throw *me* over his shoulder like that.*

And another brings on the type of eye-roll that could very well cause damage to my retinas.

Give me five minutes and a hair tie, iykyk.

They're written under a montage of clips playing with a Noah Kahan song I edited together the other day when Sawyer and Gus were hauling fallen down logs up to Gus's fire pit. Can't say I see the appeal…

I let the video replay, even though I had to watch it through no less than a hundred times while editing. Okay, *fine*. I guess Gus looks objectively attractive carrying a tree trunk that probably weighs double him with ease. He doesn't even look like he's breaking a sweat. That kind of shit gets the ladies going. I can be amenable to that opinion.

I also know how those hands wrapped around the bark feel when they're wrapped around my body. As much as I've tried to train the memory out of my brain, it's seared in there. Permanent. Life altering. Ick.

Not ick.

Whatever.

I heart the thirsty comments, along with the six other ones agreeing with the original poster, the crease between my eyebrows crinkling in disdain with every single one.

But my finger pauses at a comment I somehow missed. One that has more likes that I would prefer.

When's someone going to take one for the team and find out who mountain man is?

My eyes bulge at a reply.

Do we think he's single? I'm about to shoot my shot. Climb him like a tree if you will.

Like fucking hell you are. Something nasty comes over me. My thumb hovers for a second before I let the pad of my thumb swipe the delete button on the original comment and the reply.

Whoops.

We don't need random people with no desire to support the actual business of the riverside twittering around and being general pains in the ass just to attempt to score with Gus. It's unprofessional and rude and disrespectful.

We're an upstanding establishment in this community. Beth deserves more than hosting some impromptu small town redneck version of *The Bachelor*.

At least all of that sounds good in my head when I try to block out the ugly green-eyed monster named jealousy that occasionally likes to take up residence in my brain.

I'm not jealous. I don't even know what I'm saying. Gus is Gus. He's free to do whatever—whoever—he wants. I mean, we… did what we did once. It was a one-time thing.

A text pops up across the top of my screen.

LITTLE RED RIDING HOE

you never texted me to tell me you got
home. rude

Shit. Red's a stickler about stuff like this. Like I said, mother hen.

ME

Sorry! Sorry! Home safe and sound.

LITTLE RED RIDING HOE

shame you didn't stay. gus came by ;)

I freeze. What the hell does the wink mean? She can't—there's no way. Red wouldn't know anything. I never even leaned into a *hint* about what went down between me and Gus. Did he say something? He wouldn't.

My stream of consciousness is running at a million miles a minute, and yet I can't think of a single way to reply that doesn't throw me under the bus.

Three dots appear before I come to any sort of a decision.

LITTLE RED RIDING HOE

ohmyGAWSH. i was kidding don't ignore me

ME

Har-har. See you tomorrow, bitch.

My headphones might be noise canceling, but they don't do shit to block out the sound of my door bashing into the wall as it's whipped open.

I throw my phone down, along with my headphones, and swivel in my chair to see my nightly sleep paralysis demon.

I mean, my mother.

"What are you doing home so late?" she snarls.

"It's—" I glance down at the time on my phone. "Not even

9:00 p.m. I don't have a curfew, nor does literally any of this matter. Can I help you?"

"This is still my house, Daisy. You still need to abide by my rules." Her words are slurred. My mother's hair is tied up into a rat's nest of a bun and makeup runs down her face. Clearly it's not one of her better nights. No idea what could've set her off.

The number one rule to handling an intoxicated person is to not make them mad when they're volatile, a skill I should have perfected by now but alas, I'm still doing my silent counts to three with deep breathes in through my nose. Just like Dr. Saltore taught me.

"Sorry, Mom." I swallow. "Do you need my help with something?"

An ugly laugh escapes her mouth. "No. The twins would have starved, since you never even bothered to check if they ate. But not to worry, your father picked them up something a little bit ago. Shame they can't rely on their big sister."

Shame they can't rely on their mother. I keep that obvious fact to myself though.

Because of course she would use Hunter and Chase to make me feel guilty for being gone. She knows I'm taking off for the weekend. So hitting me where it hurts right before I leave ensures there's a damper on my time away.

Never mind the fact that I made sure our grandmother was free to host them. But, of course, Mary Jane would take offense to that. She doesn't like *any* outsiders knowing our nasty business.

"Again, sorry," I say, resigned. "Won't happen again."

Drunken Mary Jane Stiles backs out of my room, not bothering to shut the door behind her. Before slinking away, she strikes again. "Such a waste."

Ah, yes. My entire existence. A waste.

CHAPTER 8: AUGUST - LET'S GET THIS SHOW ON THE ROAD

MILLER CASWELL

If someone needed to strap something to the roof of their car, how would one begin to go about that?

ME

I have bungee cords here. Just pack your shit in your little car and we'll get it sorted before we all head out

MILLER CASWELL

Please don't tell Gwen.

I chuckle before tossing my phone back on my bed, right on top of the pile of clothes and supplies I need to get packed myself before everyone else arrives. We're supposed to hit the road to make it to Barefoot Lake by early afternoon, but we're a caravan of six, so I'm setting my expectations low.

I'm semi-hopeful we make it before sundown.

Truth is, as crazy as Margot's plan seemed to just about everyone else, I'm pumped for this little getaway. Sawyer and I used to make the trip to Barefoot Lake a hell of a lot more when we were younger. It's something I wish we kept in our regular rotation of things to do, but life happens.

Some of my best late nights have happened at that campsite nestled in the woods of New Hampshire. It's got that cozy vibe, or whatever the hell Penelope would say.

Miller invited me to stop by last night, and I took him up on the offer, given the fact that I had nothing else going on, sort of like I do every night after I finish up work. When I got there, Penelope—unprompted—gave me a play by play of how Daisy spent the afternoon with them packing and having dinner, and I *juuuuuuuuuuuust* missed her.

I'll be honest, sometimes it's hard to keep up with P. She talks a mile a minute and can change the subject about forty times in a span of ten minutes. She has these little phrases that make my head tilt, and when I don't know the answer to one of her nine hundred questions, she'll shoot me a glare that tells me I should have paid a hell of a lot more attention in school.

Then she tells me to Google the answer.

Smartass.

But I love her. In the course of the time the Caswells have spent in Merrymount, Penelope has shown me that some kids— more specifically, maybe only the kids of my friends—are kind of cool as shit.

Penelope is the first to laugh at my jokes, and even when I'm not in a good mood, she somehow can always spin it around.

It reminds me a lot of Daisy back when I first moved to town. I shake that thought away.

I finish getting my shit sorted into a duffel bag and haul it downstairs when there's a knock on my front door. Beth is already peeking through the slim window beside it. I'm sure she's looking to see if she can see me purposely ignoring her.

Which I did consider, so I guess it was deserved.

"It's unlocked, Beth," I call.

She enters before I finish saying her name. "You were going to let me stand out there and beat down the door, weren't you?"

"Thought about it." I shrug my shoulders, drop my bag by the door, and head off into the kitchen.

Beth trails behind me. "So, you all ready for your little trip?" She grabs her favorite mug from the cupboard and places it in front of the chair she declared hers years ago.

"Just about." I grab the pot of still-warm coffee and pour the liquid caffeine into Beth's waiting cup. I find the creamer on the door of the fridge, and slide the sugar pot, a gift from Beth when I moved in here, across the table toward her.

This is a well-rehearsed scene, never changing—the same pattern every time Beth Rivers pays me a visit from across the way at her place. So, I know her next move before she even starts.

Beth quietly assembles her coffee just the way she likes it. She takes the first sip and hums. When she places the mug back on my kitchen table, she crosses her right leg over her left, and sits back in her chair.

"Something's up," she declares.

"What?" I ask, amused at her style of interrogation.

"You're being funny. You've been funny since the gender reveal."

"In what way? And no euphemisms or whatever the hell you're gonna come up with. I still have to finish packing up the food locker before everyone gets here."

Beth points a finger at me, leaning over the kitchen table. "There it is! August," she sighs. "I'd like to think we've always been transparent with each other. But we also respect our individual spaces...Like when I actively choose to ignore the parade of women you normally traipse up this driveway during the middle of the night on any given weekend."

I turn up my face in disgust. Didn't need to know she was aware of that. Not sure why that thought never crossed my mind. Gross.

"Anyway, this is one of those times where I feel like I can't look away. I'm worried about ya, Gus."

"Why?" I ask, exasperated. I haven't been doing anything differently. Nothing has changed. This whole weird half-intervention thing is unnecessary. I want to tell Beth as much, but I know better. I'm not as dumb as everyone might think.

"You're being avoidant, for starters. Sawyer opens his mouth, and you're ready to rip his head off. And I'm not saying it's a bad thing, but definitely an odd thing...Maybe not odd, moreso...interesting."

"Out with it," I snap, a mistake I clock when Beth narrows her eyes. "Sorry," I mumble immediately.

"You've been following Daisy around here like a moth to a flame."

"Am not." I cross my arms over my chest and lean back on the counter.

"You kids think I'm not up with the times." Beth wiggles her dinosaur aged phone out of her front pocket and holds it up. "I follow the *Instaslam* pages."

"Instagram..." I mutter.

Beth huffs. "Whatever! I see the posts. You're in every single one of 'em this week." She somehow manages to open up the app, and scrolls through at least six different pictures and videos, all of them featuring me in some way. "You waved to the camera in this one, Gus. Since when have you ever been that damn friendly?"

"I'll be sure to flip it off next time."

"I'm just gonna come out and ask. Shoot straight from the hip. Did something happen with you and Daisy? The last thing we all need is for you two to let all this pent-up anger out in a way that's going to break people apart."

I've only lied to Beth Rivers on one occasion, and she called me out on it immediately, but I think I'm about to make the same mistake for a second time.

"Nothing happened. I'm just—We're just trying to get along for the greater good."

"Why now?"

"For the kids. I kind of thought that was obvious." I shrug.

"And I *love* that sentiment, my boy. I just don't believe it's the whole truth. I don't want to see either of you hurt. Not like last time."

Fuck. I can't talk about this with her—with anyone.

I shake my head. "No, it's not…It's not like that. I'm not a teenager anymore, Beth."

The room gets quiet. Beth takes another sip of her coffee, and I don't dare move.

"Your feelings for that girl have never been the kind that float away with age. I fear I've let this get out of control because I was hellbent on teaching you some sort of lesson I've forgotten the point of over the years. Maybe it was just easier on me to ignore and referee on occasion. Nevertheless, my boy, there are only a few people who know what rumbles behind yours and Daisy's hearts. You've both been enveloped in rage for so long, I think you forget how easy contempt can switch to adoration."

I huff. I sound so much like a fucking cow, I'm grating on my own nerves. But I do not *adore* Daisy Stiles. She drives me up a goddamn wall. She's rude and pretentious and just always *there*.

"Balk all you want. Don't think I assumed I was walking in here for an easy fight. I'm just asking you to consider everything before you run off and get yourself stuck in a position I can't argue my way out of for you."

"Noted," I say with a short nod. "You taking the kid and the cat this weekend?" I attempt a subject change.

Beth's eyes light up. I'm not the only one obsessed with Penelope Caswell's energy. "Mel's crashing with us too, of course. We're counting down the minutes 'till you lot clear out." She laughs and gets up to discard her empty mug in the sink.

Her hand claps on my elbow, probably about as high as she

can reach without standing on her toes. Beth was never tall, but she's shrinking with age.

"Please be good for me this weekend. And keep an eye on the crew, especially Margot. Lord knows she's going to find a bug to trip over."

"Isn't that Sawyer's job?" I tease.

Beth's back at my front door before she responds. "You're both good boys, but Sawyer would fall *with* Margot. You're the one there I trust to catch them before they hit the ground."

* * *

WE'RE at our fourth rest stop. Margot has to pee every half hour.

Two stops ago, Red proclaimed she had to sympathy pee, a small bladder in solidarity with her pregnant sister.

According to the clock on my dashboard, I've spent almost three hours in the car with both of them. If there was ever a time that I longed for a sister or two, that period of my life has officially ceased.

It's too hot, and then it's too cold. Can we restart the song? Margot missed her favorite bridge. Can you pass me the bag of chips? Do you have a napkin? I could use a moisturizer in my daily skincare routine according to Red. Don't worry, Margot has a great suggestion for when we get back to Merrymount.

For some unexplained reason, I somehow got tasked with driving the majority of the camping supplies—tents, coolers, chairs, and food—in the bed of my truck and Margot and Red on the bench seat in the cab.

I spent my childhood ignored, until I was needed as a punching bag. When I moved in with Sawyer and Beth, as much as they love to prod, things at the house were generally pretty quiet. Me, alone in a small space with two women who have never heard of a personal boundary a day in their life? I am weak compared to them. I'm surrendering.

I'm savoring my few moments of silence before they make it back to the truck. I can already hear the plastic bag of snacks they *couldn't pass up* rustling in my mind.

A light tap on my window has me jumping and my eyes bugging out. I look to my left and groan. I crank the handle to lower the window against my better judgment. "And to what do I owe this pleasure, Daisy?"

Miller has been carting Sawyer and Daisy in his Corolla. When one of us has to stop, so does the other. Like I said earlier, we're a dysfunctional caravan. I haven't spoken to Daisy since we left my place. She hopped in the back seat of Miller's car without a second thought and threw those big ass baby blue headphones on to block out the world.

Those headphones are sitting around her neck right now.

They match her eyes.

She rolls those ocean eyes at me. "Hey, listen. Let's pretend we just argued about something trivial so we can skip to why I'm putting myself through a conversation with you."

"What a way to start things off," I offer sarcastically.

"You went viral." Daisy holds her phone up so it's about two inches in front of my face. I have no idea what I'm supposed to be looking at.

"Vi-ral," Daisy repeats with emphasis on each syllable. She taps the picture I think I'm supposed to be focusing on.

I reach out and wrap my hand around her wrist so I can attempt to focus on the screen. "Will you hold still?"

Daisy sucks in a breath but doesn't try to pull away or say anything else.

Turns out it's not a picture, it's the same video Beth had brought up earlier, except looking at it now, I see there are hundreds of comments, thousands of likes, and that the little notification sign keeps popping up every second that ticks by.

"What the..." I let the phrase trail off, releasing Daisy's wrist.

"Believe me, I said the same thing. As much as this pains me to admit, August, you're good for business. You're the last person I want to ask for help, but I'm putting the riverside first here." She locks her phone and pockets it.

"I don't get it," I confess. And I mean it. I've never understood social media. I made a profile when Sawyer did back in school, and I scroll through people's posts when I can't sleep. But I've never uploaded a single thing. Nothing in my life is worth showcasing like that.

"Girls are thirsty for conservative-looking men with liberal opinions in this day and age. The fact that you're this beast who lugs tree trunks over his shoulder like a bag of flour and works for a woman-owned business is hot to them."

"I'm just doing my job." I'm so fucking confused.

Daisy braces a hand on my door. Her knuckles go white like she's trying to find the strength to not clap me upside the head. I gotta admit, the effort for restraint is comical.

"Fantastic, Gus. You're employee of the freaking month. Agree to let me film you doing whatever, whenever, and I won't ask for anything more."

"Whatever, whenever?" I ask, a grin forming on my face. "My, my, how the turns have tabled. I thought *it was a one-time thing?*" I go up a few octaves to mimic her voice.

Daisy's scowl deepens. "I regret everything about this entire interaction and before."

I lean over, just a little. "You don't mean that, darling. I know you don't." I see the rest of our crew exit the rest stop. "But, I'll spare ya. Sure, Daze. Paint me like one of your French girls or whatever. Doesn't matter to me."

She tracks my line of vision and steps away from the truck, an earnest look on her face. She pulls those headphones, dainty fucking white little bows on either side, back over her ears. "Rivers River's social media appreciates it."

I can't help but chuckle. It wouldn't be Daisy if she flat-out thanked me for a damn thing herself.

My passenger door flies open, and Margot hops onto the bench, scooting over to her spot in the middle. She leans her head on my shoulder and rests a hand on her belly.

"Do you mind if I nap the rest of the way?" she asks.

Suddenly, my annoyances from before melt away. Maybe I never longed for a sister, but I've somehow found myself with a couple of them. And I don't hate it, not even a little bit.

Red jumps in next to Margot and hands me a bag of beef jerky. I rip the perforated top and toss a handful of dehydrated meat into my mouth before answering Margot, who's already closed her eyes. "Sleep tight," I tell her.

Sawyer stops at my door and looks down at Margot, who might have actually passed out in record time, that dopey, lovey look on his face.

"Yeah. That tracks," Sawyer sighs. "She gets tired pretty easily these days. We ready to go?"

"Let's get this show on the road," I say, starting my truck up. We still have about an hour left of this drive, and if we have any chance of actually making it to the site before sundown, we need to get these miles behind us *before* Margot wakes up.

CHAPTER 9: DAISY - THANK YOU, AUGUST.

The Journal of Daisy D. Stiles - Thirteen years ago

An unfortunate altercation happened today.

That's exactly how Principal Rosewood described August body-slamming Ben Caponi into a locker after he tried to slap my ass in the hallway.

Everything happened really fast. One minute, I was walking from History to Geometry, minding my own business. Next thing I knew, Ben's nasty Hot Cheeto breath was in my face. He was whispering how good I looked in my yoga pants, but my vision went black and my ears started ringing after that. I was busy trying to do my breathing exercises Dr. Saltore taught me for anytime I'm feeling cornered or stuck.

Those breathing exercises didn't do shit. But the sound of Ben's body ricocheting off metal sure did the trick to snap me out of my impending panic attack.

August had Ben pinned, and he was seething. I watched Ben struggle to get a mouthful of oxygen in. A second later about four teachers pulled them apart and marched all three of us to the main office.

Mr. Rosewood asked what happened. I recounted the sequence of events in a monotone voice that felt nothing like my own. After Mr.

Rosewood expressed how unfortunate this situation was, I was sent to guidance.

I wanted to thank August, but I never got the chance.

* * *

I'LL ADMIT, the day wasn't bad.

We all definitely had a blast setting up our tent sites, and when the guys scattered to collect wood for the fire, Margot, Red, and I got to unpacking the food prep to get ready for the dinner we'd be making over said fire.

Real stereotypical camping shit.

But like I said. It wasn't bad. It was actually kind of fun.

We've had music going and conversation flowing. Gus and I have managed to keep a safe distance between us with glances to a minimum. I still remember too vividly what it felt like to have him inside me. And with the way I caught him shaking his head at me earlier, it seems he's having a difficult time not recalling the same memory.

I got some content I can use for the riverside, and Gus, true to his word, didn't object. Probably because it required minimal effort on his part. But hey, a win is a win.

But now it's the middle of the night, everyone is safely passed out in their tents, and I'm laying on the rock solid dirt of the fucking earth because the air mattress I found stowed away in the attic at my parents' house deflated an hour ago.

As you can tell, things don't seem as though they can get much worse. Until I let out a frustrated breath and hear the unzipping of a tent nearby.

I pause, hoping it's just someone up to use the bathroom. The heavy footsteps headed my way clue me in before Gus makes himself known outside my tent.

"What's going on? I've been listening to you fucking hem and haw for an hour now," he gruffly whispers.

"Bet if you smother yourself with a pillow the silence would be bliss," I offer sarcastically.

"Open up," he demands, ignoring my suggestion.

"No."

"Open the fucking door, Daze."

Should I remind him it's a literal tent? He could easily rip the flimsy material and get what he wants, but for some reason he stays firmly on the other side. I huff and sit up, throwing my blankets to the side. I lean over and jerk the zipper up so it flaps open.

I look up to see Gus is standing in front of me in a wide stance with his arms across his chest and a scowl on his face. Gus's hair is perfectly rumpled. He has one of his classic maroon flannels open over a plain white T-shirt and tantalizing grey sweatpants stretched across his thighs. They do absolutely nothing to hide every massive piece of August Burton. His work boots are untied, the laces dangling on the ground.

I fight to not suck in a breath. God, he's a vision right now. The coals from our earlier fire are still lit and glowing a dull red in the pit behind him. The full moon is showing off, casting down a light onto our site in a way only a place in the middle of nowhere like this could offer.

"Why aren't you sleeping?" Gus snaps me out of my oggling. Jesus Christ, I need to get it together.

"I'm fine. Well, I was until you practically banged down my door."

Gus peers behind me, into the tent, and his frown lines deepen. "What happened to your mattress?"

I pointlessly try to shift my weight to block his view. I pull on my oversized crewneck to try to cover my bare thighs. It might be the end of September and cold as shit outside, but I still can't sleep with pants on. I obviously regret that now. "Nothing. I told you, I'm fine. Besides, it's none of your business."

Gus's eyes linger for a moment on my exposed skin, and I

fight a shiver that's not from the dropping temperature. "You can't sleep on the ground."

You know, I somehow forgot this fact about Gus over the years of distance. He can get tunnel vision speedy quick. Once he gets something in his head, it's really hard to get him off that track. So I know that now that *he* knows I'm put out, he's going to try to fix it. Even though he hates me.

"I'll manage," I lamely offer.

He exhales and looks up at the night sky. *"Daisy."* The breath of my name causes a prickling sensation on the back of my neck.

I hear the stirring of someone in one of the tents only feet away from us, reminding me we're not the only two out here. "Go back to your tent, Gus. We don't need to wake everyone else up."

"Oh, I'll be sure everyone here knows you're refusing help. Let's see where that gets you."

"You wouldn't," I seethe.

"Just let me blow the air mattress back up, and I'll be gone in two minutes. We can pretend this whole thing never happened."

"You can't," I tell him.

"I have my pump. Let me go grab it." Gus turns, but I stop him before he takes a step.

"Don't bother. There's a hole the size of a fucking donut. The mattress is as dead as a doornail," I admit.

Gus's head rotates towards me again. I don't look to meet his eyes in embarrassment. He once again sighs, and it sounds like almost all of the fight in him leaves with it. "Listen. It's like, one-thirty in the morning. I want to sleep. I'm sure you want to sleep, even though you're being a stubborn pain in the ass." He pauses, but I still say nothing. *"Please."* It comes out pained. "Get up, and let's go. And for fuck's sake, put some pants on. You're gonna get sick," he chastises me.

I bite my lower lip, trying to think of any other reasonable and logical solution for my situation. I come up with nothing.

"It doesn't seem like I have much of a choice," I say.

I'm surprised when Gus lowers himself into a squat in front of me. I focus on the noodle-like shoelaces of his boots. His voice sounds like gravel. "You always have a choice. I'm asking you to take my tent, and I'll sleep in my truck."

That was…oddly, extremely nice. And confusing. And kind of exactly the kind of thing I needed to hear. "That's not fair," I argue. But at the same time, I reach back and grab my pillow, snatching my blanket along with it. I find my discarded sweatpants and quickly push my legs through, shimmying them up over my hips.

"I won't make you uncomfortable, Daisy."

"And I don't want to put you out," I counter while exiting my tent and silently saying goodbye to my useless air mattress. "Listen, I appreciate this. I do. I'm good to sleep on one side, if you promise to stay on yours. I'm…I'm okay with that."

I mean it, too. Throughout the years, I've given up on searching for the answer to why August Burton, of all people, is the exception to the rules my mind and body have made.

Gus searches my face for any hint of hesitation. He must find what he's looking for because he nods once and then stalks back towards his big blue tent. He really would sleep crammed up in his old truck just to make sure I'm not stuck in a position I can't mentally handle.

I don't know how to feel about that.

Gus waits outside of his tent, gesturing for me to enter first. When I kick off my boots and flop inside, I toss my pillow and blanket to the furthest left corner of the space, and crawl over the air mattress that's so big it takes up about every square inch of this tent.

"Damn, is this a king size?" I ask, moreso to myself.

But Gus still responds as he enters and zips the front of the tent closed behind him. "It's not like I'm really fitting on anything less."

I'm hit against my will with the image of August trying to contort his massive build onto my pitiful full-sized bed that still occupies my room at my parents' house. I chuckle and the next words that fall out of my mouth also feel against my will. "Remember that time when—" I freeze.

"I remember," Gus says quietly. The silence hangs, and it's so painful to attempt to sit through.

"We should get some sleep," I attempt to recover.

He shakes his head, almost as if he's shaking the memory out of his mind. Memories of days when it wasn't a battle to share space. Times when the mere thought of one another brought us both a sense of peace. It's funny how that works.

Gus finally lays down beside me. He grabs one of the pillows from behind his head and places it between us. If I wanted to start an argument about how that's immature and unnecessary, I could. But for once, I don't. I don't want to spoil the moment. He and I both know the real reason for the barrier.

I roll over, putting my back to Gus and mumble some form of a goodnight. I barely hear his reply as my eyes close and sleep finds me.

* * *

RUSTLING WAKES me a lot sooner than I planned when I drifted off earlier. It's still pitch black out when I crack one eye open. I quickly sit up when I realize the rustling noise is closer than I had originally thought.

I rub my eyelids, willing my vision to clear and make out what's causing the commotion in the dark. When I finally gain some sight back and spot the culprit, I attempt to shriek but no sound comes out.

Without thinking, I reach out and grab hold of Gus's arm in a death grip. "It's a...it's a—"

"Fuck, that's a 'possum." Gus moves quickly, trying to move

me out of the way while simultaneously—I *think*—trying to remove said opossum from the tent before all hell breaks loose.

His attempts are futile though because I unfortunately have a front row seat to watch August try to swipe at the critter. He loses his balance on the wobbly air mattress and crashes into the corner of the tent. The small opening that the opossum somehow weaseled his way through proceeds to rip all the way up to the top metal pole holding the vinyl scraps of fabric together.

The beady eyes of the opossum go wide, and I swear he looks directly at me, right into my soul, before giving Gus another glance and dashing out of the now-ruined tent. Leaving the two of us humans in stunned silence. The only sounds now are from the great outdoors I petitioned to avoid and our labored breathing. How in the hell no one else has woken up is simply beyond me.

"How did that thing get in here?" I finally ask.

I then hear the faint sound of air escaping, a wheezing that can only mean one thing.

Gus is busy inspecting the damage. A wasted effort, in my opinion, but I choose to keep that to myself. He starts gathering pillows and blankets, mine included, without a word.

"Gus?" I prompt.

He ignores me.

"Gus?" I attempt again.

"Gus, the air mattress popped."

"Do you think I don't realize that?" He whips his head to me. "Do you think I'm not aware that it's now almost three a.m., I've gotten maybe two hours of sleep, and I'm now gonna have to go back and forth with *you* for however the fuck long it takes to convince you to get out of this now junk tent? Spare me. This one goddamn time, spare me, and let's *go*."

He finishes collecting just about everything in the space up into his arms and leaves me sitting on the now half-inflated mattress. I don't make any moves to follow. Instead, I watch in silence as August gets busy building a nest of comfort in the bed of his truck.

After a few minutes of watching him rearrange pillows and blankets, he turns back to me. "I told you earlier, you always have a choice. I'm telling you right now, my patience has run out. You get this one shot to make the right decision, and yes, Daisy, there's a right decision here, and then I'm passing the fuck out."

I weigh my options. I realize I have none. I sigh and plant my hands on either side of me for balance to hoist myself up, when Gus crosses the space between us and wordlessly offers his hand. I reach up and grab it and almost fall back from the shock, but his firm grip brings me up into a standing position.

"Must be static electricity. From the blankets," he mutters. "Sorry."

"Yeah, must be," I lamely agree. Neither of us has let go of the other. It's gotten to the point where it's definitely weird now.

Gus is the first to break. He stalks back to the truck, kicking off his boots again, hopping into the bed, and crawling under one of the top comforters. I shake off the weird fog that just clouded my brain and follow suit.

I lay my back against the surprisingly comfortable makeshift bed Gus created and look up at the stars. You get a pretty good view of them in Merrymount, but I have to admit, there's nothing like the night sky at Barefoot Lake.

I peek at Gus from the corner of my eye. He has one arm tucked underneath his head and his other hand is toying with the seam of the comforter. There's a loose string that he keeps wrapping and unwrapping around his finger.

Refocusing back on the twinkling dots above, I decide to fill the silence with mentions of *before*, before things with August and me went to shit. The times that we never bring up or share, on his part because they're probably trivial, forgotten pasts. For me, because with to-the-bone honesty, it hurts too much to think about.

"It's been quite a while since I spent time in the back of this truck," I admit.

"Listening to the sound of your voice and you fidgeting with the blankets kind of makes it feel like it was just yesterday," Gus says after a long pause.

"The stars look the same," I breathe. "Still shining bright and beautiful. Still there as a guide to who-knows-where."

A trick of the light makes it look like Gus's focus is solely on me when he says, "I was thinking the same thing, Daze."

I hate to admit how much the nickname only works when it's coming from him. Whether it's said in anger or affection, it's always had the same effect on me. Can't explain it, not going to try.

"I just want to say thank you, August. For helping me out tonight, despite all of the drama that came with it. I can replace your tent. And the mattress. Lord knows I'm going to have to get a new one for my parents anyway. Because even though the thing hasn't been touched in years, it broke on my watch. So, it's my problem now," I ramble.

Gus scoffs. "I'm not arguing with you right now, Daze. Go back to sleep." He removes his arm from underneath his head and folds his pillow in half, a thing he's done all the while I've known him. It's another thing that's remained the same. Just like the stars.

I drift off shortly after that, without a care in the world that there's no barrier between us, or that August Burton, of all people, saved the day. I don't think about the fact that this isn't even close to the first time I've come face to face with this kind of reality.

CHAPTER 10: AUGUST - USE ME

Lavender. Roses. Jasmine. Lilacs. Honeysuckle. Daisies.

While my body begins its wake up process, my senses are smacked by the scent of all different kinds of flowers. It's overpowering and consuming.

My eyes fly open, and they're met with sprawled out, jet black hair that's attached to a head tucked comfortably under my chin. An arm that isn't my own lays lazily across my chest, where mine is wrapped tightly around a body still sleeping soundly.

Daisy.

Daisy Stiles. Sleeping with me. In a way that has never felt right...until now.

"What the *fuck?*" Sawyer's voice interrupts every thought ratting through my brain.

Suddenly, Daisy Stiles is no longer sleeping with me. She bounces up faster than I've ever seen, snatching the comforter that covered the both of us. She pulls it up to her chin, as if she's trying to hide something indecent.

My head swishes from side to side, Sawyer to Daisy, unsure where to land. I don't know what to say, or what I'm supposed to be doing. This looks bad. This looks really fucking bad.

Things go from bad to worse when Margot steps out from behind Sawyer with a bewildered look on her face.

"My, my, my…" she starts.

"We were sleeping!" I yell.

"We can see that, Gus," Sawyer says as he nods in slow motion.

"Sleeping…together," Margot adds. She still might be in shock.

I *know* Daisy's still in shock because for once in her entire life, she's speechless. No quip remark, no sassy comeback. But damn, are those icy blue eyes blazing.

I finally try to explain our way out of this mess.

"Daisy's mattress shit the bed. Then there was an opossum, and I fell, and well…We needed to sleep. We slept here. We just slept."

Why the hell am I acting like we did anything else? If someone else blabbed this kind of speech to me, I'd assume they fucked like rabbits all night long.

Protecting Daisy right now feels important though.

Before Margot opens her mouth, I go off again.

"And you know what? I was cold. So, yeah. I cuddled up with Daisy for warmth. She barely tolerated it, but in the name of self preservation, she stuck it out. No further questions, got it?" I toss what little of the blanket is still covering me off and slide myself out of the bed of my truck. I risk a look back at Daisy, who's trying like hell to not let her mouth hang open.

Sawyer and Margot are not as subtle in their surprise.

"Yeah, okay. Well, this is an insane turn of events. But, anyway, good morning?" Margot offers.

"Good morning," I gruffly answer. I pass by the two of them on a mission for coffee. I unlock our food bin and pull out all of the fixings for breakfast, lining everything up on the folding table. I start separating the bacon from its package, readying it to line across the grate we place over the fire when cooking. I open the can of coffee grounds and take a good whiff, clearing out all of the floral still stuck in my nose.

Sawyer makes his way over and gets to work on relighting the fire next to me. "We gonna—"

"Nope," I stop him. "We're not gonna talk about shit. I told you exactly what happened. If you or your fiancée have a differing opinion, keep it to your damn selves."

"Noted, you fucking grump." Sawyer claps me on the back, unphased by my barking.

"Red and Miller still passed out?" I ask.

"Yeah, I don't think they usually get much of a chance to sleep in."

"That's gonna be you pretty soon," I remind him.

"Oh, I am well aware. But it's nothing I can't handle. It's not like we let the day get away from us too often at the riverside anyway."

Don't I know it. I don't remember the last time I didn't catch at least part of the sunrise. Even today, the rays of light are barely up around us. The air still has that chilly bite to it.

"Do you know what time it is?" I ask.

"A little after six. We were going to take an early morning walk, but then we saw what was left of your tent. And then we saw the scene in your truck, and well, now we're here."

"Now we're here," I parrot.

"I'm sorry. I just gotta say it—a 'possum, really? That's what you came up with?" Sawyer stands up from his squat after the fire has life again.

This time the roles are reversed, and it's Daisy coming to my rescue. She and Margot join us by the fire.

"Yes! Yes, it was actually a fucking opossum. He didn't come up with anything! Oh my God, you can't actually think *we—*"

She stops. I turn to stone. No one fills the void, and the four of us stand here waiting for *someone* to speak up. But no one does, and I consider stoking the coals to stick my head in the flames of the fire pit.

I'm pissed. I'm not Daisy's biggest fan, clearly. We haven't gotten along in years, and just about everyone knows that. But now I know what she sounds and feels like when she comes. I know she still can only sleep if her hand is resting on her cheek. And she has the audacity to pretend like she wouldn't touch me with a ten-foot pole to save face in front of our friends?

Screw this.

"Calm down, Daze. No one here would ever think you'd get down and dirty with, what do you call me? A stray dog?" I shoot daggers at her, sinking right back into the comfortability of our feud, forgetting the quiet moments of last night where things felt like they might one day be different.

"What the hell's going on out here?" I hear Red call from the tent farthest from us. In the next second, I hear the sound of a zipper, and she pokes her head out. "How are you two arguing already? Why is everyone awake?" she whines.

"Good morning, sleepyhead!" Margot calls in a fake sing-song voice. "To catch you up to speed, Sawyer and I caught Daisy and Gus practically fused together in the back of his truck with his tent destroyed. They claim to have just slept. It's actually the only thing they'll agree on ever, it appears, because they are, to no one's surprise, back to fighting!" She throws her hands up and stomps off to…honestly, who knows where. She's not happy.

Sawyer exhales, and I feel the weight of it. "Guess we're going for that morning walk after all. Goddamnit. Dude, can you make sure breakfast is ready by the time we get back?" He doesn't wait for a reply. Sawyer follows behind Margot at a slight jog to catch up to her.

"Yikes, I'm just gonna…" Red closes herself back into her and Miller's tent.

Oh no.

I slowly turn my head to Daisy, who has a twisted look on her face. One that tells me I just fucked up big time.

The bet.

No way. She owes me after last night. This cannot be actually happening right now. We were supposed to keep it together. If anything, she was going to be the one to cave first. I'm not considering this a loss. She technically threw the first punch. Right?

I don't spare Daisy another glance, immediately throwing myself into camp chef mode. I throw the grate on top of the fire and line bacon across it. I pull bagels out and start slicing them down the middle to prepare breakfast sandwiches.

I remain silent when Daisy joins me. She starts aggressively cracking eggs into a bowl to scramble. I wordlessly shove the bag of shredded cheese towards her to add in. There's an edge to every move each of us makes, and yet we keep completely to ourselves.

When Red and Miller finally emerge however long later, Daisy has already started pouring coffee into everyone's mugs on the picnic table, and I'm assembling the sandwiches at my little makeshift station.

"Morning, guys," Miller greets us with a yawn. His hair is standing up in every direction, and I don't think he realizes both his shirt and sweatpants are on backwards. But I'm the one being accused of participating in nefarious activities last night. Cool.

"Morning!" Daisy calls, pretending nothing is wrong. "How'd you guys sleep?"

"Like the dead. It was incredible. Is anyone going to clue us in on the show we apparently missed last night?" Red hikes her head in the direction of Daisy's tent, the front flap wide open to show a deflated air mattress flat on the ground. And my tent...in shreds, flapping in the chill breeze of morning.

I lower my head, prepared to repeat the same story no one

here is going to even bother to entertain as the truth, but Daisy beats me to it.

Daisy slams her palms on the picnic table. "This is the last time we're doing this. My mattress had a hole. Enter Gus and his tent. Then we meet Mr. Opossum. Cue Gus shredding his tent. We manage to get maybe three hours of sleep in the bed of his truck. The *fucking* end, got it?"

Miller's head begins to nod vigorously.

Red simply picks up a mug and sips on black coffee. "Noted. We can head into town later and pick you up a new air mattress." She turns to me. "And you, a new tent, I suppose."

I wave my hand. "Honestly? I liked sleeping under the stars. I'm good with it for another night."

I see Sawyer and Margot emerging from a walking trail. I pick up my sandwich and wrap it in a paper towel. I scoop up my mug, too.

"Bacon, egg, and cheeses for everyone. Add whatever toppings you'd like. I'm taking off for a little. I haven't seen the lake this time of year in a while." I take a bite of my breakfast and don't wait for anyone's response. I head in the opposite direction of our site, off to find even a hint of the peace I felt laying next to Daisy last night, shaking off how pathetic that makes me.

* * *

"I'm sorry."

I whip my head around to find Daisy standing behind me, both of her hands clasped together tightly in front of her, eyes on the ground, feet gently patting loose dirt side to side. She's nervous, uncharacteristically shy. I guess all of this tracks when my brain catches up to the two words she just muttered.

"Come again?" I ask.

It's been hours since I've talked to anyone. I decided to spend the morning alone, not trusting myself to not kill the mood of those around me. Sure, I'm used to going tit for tat with Daisy, but I'm not used to feeling gross about how she publicly rejects me with ease. Not when things seem to have shifted in private, even just a little. It's not right, and it's fucking with my head.

"Don't make me say it again," she huffs.

"Why shouldn't I?" I step towards her. She doesn't move. I look to make sure none of our friends are within earshot. "I'm good enough to fuck. But wait, only once." I bark out a laugh. "I'm good enough to make you a bed to sleep on when you're stranded. I'm even good enough for some nostalgic *remember whens* in the dead of the night, right? But you can't twist your nasty thoughts into something decent for me in front of our closest friends? Not even one time?"

I've had a lot of time to think today, and my mind hasn't strayed once for any other topic other than the complexity that is Daisy Stiles. I don't know what shifted. If it really was the sex, or maybe the stars. Or maybe at some point, I realized my issues with her were never real, just an act I thought I had to keep up for the balance of the world.

Now I feel like I'm crawling out of my skin with it all. It's too much.

I'll give Daisy credit. She doesn't back down. She squares her shoulders, letting the earlier nerves melt off her body.

"I deserve that," she says. My eyes watch her swallow slowly move down her throat. "I am sorry."

"I gotta know," I breathe, taking another step towards her. We're only inches apart now. Her eyes line up with my chest, but she raises them to meet mine, jutting her chin out. "Which part? Which part pains you so much you feel the need to offer apologies? Because the Daisy Stiles I know would normally never."

"All of it."

"Not good enough," I balk.

Daisy looks up to the sky. I can't help another frustrated laugh escaping me. "No one up there is gonna help you with this."

Her brows furrow, and that little crease in between makes its familiar appearance. "I'm sorry. I used you for sex. I shouldn't have done that. I don't...I can admit, I don't regret the sex. I'm not ashamed. I just don't want to complicate things with them." Her arm gestures in the direction of our group of friends lounging around the fire pit. "And I'm sorry for how I acted this morning. I felt cornered in a glass box, on display for everyone."

"You always assume everyone is judging you."

"*You* do." It's faint. I can barely make out those two words, but they crush me all the same.

"Yeah, well..." I want to lighten the mood, take back my pressing for an apology. "It's always been different with us, right?" I offer her a crooked smile.

Daisy's face softens, just a little. Then she takes a step back, shuffling on the ground with her little fucking tennis shoes again. The dirt is already ruining the bright whites of them. "Please don't brood all day. I think it defeats the purpose of Margot dragging us all out here."

Accepting the fact that my question will remain unanswered, I move on. "I wasn't dragged. I love coming here. But, I know. I'm good. I appreciate...this." I don't explain further. She doesn't ask me to.

"*Shit*," Daisy exhales. "Oh, and I have some semi-bad news. We went into town, and because the camping season is practically over..." There's that weird hesitation again.

"Daze, out with it."

"They only had one air mattress and no tents."

"Oh," I say. That's it. Oh.

"This man offered to let us borrow one of his when he heard us inquiring with the cashier, but I felt really weird about that. I didn't accept. I said no. But if you're uncomfortable, I can go back. I mean, I didn't get his name or anything—"

"Daisy," I stop her. She looks up at me, hands twisting together this way and that again. "I said I was fine to sleep like I did last night. I meant it. Feel free to join me if you want." I raise my hand to cup her shoulder, but my palm hovers about an inch away.

Daisy doesn't like to be touched.

I take a step back, separating us further and feeling the air change with it. I turn to finally walk back to join our group, putting everything before right now behind us. "And Daze?"

Ocean blue eyes find mine instinctively, a curious gleam in them.

"Use me whenever you want."

I don't wait for a response or any form of acknowledgment.

CHAPTER 11: AUGUST - THE FUZZY LEAF

I told Daisy to use me.

I looked her dead in the face and offered myself to her. I fully thought she'd take me up on it too, seeing as I'm more than aware I can deliver in that department.

That was almost two weeks ago, and besides pulling me aside to "shoot content"—fancy way of saying take *way too many pictures and videos of me doing boring shit*—I haven't heard from her.

No arguing, no lame remarks, definitely no comments about a good old fashioned friends with benefits situation. Only complete and total professionalism.

I fucking hate it. I'm going out of my damn mind trying to figure out what changed, how it did, and if there's a chance of switching things back.

Not back. I don't really think I want to do the sworn enemies thing anymore. Things have…shifted.

I'm confused, okay?

Margot has a doctor's appointment, so Sawyer and I finish up work a little early so he can head out with her. I ask Beth if there is anything else that could be done to keep my hands busy, but she waves me off.

So now I'm home, showered, and planted on my couch with fuck all else to do.

I find myself on the riverside's Instagram page to pass the time. After checking out everything there, I realize Daisy must have her own account. She pops up easily with a quick name search, and now I'm poking around her page and through her posts.

It's weird. Normally you see everyone's travels, big smiles, holiday pictures, family photo shoots, all of the selfies. There's no sign of Daisy in this entire feed. Sure, there's her hand holding the ceramic handle of a coffee mug. And yeah, I spot the back of her head, covered by one of her crocheted bandanas in a few snaps. But swipe after swipe, it's all objects and scenery. It looks nice. Don't get me wrong. But it's fake, better off staged for a magazine or something.

Time goes by, couldn't tell you how long, and I'm still scrolling. I get all the way back until the pictures start looking grainy with some heavy-ass filters on them. When I look at the dates, I realize I've made it to when we were in high school.

One single square stops me dead in my tracks. It might be the only picture that shows Daisy's face on the whole fucking internet for all I know. And me. I'm sitting right next to her. My arm's around her shoulders while she leans into my side. And I wish I could see her eyes, but I can't because they're not focused on whoever had the camera.

No, those blue eyes that always held way too much pain for anyone to carry by themselves are looking right up at me. And I don't even notice, a goofy fucking grin on my face.

We're sitting against the wall of Merrymount High's gym. Daisy has her hair tied up in a high ponytail, letting her dark curls fall over one shoulder. She's wearing one of those white frilly dresses. God, has she always had a different one for every occasion? I'm in a pair of dress pants and a white button up Beth picked out for me the day before this. Daisy's barefoot, her heels sitting in a pile next to me. I remember I carried them for her when she said her feet started to hurt.

Suddenly I'm transported back to a time I've never cared to revisit. Sitting here alone, clutching my phone, I can admit it's because the few times I did think back, it hurt.

It hurt like hell to know I had someone, a friend—*maybe more than that*—like Daisy Stiles next to me, and then I lost it all.

So I forgot about it. Just like I do with most of my heavy thoughts and feelings. I clung to our mutual disdain for each other based on one night of mistakes and left the past in the past.

But now a memory comes flooding through my brain, and I can carry a lot of shit, but I'm not strong enough to hold this back.

"I can't believe I agreed to show up to this thing," Daisy giggles, hopping down, out of my truck. She never waits for me to come around and open the door for her. I tell her it pisses me off every time, but she waves me off like it'd be a bother or something for me to help her.

"You're getting an award, Daze. None of us were going to let you miss it," I remind her.

"Yeah, but it's family night. And as you can see"—Daisy twirls, letting the dress float up her thighs, her arms raised in the air—"I'm arriving family-less." She tries to play it off like it isn't a big deal.

"Fix your scowl, August. Your face is going to get stuck like that," Daisy jokes, tapping a finger on my forehead.

My acting skills aren't on par with hers.

"What am I then?" I ask her.

There's a bounce with every step she takes. It's been like this the whole week. I think because with every day, we get closer and closer to graduation. For Daisy, it's the means for a way out. There's a lightness to her that I usually only get to see in small bursts. In the quiet, when it's just me and her.

She turns around, impatiently waiting for me to catch up when she sees I'm still standing on the passenger side of my truck. A smile breaks out across her face, and she answers me like it's the most obvious thing in the world. "You're August Burton, and I'm Daisy Stiles. It's just as simple as that. Always will be."

She's not wrong, I think to myself.

I make sure I'm the loudest to cheer when they call her name for her art award. Sawyer, Beth, Red, and even Katie, yell right alongside me. I'm so fucking proud of Daisy.

Her eyes find mine, because they always do, and I fist pump, making sure she knows I'm here for her and her alone.

We meet up after the ceremony with our friends behind the gym. When we're sitting against the chipping paint of a mural former Merrymount High kids worked on however many years ago, Beth finds us. Daisy holds out her phone, asking Beth to take a picture.

Beth's never been good with technology, so I know we have one shot to get this right. I plaster a giant smile on my face, pulling Daisy tight into my side when the flash goes off.

I never see how the photo comes out. We graduate the following day, and I forget what it feels like to be so sure that there's a world with August Burton and Daisy Stiles.

I stare at that picture, replaying that memory until I fall asleep on the couch.

MY PHONE WAKES me up when it slips from my hand and smacks me in the face. After shaking off the sting, I lift my phone back up in actual fucking horror, because my big ass nose apparently *liked* the goddamn picture. From twelve years ago. Daisy's going to think I'm cyber stalking her…on account of the fact that I basically have been.

You know what? Not an issue. I tap the little red heart and the like disappears.

Crisis averted.

I sigh at my own stupidity and lift myself up. I'm not gonna be able to focus on shit unless I lay it all out on the table for Daisy. Maybe she took my offering of "use me" to mean just like, strictly riverside bullshit.

I'm still fine with that, but she should know I also meant that I'm available at any given time to fix her…frustrations. I lost the privilege to any other part of Daisy a long time ago. But this…I can assist with this.

Pocketing my phone and grabbing my keys on the rack beside my front door, I march off to my truck. I'm on a mission to clear the air, or whatever. My truck beats down the backroads that lead to Main Street, and I try to go over how I'm going to approach this in my head.

"Hey, Daze. I know you can't stand the sight of me, but if you're ever looking to get dicked down—"

No.

"What's up, Daisy? Why am I here at your parents' flower shop? Oh, no reason. Just offering sexual services—"

Good God, nope.

"Daisy. You. Me. Sex?"

Yeah, I'm screwed. And not in the way I'm trying to be.

I'm no closer to nailing a good opening line by the time I throw the truck into park outside of The Fuzzy Leaf.

I haven't paid a visit to this building in over a decade. Never really thought I'd see the inside of it again. No reason to, when the entire family turns their noses up in disgust when they see me. I brush off lingering nerves as I enter through the door, the jingle announcing my arrival. My shoulders hit huge leaves jutting out on either side of me, and I turn slightly to avoid wrecking anything.

The place could've been cool if the owners (a.k.a. Daisy's mother and father) weren't such dickheads. The back wall is made entirely of greenery, and the arrangements you see throughout the store are so different from what you'd find anywhere else. I'm sure it's all thanks to the girl lost in thought in front of me.

Daisy lifts her head from the notebook she's writing in while standing behind the counter. It's an image that transports me back in time. Buckets of about thirteen different flowers are crowded around her, and she has half of her hair tied into a bun on the top of her head, fastened with what looks like a pencil or a chopstick.

Her mouth falls open and stays slightly ajar like that for well over a minute.

"Hey." I don't move towards her. I keep my feet firmly planted where they are, assuming I'm going to be thrown out of here in the next second.

"Gus?" Daisy finally asks after another drawn out pause.

"It's weird I'm here, right?" I ask, exhaling with an attempt at a laugh.

"That's an understatement," Daisy mumbles. "Is everything... Are you okay?"

I decide it's safe to commit to walking up at least to the counter. "Yeah, yeah, of course. I'm fine."

Daisy breathes a sigh that almost sounds...relieved? "Cool. Cool, cool. So..."

"Is anyone else here?" I quickly try to confirm.

"Jeez, do you plan on murdering me?" Daisy jokes. I hope she's joking.

"What?" I balk. "No, I just—I wanted to run something by you."

"Is this because you accidentally liked my picture on Instagram?"

"*What?*" I practically shout. How does she know? I took the like back, damn it.

"Unliking the post doesn't take back the notification, August," she informs me while shaking her head.

"Daisy? Are you out front?" a barking voice from the back

calls. "Ugh, that Burton boy parked his nasty truck right—Oh." Mary Jane Stiles walks through the back doorway and stops dead in her tracks when she sees me.

"Hi, Mrs. Stiles," I greet her through gritted teeth.

I fucking hate this woman, always have, always will. Which is perfectly fine, since she feels the exact same about me.

Mary Jane doesn't bother with niceties, she never deemed me on a level deserving of her hoity-toity act. Again, more than fine with me. Keeping up appearances is nothing I've ever practiced anyway. "What're you doing here?"

"The door was unlocked, and the sign says open, Mrs. Stiles. This is still a business, correct? Or did you run it into the ground before Daisy could clean up your mess?" I adjust my footing and cross my arms over my chest.

"Gus," Daisy whispers. Her voice never reaches much higher than that when either of her pathetic parents are around. I hate to see that hasn't changed.

"Get out," Mary Jane seethes. She snaps her head in Daisy's direction, and I already know I won't be leaving unless it's with Daisy in tow. "Why would you let that trash in here?"

Daisy opens her mouth to respond, but I cut her off. "I let myself in. Daisy had nothing to do with this."

Daisy's mother scoffs, and I clench my jaw at the dismissive sound. "I don't want to hear it. Just *get out*. I don't need you around my business or my daughter."

I really should go. I really do not need to be arguing with some middle-aged drunk woman in a flower shop on a Wednesday afternoon. Mary Jane's eyes are sunken in, and her skin is pale despite the fact that we just wrapped up our best weathered summer Merrymount has seen in years. She resembles a Tim Burton character more than an actual human being at this point.

"You care who's around your daughter now? That's rich." I stop myself before I take it any further. I know if I go down this road, I'll end up behind bars. Again. "Daze, come on." I tilt my head in the direction of the front door. Silently praying to fucking God she doesn't argue with me right now. Or worse— stand beside Mary Jane. I find a discarded kernel of hope that even if she despises me, she still despises her parents more.

Daisy looks at me with big doe eyes, filled with so much confusion and anger and…maybe, just maybe a little appreciation. She nods once before reaching below the counter, grabbing her tote bag, stuffing her notebook inside, and crossing the room. She stops at the door. "I'm going. Orders are set for the rest of the week. Slips are in the register. Books are updated. Hunter and Chase are home, schoolwork finished and fed. You'll probably find them already sequestered in their room by the time you make it back to the house."

"Daisy Daf—"

"*Don't* use my middle name," Daisy growls. "I'm. Going." She whips the door open and leaves without another word. Mary Jane doesn't move from where she stands. I decide it's not worth the risk of me saying anything more, and I follow Daisy out.

She's doing deep breaths in the passenger seat by the time I make it back to the truck.

"What the hell just happened?" she asks when I enter the driver's side.

"I gotta be real with you, none of that was my intention when I showed up," I admit. I run a hand through my hair.

"No shit, Gus. You didn't plan on going to The Fuzzy Leaf for the first time in probably a decade to square off with my mother in my defense? Another thing you haven't done in over ten years? Crazy. Wild. Color me *shocked.*"

It's best I say nothing. Key in the ignition, I start up the truck, and reverse onto Main Street.

"Wait, where are we going?" Daisy asks, snapping her head to face out of her window as I drive down the street.

"Oh. Right. Do you wanna come back to my place? I still need to talk to you. Unless you want me to drive you home—"

"No," she interrupts me. "The very last place on the planet I want to be is my house."

"So, mine's okay?" I double-check.

Daisy leans against the seat, head tipped back, and closes her eyes. She pulls her legs up to wrap her arms around them, just like she used to. "Yeah. Your place is fine, Gus."

CHAPTER 12: DAISY - THE LAUNDRY LIST

The Journal of Daisy D. Stiles - Thirteen years ago

*A*ugust sat next to me at lunch today. He didn't say a single word, and he only moved over to my table after Sawyer Hale sat at his, trying to get him to engage in a conversation with him. But, we ate food at the same time at the same table.

I'd consider that a real bonding experience, wouldn't you, Journal?

I have got to stop doing that.

Anyway, my parents are going out of town next weekend for some florist convention. They're calling it the Babymoon they never had, since Mom won't be able to travel much longer due to her pregnancy being considered high risk.

If I was a normal girl with normal feelings and the capability of having a normal relationship with people, I could have thrown a party. Maybe I could have invited August over. Or at the very least, Red, for movies and popcorn and face masks, or something.

But instead I have a heaping pile of trauma, a basket of diagnoses, and the blissful silence of an empty house. At least for forty-eight hours.

Beggars can't be choosers, so I'll take it.

* * *

I'm grappling with the current status of my life.

I just willingly got into August Burton's truck. And even more bizarre than that one fact, is that I agreed to be driven *by August* to *his* house. Alone.

Not alone. The two of us. Together.

For what? I literally haven't the slightest clue. Well, I needed to get away from my mother. I'm lost as to how Gus requires my aid for anything.

I should ask what's going on. That would be the reasonable thing to do. We don't need to have this uncomfortable silence of build-up. It takes approximately twelve minutes to get from Main Street to the Rivers River piece of land, and I don't think I'll survive sitting with so many unknowns in that amount of time.

Turning my head to rest my cheek on the tops of my knees, I open my mouth to break the dam of quiet. I close it immediately after taking in the sight of August.

Gus has his left hand on the steering wheel, the other resting on the empty space of bench between us. His palm lays flat on the leather so I have full view of the thick veins that rope up his arm, the dark hair scattered over them. When he flexes, the rippling of those veins does something to me.

Suddenly I'm being transported back to a day however many weeks ago when those arms and hands were holding me in place while he fucked me from behind, making me forget every worry I've probably ever had. And it was effortless for him. I try not to squirm in my seat.

I'm confused and horny, not a good combination.

His facial hair has started to grow in, covering his jawline. Knowing Gus all these years has taught me that he shaves once a week, but when the weather starts to cool down, he leaves the beard. He keeps it trimmed and neat, sure. But it really adds to that mountain man thing the obsessive fangirls online keep yapping about in the comments on every post that shows even a glance of Gus.

Personally, I used to be a fan of his *pornstar mustache*. His words, not mine. It made him look rugged and sexy like Tom Selleck. And if you don't think Tom Selleck is sex on a fucking stick, I don't know what to tell you.

Rather than dive further into a spiral about the social media stardom I accidentally created regarding Rivers River and Gus, I attempt to start the conversation I intended on having just a second ago. You know, before I let Gus take over my brain. Again.

"What do you want to talk about?" I ask.

Gus bristles. "Just stuff. It's best we do this at my place."

"You say that like you didn't journey into town to find me," I argue.

He looks like he wants to hang his head, maybe regretting his earlier kindness. Because, yes. Even I can admit that August getting me out of my mother's way was a very kind thing to do. But he swallows and the look is gone. We take a right, and the tires start rolling over dirt, rather than smooth concrete, signaling our imminent arrival to the Rivers' compound.

"Just let me get us to my house. I don't want to do this while I'm driving."

With a harumph, I decide to leave things be. Fine. Be weird, August. See if I care.

I do. I care far too much.

We pass the Rivers River sign and hang a left to travel up Gus's driveway. His two-story house sits up on a little hill. A dark green roof covers the dark stained wooden walls of the exterior. And if the grumpy man on my left wasn't its sole occupant, the open front porch—perfected with two adorable handmade rocking chairs—would be the most beautiful, welcoming hello to everyone who visits.

I've never been inside, and my body catches up on that fun

fact by the time Gus slows to a stop. The back of my neck gets hot and my insides twist with nerves.

When Gus switches the gear into park, he finally faces me. Confusion and worry find their way onto his face. "Daze? What's wrong?"

"This is my first time at your house," I admit in between chewing on my bottom lip. My hands tremble together.

Those dark brows of his furrow. "What? Really? I mean—" He stops. It's like I have a front row seat to watch the last ten years catch up to him. "Yeah." Gus blows out a breath. "I guess you're right. Well, Beth handed me the deed a year after we graduated. She told me I proved myself independent and capable. You see the front door there?" He points up ahead, and I nod.

"That's the door I use ninety-nine percent of the time. The back door is a slider to a small deck. That's where my grill is. There's a small staircase that leads down to the backyard, but honestly? I haven't had time to really reinforce the wood there, so it's kind of rickety, and I don't recommend using it. There's a basement with a bulkhead door. No garage."

Gus continues to list off fact after fact of his unfamiliar house with ease. My anxiety dissipates a little more with every token of information he bestows on me. He never once pushes me to leave the truck, or asks why all of this knowledge might mean something to me.

Because he already knows it means more than I'll ever be able to admit. He knows still—after years of therapy—that I struggle to handle new places without extensive research into exits and safe spaces.

Even after all this time and the hell I've willingly put him through, August still prioritizes finding light in my dark past. For me.

He wraps up his verbal tour. "And I'll walk you through everything again once we get inside if need be."

For as mean and giant and dirty and brutal August can be, he's also gentle. When he wants to be. I've just let myself forget that over time, but that's hard to do now, when he's sitting next to me, coaxing me down from an impending anxiety attack without even trying.

"Gus," I start. I pull my bottom lip in with my teeth, and I watch his eyes follow. "Are we—Do you think we could be friends again?"

His cheeks go pink, and Gus doesn't even pretend to hide the shock on his face.

I don't know if it was the sex or the camping or how quick he was to pull me away from my mother. Maybe it was how as soon as I said I needed him to help with riverside stuff, he didn't object or make it a *thing* like I would've assumed he would have. It could've been witnessing every interaction between him and Penelope, watching the sweetest of little friendships form over the past couple years. I replay the moment right before this. Gus's immediate response to my anxiety wasn't to freeze or scoff. It was to help. In every single way.

It's quite possibly a compilation of all of those moments, a collection of the last two or so years where I found myself questioning the solidness of our disdain, choosing to wave off such a ridiculous feeling.

But maybe it wasn't so ridiculous. Maybe we've both just been too stubborn, stuck in our ways. Hellbent on each of us winning or being right or what-the-fuck-ever we were trying to convince ourselves of.

When Gus doesn't respond, I feel the panic rise in me again. What a stupid thing to say—to suggest. Friends? We...Was the term *friends* ever an acceptable description of our relationship? Or was it always some grey area that only existed for us?

I try to backtrack as fast as humanly possible, my old insecurities creeping out in the worst kind of form.

"Kidding!" I laugh, fake in every way. "Obviously just joking. We weren't, or rather, we can't be friends. Right?"

I don't count the seconds of silence that stretch, longer and longer, to the point where I think walking back home in the pitch black dead of night would be a more pleasant alternative than dying in the quietude of this godforsaken truck.

Gus chuckles, humorless. "Yeah, you assuming we were never anything to each other tracks, Daisy."

"That's *not* what I meant," I practically shout.

In the small space of the truck's cab, Gus turns his whole body to face me. "Forget it. We don't need to rehash the past. We both have proven we can't handle it. I'll just lay it all out here. I want to fuck you."

I try to stifle my gasp to no avail.

Gus reaches up to rub the back of his neck. "That was aggressive, sorry. We don't have to be friends, you can continue to hate me—"

"I told you I don't hate you," I slip in.

"Whatever. We both know where we stand. This can be just sex."

Do we know where we stand? He seems confident in that whereas I…I'm lost.

"Just sex," I confirm. "That's what you wanted to talk to me about?"

He nods in answer.

"I feel like you could find this arrangement with just about anyone else," I say.

"I don't want to." It sounds like an admission.

"Is that why you brought me here? To fuck me? You were so sure I'd be desperate enough to say yes and jump in your pants whenever you commanded it?"

I watch Gus's restraint slip right in front of me. "Jesus Christ, *no*. Yes, I came to you to ask about some sort of friends with benefits situation, like the movies, or whatever. I thought it'd be mutually beneficial. But I brought you here to get you away from that fucking mutant you call a mother. No other motive behind it. Take a goddamn break from the theatrics, Daisy."

"I'm just reviewing the optics of the situation, August."

Gus wags a finger at me. "Careful, Daze. You look like Mary Jane in this light."

The accusation feels like a slap to the face. "Take it back," I demand.

"Nope." Gus pops the P, and irritates me in a way no one else is capable of.

"Whatever," I say in defeat. "Fine. I flew off the handle. I'm just kind of caught off guard. And I'm not saying *no*—" I mull things over. No-strings-attached sex with one person does sound sort of…nice. And while I can't definitively label what we are, this could work. Maybe. "We need to add to our rules."

"What, are you going to make me sign a contract?" Gus scoffs.

"That's not the worst idea, actually." I reach down and pull the notebook out of my tote bag.

"Daisy, I'm not signing a sex contract." He swipes a hand down his face.

"Why not? This way there's no grey area. We can just do… whatever—be safe, get off, and then be on our separate ways."

I open up to a fresh page of lined paper and uncap my pen. I cheekily title the top *Laundry List.*

Gus leans over to inspect, the breath from his laugh reaches the side of my neck, and I feel goosebumps break out across the small bit of exposed skin. "Ha, okay, wait—That's good. I like that."

Pretending his praise has no effect on me, I start writing out the first bullet point. My most important rule.

No kissing.

"I still don't entirely agree with that one," Gus adds.

"And I still don't care." I move on to number two.

Not a soul can know.

"Ah, yes. Because I was planning on actually using this arrangement as my first post online. Y'know, really start off with a bang." Gus's commentary earns him a giggle from me. I hate that he's funny.

"Do you have anything you'd like to add?" I offer him the pen.

Gus takes the notebook and pen, positioning the notebook on the steering wheel so he can write. He takes several minutes to finish whatever he deems important for this list of rules, and then wordlessly hands it back to me to inspect.

His handwriting still sucks, but it's always been legible to me. He's added three bullet points.

Safe word: Shrimp

Okay…sure.

I'm not sharing.

He underlined that one.

You gotta sleep over.

"You know I need clarification on literally all of these, right?" I confirm.

"Sure. I just didn't…I didn't want to be too specific just in case someone found your precious list."

Oh. Well, that was honestly really smart. "Proceed," I tell Gus.

"A safe word is kind of non-negotiable. You need to feel

secure in anything we do. I picked shrimp because…It's dumb. We can change it, use a regular one. Just not *stop* because that one isn't very safe in my opinion."

"You picked shrimp for Bubba Gump Shrimp, didn't you?" I interrupt.

His cheeks go pink again. "I thought it was funny."

It has nothing to do with the fact that it's your favorite movie, Daisy. Get it together.

A small smile finds its way onto my face. "It is. Shrimp's good with me. Onto the next," I urge Gus to continue.

His face hardens. "While we're doing this, it's just me and you. I'm not into sharing."

"Really? I pegged you as a threesome kind of guy," I tease. Although, I really wouldn't be surprised if he was into it. Or has been a participant, or—I don't want to visualize that, actually.

"Nah. Not my thing," Gus says. "I'm not into pegging either, for the record. To each their own, but no, thank you. What I really meant is, I won't be sleeping with anyone else outside of this arrangement. And I'm asking the same of you in return."

Does he actually think I have a mile-long roster I can fuck my way through? "Yeah, Gus. No one else. Got it."

"Cool," he sighs. "Alright, last one, the big one. I don't feel good about giving you the boot after we're done. I have a spare bedroom if you want it. But really, Daze, I'm not cool with you leaving as soon as we get cleaned up."

That's a lot more than I thought this would be. "Is this a regular thing for you?"

I watch Gus's mouth open and close, clearly ruminating on how to answer my latest follow up question.

"No, actually. I've never had anyone spend the night. Unless you count the one time a woman slept over without my permission. She was weird. It's…different. With you." Every word drips with honesty, so much so that I suck in a breath.

"Do you want to elaborate on that? Because to me, it sounds like there's some unpacking we might need to do before we can do…whatever it is we want to do. No pegging, of course," I add to lighten the mood.

The joke doesn't land, unfortunately. Gus remains steely serious. "I couldn't tell you a single fact about any of the other women I've slept with. I'm not bragging, I'm not proud of it or whatever. I don't think it makes me a bad guy either though. Because I've always been upfront. But Daisy, shit. I *know* you. Or, I did. I still do? It's confusing as fuck to me, but I wouldn't be able to live with myself if this was completely transactional. You can say we're not friends, whatever makes you feel better, but—"

"Okay," I say, gently placing my hand on top of his. I have to admit to myself that my perception of our strained relationship might not have been the whole truth. But currently, I can't bear diving into specifics.

Gus turns his hand over to hold mine. The move is so delicate. Light. Featherlike.

"Is there anything else you think we should add?" he asks, his tone changing slightly.

The air in this truck becomes stifling. I shift in my seat and pull at the fabric of my skirt to adjust.

"Uh, no. I think that covers things." I flip the pages closed. Gus reaches out to grab the notebook, and tosses it to the floor.

"And you're staying over tonight?" Gus questions, his massive body taking up so much space. And yet, he's still able to lean further into me.

Inches. Fucking inches separate us. The hand not holding mine reaches below my skirt, grazing my skin up my calf to my thigh.

"Well, I told Mary Jane I wasn't coming home," I think out loud. Gus grips my thigh, shifting me until my back leans into the passenger side door, my feet still resting on the bench seat.

"Say yes," Gus commands, and my body betrays me by agreeing immediately. My insides light up like the freaking Fourth of July. A devilish smile breaks out across his face.

I'm so screwed.

"Yes."

CHAPTER 13: DAISY - WHAT'S MY NAME, DAISY DARLING?

The Journal of Daisy D. Stiles - Thirteen years ago

*A*ugust loves the color yellow, and he's never seen the movie
Forest Gump.

*He asks what I'm writing about daily, and every day I say the same
thing: Just stuff.*

*The truth of the matter is, if I ever actually let it slip out that I've
hyper fixated on each little thing he utters to me over the course of our
days in Merrymount High's guidance office, I might never see him again.*

That would crush me.

*So I pocket whatever fact he decides to bestow on me and reply with
numerous follow-up questions. Sometimes he answers. Sometimes he
doesn't.*

*I couldn't tell you what got him to start talking, especially to me.
One day it was the usual silence. The next, curiosity—or something—
got the best of him. And now we're here.*

*I don't have his phone number. He's never offered it or asked for
mine. Maybe that's a line for him. It's sort of pathetic how okay I am to
just take what I can get.*

But despite all of that, I've decided we're friends now. Even if it's only within these bland walls.

* * *

AUGUST LOOKS up at me with hooded eyes, and I already know I'll agree with just about anything he's going to say with the way his gaze is turning over hot coals in my core.

"You gonna let me eat your pussy?" he asks unabashedly, continuing to guide the long fabric of my skirt up my body, until the purple lace of my impractical underwear is exposed. He separates my thighs, and he looks at me for a long while. I fight the urge to tremble beneath his gaze.

"Do you *want* to eat my pussy?" I taunt him. Because while I know I'm ultimately giving in, I still have to play with him. Keep him on his toes.

"More than I want air to breathe, Daze."

My mouth falls open in the shape of a big ole O. August's face hovers low over me, close but absolutely not touching. So close the only piece of himself he's offering is his breath. It tickles my exposed skin, and I have to stop myself from writhing on this seat.

Where is he even finding the space for this?

"Daisy darling," he says low while keeping his eyes on mine. I avert my gaze down. His left hand lowers, smoothing over my thigh. His hand covers so much of my skin. The tip of his thumb brushes towards the inside, just hitting the sensitive part, and I jump. His hand continues its journey up until it reaches the crease of my hip. My eyes snap back to his when his grip tightens on me. "I asked you a question."

"Oh." Right. He did do that. "You're waiting for me to answer?" Is my brain broken?

His tone is serious and absolute. "Your body, your rules,

Daisy. I need to hear a resounding yes before I make you see fucking stars with my tongue."

"*Yes*," I half-cry. "Yes, please." I throw my head back when he wastes no time pushing my thong aside to devour me. I don't know when consent and absolutely justified cockiness became my kinks, or if I'm broken and only get this worked up for August Burton now. But either way, I'm fucked.

His right hand mirrors his left, gripping my hip. He pulls me into him, lifting my ass off the seat to get a better angle. His tongue swirls while he sucks, and I'm lost to the feeling immediately.

For every gasp of pleasure, Gus meets me with a satisfied moan into my core.

I've never met a man who treats going down on a woman like it's his last meal the way Gus apparently can. It's like gasoline on the fire inside me.

It's almost as if his face was crafted just for this, just so he could fit perfectly between my thighs and unravel me with his tongue while his eyes refuse to leave mine, eliciting every feeling —both physical and mental—from me without my permission.

"You taste so good, Daze," he mumbles between strokes of his tongue. I gasp when his teeth graze my clit.

"Fuck, that's nice," I pant. My head hits the glass of the window behind me.

Gus pauses, and a fucking *whimper* escapes me.

"Are you okay?"

"You stopped," I breathe.

"Your head," he counters.

"My head is fine, August."

His mouth is back on my pussy without a second thought. His teeth graze my clit again, and my hips buck in answer.

"*Fuck*," I exhale.

Gus's tongue continues to lap at me, switching to a torturously slow pace that has me writhing in his grasp. I feel myself getting wetter with every second, the build-up becoming too much. And yet at the same time…"Gus," I attempt to get out in between gulps of air.

"What did I tell you, Daze? It's *August*." His right hand releases my hip. He smacks my pussy, jolting the lower half of my body into the air.

"*Did you just—*"

"What's my name, Daisy darling?" He leaves light kisses everywhere except where I need them. His finger starts to toy with my entrance, giving me centimeters instead of filling me like he knows I want. Like I *need.*

"August, I want to come. Please make me come," I beg. It's pathetic, and right now, I don't fucking care. Right now, I get to forget everything—my mother, the flower shop, my brothers, my issues with my miserable fucking life, everything. I get to just enjoy the company of someone who so easily knows what works. I'm going to selfishly bask in that for however long I'm granted the privilege.

Even if it is because of August Burton.

Forgoing the ruse of working up towards anything, August's eyes darken. The last thing I see is his wicked grin before he thrusts two fingers deep inside me, fucking me, while his tongue once again paints a fucking portrait on my clit.

I reach up and find the grab handle, letting myself ride August's face through my orgasm. He doesn't stop—not until I'm panting and begging and squirming from how sensitive I am.

August lowers me back onto the seat and shamelessly wipes his mouth, my release practically glistening there, with the back of his hand. I know without confirmation that I'm blushing.

"You're beautiful like this," he says.

"Like what?" I stupidly ask, readjusting my clothes and myself.

"Sated. Taken care of. C'mon, let's go make dinner." August

reaches down, grabbing my notebook and bag, taking them both with him when he exits the truck. My body hasn't caught up to the rest of me by the time he makes it around to my side, tapping on the window so when he opens the door, I don't fall out.

For some reason, though, I think he'd catch me.

I gather my wits and let August open the door for me to step out. An eerie sense of familiarity wraps around me as we walk side by side up the path leading to his porch.

Once inside, August makes good on his earlier promise, giving me a full, extremely detailed and extensive tour of his house—basement with spider webs and potential mice included —until we arrive back at the front door.

"Good to stay?" he asks.

"Yes?" I answer with a laugh. "Didn't I say that earlier?"

"Doesn't mean you couldn't have changed your mind," he answers. He hangs my tote bag up on the coat rack beside the door and then holds his arm out, gesturing for me to lead the way into what I now know is his kitchen.

"Your house is beautiful, by the way. I forgot to mention that while you were showing me around," I tell Gus, and I mean it.

Sure, it's lacking some decor. The walls could use, well, just about anything on them. But every piece of furniture looks like it was chosen very purposefully. Everything screams *August*. Dark wood, deep maroons, and juniper throughout.

A sheepish look crosses his face. He rubs the back of his neck. "Thanks. It's not much but—"

"Shut up, August. It's a home." I don't like him downplaying something he clearly has put a lot of time and effort in over the years. August has never been bashful or self-conscious.

His eyes widen slightly, but he shakes off his surprise in the next second. "Yeah, I...I really like having a place to call my own."

God, when he speaks candidly like that, I feel so much like we're our old selves.

I make myself comfy in the breakfast nook that overlooks the backyard. Fallen leaves have already been sorted into piles. There's a fire pit with a couple chairs around it and a few logs stacked nearby, presumably ready for whenever Gus decides to have himself a night by said fire. I find myself halfway hoping I might be included in that kind of night.

Which is silly, because well—actually, I guess I don't have much of a reason to assume it'd be silly to want that now when I've already waded into friendly waters with August.

He gets started on dinner and declines my offer to help. I go and retrieve my headphones from my bag. But right before I place them over my ears, Gus turns from the stove to face me.

"What are you planning on listening to?" he asks.

"Audiobook," I tell him. "I have like thirty percent left of this one, and everything's gone to shit in the story. I've been dying to finish it."

He walks over to me, mixing bowl of whatever he's putting together in one hand, and plucks the headphones from me with the other.

"Connect to that thing." Gus gestures to the little sphere speaker with an owl design that's perched on his counter. "But wait, before you hit play, catch me up, so I can follow along with you."

"It's a romance," I attempt to warn him.

"And?" Gus questions, heading back to his workspace next to the oven.

"Aaaaand," I drag out. "I don't know. I'd assume you wouldn't be into that sort of thing."

He doesn't turn around again, letting me take in the sight of his back muscles stretching the thin material of his shirt as he starts pounding the chicken with a meat cleaver. Damn, he just got me off in the truck no less than a half an hour ago, and I'm ready for round two.

Once he finishes with the first chicken breast, he pauses. A quick chuckle escapes him.

"You say that like I didn't spend a significant amount of time listening to you recap every smutty book you got your hands on in high school. This isn't new to me, Daze. Let it rip."

CHAPTER 14: AUGUST - THE FAMILIARITY OF THE DARK AND QUIET

I told Daisy she looked beautiful earlier, right after I made her come. I didn't want to look away from the way her cheeks flushed and her chest heaved, almost breathless. And I meant it, she really did. She always has, even when we're fighting. Actually, especially when we're fighting.

But God, it doesn't hold a candle to how beautiful she looks right now. The light cast from the moon and the stars are shining bright on her in the most magical way while she sleeps soundly next to me on the couch. She fell asleep about an hour ago, and I didn't have the nerve to wake her up to move her.

I know I could scoop her up and carry her upstairs without issue. But we never discussed sleeping arrangements, and I don't want to assume. I can't assume.

Not with Daisy.

If I brought her into my bed, I'd be assuming she was okay with sleeping next to me. A line might be crossed. If I carried her into my spare bedroom, she might wake up alone and panic—needing possibly more than a minute to get her bearings. If I just left her here on the couch…Well, that's just not a fucking option.

Sometimes, people think because I'm the big guy who doesn't

hesitate to throw my weight around that I don't have a lot going on in my head. And I guess those who assume that might be half right—I'm not winning awards in academics or anything, but I can overthink a lot. I never want to be the worst guy in a room. I want…I hope, maybe someday, I can make someone proud.

Having Daisy here is…I don't know how to describe it. My head has felt underwater—borderline drowning—all night. It's like old times, but there's more. It's like every curiosity I had about Daisy Stiles was held in a limbo for a decade and now that the ice has cracked, I'm unsteady with no sense of balance.

I kept everything locked up. I chalked my teenage feelings up to be nothing more than that. Because there never could be more. There still can't. I look over at Daisy, the blanket I gave her before we turned the TV on pulled up so it's resting on her cheek. The steady rise and fall of her breathing has a perfect rhythm I find myself counting.

She'll always deserve better than the cards she was handed.

This thing we're doing…It's probably not healthy. It's absolutely going to fuck with my head. But, I can handle it. To get quiet moments like this, I'll take it.

My phone pings with a text, and I reach out toward the coffee table to grab it.

It's a notification from a group text Sawyer added me to against my will. There's an unknown number included. Quickly putting the dots together that it's Daisy, I save her as a new contact. I ignore how bizarre it feels to finally have something as trivial as her phone number after so much history between us.

RED BOZELLI

i think a night out is in order for this weekend, whooooooooo's in??? p's chilling with me!

MARGOT

Me! Sawyer! Us!

RED BOZELLI

yes, my honey bunny pregnant queen. i assumed
your rsvp would include sawyer

RED BOZELLI

okaaaay, just waiting on gus gus and miss daisy
to grace us with responses

ME

Sure.

SAWYER HALE

Aye, Gus in the chat!

RED BOZELLI

daze? we're waiting on u girl

MARGOT

DAISY STILES, YOU CAN'T IGNORE US
FOREVER

MILLER CASWELL

She probably got scared off by Gus being here.

RED BOZELLI

daisy i swear on all that is holy if you don't text
us back in the next 2 minutes i will find you

Shit. I can't respond on her behalf because then they'd know she's with me. And these lunatics—no matter how much I love them—cannot know Daisy is staying at my place, not on night one of whatever this situation is between the two of us. But I don't want Daisy to not answer, because then everyone might worry and start asking questions.

I could...I peer over at Daisy's phone resting on the couch beside her. No. Bad idea. Invasion of privacy. Not to mention, weird as hell.

I opt to sacrifice the peacefulness of her sleep and gently shake her shoulder to wake her. "Daze," I whisper.

I'm not shocked by her jolting awake. "What?" she yells. "Ah! I fell asleep." Daisy slumps back into the couch cushions.

"It's okay. You're okay. Sorry to wake you. Umm, I didn't know where you wanted to sleep. Also, our friends want us to all go out this weekend, and they're about five seconds away from sending out a search party if you don't respond to our group text," I say in one breath.

"We're in a group text?" Daisy asks, rightfully confused. She gathers the hair that's fallen out of her ponytail while sleeping. Her loose sweater creeps up, exposing a thin line of her soft belly. She pulls the elastic out of her hair and twists her curls into a pineapple-shaped bun on the top of her head. It's messy and honestly?

It's cute as fuck.

I shake the thought away and hand Daisy her cell. She scrolls through all of the unread texts, eyes going wide at the last one from Red. But then her face relaxes.

"It's not like she'd go looking for me at your house." Daisy laughs. "My car's not even here. And it's ten o'clock at night. Red isn't leaving her house for shit." I watch her type out a quick reply, and my phone pings with the notification.

DAISY DARLING

Dramatic little bitches. I'll be there.

She tosses her phone on my coffee table, not bothering to wait for anyone else's response. I copy her, placing mine next to hers.

Daisy huffs. "Damn, your couch is comfy as hell."

I stretch my arm out over the back of it and throw one leg on the ottoman. "Thanks, did a lot of saving to get the big one. I drove out to that furniture store with the 3D movie theater."

"The one with the funky mirrors in the bathrooms?" she exclaims.

"Yeah." I laugh. "That one. Place is fucking ginormous. I got lost like, seven times. But she was worth it." I smooth my hand over the fabric.

"I have to agree with you. I'm okay to sleep here, by the way. You didn't have to hang out down here and watch me drool."

"A Stiles drooling? Can't be. Your genetics wouldn't allow such a disgrace to the family name."

Daisy's shriek could probably be heard all the way back to Main Street. "Fuck off!" She playfully swats my arm.

"Such *language* from a Stiles," I keep the mockery going.

And Daisy just keeps laughing, and shit, does it sound fucking pretty.

So much so, the next words just fall out of my mouth. "I like the sound of that."

"What?" Daisy asks in between hiccups of giggles.

"You. Laughing. This." I gesture to the dark, quiet house around us. "It's nice."

Daisy criss-crosses her legs, scooting back into the cuddlier part of the sectional.

"I actually thought about something like this when we were camping. Do you remember the time I tried to sneak you into my bedroom? And we couldn't fit ourselves on the bed together but kept trying until you crashed to the floor?"

"And Mary Jane came storming in to throw me out, but I was already halfway out your window?" I finish the memory, not bringing up how she *did* start to reminisce out loud on this particular one a couple weeks ago.

"She sucks," Daisy says with a sigh.

"Things never got better, huh?" It's a dumb question that I clearly already know the answer to.

Daisy starts smoothing out the blanket on her lap, her earlier playfulness gone.

"No. I mean—she tries. And I can't say the same about our dad, so I guess she earns that point. For Hunter and Chase. Not sure what good it does seeing as Hunter is basically gearing up to be the next Dean Fitzgerald, and Chase…I don't know what to say about Chase."

"What do you mean?" The twins were babies, barely considered functioning human beings when Daisy and I fell off. I see them around town. That's a given in a small place like Merrymount, but I couldn't tell you a single thing about them other than the fact that they're practically carbon copies of Daisy in lanky, boy form.

Daisy blows out a long breath. "About two years ago, right around their tenth birthday, Chase stopped talking. And not like, in some bratty, defiant way. I mean, completely mute. My parents, to no one's surprise, lost their ever-loving minds over it, but the answer remains a mystery to everyone but Chase. He's such a good kid, always focused on school, kind to everyone, sweet. He's just such a sweet kid. It kills me, to be honest."

That's some heavy shit. I don't even know what I could say.

"You don't have to say anything, August," Daisy comments, basically reading my mind. "Chase being silent is honestly the least of my worries. He and I understand each other. Now, Hunter on the other hand…"

"Comparing him to Dean sounds rough. I can't lie." None of us have complained about the lack of Dean Fitzgerald since he skipped town earlier this year after getting arrested for drinking and driving, resulting in him losing his precious job at the police station. Good riddance.

"He's a real fucking peach. I'll tell you that much. But, maybe that's all twelve-year-old boys. I don't know. I'm not their mother. I'm just trying to make sure they turn out half decent. And well, you've met my parents. There's not much help in that department. But what do I know? It's not like I'm any better, right?" She sounds so defeated. It makes me feel instantly guilty for adding to her pressure all these years.

I've only let myself think about it three times—maybe four. A set amount of time to feed that nagging, pest of a spot in the back of my brain that asked, *Why did you stay?*

Why remain in the house you always referred to as a prison? Why put up with two failures for parents? You wanted to get out. You were getting out.

But her face says it all, no words needed.

She saw little two kids, with no different of a start than each of us had, and saw the fork in the road. Daisy made the decision to not leave her brothers' lives up to the same chance we had growing up. She took on a burden that wasn't hers without complaint.

For all of those same years, I laid into her every chance I got. I threw around words like selfish, pretentious, and self-centered. And she never even made the time to deny it, only throwing my own ugliness back in my face in repayment.

Well fucking deserved and more on my part.

When she decided to stay, I have no idea. Was it before everything, and she just didn't tell me? Was all of it…for nothing?

I feel like the damn wind just got knocked out of me.

My socked feet abruptly hit the hardwood floor, and I pull myself up to stand. I'm not nearly ready to let this conversation go any further. I'll say the wrong thing and—just nope.

I click the muted TV off and toss the remote on the couch.

"You'll never be your parents, Daze. And you're not sleeping on the fucking couch. The spare bed has fresh sheets, and mine is available too. Well, the left side is. I sleep on the right."

Daisy doesn't move, twisting the blanket between her fingers. She refuses to look up, but I can see her toying with that pouty lower lip of hers.

"No, really. The couch is perfectly fine," she says stubbornly.

I don't bother arguing. Fuck this coy act she has going on. I take a chance and bend over, hoisting Daisy up over my shoulder, blanket in tow, dangling and swishing on the floor.

"August!" Her fists rap against my ass, and I chuckle the whole

way up the stairs. While she puts on a little show, her body is relaxed against me. Once on the second floor, I gently place Daisy back on solid ground in between my room and the spare. A bathroom door sits between, with a second door connecting to the spare bedroom. There's another full bath in my room.

Daisy plants those same fists on her hips. "I have a say in this! You can't just throw me around like a sack of potatoes!"

I attempt to imitate her pose, and I swear I see her want to break character for half a second. "Just did. Get over it. I gave you two perfectly respectable options. Pick one."

I think she's about to actually stomp her foot when she pivots left, marches in, and turns again to slam the spare bedroom door in my face.

"Goodnight, August," Daisy ends the conversation on her terms. Just like she always does.

Except this time it doesn't grate me like it normally would. This time, I have to really respect when a woman like Daisy takes what she wants, and accepts nothing less.

I change into a pair of sweats and halfway through brushing my teeth, I realize I forgot to bring Daisy one of my extra toothbrushes. Mouthful of toothpaste and balancing my toothbrush between my teeth, I cross the hallway, peace offering in the form of dental hygiene in hand, when the door opens before I can knock.

My toothbrush bobbles almost out and onto the floor when my jaw falls open on its own accord.

Daisy stands in the doorway, right hip popped out wearing a T-shirt that's entirely too big for her, the dark grey cotton skimming maybe an inch or two above her knee.

My T-shirt.

She's wearing *my* shirt, and wildly possessive caveman instincts try to break through. I swallow them down, keeping my shit in check.

"I was literally just coming to ask you for one of these. Thank you," Daisy says, plucking the toothbrush I'm still stupidly holding up from my limp hand.

"Glad you found pajamas," I stammer.

I think things can't get worse, and then her cheeks darken. What the fuck is *wrong* with me right now?

"This is okay, right? Sorry. Should I have asked? There's a pile of T-shirts and shorts—"

"Daze." I go to cup her shoulder, but I stop an inch away and now my hand is just awkwardly hovering. I don't trust myself to touch her right now. I need to get back to my room. "It's cool. You didn't exactly have time to pack a sleepover bag. Looks good on you." I retreat back and turn to shut the door. "Night."

I jerk myself off later in the shower to the image of Daisy standing there in the low hallway light with a deep blush on her face, looking back at me in only my thin T-shirt, whispering an almost silent *goodnight*. One of her small hands, nails painted a blue that matches her eyes, wrapped around the doorframe.

I thought it felt like old times before, and it does—to an extent. But I'm starting to realize the new I'm finding might be even better.

CHAPTER 15: AUGUST - GOOD MORNING, DAISY MY DARLING

It's about seven a.m. by the time I'm turning the burner off on the stove. It's a lot later than I usually start the day, but I'm letting Daisy sleep. Plus, my workload is light today, and it wasn't difficult for me to push my tasks around so my tardy arrival didn't look suspicious.

Daisy has rules, and I gotta follow them. Can't tell a soul. Got it.

I barely fucking slept last night. Knowing Daze was in the room across the hall, in my goddamn shirt, unsure if she was comfortable enough to fall back to sleep drove me nuts.

Everything's driving me nuts.

I had no plans to switch my life around whatsoever, and now I'm over here making friends with benefits contracts with the one person I'm usually trying to avoid in every crowd.

And I'm asking myself why I was avoiding her, and that's pissing me the hell off. Because Daisy and I not getting along was something I was sure would never change. A constant.

What the fuck ever, not a now problem.

I bring two plates down from the cabinet and think through

how I'm gonna get Daisy up and out of here without a fight, someone seeing us, or any other dramatic shitshow.

My phone lights up on the counter beside me.

@riversriverco posted a new story!

Did I turn post notifications on for the riverside and Daisy's personal page? Uh—

Yeah. Not my proudest moment, but it fucking beats refreshing each page two hundred times a day. Which I'm not admitting to doing.

I wait for the post to load and take in the picture of the sunrise, surely taken a couple of days ago, above some blurb written about early mornings best spent by the water. Daisy paired it with another Noah Kahan song, her favorite artist for riverside posts. It's not surprising and definitely on brand for what we got going on here.

It dawns on me that if this just went live, she's awake.

I toss my phone. "Daisy!" I yell, walking towards the staircase.

I hear the creaking of floorboards and a door opening. "Why are you yelling?" Daisy calls.

"Breakfast! Let's go, or you're walking your ass back to town!"

I retreat back to the kitchen, making myself busy with the food, and wait until I hear footsteps descending the stairs.

When I turn and find Daisy sauntering in still wearing that flimsy-ass shirt, I swallow hard.

It appears she also found a pair of my grey wool socks to match. They're simultaneously hiked up her calves and slouching. And when the hell did something like oversized, comfy socks become sexy?

Her hair is messily tossed to one side of her head, and she's got sleepy eyes, a fist rubbing one of them. I can see her nipples poking through the thin material, and I have no idea how I'm going to get through this meal and get us out the door without combusting.

"Good morning," she offers. Daisy's eyes trail up and down

my body, sight landing south, right where I know my sweatpants hang low.

"You saying that to my magic carpet, or to me?" I joke.

Daisy rolls her eyes but otherwise ignores me, journeying right past me to grab one of the plates I pulled down. I don't move to give her any room, half stuck in place, half desperate to be close to her.

There's a lot of confusing shit going on in my head.

When she turns to scoop a spoonful of scrambled eggs onto her plate, her backside brushes against my front, and all rational thought ceases to exist.

My hands smack on the counter, arms caging Daisy in from behind. She freezes, dropping the spoon back into the pan. I lower my head to the side of her neck. "Is this okay?" I whisper.

Daisy tilts her neck, giving me access, a silent invitation I instantly take. She leans back into me with a quiet sigh. I begin kissing and sucking lightly along her neck, breathing her in, thankful that no kissing rule apparently doesn't apply to this. Fine by me.

"So we're really doing this?" Daisy questions as I lightly nip at her neck.

"I had to finish myself off in the shower last night, Daze," I say into her skin. "I came so fucking hard, picturing you coming undone in my truck." I lick right below her ear, and I feel goosebumps rise. "Picturing you in this shirt. *My* shirt." I grab a fistful of the material.

She shakes her head and arches her back so her ass presses right up against my hard cock.

"You feel that, Daze? You feel how easy it is for you to get me going?"

Next thing I know, her arm is reaching back, and she grips my cock through my sweats. "Wow, Gussy," she breathes. "You gonna blow in your pants?" Her fingers squeeze around my length.

I growl and lift my right hand from the counter to snake

underneath the hem of her shirt. My fingers graze her bare pussy. "No panties?" I ask shakily.

"You ruined them last night," she says matter-of-factly as I start to play with her. She's trying to act like she's unfazed, or maybe she really thinks walking around my house like this wouldn't drive me fucking mad.

I grab Daisy by the waist, turning us both together, and bend her over the island. She wiggles, desperate for friction. Her breath hitches, and satisfaction rumbles inside of me knowing I finally brought her up to the level of insanity I'm currently barely surviving in.

I hike the shirt up, exposing her backside to me and revel at the sight. "I don't want to assume," I start as my palm massages up and down her perfect ass that's sitting so goddamn pretty up in the air with the way I have her bent over. She moves her lower half in answer, balancing on her tiptoes. "But it sounds like you wanna be taken care of right now, Daisy. Fucked nice and deep and hard. Right here in the kitchen after a full night's rest. Tell me that's what you need, Daze."

She tosses her head back when I smack her right ass cheek after a beat of silence. "Condom, August. Get a condom."

I reach behind me to my junk drawer and extract a loose condom I'm thankful as hell I tossed in here however long ago.

Daisy scoffs, looking over her shoulder. Fucking beautiful, messy bedhead swaying. "How frat boy of you."

Smack.

Daze jumps and gasps, and the way her bottom bounces has me groaning.

I pull my cock out and roll the latex over my length and give myself a few pumps. I lean over to press a single finger inside of her, confirming she's wet and ready for me.

She moans, moving her ass back into me—searching for more —as I add a second finger at a languid pace. Next time I'll drag it out, make her beg. Get her real fucking needy. But I don't have the patience right now, and clearly neither does Daisy. I line my head up with her entrance and thrust. She gasps as I fill her to the hilt.

"I don't fuck like a frat boy though."

Her hands flatten, pressing hard into the black granite.

"*Oh—*" she pants.

"*Fuck,* baby. Fucking perfect," I breathe in between strokes. I let my hand roam up her curves, tracing her spine, and get it tangled up in that sexy bed of curls. Her head leans into my touch, and I grip steadily to guide her up so my lips are at her ear again.

With shallow breaths and her body still adjusting to my size, Daisy lets out satisfied moans that shake me.

I'm not gentle. That's not what Daisy wants—needs. I know because the smile that breaks out on her face is lethal when I repeat, "Fucking *perfect.*" I release her hair and snake my hand down her arm. I wrap my fingers around hers still splayed on the island.

"This is how you're supposed to start the day," Daisy says, bucking perfectly in rhythm with me. And I have to agree, it's like we were fucking created to come together like this. Like we've been doing it all along.

I feel her muscles flex around me, somehow making it a tighter fit than I thought possible. I lose any restraint I had, pounding into her, the right side of her face now pressed into the granite as she continues to moan loudly.

"That's right, Daze. It's just me and you in here. This is my house. Make as much noise as you need. I wanna fucking hear it."

"*August,*" escapes her lips.

"Forget everything else. Just me and you. You feel so fucking good." I love how her body responds to praise. I adjust my grip, lifting her slightly. My hand starts to travel over every inch of her soft skin, under the shirt and against the countertop until I'm cupping and squeezing her breast. I pinch her hardened nipple in between my fingers, and Daisy gasps.

There's something so right about all of this that it's enough for me to not fully realize how fucked up what I'm saying sounds. How much it *doesn't* make sense that she's her and I'm me. Or what we think the other is. I choose to revel in feeling the build up of Daisy's climax, pussy flexing around me, getting me to the same point.

"Yes, August, yes, please. *Oh my God*, just like that," she coaches me. I do exactly as I'm fucking told, easily flipping the dynamic, letting her take full control.

I grunt as Daisy rolls her ass backwards, the tip of my cock hitting a spot that has her moaning again, head tipped back.

"Daze—" I start.

"I'm right there, August." She reaches back, pulling my hand to her. I rub two fingers in circles on her clit, applying pressure. "*Yes—*"

Not a drop of control left, I spill into the condom. She comes around me, and I keep slow strokes until we're both panting, heaving messes.

Seconds tick by, and I finally pull out to toss the condom. Daisy doesn't change position, the front half of her still resting on the island. Taking in the sight of her, I'm hit with the intrusive thought of Daisy bent over like this with my come dripping down her thigh. I picture swiping a finger up to push the mess back inside of her, where it belongs. Satisfaction rumbles throughout my chest.

Holy fucking shit, what the hell is wrong with me?

I've never fucked without protection, never planned on it, considering the fact little Burton gremlins have never been on the table. I don't daydream, or whatever the fuck that was, about knocking anyone up. I like to get off and get out. It's always been just sex.

I shake my head, clearing my thoughts to get back to Daisy. I run a hand up the length of her spine, and when she hums in response, I swear my dick twitches for a round two.

She slowly rises, letting the T-shirt fall to cover her again, and she turns to look up at me.

As the pink on her cheeks fades, we share a quick moment where I forget just about everything else that exists in the universe. It throws me off so much that while I watch her mouth open and form words, I couldn't tell you what a single one was. I hear nothing.

"Hmm?"

Daisy doesn't repeat herself. She pats me on the arm in a way that feels like *"good game"* and waltzes out of the kitchen.

I have half a mind to follow her. Where's she going? Why am I so screwed up, and she's unphased? I'm gonna say it again. What's wrong with me?

After a couple minutes of me regaining my ability to function, throwing an unbuttoned flannel on, washing my hands, and resuming the breakfast prep, I hear a toilet flush and the running of the sink's faucet. Daisy reenters the kitchen with her hair piled high on the top of her head.

"What's wrong?" she asks, a confused look on her face.

"What do you mean? Nothing's wrong. What's wrong with you?" I counter defensively.

"August," she sighs. "You fucked me so good that for once I'm going to ignore how truly insufferable you can be."

Daisy hip checks me to reclaim her plate and continues assembling her breakfast. She scoops up her previously abandoned scrambled eggs and sprinkles shredded cheese on top. She lifts the plate, and I grab it from her hands to reach up and put it in the microwave for her.

"I was going to melt the cheese for you earlier, but we got distracted." I punch in thirty seconds on the keypad and hit start.

"Oh." Daisy doesn't hide the surprise on her face. "Thanks," she adds.

"Just go sit down and let me *insufferably* get your breakfast for you, okay?"

"Oh…" she hesitates. "'Kay…" Daisy slowly backs away, rounding the island to mercifully take a seat without protest.

I realize all of the breakfast components are cold. I flip one of the burner's dials back to low heat to warm the potatoes and bacon, not wanting everything to be nuked in the microwave.

I bank on my probably-outdated Daisy Stiles knowledge and dice up a rogue tomato and an avocado I hope is ripe. Beth drops off random vegetables, hoping I'll add them to my meals. Like I'm a toddler. But hey, the mother hen energy is coming in clutch right about now.

I retrieve the plate from the microwave, add a portion of breakfast potatoes, a couple slices of bacon, and the veggies. I sprinkle salt and pepper on everything, and grab the bottle of hot sauce from the fridge along with a fork from the utensil drawer before placing everything in front of Daisy.

Her arms remain at her sides. She stays frozen in place staring at the plate of food. Silent.

"Daze?" I prompt. I really don't want the food to get cold again.

Did I fuck this up that bad?

"You…made me food. And plated it. And served it." She finally picks up the fork, spearing a chunk of avocado, and holds it up. "This is an avocado that you cut up."

And with this, I come to the conclusion that we're both extremely broken people.

Because if Daisy's brain can't compute someone putting together a ridiculously simple breakfast, and I can't tell the difference between the moan that escapes her lips when she comes, or the one she makes when she tastes a bite of a seasoned potato—we're fucked.

"Eat up," I tell her before turning to make my own plate.

We eat across from each other, neither of us bothering with

conversation in between bites. There's not a drop of tension in the air, and I have to admit it's nice to sit in companionable silence.

As we're finishing up, a knock causes us both to freeze. Our forks clank down onto our respective plates. I lean forward to get a clear view of my front door while Daisy springs out of her chair.

I hear the doormat flop, and realize we have less than twenty seconds before Beth Rivers uses the spare key and is in my fucking house.

"It's Beth," I whisper. "What do you want to do?"

This is Daisy's call. Nobody knowing is her rule, after all.

She dives to the closet behind her, throwing herself into my mess of bath and beach towels. I throw our plates and silverware crashing into the sink.

The key enters the lock, another knock accompanying it, along with Beth's raised voice. "August, my boy, you're awfully late. Sawyer's already running his mouth. I'm coming in. Be decent!"

"S-sorry, Beth," I stammer. "Morning—Good morning." I try to peer down and confirm I look presentable. I quickly fasten a couple of the buttons on my flannel closed and pull my sweatpants further up.

"Smells good in here. Are you okay?" Beth stops at the entrance to the kitchen with a hand on her hip. She has a denim baseball hat covering her short grey hair and is wearing her usual pair of work jeans, boots, and a white thermal long sleeve under a Rivers River T-shirt.

"Fine. I'm fine. I just, uh, I needed a slow start. Headache." I point to my forehead.

Beth narrows her eyes, inspecting me for injury or ailment. "Have you started taking your allergy meds? You know this is your season."

"Forgot." I shrug. "I'll pick them up next time I'm at the store.

You know you could have just texted or called, right?" I mean this in the nicest, most respectful way possible, I need Beth out of my fucking house five minutes ago.

"Oh, really?" she asks. Beth's eyes scan the kitchen, and I don't know how I know, but I know I'm screwed in some capacity. "Funny. Because I did text *and* call. Both unanswered. So, now I'm here to put eyes on you."

"Beth—"

"Save it, my boy. Get dressed and get to work." She pivots, and I'm convinced I survived this interaction with a very minor reprimand for tardiness. This is something I can live with.

She's halfway down the hall to leave when she pauses. "Oh, I mean, after you bring Miss Stiles home. Good morning, Daisy, my darling. I'll be seeing *you* later," Beth calls. A few footsteps and the front door slamming later, she's gone.

I basically turn into a statue.

The accordion door of the closet flies open, and Daisy's wide eyes meet mine.

"Oh my fucking *God*," she shrieks.

Warranted. Very fair, given the situation.

"It's not that bad," I try to offer.

"You're kidding right now, right?"

"Okay, it's bad," I concede. "But you know she won't say anything."

"August, she's going to make our lives hell."

She is. I can't deny this. But admitting that out loud right now does feel dangerous.

"I'll talk to her, " I assure Daisy. Don't know what good it'll do, but I have to try.

"Can't wait to hear how that conversation goes!" Daisy shouts, face reddening. "Oh, hi, Beth. Yeah. Daisy and I can't agree on the color of the sky most days, but we're fucking because the sex is really good." She paces the kitchen, flailing her arms with every step. "No, there's absolutely nothing that could go wrong! Why would you ask that? Oh, because we're already walking on thin ice with our close knit group of friends? *Psh—*" Daisy waves to an imaginary Beth Rivers. "Nah! This is fine! Everything's fine!"

"Well, when you word it like that…" I admit.

"It's not the wording that paints this in a negative light. It's us."

All right, that was unnecessary.

"We can stop. I can tell Beth there was an emergency that has been taken care of, and we go back to normal," I say with a bite of bitterness to it.

Daisy's face softens slightly. "I didn't say that's what I wanted. I'm sorry, I'm just—This is a lot, okay?"

I take a step towards Daisy. I want to reach out and grab her, comfort her maybe, but I don't. "I know. I'm sorry. Let's just get dressed. I'll drive you home."

And that's exactly what we do. Before she leaves the truck, I hand her her tote bag and remind her she has my number now, and that she can text me for…for whatever.

She quietly confirms she will, and I risk another Mary Jane Stiles altercation to wait until Daisy gets inside before pulling out of the driveway.

Well, it is what it is. Beth knows.

Beth knows it all, I admit only to myself.

She remembers trying to pick me back up when things fell apart the first time with Daisy. She doesn't want a repeat.

Well, no fucking worries there.

I'm not letting things fall apart again.

If this morning has shown me anything, it's that no matter what goes down or how things play out, things with Daisy Stiles will always be the exception to the rule. It'll always be different.

CHAPTER 16: DAISY - I AM THE DEFINITION OF CONFUSION

The Journal of Daisy D. Stiles - Twelve and a half years ago

August found me sitting outside against the gym this afternoon. Normally, this would have made my entire day, week, month, year. But I was mid-breakdown, and August Burton is the second-to-last person on my list of people who I'd want to see me like that.

He asked what was wrong. I refused to tell him.

So—he sat. Right next to me. And didn't leave until the parking lot had cleared out and the sun had set.

He didn't offer words of encouragement or meaningless "it'll get betters."

I think somehow he knew none of that would have mattered to me.

But being there? Not leaving my side?

It was everything.

* * *

I'm more than embarrassed to admit for the first time in my life, I'm avoiding Beth Rivers.

I've kept myself holed up in my bedroom and the flower shop for a few days now, dodging calls and texts. I quietly celebrated my thirtieth birthday and the twins' twelfth. But I know it's only a matter of time before she beats down my metaphorical door for a conversation.

A conversation involving August and me and what we've done.

Not. Happening.

Today's chosen place of hiding is Merrymount Middle School.

When the twins came home on the first day of seventh grade, there was a mountain of paperwork to sift through between the two. I noticed Chase's gaze lingering on one about a new art program the school was introducing as an extracurricular activity. After a handful of nights pestering him on whether he was interested, he slid the filled-out form under my bedroom door. It just needed a signature.

So now, every Wednesday, I wait for him to trot out of the building with whatever project he got to work on that afternoon. His joy is infectious. The smile I get to witness overtakes his whole body, and for a minute, I get the honor of basking in Chase's undiluted happiness.

"Hey, my dude!" I call from my spot outside my car, waving like a lunatic. He pretends to be embarrassed, but I know he likes it.

You can tell by the playful shake of his head, and his smile never breaking. He waves back at me in greeting. But then I watch confusion alter his sweet, little face, and I turn quickly in fear of finding something wrong.

The familiar jalopy of a truck turns into the parking lot, pulling up right next to my car. Gus rolls down his window and sticks his head out, arm resting on the door.

"Hey, Stiles." He tilts his head to face Chase. "Hey, little Stiles."

Chase gives a very hesitant wave, but a greeting nonetheless.

"Gus, what are you doing at the middle school?" I ask.

"I was putzing around. Saw your car. I dunno." Suddenly his usual bravado has evacuated the premises.

"Well…" I start. I'm not sure where to go from here. "Chase, this is—"

August thrusts his hand out and cuts me off. "August. Just August. I'm an old friend of your sister's. It's Chase, right?"

That's one way to word our situation, but go off.

Chase takes a few steps forward, nods, and shakes August's hand.

"Nice to meet ya, Chase. Whatcha got there?" Gus gestures to the poster board Chase has rolled up in his other hand.

Chase hesitates but then unfurls his latest creation. Gus doesn't move, and neither do I. Chase holds up a charcoal drawing of a set of eyes. They look fucking devastating. Familiar. Beautiful, yes, Chase is so incredibly talented, but these are eyes that are going through such a deep level of heartbreak, it's hard to look away from them.

I don't realize I'm holding my breath throughout this entire interaction until I notice there's a serious lack of oxygen in my brain.

"Damn, kid," Gus finally says. "You're good."

I'd give just about anything to hear Chase utter the word thanks. Any word at all. But his quick nod is acknowledgment enough for Gus.

"It's beautiful, Chase," I add, ruffling his raven black hair. "I swear you get better every week. We should get this framed."

Chase shrugs in answer. I wrap my arm around his shoulders. "Well, we better get going. Homework to be done, dinner to be had."

"Where's Hunter?" Gus asks, ignoring my attempt to segway out of here.

"Home," I reply. "The place we're headed."

"Do you wanna grab him and meet me for some pizza at George's?"

"Do I…*What?*" I stutter, completely dumbfounded. There's no possible way August just suggested sharing a meal. Together. In public. With my *little brothers.*

But then Chase reaches his hand out to grab my wrist. His grip tightens for a split second, and it takes me another to realize he wants me to say yes.

And I'd do anything for him.

Well, just about anything. I clear my throat, preparing to offer a compromise. "Uh, you know what? Sure. But, could we do a pick-up and maybe head toward your house? If that's okay?"

"As long as it's cool with Chase here, I'm down," Gus answers easily, like nothing is weird about this entire ordeal.

Chase nods more enthusiastically now. He doesn't wait for further comment and walks over to my car, letting himself into the passenger seat.

It hits me that there *is* nothing weird about this to Gus. He loves to sit in silent company. It's how our friendship started all those years ago. Maybe he sees a little bit of himself in Chase.

My heartbeat skips, and I remind myself to do a blood pressure test or something in the near future.

"Is this some part of the friends with benefits contract I missed?" I ask when Chase is out of earshot.

August chuckles and starts his truck back up. "Yeah, Daze. Call it the friends part. Text me the boys' order, I'll call it in on my way over. Meet you at my house in about thirty."

* * *

I COULDN'T TELL you what drugs the pizza we devoured must have been laced with, but Hunter's been on his best behavior since we arrived at August's house.

He said *please* and *thank you.* He even brought Chase's empty plate to the sink when he was finished. I'm fucking gobsmacked. It's like the change of scenery has temporarily rewired his brain.

Or maybe being introduced to Gus while Gus towed over him with his arms crossed over his chest on his front porch with a look that oozed *don't fuck with me* scared him straight.

Regardless, I'm eternally grateful for the break from bickering with a twelve-year-old boy.

Instead, I get to listen to my little brother rattle off the ins and outs of the club lacrosse team he's been following all summer. He's animated and so deeply invested, if I were a crier—which I am so obviously *not*—I'd be swiping my eyes right about now.

Chase has kept up with conversation in his own way, nodding along and letting his eyes zoom from person to person. I swear when Gus made some highly inappropriate joke earlier, Chase was so fucking close to laughing.

I watch August involve Chase in everything effortlessly.

After ten years and then some of total rivalry, I suddenly want to throw it all away for even just one more simple night like this.

The clock on the wall tells me I should've had the boys home at least an hour ago, but they're having fun. I'm having fun.

I feel like I'm living someone else's life, and I can't help but ruin it for myself by wondering why August pulled into the school parking lot. Or why he invited us over. Why do any of this?

I don't like the unknown.

The new thing that's occupied Hunter's attention is pilfering through August's cabinets, which I did try to object to, but Gus waved me off.

"What the heck are these?" Hunter asks, pulling a tiny ceramic house down from one of the shelves.

A searing pain rips through my chest, blocked out and suppressed heartbreak crashing through me.

Gus's eyes go wide and the sip of water he just swallowed must go down the wrong way because he coughs violently. Once he's done choking, and I accept I won't need to attempt CPR, August jumps up from his seat and plucks the red brick-roofed house of cinnamon out of Hunter's hand, placing it back on the shelf and shutting the cabinet door.

"Spice rack, nothing exciting," Gus finally responds.

"They look kind of girly, no?" Hunter asks.

"Spices have genders now?" Gus raises a brow in Hunter's direction.

I tune them out. *Nothing exciting.*

The original spice village is my fucking Roman Empire. I spent a week every summer for seven summers with my grandmother perusing through the biggest flea market in the state, scouring every booth for each individual building in the set until it was complete.

They're riddled with lead so I never actually planned on using them, but they were my favorite decoration to display on the wooden shelves I also found at the same flea market above my bed. Nothing was more fun than the high of the chase to find them, and the satisfaction that filled me when I had them all in my possession.

Until one day when I said the wrong thing. I don't even remember what it was now, but it was clearly poorly uttered at the worst of times because in an alcohol-induced rage, Mary Jane Stiles decided to take a swing at my shelves. She didn't stop swinging until all twenty-four little ceramic buildings were smashed to bits all over my room.

She left me to clean up her mess afterwards.

I didn't let myself shed a single tear. Void of any emotion, I stripped my bed, replaced the sheets, and vacuumed every inch of my room. At some point, I drifted off to sleep. I went to school the next day and lasted through six hours of normalcy, and then found myself ditching the last two periods to completely lose my shit out back by the gym.

August found me that day, and I never even told him what was wrong.

The conversation continues on with no notice to my internal sorrow over another blip in my shitty past.

When my mother calls Hunter's phone to find our whereabouts, he gives a half-truth effortlessly, saying I brought him and his brother to get pizza. He assures her we'll be home soon, and he and Chase are perfectly fine. Another part of my heart cracks knowing that despite giving it my all to shelter them, they still know how and when to walk on eggshells.

My very best attempts at breaking the generational trauma won't ever be good enough.

That fact feels like it could crush me.

Once Hunter gets our mother off the phone, Gus declares it's time to clean up. To my surprise, both boys jump to help without further comment. I see Gus take his phone out of his pocket and type away. My phone vibrates with a text.

AUGUST

Bring them home and come back? I could start a fire.

ME

Depends on the state of Mary Jane...But most likely no.

I chance a quick look at Gus. I watch his shoulders droop slightly, and I find myself reverting back to my old self, the one that finds me desperate to change my answer and spend any amount of time with August.

But I vowed to keep Hunter and Chase safe. I can't be too selfish with my time.

There wasn't a fraction of a moment tonight where I found myself annoyed or scoffing at Gus's usual antics. I got to see him in a new light, or rather, a light I haven't seen in quite some time. Funny, kind, *thoughtful.*

I can't get over how he made sure Chase was included in everything, waiting for his cues. He was so firm with Hunter, leaving no room for backtalk, but made sure to razz on him too, letting Hunter take digs at Gus's expense in a fun way.

August told me he doesn't want kids. He hasn't really spent too much time around kids. But it's so obvious he's a natural. I won't tell him that though. That's, for one, incredibly out of left field. And two, wildly inappropriate. I don't want him to think I'm envisioning something else or trying to change his mind.

August doesn't reply to my text. He pockets his phone and answers whatever question Hunter just lobbed at him. I make my way towards the front of the house, gathering the twins' backpacks and coats.

"Alright, boys, time to head on out," I call with almost zero umph.

The fact of the matter is, I don't want to leave. With the way Hunter and Chase are dragging their feet down the hallway, they don't either, and the look Gus is trying to hide on his face mirrors my feelings.

"Can we come back?" Hunter asks while slipping into his shoes.

"Anytime," Gus answers before I can. "Instead of bothering your sister about stupid shit, bother her to bring you here."

"Cool," Hunter mutters to himself.

"Gee, thanks, Gus," I joke. "Go get situated in the car. Both in the backseat, I'm not refereeing a stupid shotgun argument. I'll meet you there in a minute," I say to the boys.

Hunter peers at Gus, sees his stern face, and with no argument about seating arrangements, thanks Gus for dinner. Chase offers a wave with a closed-lip smile as his own form of a proper goodbye.

I lean against the doorway, pressing my back against it. I've been saving this question for hours now.

"What was tonight about, August?"

He takes a small step forward, right on the thin line of invading my space.

"I'm sorry. Did you have better plans in mind?"

"No," I answer truthfully. "I just don't get what we're doing. I'm confused. Like, really confused, actually."

"I wanna be friends, Daze."

"Friends with benefits?" I tilt my chin up.

Gus reaches his arm out, placing his palm on the wood right above my head. I can feel his body's heat on me now. We're back to being inches from each other, and the air is thick with a need to close the gap. He has a smirk on his face like he knows something I don't. This is wrong. We shouldn't be doing this. This isn't us.

We—We're—

"Daze?" Gus whispers.

I blink three times in rapid succession to try to clear my vision and my brain. "Hm?"

"Tell yourself whatever you need to. I'm more than okay with letting you be confused right now. I actually think it might be good for you." He releases his bracketed arm from the doorframe and uses the very tips of his fingers to brush my bangs out of my face. "Get Thing One and Thing Two home. And for fuck's sake, if you don't let me know you got home safe, I have no problem marching over there."

My breath hitches at the authoritative tone in his voice. I *hate* being bossed around.

Well, I did.

I do.

By anyone who apparently isn't August, according to the irritating firework show popping off in my lower belly.

"Goodnight, August," I breathe and practically sprint out the open front door, down the three porch steps, and into my car.

He waves from the porch until we're out of sight.

CHAPTER 17: AUGUST - YOU BIG SOFTY

"These guys are fucking morons, Sawyer," I tell my best friend for probably the sixth time just this morning. It may be redundant, but it's the truth. I swipe my hand down my face in exhaustion from watching the shitshow unfolding in front of me.

When Sawyer got all of the plans approved to add an extension to one of the cottages, we both quickly realized it wasn't a two-man job if we wanted to have it done by the time the twins finished cooking, especially with the winter creeping up on us and with our actual work at Rivers River.

So, we outsourced. Got a small local construction crew that's, sure, *fine*. They're not half bad. If your version of half bad is taking a goddamn fifteen minute break every hour, dropping every tool and two-by-four you pick up, and bitching about just about anything and everything under the sun all while listening to the worst EDM house music you could find at full *fucking* blast.

Sawyer sighs, hands on his hips, head hung. "As long as they can manage to frame this out before the first snowfall, I don't really care."

"I care," I grumble. "We could've—"

"No, we couldn't have. That's why they're here. I realize they're lazy. I know they're nothing like us, but this is a situation where more hands on deck matter. You bitching about their bitching isn't gonna fix shit."

"*Alright!*" I bark. "I get it!"

Sawyer stalks off to check in with one of the guys manning the sawzall.

I really need to stop pressing Sawyer's buttons. His patience has run thin with taking care of Margot and worrying about if they're gonna have a solid place to take their newborns home to by her due date. Or earlier, since apparently that's more than likely with twins.

I now have way too much knowledge I never planned on gathering on how pregnancy and childbirth and newborns work, thanks to Sawyer. He has a constant flow of information spouting out of him—I think out of nerves—and I've been the recipient of it all.

It feels like a waste, seeing as how I'll never use any of it. But if it helps Sawyer out in any way to talk it through, I'll listen. I owe him.

I pull out my phone and see two notifications. Both are Daisy-related, and nothing feels weirder than being excited to see that.

@riversriverco posted a new story!

DAISY DARLING

I just stopped by Red's. Penelope's home sick today so they're not sure if plans are still a-go for tomorrow :/

I ignore the Instagram notification, quickly typing a response to Daisy.

Shit, P's not feeling good? A wave of worry crashes into me. I'm at least four times the size of Penelope, and when I'm sick,

I'm down for the count. What happens when a person that little gets a cold? Or the flu? Or worse?

ME

Is she okay? What's wrong?

Thankfully, Daisy answers almost instantly.

DAISY DARLING

Chill, Uncle Gussy. Just a regular ole stomach bug. Those things get passed around the elementary school like candy. Miller's home with her. I just wanted to give you a heads up.

ME

Poor kid.

DAISY DARLING

I'm gonna tell everyone you're actually just a huge teddy bear.

ME

Not funny.

I blow out a breath and swipe into my text thread with Miller.

ME

How's lil P? Does she need anything?

He doesn't answer, and I tell myself it's because he's busy being a dad or napping with P. Everything's fine, just like Daisy said. I pocket my phone to resume monitoring the construction, seeing if there's anywhere I can lend a hand to move this along.

I replay last night, just like I have about six hundred times over already.

I forgot how addictive it is to hear Daisy laugh. She doesn't offer the sound often, usually never in my vicinity. And she cares so much about her brothers. It's…Well, it's beautiful, honestly.

And maybe she doesn't see it because it's hard when there's so much on your plate, but they respect the hell out of her. I'm sure I didn't get the full picture after only spending a few hours with them, but to me, it was clear that there was a level of trust and love among all three that couldn't be dismantled.

I feel lucky to be a part of it, even if only for a short time. I could see us doing it again. I was serious when I offered, too.

They say there's a fine line between love and hate.

I've been walking that line with Daisy Stiles for so long I don't know how to stop or which way to lean.

Maybe it's all been an act. Maybe I've just been some variation of in love with this girl for the better part of my life, and there's nothing that can be done to stop it.

Wait—not *in love.* I'm not a romantic, in love, touchy-feely-gooey kind of guy. Never have been, never will be.

But I can be into the idea of spending as much time as I can with Daisy until she's ready to commit to her escape.

Because she will get out one day. I won't be the reason to make her stay somewhere she doesn't want to be.

* * *

MILLER NEVER TEXTED ME BACK.

I'm now standing on Red's front porch with a six-pack of yellow Gatorade and an open bag of Sour Patch Kids with only the red ones remaining, because those are Penelope's favorite.

Daisy said P had a stomach bug, so she might not be up for sweets right now, but when she's better, she will be. Right?

I don't know shit about fuck when it comes to kids or taking care of them, but P hasn't left my mind all day. I don't want to picture her down for the count, weak on the couch, pale in the face. She's Penelope fuckin' Caswell, everyone's favorite little spitfire. She deserves to be running around, cracking jokes, and just generally messing with everyone like she always does.

I just need to get eyes on her. As soon as I know she's okay, I won't bother anyone further. Jesus, Beth's rubbing off on me.

"It's me—Gus!" I yell as I knock three times.

I pretend I don't count the minutes it takes for Miller to make his way to the front of the house and open the door.

It was two and a half.

"Hey, man. What's up?" Miller greets me. Their family cat, Ladybug, weaves between his legs.

"Where's P? How is she?" I ask, skipping formalities.

"Uh…" Miller leans back to peer into the living room.

Penelope, dressed in a nightgown with princess crowns all over it, comes barreling into Miller's legs, wrapping her arms around his torso.

"Gus? I got to skip school today!" she exclaims. She releases her dad to face me.

A mixture of relief and confusion washes over me in a wave.

"P!" I squat down to get on her level. "I heard you were sick. I wanted to check on you, but you, uh, you seem fine?"

"Oh, yeah. I threw up three times. Gross." She shudders. "But I'm all better now! Daddy stayed home with me and we watched all of the *Halloweentown* movies and ate Mom's lemon chicken soup and—"

"Hold on, P. Slow down. You're okay? You're not sick anymore?"

Penelope gives me a classic eyeroll. "I *just* said that, Gussy. Whatcha got there?" She points to the plastic shopping bag dangling from my hand.

"Oh." I hold it out for her. "Got this stuff for you. Just like—"

"*Red Sour Patch!*" Penelope screeches when she peers into the bag. She throws her arms around my neck. "Thanks!" She releases me, snatches the bag, and trots back into the living room, goodies in tow.

"Damn. Thanks, Gus. You didn't have to do that. Wait, hold up. How did you know P was sick?"

I rub the back of my neck, trying to weave some sort of tale that won't end with me admitting I got my intel from Daze.

"You know Merrymount. News travels fast," I offer.

Miller eyes me skeptically, but then shakes it off. "Penelope projectile vomited down the entire staircase this morning after Gwen left for work. I've just decided I don't have the energy to figure out why you're being weird as fuck. And I'd invite you in but…"

"Nah, I get it. I just wanted to make sure the rugrat was okay." I wave him off.

I really am glad Penelope doesn't seem to be suffering from the bubonic plague or some shit, but I'm also not trying to get whatever germs ran through her system.

"It's nice you stopped by, though. You probably made her whole day," Miller says.

I scoff. "It's nothing. I'm gonna take off." I step back and offer a wave. "Text the group, or whatever, about tomorrow?"

Miller assures me he will before closing the door. I'm just about back to my truck when Red's Mini Cooper flies into the driveway like a bat out of hell.

When she emerges from her driver's seat, I greet her. "Anyone ever tell you to slow it down?"

"Shove it, Gus," Red snaps. "I've been trying to escape the café for like, two hours now with no luck. All I wanted to do was get home to my sick kid, but everyone and their goddamn brother was up my ass. Chris called out," she explains.

"Where's Margot?" I ask.

"I sent her home. Chris has the same bug P has, so it must be going around. I don't want Margot sick on top of everything else she has going on. Wait, hold up—What're you doing here?"

"Checking on your sick kid," I say.

This gets Red to stop in her tracks, and her face softens instantly. "Really?"

I'm not even able to acknowledge her question before Red throws her arms around my neck, pulling me into a tight hug.

"You big softy." She releases me and tears shine in her eyes.

I didn't sign up for some emotional moment. I literally was just here to assure myself Penelope was alive and well.

"Anyway, she's fine. I'm going home before I contract whatever nastiness you got floating around your house." I open my door and hop into the truck, starting her up.

I crank the window down to wave bye to Red when she stops me again.

"August." A raised eyebrow has me thinking I screwed up. I'm not sure how, seeing as she was just embracing me like I pulled a kitten from a burning building.

"Yeah?" I urge.

"I told Daisy about Penelope. *Only* Daisy."

I try to skirt around admitting anything. "And?"

Red's eyes narrow.

"Bye, Gus." She pivots and marches up the porch steps.

I brush the interaction off. Red's running her mouth based on a hunch, and I won't fuel that fire.

CHAPTER 18: DAISY - IT'S THE SEAT FOR YOUR RIDE LATER

The Journal of Daisy D. Stiles - Twelve and a half years ago

I'm mad at August today, and I feel really fucked up for saying that.

We were in this together, and now he's run off and found a new life with good people.

Sawyer Hale and his grandmother, Beth, really are the best kind of people.

I've watched through people's windows for years to see what real, unconditional love looks like, and those two are the perfect example. Now August gets to be a part of that while I'm still here.

Alone.

I'll always be alone.

At least, that's the last thing my father said to me that held any meaning. That was, what? Three? Four years ago?

I forget. I guess it doesn't matter anyway.

August just walked in. He got a haircut. And new clothes. Nice.

He still visits me every day. It's probably out of pity. He probably feels bad.

Whatever.

* * *

I'M STILL REELING about the other night with August and my brothers. We had fun. It felt so *normal* to sit around a table with the three of them. After I let him know we got home safe, I ended up texting back and forth with August late into the night until my eyes couldn't stay open for another second.

The conversation continued the following morning.

We just kept talking. About everything, catching up on things we missed. And yet, it felt like we never skipped a beat. My paragraphs of texts were met with equally long replies, and I found myself laughing out loud at parts.

Gus is so funny. I can't believe I let myself forget.

Gus also has an incredible memory, bringing up little facts about me I forgot he was privy to, like when he asked me if I still had never tried an olive.

I haven't. Those little fuckers freak me out.

I woke up this morning around three a.m., like I always do, to two texts that came through after I passed out earlier in the night. I've been rereading them over and over again with every spare minute I have.

AUGUST

I watch Forrest Gump to fall asleep most nights. You were right, you know. It really is the best movie. But I think about Jenny a lot. One night I read through pages of Reddit threads about how people think she's the villain. Daze, I was so fucking pissed off lol. She's my favorite and no one gets it. And another thing, she got out, but at what cost? Do you think she was happy in all of the places she ended up? I think she deserved a better ending. The kid is cute though.

The familiar jingle of the bell on Red's door makes me look up from my phone. Gus waltzes in, and I feel my eyes bulge out of my head at the sight of him.

No. No, no, no, no.

There is absolutely no way. This simply can't be true. My eyes are deceiving me, or I'm dreaming, or I don't know but—

Yep.

My actual kryptonite come to *fucking life.*

I haven't seen August in almost two days and in that extremely small window of time, he shaved his face. He left a perfect mustache right above his insufferable, soft, almost cloud-like, extremely kissable lips. I have half a mind to forget every dumb rule I've imposed on our little arrangement to test out those lips.

Wait, what the fuck am I saying?

"What's that on your face?" I greet him when he reaches the table I'm occupying. Yeah, that sounds more like something I'd say. I don't linger on the fact that he came straight to me, rather than the counter to order the coffee he's probably here for.

"It's the seat for your ride later, Daze." Gus smooths the hair above his top lip with two fingers. It pisses me off that he should look goofy and instead, he just looks hot as fuck.

I scrunch up my nose, pretending like I'm not squeezing the muscles in between my legs in answer. "That's foul, August."

He leans into my space and the mustache in question tickles my ear. His voice drops so low that I know for certain I'm the only one who can hear him. "Oh, yeah? How much would you bet that if I wiggled my fingers into that tight cunt of yours, you'd be wet right now?"

The goosebumps that break out across my entire body do

nothing to hold up my end of the argument. His deep chuckle sends a flare of heat up my neck, and I have to stop my hand from chasing it.

"I hate you," I say through gritted teeth. I hate that he's absolutely right.

"Save the foreplay for later, Daze. You know that shit turns me on." He mercifully backs away, and I'm able to regain control over my senses again.

What the hell is happening to me?

"Are you working today?" My pathetic attempt to continue a conversation that only weeks—hell, *days*—ago I wouldn't have found myself participating in makes my head spin. I ignore the dancing poppies in my stomach when Gus turns back around and shoots me one his crooked smiles.

"Yeah, Daze. You?"

"Not at the flower shop. But I had this idea last night for something at the riverside that I think Beth's gonna love. So, I'll probably be swinging by. Business might be winding down for the season, but never too late to plan for next year!"

"You want me to give you a ride? How much of whatever it is you got going on there do you have left?" he asks, gesturing to my laptop and brainstorming notebook spread out on the table. He again abandons his journey to the counter, instead choosing to slide into the seat across from me.

"Uh," I hesitate. This is as friendly as we've gotten publicly probably ever. The mustache is doing something. It's messing with the ways of the world. "You're sure?"

"Oh, I'm sorry, darling. Did you not plan to sit on my face tonight? We're going out, remember? There's no sense in driving your car over to the riverside when I'm already on my way. I'll bring you back in the morning. Come on, we can even make a pit stop so you can pack a sleepaway bag. Pretend like it's camp. You know, minus the critters." Gus wiggles his eyebrows, reminding me of the last time I found myself in a camp setting with him.

"We canceled tonight, *remember?*" I remind him.

While Penelope recovered from the stomach bug rather quickly, poor Miller is now going through it.

"No...*Red and Miller* canceled. And Sawyer and Margot backed out because Margot's exhausted. Last I checked, we don't have any ailments stopping us from having some fun."

I can honestly say with every true bone in my body that I haven't the slightest clue as to what's gotten into August Burton in the past several days. It's Gus. But not. Agreeing to this would be insanity.

And yet, I find myself going along with the plan anyway. I slam my laptop shut. "You know what, fine."

"Reluctant agreement? That's the spirit!" Gus pumps his fist in the air in victory. I roll my eyes, but I'm smiling through it. I'm doing that a lot more often now than I used to.

This whole thing screams dangerous. We're wading into a familiar territory of the past, and I'm not sure I'm comfortable enough in these waters. What's that saying? Fool me once, shame on you. Fool me twice...

"You're being weird," I tell him, avoiding my real feelings about this whole ordeal.

"You like it, Daze. Admit it."

"Like what?" I roll my eyes as I start to gather my things into my tote bag. When I shimmy out of the booth, Gus stands and scoops the strap of my tote from the table, hiking it up over his shoulder.

"Spending time with me. And the 'stache."

The man has the audacity to fucking *wink* before taking himself and my bag to the counter. He greets Red as if this isn't the most bizarre morning I've ever experienced, grabs his coffee, and slides cash across the surface.

"Since when do you two get along?" Red eyes us suspiciously. I feel as though I shouldn't be grouped into this question, seeing as how I'm not the one acting like a crazy person before nine a.m.

"Don't look at *me*," I argue when I reach the counter. I try to retrieve my tote from Gus, but he doesn't budge.

"Mhm," Red mutters while looking me up and down—multiple times.

"Take a picture. It'll last longer." I purse my lips for good measure.

"Don't tempt me, I thought about it. Since no one in this entire town would believe me if I told them without photographic evidence that Daisy Stiles and August Burton were canoodling in my café."

"Canoodling?" I scoff. "You're dramatic. He's just..." I try to yank my bag free again with no luck. "Jesus Christ, Gus. Give me my shit."

"No." Gus readjusts the strap on his shoulder and marches towards the door.

Red shrugs. "Ah, well. That lasted about as long as everyone would expect. Back to business as usual. You kids have a good day! See ya later!" She blows us a kiss and saunters off to the back.

"Bag, please, Gus." I hold out my hand.

"Would you just march your ass out the door so we can get a move on?" He gestures with the hand holding his coffee cup to the front door.

"Your idea of chivalry is distorted," I mumble on my way out.

Gus continues his weird gentlemanly act by opening my driver's door for me. "I'll follow you to your house," he says once I'm in my seat, finally passing me my tote. He shuts the door without waiting for my reply.

Mercifully, there are no cars in the driveway when Gus and I pull up to my house. I assume he'll wait in his truck for me while I run inside to gather a fucking *sleepaway bag*. I almost laugh to myself when I hear a second door slamming closed. I turn to discover I clearly assumed wrong because Gus is marching up the walkway to the front of the house.

"I don't need a bodyguard, August. No one's home," I tell him.

"Maybe I'm trying to get a quickie in. You know, start the day properly. You said something like that, right?" He nudges me playfully with his arm.

This time I let myself giggle. God, since when is it fun to joke around with August?

Yeah, Daisy. Pretend like it wasn't always like this after he let you in.

"I'm not showing up to face Beth freshly fucked. I can barely make eye contact with her as it is."

"You know, I think she's choosing to be chill about this," Gus tries to assure me.

"Ha!" I bark. "She's saving it. She's waiting for the perfect moment to rip us to shreds," I say as I unlock the door and make my way upstairs, Gus still on my tail.

"There are no pictures of you," Gus observes as we walk along the hall to my bedroom.

He's definitely referring to the school pictures of Hunter and Chase lined up on the wall. And while he's right—there isn't a single one of me—I'm used to it. I don't notice it anymore.

"Yeah," I say offhandedly, trying to breeze past the fact that I have two parents who actively choose to pretend I don't exist.

"Fuck them," he mumbles under his breath.

Gus doesn't offer more conversation as I pack my essentials. He grabs my duffel bag and lobs it over his shoulder before I can get it myself. He marches down the stairs and out the door without another word.

When we pull up to the riverside, all ideas of no one spotting us together wither away into nothing when we both see Melanie LeClair rocking on the porch of the main building's cabin.

"Howdy hey, you two cuties!" Mel calls, waving one arm dramatically, as we pull up to a stop.

A smile breaks out across my face. Margot's mom is the best

addition to Merrymount, and I feel guilty I haven't seen enough of her since she moved to town.

She's the mom everyone wishes they had. At least, I know I wish she was my mom.

I forget any reason I would be hiding and shoot out of Gus's truck once we're parked.

"Mel!" I call.

After I run up the steps, Melanie stands and pulls me into her arms for a tight embrace.

"Oh, it's so good to see you, my girl!"

I breathe in the faint smell of chlorine that apparently still hasn't left her clothes since moving and leaving her career at the community pool back in the town she and Margot used to live in.

"You too! How's the apartment? You hanging around today?"

Mel releases me and ushers me to sit in the rocking chair next to the one she was occupying.

"The apartment is perfect. It's the right amount of space in the best part of town." She winks. "I'm still unemployed, which feels odd, I have to admit. So, I'm pestering Beth today instead of my moody daughter."

That causes me to laugh. "Can't say I wouldn't be moody too if I was baking two babies at once."

Melanie pats my thigh and chuckles. "God knew I couldn't handle it. Margot, though? Small but mighty she is."

Gus's footsteps cause wooden steps to creak.

"Morning, Mel," he greets her.

"Hello, Gus. Or should I say *mountain man?* The women are going to have a field day with the new look." Melanie wiggles her eyebrows and barks out a laugh she for sure was trying to hold in.

I reach my hand out to grab onto Melanie's arm.

"*Mel,* you read the comments?" I say shrilly.

"Of course I do!" she confirms. "Scrolling through those is better than anything I could watch on TV."

August's cheeks turn a dark pink as he pieces together what we're referring to. "I don't think I like being objectified."

"Oh, get over it," I say.

Gus narrows his eyes at me.

"You know, it's funny seeing you two together," Melanie observes.

"We're not together," Gus and I both practically shout simultaneously.

Melanie stands and brushes off seemingly nothing from the front of her jeans. "Ah, yes. And Sawyer and Margot were just friends. But…Beth told me no meddling."

"Beth?" Gus and I, once again, yell at the same time.

Melanie pauses with her hand on the door. She looks at us with a soft, all-knowing, motherly type of smile. "I will say, I find it interesting that you think you're still putting on a show. And maybe you are. But I think it's more for your own benefit, protecting your own hearts, than anything else. I'm walking away after one teensy bit of advice: don't forget who you really are, the Daisy and August behind the curtain, off stage. Have a good day, you two. I'm sure I'll be seeing you around."

Once the door closes and Melanie is out of sight, Gus lets out a nervous laugh. I mimic it.

"That was odd, right? Like, I love Mel. But she's laying the wise owl speeches on thick, don't you think?" I ask.

Gus hesitates.

"Yeah," he finally breathes. But for some reason, I don't know if he's actually agreeing with me.

CHAPTER 19: DAISY - THAT'S INSANE. YOU'RE INSANE. YOU KNOW THAT, RIGHT?

The Journal of Daisy D. Stiles - Twelve and a half years ago

August invited me to a party tonight.

Everyone is celebrating summer, and I should have said yes.

A big part of me wanted to say yes, mostly because he asked.

But also because I'm desperate to feel normal, just once.

I said no, though.

Alcohol is the worst drug in the world, and I refuse to take part in it.

* * *

NEVER THOUGHT I'd say this, but I wish I was home. Actually, scratch that. I'd rather be anywhere but here right now.

The Bar, our usual staple of a hangout when our group goes out, is closed because Rodney, the owner, is replacing the floors before Thanksgiving Eve. So Gus and I decided to hop two towns over to a place I'm not totally familiar with.

It has some honky tonk embarrassing small town kind of name like the Flying Boot Buckle or some shit.

I've never liked the smell of alcohol, even before things got bad with my parents. And right now I'm holding back the need to projectile vomit all over the seemingly harmless guy next to me because all I can focus on is the smell of his stale beer breath as he goes on about…Jesus Christ, I don't even know what he's rambling about.

He's not bad looking, I guess. But it's in a stuffy financial bro sort of way. The pants he has on are a little too short with his ankles poking out, and his shirt just *looks* crunchy. From what I can see of his loafers, he's not wearing any socks, and that's giving me an ick no one on the planet could come back from. His personality so far has matched his appearance.

All that to say, I'm crawling out of my fucking skin.

Gus left for the bathroom realistically about four minutes ago, but to me, it feels like forty.

For not the first time in my life, but definitely something I actively try to avoid, I'm scanning the room for Gus. I desperately need an out, and he's the only person in this bar I trust to help me.

Not even bothering to wait for the dude to finish his latest thought, I cut him off.

"I'm just gonna…go." Not my smoothest delivery, but my senses feel kind of warped right now. I'm on edge, but I don't know why. It's bothering me. I hate not being in control. I'm always in control.

His hand falls to the top of my thigh, and I lock up.

"I thought we were having a good time," he says, leaning in and wiggling his eyebrow in a very unattractive way.

I try to laugh him off. "It's definitely been a time, and thank you for the drink. But I'm ready to call it a night." I motion towards the untouched glass of whatever he ordered me without my asking, and fake a yawn.

Instead of the man's hand releasing me, his grip tightens. When he leans in, the hairs on the back of my neck stand up. His words send a chill down my spine. "I don't feel like I've been properly thanked. How about a little kiss, pretty girl?"

There's no hiding the look of pure mortification on my face. "Ew. Get the hell off me." I move to shove him so I can hop off this barstool with no luck. His fingers dig into my skin, so much that I know each print will leave a bruise. I only like the bruises August leaves.

"Don't be a bitch," he hisses.

I should yell. Cause a scene so someone—fucking *anyone*—interjects. There are a lot of things I should be doing to help myself, and yet I'm paralyzed in fear. Because I know this feeling. I know what happens when someone's touch feels like that. I remember what comes next—

The ringing in my ears starts first.

The black spots in my vision come next.

I taste metal on my tongue, and I don't have the wits to realize it's my own blood because I'm biting down on the inside of my cheek.

I close my eyes and breathe in through my nose. I can get out of this. An eerie sort of calm takes over, the boxes in my brain opening up to stow away bad feelings and memories. My survival skills are finally kicking into gear. I slowly open my eyes back up to see this piece of shit loser hasn't budged an inch. He's so dangerously close until I kick my leg out, and he stumbles.

"Well, unfortunately for you, I am a bitch. Get. Off."

I grab hold of the bartop and look around to see that while this whole situation has rocked me, it really hasn't disturbed the rest of the patrons. Seemingly no one noticed a man trying to take advantage of a woman. Which, I guess, shouldn't be too surprising.

But in the next second, all I see is the blur of a mass of a man roughly dragging the asshole out the back door of the bar.

My senses catch up to the scene, and I realize, the mass of a man is August.

Oh, no.

* * *

I RUSH out the back door to see Gus crashing the two of them into the alley. Since I didn't get the guy's name, let's go ahead and call him Douche Canoe for right now. Douche Canoe stumbles, trying to right his footing before Gus has the chance to cause more damage.

No luck for Douche Canoe though.

Gus gets in his face, so close their noses are almost touching. The asshole tries to back up, not realizing Gus has him up against a wall with no out. Idiot. He turns his head to the side, desperate to find an escape. But there is none. Not when all six foot, five inches of August Burton is towering in front of him with the guy's shirt in a vice grip in his fist.

"Who taught you it was okay to lay a single unwanted finger on a woman?" Gus is seething.

Douche Canoe doesn't answer. He inhales with a shake. I'm sure if I checked, I'd see he pissed himself.

Honestly? It'd be deserved.

I continue to stand back, not really having a clue about what I should be doing. Am I supposed to be putting a stop to this? Intervening sounds like not the brightest idea. Gus is unhinged, and I'm really only used to his anger being directed at me. But never like this. But also never in my defense.

"Let's play a little game, okay? Every time you don't answer me, I rock your head against this brick." Gus proceeds to make good on his word, hauling the guy against the wall. I watch his head bounce once.

"I'm asking again. Who told you it was okay to touch someone without their goddamn permission?"

"I'm sorry!" Asshole chokes out.

Gus whips him forward so he's under the light, and I can fully see him. And yep, he definitely peed his pants.

"Say it to her fucking face."

"I'm…sorry," the pathetic man pants.

"Daze?" Gus looks at me. For what? Not a clue.

My brain finally catches up with the scene in front of me. I think, and again, I'm not entirely sure, but I think Gus wants to know if that's a good enough apology for me. I don't want to know what would happen if I said it wasn't.

"Uh, yeah. Get fucked, dude. Gus, let him go, please. Come on."

Gus tosses the creep into a pile of cardboard the bar has piled in the back alley. He crouches low and whispers something my ears can't pick up. When he walks over to me, his hand finds the small of my back, urging me forward without another word. I hate that the feeling of him on my back is comforting.

"You can't handle things like that," I say in a low voice.

"Daisy, shut your mouth before I turn around and knock every fucking tooth out of his skull. I'm barely keeping it together right now." I'm inclined to believe him, due to the fact that I can feel his hand shaking over my jacket.

"That's insane. You're insane. You know that, right?"

Gus stops in his tracks, taking me with him by wrapping his hand around my biceps so I halt too. "Yeah, I do. I need you to remember that the next time you ever think it's okay for a man to put his hands on you like that with zero repercussions, got it? You find me, and I handle it."

"I could have taken care of myself," I argue.

"Never said you couldn't. Now, let's go." Gus continues to usher me forward and for some reason unbeknownst to me, I continue to let him lead.

He leads me right out of the bar and down the street til we stop in front of his truck.

Gus spins me around and walks us until my back hits metal.

"What do you need right now, Daze?" he huffs with barely contained restraint.

I close my eyes and inhale, willing every bone in my body to let go of the feelings seeping into my pores. This isn't like before. It's different. I'm safe.

I focus on Gus's thumb kneading into the skin on my hip, holding me in place.

I'm safe.

I know I'm safe, and now all I want—

"I want to forget," I admit barely above a whisper. I clear my throat to find my voice. "I want you to make me forget what just happened. I want to remember what it's supposed to feel like," I say more clearly, reaching out to run my fingers down his chest.

When I open my eyes, Gus is staring at me so intensely, I almost jump. It's like he's trying to read my mind or get lost in the sight of me. It's overwhelming.

"You trust me?" he breathes.

I nod.

"Gentle?"

I shake my head slowly.

"Words, Daze," he commands, and it sends the good kind of shivers through my core.

"I want *you*," I tell him with painful honesty.

He pulls me aside and whips the passenger door open. "Get in the truck."

I don't move quickly enough for Gus apparently because all of a sudden, he's scooping me up and placing me on the bench seat himself. He reaches for the seatbelt and pulls it across my chest until it locks into place.

Another part of my not-so-impenetrable shell cracks, and I unbuckle and scoot over to the middle before Gus enters the driver's side.

He looks at me like he's about to ask what I'm doing, so I tell him before he even opens his mouth. "I just want to be close to you. Is that okay?"

August puts the key in the ignition and starts his old truck up. I lean into him and the old memories of my time in this cab. He wraps one arm around my shoulders, tucking me into his side.

"Always, Daze."

CHAPTER 20: AUGUST - THERE MAY BE SOMETHING THERE THAT WASN'T THERE BEFORE

"Ooooh, this towel is toasty," I hear Daisy acknowledge from the room over.

Should be. I tossed it into the dryer for ten minutes to warm it up for her while she was showering.

There's so much adrenaline coursing through my body, I feel like I'm a live wire. The energy is humming inside of me, and I need to release some of it. At least a little bit.

I know exactly how to accomplish that, too, while also satisfying the woman who drives me wilder than anything.

I push away the rage I feel for that piece of shit who was messing with Daisy at the bar. I wasn't gone for more than five minutes. I only stepped outside to take a call from Sawyer, who was having issues with one of the fuses at his house. Lesson fucking learned, Daze doesn't leave my sight when we're out now.

I focus on Daisy, whose hair is sopping wet, a mess of tangled jet black—almost blue—curls falling every which way around her face. She insisted on a shower when we made it back, and I didn't try to object or insert myself. She was asking for a minute. I understood with no problem.

I stripped down to nothing, rinsed off in the guest bathroom, and didn't bother getting dressed afterwards. Daisy apparently decided to waste time putting on the same shirt she slept in the last time she spent the night here, and it's bringing up those feral feelings inside of me all the same.

The only difference between then and now is I'm not thinking about entertaining the idea of Daisy prancing across the hall to sleep in the guest room. I want her with me. I think I need it.

"Get over here," I tell her, slowly stroking my cock as I watch her twist her nervous little hands together. "And take that goddamn shirt off before I rip it off your body."

Daisy's mouth gapes. "Excuse you?"

"Don't even start. You don't want soft, Daze. You want me. I won't make you repeat it." Her eyes drop, and I watch her pupils track the movement of my hand around myself. She tries to adjust her footing. I know she's trying to give herself a tiny bit of relief with a small amount of friction between her legs. "Shirt. Off."

Her hands release each other, and she finds the hem of the oversized T-shirt swallowing her body.

Fuck. I've never seen Daisy naked. The fact that I've had myself so deep inside of her but never have gotten to take in the sight of her completely bare for me feels like a crime.

I can't let this be quick.

"Wait," I say before Daisy starts raising the fabric. She pauses, eyes wide, silent. I release my cock and push myself up until I'm sitting against my headboard. "Go slow."

"Is this a striptease?" she teases.

"Call it whatever you want. I want to enjoy this." I put my hands behind my head.

"And what's in it for me?" She pinches the shirt with her right hand and raises it slowly up and over one hip. The crease that connects top of her thigh to her hip has me ready to blow on the fucking spot.

"How many times do you want to come?"

"What?" Daisy laughs and the sound makes my cock twitch. She has her other hand on the shirt now and has it pulled up so I can see the beautiful fucking soft curves of her stomach and the peaks of her nipples.

"Do you need me to repeat the question?"

"How many orgasms are you offering?"

"Whatever number you're thinking, double it. Now, Daze—I said strip."

She bristles. But the pointless sleep shirt finally lifts up and over Daisy's head. She throws it onto the bed beside me, and I'm back to stroking myself to keep my composure.

She's perfect. Downright fucking *perfect.*

Pale skin with stretch marks decorating the lower plain of her belly and hips cause an unprompted groan to leave my mouth. Her breasts sit heavy, and her pink nipples are hard, begging for me to get my mouth—maybe my teeth—on them.

There's nothing dainty and breakable about Daisy. I've always known that. She's strong, solid; a goddess. It's the only way to describe her.

"I'm not skinny," she says with a soft, almost pained voice. I watch her shuffle her feet, uncomfortable with my attention on her. I'm immediately hit with a wave of confusion.

I pause. "Yeah?"

"I don't hate my body or any other self destructive thing you might be thinking. I've spent a lot of time working on that. But... I've, uh, I've seen the girls you bring home, Gus. I don't look like those girls."

All right, we're pumping the fucking breaks on this bullshit right now.

I spring from the mattress, crowding her space. I grab her chin with my fingers, forcing Daisy to look me in the eye. I watch her cheeks go from pink to red.

"Do I look like I give a fuck?" I take her hand and move it until

I feel her fingers wrap around my shaft. "Does it *feel* like I care about whatever numbers pops up when you step on a damn scale?"

A small shake of her head.

"I wanna bury myself in you, Daisy. I want you to ride me so fucking hard, I get to watch all of you bounce. I want the sight of you seared into my brain for the rest of my goddamn life." I release my grasp from her chin to let my hands start to roam. I start at her hips, letting my fingers find their favorite place to grip. She shudders at every touch, her hand not moving, but still wrapped around me tight. She squeezes, and it's almost too tight.

I lean over, my lips grazing the sensitive skin on the side of her neck. "You drive me fucking insane. This body"—I nip at her, and she gasps—"is fucking insane. And right now? It's mine."

My hands find the bottom of her ass, and I swiftly lift her up into my arms, walking backward until the backs of my knees hit the side of the bed. I let us both fall until my back hits the mattress.

Where I should feel her pussy on my cock, Daisy hovers.

"What the fuck are you doing?" I ask, kneading into the pillowy feel of her ass cheeks.

"I don't want to—"

"Sit," I growl, gripping her hips and pulling her down.

She gasps when our skin connects. No barrier. Just us.

I want to be inside of her like this. I don't want there to be anything between us when I feel her pulse around me each time I bring her to fucking climax tonight.

My hands glide up her thick thighs, and I revel at the sight of my rough, marked skin contrasting with the untouched plain of hers.

"Do we need a condom?" I ask, shocked at my own question.

Daisy raises her arms, gathering her hair in her hands, and pulling it all to hang over one shoulder. My eyes take in the sight of her, and *damn*—it's a sight.

She's like fucking Aphrodite.

Daisy stills, mouth popped open, pupils dilated. "Do we—I mean, I'm—"

I massage her pillowy skin. "What's your birth control situation?"

Her hips move seemingly against her will, grinding into me for relief, and I groan.

"*Fuck,*" I mumble.

"Copper IUD. Nonhormonal." Daisy braces her hands on my chest. "They told me it was like, over 99% effective."

"I can pull out." I shallowly thrust. My cock practically glides against her center from how wet she is.

A whimper escapes Daisy. "And there's no one else."

"No one else," I confirm.

"This is stupid," she says with a moan, leaning over me to suck on my neck.

"Real fucking stupid," I agree, but reach down to notch my tip at her entrance anyway. She raises herself up to accommodate me, placing her hands back on my chest. "Last call, Daze. And then I don't stop until you say the safe—"

I'm cut off by Daisy sinking onto my cock in one swift motion. "Safe word. Got it. *Fuck.* This is it." She swivels her hips forward, and I throw my head back ready to fully enjoy the ride.

My thumbs find homes on either side of her, and I hold on tight, pretending I'm running this show in any way.

"That's right, Daze. Ride me. Chase the high."

She continues to fuck me, pulling her hands up to cup both breasts, twisting her nipples. Her body moves effortlessly on top of me and the room fills with my deep moans of satisfaction.

I'd never get sick of this. I would consider it a nice life and die a happy man if all I ever had was a full workload at the riverside and Daisy Stiles in my bed every night.

"You look good under me, August," she says in between pants.

I can't explain why my cock feels like it somehow gets harder hearing her call me good about anything.

My grip tightens, and I move Daisy's hips, adjusting the pace, kicking things up a notch. Her hands fall, and her breasts bounce free. I lean up, capturing a nipple in my mouth.

Daisy cries out. "*Yes. August, yes.*"

I feel her muscles flex around me and her body shudders. I don't relent though. I'm not done yet, and neither is she.

Another whimper falls from Daisy's lips when I release my grasp and my thumb finds her clit. I apply pressure and rub quick circles until she's draped over me, panting, as I fuck her deep and hard.

"Give me another, Daze. Let me feel you come again," I gruffly whisper in her ear.

"I—God, it's so much, August," she whines, followed by a moan of pleasure.

"But you can take it, Daze. You can take it," I chant.

Her words fall apart and become senseless cries as I continue driving her down onto my cock. I feel a tightening inside of me and reach down the long mental tunnel to my willpower to pull out. But I need to feel Daisy come again, she's right there...*I'm right there...*

"August," she pants. "August, I'm gonna come again. Don't stop, please, please don't stop," she begs, matching my thrusts again.

"Daze, I'm right there. I'm not gonna—"

Daisy's pussy squeezes my length so tight, I practically fucking black out as I spill into her. She rides me harder, chasing her own orgasm.

"*Oh my God,*" she gasps, and I pull myself out. Daisy collapses on top of me.

I rub up and down her back, using the tips of my fingers to trace her spine in long strokes as we both try to regain control of our breathing.

Every tiny movement from either of us causes the other to jolt in shock. We're both too sensitive. I'm hyper-aware of my every move.

Daisy's labored breaths start to even out, and I chance disrupting whatever bubble we've found ourselves in. "I gotta get you cleaned up."

She mutters something inaudible into my neck, and I huff out a laugh at the air of her breath on me. "Come on, Daze."

She springs up.

"Don't move." She shimmies off me and stands. "Please," she adds quickly before walking into the bathroom. I do as I'm told and stay exactly where I am until I hear the toilet flushing and water running, and Daisy practically dancing back into the bedroom.

She crawls back on top of me and inexplicable warmth floods me.

"Hey," Daisy whispers.

"Hi, darling," I answer, rubbing the tops of her thighs, lost in so many thoughts.

All of them surrounding the chaos that's me and Daisy.

Daisy's fingers start tracing the line work of the tattoos I have covering my torso. The lust-filled tension in the air shifts, and everything feels like it softens. She lingers on faded ink, a reminder that I need to reschedule a touch up soon for the ones I got while I was underage.

"You know, I've waited years to look at these up close," she says quietly. Admiringly. It halts me. "I remember seeing glimpses of them when you'd raise your arm or something. And I thought it was so taboo to be in high school with tattoos. Like, driving a motorcycle without a helmet." She laughs. "You've always been this almost untouchable, definitely unbreakable, and not to fuck-with-able being to me."

"*Daze*," I say, my breath getting caught in my throat at her honesty.

"Just let me look, please."

Her face is shadowed by her hair and the lack of lighting. Her eyes are glazed over, so focused on my body that she doesn't notice me watching her.

I'm…Shit, what's that word?

I'm fucking captivated by Daisy Stiles.

Again, I remind myself.

Her slow perusal stops right where I know my first tattoo sits along my right rib cage.

I'll never forget walking into that semi-questionable tattoo parlor when I was barely sixteen. I grabbed their book of flash designs, pointed at the first one that looked thick and dark enough to cover cigarette burn marks, and told the artist to pack in as much ink as possible.

I sat in that chair for six hours with no break while Jessi drilled that tattoo gun into me, shading as dark as she could. I went back to her every six months until everything was covered. Sometimes I picked from that flash book again, or took a suggestion from Jessi when she had a design she was dying to work on. The best sessions were when I came in with my own idea. Getting to see a finished piece that held meaning. Even if I was the only one who ever knew what those ones meant.

Daisy's breath hitches. "August."

"Hm?" I offer, bringing my hands over her hips to rest on her waist.

"There are…There are so many *scars.*"

"Not anymore," I try to assure her. I reach up to grab her chin. She lets her eyes flutter closed. "Look at me, Daisy."

When she opens those pretty blues up, fresh tears are held at bay on her water line. "I made my peace with that part of my life. These"—I take her hand in mine and drag it across my chest—"tell the story I want to share. The one where I got out and things got better."

She nods in an unspoken understanding. Before I can figure

out what she's doing, Daisy's moving herself down, bringing her legs together to sit on her knees in between mine. She leans over and starts outlining that first tattoo with her lips, leaving feather-light kisses silently.

I don't move. I hold myself as still as I can as she continues her journey of acknowledging every bit of ink that covers me with her mouth. I find myself running my hand through her hair, using the chill of the damp strands to ground me.

She doesn't stop until I'm sure she left her mark.

"Are you okay with everything that just happened?" Daisy asks.

"Yes," I answer immediately, surprised by how sure I am of this. More than okay, actually. Well, I would be if Daze ever gave me the time of day and reneged on rule number one; moving those lips from my inked skin to my own. Fulfilling a broken promise on my end from all those years ago.

It's like Daisy reads my mind. She readjusts, laying down to tuck into my side, face out of sight and reach.

"You don't smell like beer," Daisy says almost absentmindedly as she restarts her tracing on my chest with a finger.

"Well, that makes sense, seeing as I didn't have one."

"For any particular reason?"

"I haven't had a drink since the gender reveal party."

She pauses. "And is there a reason for that as well?"

"You don't like the smell of alcohol."

"*Oh*," Daisy utters, so softly.

We lay like this for a while. Silent and thoughtful. It's delicate and intimate. It's new; everything about this feels like the first time.

But the first time for what?

I don't know.

CHAPTER 21: DAISY - A PROPER LADY DOESN'T KISS AND TELL

The Journal of Daisy D. Stiles - Twelve years ago

I've made a decision.

Well, first let me back up to my realization.

I love August Burton.

I know, I know. A teenager in high school doesn't know the first thing about love, and maybe that's usually true. But, I know this is the real deal.

That leaves me at a crossroad. Do I act on this feeling?

My answer: no.

Because the way I love August feels all-consuming and like forever type shit.

We don't have forever. Or rather, we don't have a shot at forever right now, under these circumstances. And I'm too selfish to risk losing him.

* * *

"Have you thought about names yet?" I raise my voice to ask Margot over the hammering and power tools drilling around us.

I texted Margot earlier, asking if it was okay if I stopped by the cottages. She said yes as long as I was okay with incessant banging and boys arguing over simple tasks.

"That's been the easiest thing about this whole pregnancy!" she exclaims, laughing.

If you looked up *World's Worst Friend* in the dictionary, you'd find a picture of me. I look at Margot, round bump finally popping, and realize I've missed so much. I *always* miss so much, purposely keeping myself on the outskirts to avoid fallout.

This is hard for me to admit, but spending so much time with August has me bending and reconsidering a lot of my self-imposed rules, the ones regarding how close I allow myself to get to the people I care so deeply about. Sort of. Maybe.

"Are you willing to share?" I ask.

Margot readjusts her growing self in her wicker, egg-shaped chair. I'm pretty positive she's reached the end of her time to be able to contort her body comfortably in there, but I'm not going to be the one to shed light on that fact.

A dreamy look takes over her face once she's situated, despite the fact that we're attempting to hang out normally in the middle of a full-blown construction zone in early November. Sawyer's trying to have the addition finished as fast as possible, racing a biological clock with the twins and mother nature, who's mercifully kept the weather at bay.

"Watch where you fuckin' swing that thing!" I hear Gus bark at some poor construction worker who didn't know what he signed up for when his boss sent him on this project. Margot and I snicker into the hot drinks warming our hands.

Margot's boob-shaped mug is filled with what she calls a *half caf*—half hot chocolate, half coffee—because she's been told to lower her caffeine intake. She gave me a dainty tea cup that says *Kindly Fuck Off* in fancy cursive along the inside rim filled with a really nice apple spiced tea.

"We're naming them after Sawyer's parents." Margot takes a

sip. "Nora and Drea. I guess we could have gone with Andrea, because technically his dad was Andrew. But the initials on the tree say D & N so we're sticking with Drea! Besides, it's good to be different. I'm different! I'm having a baby before I get married. I'm having *two* babies before I get married." A shaky laugh escapes her. "And that's totally fine, right?" Margot's wide green eyes meet mine.

"Margot?" I test, setting my cup down.

"You think I'm crazy," she accuses. "Ugh. Everyone thinks I'm crazy. And okay, maybe I am a little. I know I haven't really been myself, but I can't help it. Every day I wake up, and something's different! The babies go from the size of lentils to lemons to some other fucking random object. Who even comes up with those comparisons, huh? And I don't know what's going on with my body. I thought I'd have more time to see my feet. I was definitely wrong about that. And as soon as I get a goddamn grip and come to terms with the fact that they're growing in there, they're going to be out here!" Margot gestures wildly with her hands around us.

"I feel like a teen mom at thirty. An unplanned pregnancy as an adult? That's embarrassing." Margot slumps back into the chair, and I believe I have a second to finally, maybe get a word in.

I reach over and pat her leg. "First of all, their names are beautiful, just like Sawyer's parents. Second, there's nothing embarrassing about this. And it's also normal to be freaking out at the same time. Both can be true."

"I'm not freaking out!"

I chance leveling her with a look that lets her know that I know she's full of shit.

"Okay, I'm freaking out a little. It's just…Can I be honest?"

"That's my preferred method of communication." I laugh.

"I never pictured having kids. Not that I thought I didn't want them—I just couldn't see it. Mostly because it either takes a shit-ton of money I never had to make one on your own, or you need a willing participant to create said kids. And until Sawyer, I didn't have that. I'm *so* sure of Sawyer. I'm absolutely positive about Merrymount and everyone in it. But we just got engaged, and I don't want anyone thinking I'm not over the fucking moon happy…" she trails off.

"You thought you had more time to wrap your head around everything?" I suggest.

Margot puffs out a breath, sending her wispy bangs flying, and wraps the wool blanket closer around herself. "I'm a piece of shit."

"You're not a piece of shit, Margot. You're juggling so much. You're still putting in hours at the café, which let's be honest— Red's gonna cut you off soon. You're still getting your photography business off the ground, adjusting to living with someone and amongst this chaos. All while pregnant. With *twins.* It's a lot."

"Do you think you'll ever have kids?" she asks.

"I have Chase and Hunter," I answer automatically.

Never mind that they get older every day, and I feel like they need me less and less. Never mind that I've been leaving them every other night in favor of sleeping at August's, a fact that makes only me feel incredibly guilty since I haven't had a meaningful run-in with my mother to let her add to that guilt. But it's there and it's strong.

"Your brothers don't count. I'm serious, Daisy."

"I don't know," I admit. "I guess I'm like you. I never really gave it thought."

"So, give it thought now! What if you wound up pregnant tomorrow? What would you do?"

"I wouldn't," I balk.

The image of August unable to stop himself, finishing inside of me a couple weeks ago flashes across my mind, and I shake my head to clear it. It was an adrenaline-fueled one-time mishap that hasn't been repeated. *He pulls out now,* I stupidly think to faux-assure myself. As if that's actually an acceptable replacement to a condom.

But I have the IUD. We're responsibly exclusive friends who fuck.

"Oh," Margot mutters. "Well, that's an answer."

"What's that supposed to mean?"

"I try to respect your privacy, Daisy. I know how much you value it, and I never want to cross a line." Margot starts fidgeting with her hands. "But you've sort of been distant lately, a little more than usual. And I was kind of hoping it was because you were seeing someone. But if I did or said something, I hope you'd tell me. I didn't mean to pressure you about getting along with Gus, that was dumb and—"

"Margot."

"I'm sorry, I just really wanted everyone—"

"*Margot*," I snap, cutting off her ramble of an apology that's not needed in the slightest. "I'm the one who should be sorry. I *am* sorry. I don't want you to feel like that. You're right, I haven't been around the way I should be. And you had every right to put Gus and me in check."

"No, I was meddling in your business. I just thought…I know I'm the new kid in town when it comes to our group. But it felt like there was something there."

There is, I want to tell her. There's something between me and August, and I don't have the slightest clue what to do with it all. I want to tell Margot everything, and then maybe she'll be able to help me untangle myself from this mess I've landed myself in. But she has enough on her plate. Now's not the time to make this about me.

"Gus and I are fine. I'm fine," I assure her.

"So…You're not seeing someone? Where have you been? Don't tell me holed up at home."

Margot is now asking very direct questions that I don't know how to respond to without flat-out lying, something I try like hell to avoid at all costs. But she also has a right to ask because I really haven't shown face aside from the small party we had to celebrate Penelope and Miller's birthday the other week.

I hesitate a second too long.

"You totally are seeing someone!" Margot shrieks, and I pray with every non-believing bone in my body that no one else heard her.

"Pix, why are you yelling?" Sawyer calls, busting through a frosted plastic tarp.

My prayers fall on deaf ears, apparently.

"She's fine!" I shout.

"Daze?" Gus asks, following behind Sawyer.

Oh, fucking *marvelous.*

"I'm interrogating Daisy here on her dating life," Margot clues the guys in, and I consider making a guillotine for myself out of one of the saws they have on the side of the cottage.

"When did you get here?" Gus ignores Margot, focusing on me.

"I dunno, like an hour ago?" I offer before picking my tea up and pretending to sip it to avoid further conversation.

"Never mind that! Daisy, what's going on?" Margot continues her witch hunt.

"Yeah, Daze." Gus obnoxiously leans on the porch banister and crosses his arms with a scandalous smirk on his face. "Let's hear about that dating life."

I'm going to fucking kill him.

"I'm not dating anyone." Truth.

"Sleeping with?" Margot asks with a raised brow.

"A proper lady doesn't kiss and tell, and we all know Daisy Stiles here is the most proper," Gus offers as an answer for me, patting the back of my chair.

I want to throttle him and smack my lips on his face at the same time.

"Booooooring," Margot huffs.

"And on that note"—I stand—"I'm gonna go grab the boys."

Margot lets out a whine that could rival Penelope's when she's overtired.

"Now I'm gonna be stuck here with *them*." She hikes a thumb in the direction of Sawyer and Gus. Both look utterly offended. It makes me laugh.

"Actually, you only have to deal with Sawyer. I'm taking off, too," Gus says.

"Wait, where are you heading?" Sawyer swivels his head, surprised.

"You know, I don't have to tell you everything," Gus says.

"What do you mean? Yes, you do. We're brothers."

Gus claps Sawyer on the back, hard. "Uh huh. Love you, too, you clingy motherfucker. Margot, take care of the big baby, will ya?"

"My first baby," Margot jokes. "Hey, Daisy, do you think you could help me with the baby shower favors next week? I ordered custom M&Ms and I need to get them sorted into little gift bags. We could make it a girls' night?"

"Of course," I say easily. I'm so glad that despite my ability to push everyone out, the people around me, like Margot, insist on pulling me back in.

We all say our goodbyes, and Gus walks with me over to our vehicles, parked side by side.

This was close, too close. I risk a look in Gus's direction, and his eyes are already on me. He has his brows pinched together in concentration, like he's trying to read my mind, wondering if I would have ever answered the question Margot threw at me, or what I would have admitted to.

Would I have claimed Gus as mine as easily as he does me every night we spend together?

* * *

"HUNTER, come on, let's finish this page please, and then I promise we can be done with homework," I bargain.

Hunter groans but thankfully picks his pencil back up and begins concentrating again on the question at hand.

We've been battling history homework for an hour now. I hate it. He hates it. It sucks. But I don't want him falling behind, and we're so close to being done with the fucking Middle Ages. The curriculum hasn't figured out a way to make feudalism cool yet.

I also have one ear on alert for the arrival of our parents. Wherever they ran off to after work, I have no idea, nor do I care. But I really don't want to deal with them when they decide to return home.

"Do you know what we're doing for Thanksgiving this year?" Hunter asks, not looking up from his workbook.

"No clue," I answer.

Touchy subject. Thanksgiving ended so poorly last year that it appears none of us have approached handling this year's holiday. I know I've been avoiding it like the plague.

My mother's sister, Aunt Michele, came into town to join us. Everything was as fine as it could have been until poor Aunt Michele asked my dad where his best friend Aiden was. Because Aiden used to join us for every holiday.

Aunt Michele doesn't come around often. I think she sees through her sister's act, at least enough to not want to spend a lot of time with her. It was an innocent question. But it kind of blew up the entire day.

Or rather, *I* blew up the entire day. The mention of that man's name had me jumping so high in my seat that it jostled the table, knocking over glasses, and they smashed to the floor.

Yelling ensued. Words were said, things that couldn't be taken back. I left and found myself at Red's doorstep to crash and burn at yet *another* Thanksgiving dinner.

I've tried to block it all out. It's been a wasted effort.

"I'm guessing Aunt Michele won't be coming?" Hunter follows up.

"No, probably not. But it'll be fine. Me, you, and Chase can make it fun. We can watch the parade in the morning like we used to!" I ruffle the hair on the top of his head.

"What's Gus doing?"

"Uh, I'm not sure." I haven't thought to ask, to be honest.

"Eating pizza at his house would be better than anything here," Hunter mumbles, lazily resting his chin on the table while he finishes up one of his last open response questions with messy handwriting.

I'm inclined to agree with Hunter, which is something I'm not used to doing. It rattles my heart in more ways than one. A part of me really likes that the boys have a male figure like Gus to turn to when the one we were biologically given for a dad is essentially a waste of space now. The other part is pained, knowing Hunter and Chase are just as miserable as I am here.

As if his ears started ringing at the mention of his name, a text from August lights up my phone on the table.

AUGUST

Whatcha wearing? Something sexy?

My hand flies up to cover my mouth as I bark out a laugh. Hunter looks up from his homework with his head tilted. I wave him off.

ME

Are you seriously sexting me right now?

AUGUST

You looked so good earlier.

ME

I was in jeans and a parka, August.

AUGUST

Fuck, I'm hard just thinking about it.

"I'll be right back," I tell Hunter as I scoot my chair away from the kitchen table and walk into the living room, out of earshot. I hit call on August's contact.

He's chuckling when he answers. "Hey there, Daisy darling."

"Don't you *Daisy darling* me. What's going on?" I pace the living room with the phone to my ear. I don't want to admit how big I'm smiling.

He clears his throat. "*Missedyou.*" It sounds so grumbly and mumbly I barely understand him.

"August Burton, did you just say you *missed me?*"

"Don't get a complex about it. Actually, forget I said anything." I can practically hear him waving me off through the phone. "Anyway, the boys in bed yet?"

I double check the time. "Gus, it's not even seven p.m. No, they're not sleeping."

"Come over when they are?"

I don't get the chance to respond because I hear the front door unlock, and both of my parents walk in. I end the call like a teenager caught doing something I'm not supposed to.

"Hi." I whip around, hellbent on getting out of their line of fire as fast as possible.

"Daisy, hold on," my mother calls. Her voice hasn't quite reached slurring territory, so I pause long enough to give her the slightest bit of my attention and time.

"Yeah?" I feel my phone start vibrating in my pocket.

"I'm not sure what's gotten into you lately. Frankly, you reverting into your old ways isn't something I believe we should be surprised about. But alas, here we are. While you live under this roof, for free I might add, there are rules you need to abide by."

I turn in her direction, facing both of my parents head on.

Something I haven't done in…Jesus, it's been a while. "Enlighten me."

"Your father—"

"Does he speak?" I cock my head in my dad's direction. Another call comes through, and I hit the silence button through my jeans, knowing August is probably freaking the hell out back at his house.

"I owe you nothing," he spits. There's so much hatred in his voice, it's comical to think we're related. Funny to think we once spent any amount of time together as father and daughter.

Mary Jane ignores both of us and continues. "Your father has been hearing stories. Stories involving you, the Burton boy, and the twins. Why the hell would any of you be grouped into anything?"

I give myself a minute to collect my thoughts and decide how I want to handle this. It'd do no good to blow up and get myself kicked out right now. The money I have saved doesn't matter. I can't leave Hunter and Chase. Not like this.

But I also can't handle these two stripping what little happiness I've rediscovered.

"Because August is my friend."

"He has no respect; he's *trash*," my mother scoffs.

Yeah, you know what? I've changed my mind.

"You have no right talking about him like that. Not when he's done more for each of your children than you *ever* will. You hide behind this facade. Newsflash, everyone sees right through it! *Everyone* in this town knows you're a drunk." I look my dad dead in the eyes. "And you?" I huff, I lose my momentum when I realize I might never be able to articulate the kind of permanent pain he left me to suffer through.

"Daisy?" Hunter calls from the kitchen, unaffected by the brawl happening only feet from him. "I need help on the last question. They're asking about the Crusades."

"Be right there!" I assure him. I lower my voice again. "The only reason I'm still attached to you in any way is because of those boys. And you know damn fucking well that without me, you'd be screwed with them and the business. Leave me alone." I rush out of the living room, not bothering to wait for a response.

Neither of my parents acknowledge me further when they enter the kitchen. They quickly and quietly greet Hunter before retreating to their bedroom. I only breathe when I finally hear the lock click.

When I check my phone and see the dozens of missed calls and panicked texts, I realize that Gus is probably halfway across town already. I quickly shoot him a text, summarizing as best as I can while also attempting to keep the events casual enough that he doesn't bust down the door to find my parents.

I try to help Hunter with half of my mind focused elsewhere. I check on Chase upstairs after we're finished. Going through the monotonous motions helps ease my brain a little, but my nerves never fully settle.

It's a combination of things, the mention of Thanksgiving last year and what that time of year means to me, my parents bursting my small bubble of happiness with August and the boys.

I'm trapped. I've gotten myself so deep in this hole that I might never get out.

All I wanted to do was get out.

CHAPTER 22: AUGUST - THE STILES STACK

J've never pulled up someone's contact so damn fast in my life.

"What's wrong?" I bark into the phone once I hear the call connect. I'm still on edge from whatever the fuck happened with Daisy's parents the other night. She talked me off the ledge of going over to give them a piece of my mind, but still, the feeling lingers.

"Nothing!" Daisy assures me. "Okay, there is something wrong, but it's not earth shattering. Pump the brakes, mountain man."

"Daisy," I say gruffly. "What's going on?"

"I forgot there's an early release today for Thanksgiving break, and I'm stuck on a deadline for this arrangement. My parents are MIA, and as much as I would love to use this to throw in their faces, I'm more worried about Hunter and Chase not having a ride home from school. I don't want them standing out in the cold waiting. And if the school calls my parents..."

"I'll get them."

"What? No, that's fine, Gus. I wanted to see if you could maybe come pick up this delivery."

I quickly run the plan through my head.

"I'm closer to the school," I tell Daisy.

"So?" She sounds frustrated. I get it, I would be too if everyone else's responsibilities fell to me without even the thought of a fucking thank you.

"So it makes more sense for me to get the boys. You finish up what you're doing, deliver the flowers, and meet us back at my house. We can hang. I'll have dinner for us."

"This is turning into way more than I was planning when I texted you, August."

"So?" I throw her sassy retort back at her.

"It's Thanksgiving eve," Daisy informs me. As if I wasn't aware.

"Uh-huh." I wedge the phone between my shoulder and ear while I start packing up my tools.

"Aren't you going out?" she asks.

"You sure have a lot of questions for a girl on a deadline, darling. No, I'm not in the mood for Thanksgiving eve, not after last year's shitshow. I think we're all old enough to take a break."

The truth is, it never even crossed my mind. I don't find myself itching to go out at all now that I have the option of spending quiet nights with Daisy.

I listen to the sounds of papers rustling and the distinct swish of a shear slicing into a plant of some kind. "They probably need a snack, and I'd like to get their homework out of the way—"

"Daisy," I interrupt. "I can handle a couple of preteens. Say thank you, and we'll see you later."

I'm halfway to my truck, waving a hand in Beth's direction when Daisy finally says, "Thank you, August. Seriously."

* * *

"CAN I ADD A CHOCOLATE SHAKE?" Hunter asks from the passenger seat.

"And a small chocolate shake please," I sigh into the drive thru receiver. "Dude, how much do you eat?" I turn my head, looking past Chase in the middle, at Hunter.

"Says the guy who just ordered three burgers...for himself," Hunter grumbles as I thank the cashier, and we're directed to pull forward to the first window.

Chase huffs next to me, and I know it's his version of a laugh. I bump his shoulder with my own. "Oh, you think he's funny, huh?" Chase shakes his head with a smile.

Neither of the twins objected when I pulled up to the middle school to pick them up. In fact, they seemed stoked I was there. Not a single question was asked aside from who got to sit shotgun, and who would be squished in the middle.

It made me feel real good to be chosen by some twelve-year-olds.

So I drove the three of us to the best fast food place near Merrymount and told the boys they could order whatever they wanted.

Hunter, much like the first time he showed up at my house, has nine hundred questions ready to fire off at me whenever there's a beat of silence. Chase nods along while halfway engrossed in the book he has perched on his lap.

They're polar fucking opposites, but when I park and hand out their meals, the way they identically stuff French fries in their sandwiches and dip them into barbecue sauce has me howling.

"Who came up with that?" I ask.

"Chase invented it," Hunter mumbles while chewing. "We—well, *I*—call it the Stiles Stack."

"Hey." I put my burger down. "Don't fucking do that."

"Do what?" Hunter tries to sound oblivious.

"Purposely exclude Chase again, and you can walk home. Got it?"

Hunter dips his head down and nods once with no further comment.

I'm pretty sure I'm not supposed to threaten a kid, and Daisy will probably have something to say about how I just handled that, but right now I don't care. Hunter is capable of good. I see he has it in him. And maybe he doesn't let up on his brother's lack of verbal bonding because it's hard for him and he doesn't know how to process it. But bullying isn't the way.

"Stiles Stack has a nice ring to it," I say before resuming eating. I reach over and grab two fries to add to my burger. When I take a bite after dipping in the apparently communal sauce Chase holds up for me, I realize it tastes as good as it sounds. "Damn, ya know what? Chase, you had a genius idea with this."

The time it takes for Hunter to recover from the scolding is short. Some would argue too short, but I kind of really like listening to this kid talk.

"He came up with it when we were eight! Dad used to take us to get food after our football practices, and we'd always try different combos. This one was the best. We don't play football anymore. And Dad doesn't really have time to take us out to eat either. So this is cool. I forgot to say thanks. So…thanks."

"Anytime, guys. I mean it, too."

We ride back to my house listening to Hunter fill the cab with different stories covering a wide range of topics. Hunter doesn't realize it, but each one drives home my opinion about how much their parents continue to royally fucking suck, and how these boys and their sister have always deserved a hell of a lot better.

When we pull up my driveway, I notice Sawyer loitering on my front porch. I kill the engine and hop out.

"What's up?" I call.

"Who do you got in your truck?" Sawyer asks, squinting to peer through the windshield.

"Hunter and Chase, Daisy's—" I stop mid-sentence.

How the hell do I talk myself out of this? What logical reason,

197

besides the truth, do I have to offer Sawyer as to why I'm carting around Daisy's younger brothers?

"Brothers?" Sawyer finishes.

"Yeah," I confirm with no other option coming to me in my time of need.

Shit, I wish I had a halfway decent working brain right about now.

"Should I be worried you kidnapped them as revenge against Daisy or something?" Sawyer cocks a brow.

"For fuck's sake." I slide my hand down my face.

A door slams, and I hear two sets of feet walking towards us. "Do we have to sit in the truck until Daisy shows up?" Hunter asks.

"No." I turn towards the boys, gearing up to get through this awkward encounter. "Hunter, Chase, this is Sawyer."

"We know Sawyer Hale," Hunter informs me with a scoff. "Hey."

"Hey, kid. Hey, Chase." Sawyer offers a friendly wave, and I can't control it. The feeling hits me like a tidal wave. I'm jealous of Sawyer. I don't really like that he has a sense of familiarity with Daisy and her family.

"Oh. Right. Well," I huff. "We're gonna head inside since it's cold as shit. And you can…" I look at Sawyer, realizing he must be here for a reason. Forgot about that. I pull my keys out of my pocket and toss them to Hunter. "Go watch some TV. I'll be inside in a minute. Key with the house on it is—"

"For the house. Yeah, dude. I could've guessed that. See ya, Sawyer," Hunter snickers, and he and Chase make their way up the stairs and into the house.

"Bye, guys!" Sawyer calls. He then turns to me with a scowl. "What the hell are Daisy's little brothers doing in *your* care?"

I don't really like the way Sawyer just phrased that. I don't appreciate the insinuation that I'm not capable of taking care of anyone. "What's that supposed to mean?"

"You're kidding, right? Last I checked, you and Daisy couldn't handle being in the same room together. Unless…"

I don't offer an alternative. I made a promise, and I intend to keep it. As much as Sawyer means to me, I won't invite him into my business with Daisy.

"Something happened. With you and Daisy," Sawyer guesses with annoying accuracy.

"I'm helping out where I can. Let's not dive further into it."

Sawyer heaves a sigh, and his hands land on his hips like an exhausted dad. He's leaning into the role a little early, but this doesn't feel like the time to touch on that…

"I knew it. That's why I came over here. I wanted to have an honest, face-to-face conversation with you, but I'm guessing that's all the answer I'll be getting. Listen, Gus. This…thing with Daisy. It's not healthy. You let her follow you around like a lost puppy when we were younger and then kicked her to the curb."

"I think it's best you don't speak on things you know nothing about." I'm seething. He has no right, even if it is coming from a place of good intention.

Sawyer is apparently in a don't-give-a-fuck mood today, because he keeps going.

"You fought and fought. And honestly, it was manageable. And I know Margot got it in your heads that you had to get along, but this sneaking around is bullshit. Things have gotten so tangled with the two of you that you're babysitting now? You know who this is going to hurt in the end when it all blows up in your faces? Everyone. Including all of us around you."

"Back the hell off." I step towards Sawyer.

He holds his hands up. "Fine. I'll leave. I'm just saying, think about how this ends."

I don't bother with a response, stalking into my house. I grumble to myself about how bullshit that whole interaction was.

Sawyer and I don't fight. But I'm not letting anyone swing in here telling me how my life is going to pan out. Especially not with Daisy.

Shit. Speaking of Daisy…

ME

> All 3 of us are back at the house. Fed and happy. Hunter says there's no homework during Thanksgiving break but I'll let you be the judge of that.

* * *

IF SAWYER'S attitude earlier didn't put a damper on my night, the mood Daisy's in right now would have done it.

She's busy using Hunter and Chase as a buffer between us to avoid any sort of conversation surrounding the way she walked into this house looking like a ghost of herself. I clocked it immediately, and I can tell she's not happy about being seen like that.

Daisy loves to hide in the comfort of the shadows. She forgets that I know it's always the first place to look for her.

She jumps when I reach my arm across the back of the couch to rub her shoulder. I bet Daisy doesn't even realize I noticed her staring blankly at the wall beside the TV.

"Hey," I mouth silently to not disrupt Hunter and Chase watching the movie.

I motion with my head to her phone sitting on the arm of the couch beside her. I pick mine up and type out a quick text.

ME

> What's going on?

She rolls her eyes when she reads my text, and based on how fast it takes her to respond, I know I'm going to be annoyed.

DAISY DARLING

> Nothing.

I'm not buying it.

ME

> Bullshit. I don't want you leaving tonight. I'll drive H & C home. You can ride with us, but you're sleeping here.

DAISY DARLING

> Thought I always had a choice.

I exhale. "Daze, I need help in the kitchen."

She doesn't look in my direction. She keeps her eyes focused ahead. "No, you don't."

Hunter looks from his left to his right at each of us. "Are you guys fighting?"

For some reason, that triggers something in Daisy, causing her to spring up. "No! Absolutely not. We'll be right back." She practically sprints out of the living room, not waiting to see if I follow.

When I enter the kitchen on her heels, I continue my pursuit to get to the bottom of whatever storm cloud is hovering over her head.

"Daisy."

"Stop!" she whisper-shouts.

I hold my hands up. "Sorry."

Daisy grips the edge of the kitchen island, letting her head hang. "It's okay. It's just—I'm fine. But I'm not fine. I don't let people see this. It's killing me trying to put on a show out there."

"You know how you appreciate honesty?"

The look she gives me when she turns her head confirms I'm about to play with fire.

"You're doing a shit job of hiding whatever's going on up there," I say softly. I take a chance winding my fingers through her hair. Surprisingly, Daisy leans into my touch. When she closes her eyes, I revel at her beauty for a minute. Lost in a daze.

"I know," she breathes. Those crystal clear blues shine up at me. An unspoken conversation passes between us. She's not ready to talk, but she's willing to let me sit with her through whatever this is. I'll take it.

It's at that moment that for the first time in a long time, I feel like I have Daisy Stiles.

And I don't want to let her go.

CHAPTER 23: DAISY - NOVEMBER 28TH

The Journal of Daisy D. Stiles - Twelve years ago

They forgot my birthday. Or just decided they didn't need to bother with acknowledging it.

Again.

Thanks a heap, Mom & Dad!

Then again, I think my dad has forgotten my entire existence. Or he's trying to. Probably less painful for him. That's nice for him.

Sometimes I'd like to forget my entire existence, too.

THE THING with depression is that some days, you forget it's there. You don't remember that nasty, dark, lingering feeling in the back of your brain that's ready to pounce at any given moment. You experience real joy, and you find comfort in people and places that matter in the best kind of way.

And then you wake up the next morning with the inability to find a reason to keep going. You feel weighed down by hundreds of bricks. You wade through a never-ending fog, searching for your purpose.

You find a million and one reasons why waking up the next morning doesn't feel worth it, and you cling with all of the hope in the Goddamn world to the one reason to stay. Because you *do* want to stay. You just don't want it to feel like it's always going to be this hard.

Why bother?

What is this even all for?

How can it get better?

It's all-consuming and finding that one tether of hope and light to cling onto feels like the world's most impossible task.

There's no cure. You just cope.

I've been coping, in a way I would deem acceptable, for quite some time now. So it shouldn't be a surprise to me that I've hit a snafu in my journey. The only problem is, I'm finding it difficult to pull myself out of this bed, and I don't know how I'm going to explain that to August.

August, who woke up before the sun. August, who kissed the top of my head when he thought I was still sleeping. August, who —above all else—cannot see me broken like this.

I remove the pillow from my face and let my eyes adjust to the blinding light coming from the windows. I do some breathing exercises and run through my list of prepositions. A Dr. Saltore-approved tool.

About, above, across, after, against, among, around, at...

I get my bearings and attempt to sit up, falling back into the pillows almost immediately. I huff in frustration with myself, angry at my brain and my body for constantly failing me.

Maybe I don't have to explain shit to anyone. Maybe I can just let myself become one with this mattress, sink into nothingness, and disappear.

That'd be nice.

It'd give me a break, for once. I wouldn't have to think about how fucking screwed up I am. That no matter how much time passes, it never seems to get better. I don't have to harp on the fact that I just keep figuring out new ways to hide it all, no one around me noticing.

No one except August. But I think I've pacified his worries enough over the last few days.

I hear the front door open below me, and I dive back under the comforter. Gus must have come back for something, something he forgot before heading to work. His lunch maybe? I'm sure there's no reason for him to come back up here.

I should've stayed in the spare room. It was dumb of me to selfishly want to sleep in his bed.

Giant footsteps coming up the staircase force me to come to terms with the fact that quite literally nothing ever goes the way I need it to.

"Daze?" Gus calls, rapping his knuckles on his own bedroom door before entering.

I don't answer. I don't think I can. There are no words to be found.

"Daisy," Gus attempts again.

One knock.

Then two.

I hear him sigh on the other side of the door. I can't imagine how frustrating this must be for him, having someone he tolerates at best taking up space in his house—his *bed*—who now won't even pull herself together enough to acknowledge him when he calls.

I'll just wait until he can't take it anymore and throws me out. Then I'll figure out my next plan to achieve nothingness. I'll figure out a how-to on becoming an inanimate object, void of emotions and feelings and pasts too fucked up to overcome.

"I gotta open the door, Daze. I saw the signs last night before we went to sleep. I know what kind of day today is for you. I woke up earlier to get my work done as fast as I could to get back here. I'm not leaving."

He…what? I peel the blanket down an inch to get eyes on the bedroom door as it slowly creaks open. Gus's head pokes in, and my eyes well with tears seeing the dark circles under his eyes. His forehead is coated in sweat, probably from doing too much in such a short amount of time to get back to me before something bad happens. His hair is standing up straight in some places, and is just plain messy in others.

He's exhausted. Being around me, dealing with me, is exhausting.

"Hi, darling," he says softly. Gently.

Gus remains in the doorway.

I don't deserve the patience he's reserved for me.

"If you give me like, five minutes, I'll be out of your hair," I say through the sheets, my words muffled.

"You're not going anywhere, and neither am I." Gus pushes the door so it opens. He steps into his bedroom, closes the door, and sinks to the floor. "No one's gonna bother us today, Daze. It's just me and you, okay?"

God, he's talking to me like I'm a baby deer.

I have to push him away, scare him so he runs for the hills. No one should be subjected to my company.

"I stay here for sex. I promise you I'm not delivering in that department today, so I might as well—"

"Save it, Daisy," he snaps.

"What?" I ask, taken aback by his tone.

"You're about to spout off some bullshit, and I'm here for just about anything with you today, I really am. But I'm not about to sit and listen to you lie to my face. You stay here because you're safe. Because you *know*—" Gus stops. I need him to finish. I need to know what else could possibly come after.

"You know this is more than sex."

"What?" I drag myself up to sit against the headboard. "No, this is…We're just…"

"Did I fuck you last night?" Gus cuts off my train of thought.

"No," I admit.

"And yet, here you are, in my bed."

"Yeah, but…"

Gus, with his hulking, oversized body, *crawls* the feet between the door and the bed, and positions himself on his knees by my side. He rests his forearms on the mattress, just out of reach. He blows out a breath that sounds like he'd been holding it in for a while.

"Let me in, Daze. Let me in your head. I'll do anything."

My hands shake as I twist the corner of the blanket around my fingers. August knows…things. He has a general idea of what happened to me, what could cause this kind of mood, or whatever you want to call it. And why, I guess, I am the way I am.

Or he did. Kind of. I never fully let him in like he's asking, and maybe he forgot the pieces I gave him over time.

I wouldn't blame him. I don't want this shit either.

Dr. Saltore used to ask about my circle of trust. Who did I count on outside the walls of his office to help me carry the weight of my feelings? I always answered with no one.

I had one fleeting period of time where if Dr. Saltore had asked just once more, I would have said August. I thought maybe, just maybe, his dark and stormy matched mine in a way that could handle this. After things fell apart, or rather, *disintegrated*, I told myself I'd never have false hope like that again.

Grappling with the idea of going back on that promise to myself, I chance another look at Gus. So many emotions swirl through his eyes and yet, I feel like I can pick out each and every single one. It's so easy for me to read him when he looks at me like this.

He's not Gus, my enemy.

He's just…He's my August.

My decision is made in the next second. I close my eyes to gather the courage to finally hand a tiny bit of trust to someone other than myself.

"It's been eighteen years," I begin quietly. "Today marks eighteen years, and I still can't bear the thought of existing when this day rolls around. The other three hundred and sixty-four days could be downright perfect, not a single flaw. But I look at the calendar and spot November twenty-eighth and suddenly, nothing else matters. It's me in that room with him, and there's no escape."

Gus remains silent, but the change in the air is obvious. His back sits ramrod straight, and I notice him trying like hell to not clench his fists. He doesn't want to seem phased. He wants to hide all of those emotions, not realizing I see him. Probably like he sees me.

"Some years I try to distract myself, like I can trick my brain. And it always works for a little, just long enough for me to think I might actually have a shot at being a normal person. Someone who didn't—Someone who wasn't—" I choke back a sob.

"Damn it!" I yell, all of my resolve falling away into nothing. I swipe at my soaked cheeks, tears continuing to spill down my face. "I'm so fucking broken," I say into the comforter as I cover myself again.

"Daisy," Gus prompts. "Daisy, look at me. Please."

I don't give in to the request.

"Can I touch you?" he asks. I feel a dip in the mattress as he puts weight on it.

I blindly reach my hand out, and when my fingers connect with his warm skin, I pull. Gus picks up exactly what I'm saying without words and moves onto the bed, wrapping me up in his arms. The next thing I know, he's pulling the comforter up until he's underneath with me.

My crying doesn't relent, and I don't feel moved to try to make it stop like I normally would. If this wasn't the worst possible timing ever, I'd laugh at the sight of the two of us basically making a fort in August's bed.

"I'm not going to tell you how you feel. But if you think you're broken, I'll carry all of the pieces." He rubs the length of my arm, up and down, soothing me.

"I don't want to carry this anymore."

"Then give it to me," he urges.

"He was my dad's friend. His best friend. He picked out my middle name. He was there when I learned how to ride a bike. He came to all of my birthday parties. If there was an emergency, his number was on the fridge to call. It was that number I dialed. Because I knew—I *thought*—I could trust him." It's the first time I've ever said it out loud.

Gus rests his head on mine, continuing to rub my arm.

I finally find the air to take a deep breath to continue. "It was late and my parents weren't home. We had just moved into the house. Everything was so new. I just wanted to know where they were, or when they'd be coming back. He said he'd be right over. I didn't ask him to come over."

I feel like I'm being transported back in time. The confusion of seeing Aiden at the front door with a demented smile on his face under the dim porch light feels fresh. I can practically smell the alcohol seeping through every part of him. A shudder racks my body, and August continues to hold me tight through it.

"He told me my parents were out, as if I didn't clearly already know that, and he'd be happy to wait with me. Things kind of go dark from there. The psychiatrist explained how sometimes your brain blocks certain memories as a preservation tactic. Which I guess I'm grateful for because if what I can recall is the lukewarm stuff—" A humorless laugh hiccups out of me.

"Daisy." Undiluted pain laces the singular word from Gus.

"I said no. I *screamed* it, until I was choking to breathe through the pillow that covered my face. I thrashed, I kicked. And then it was over. He left. My parents still weren't home. So, I walked. I think I walked the entirety of Merrymount that night until Officer Holstrom found me."

"Mark?" Gus asks.

I nod. "I don't remember what I told him. But next thing I knew, I was sitting in a chair at the station, listening to my parents drunkenly argue with Mark and his deputy."

"Why were they arguing, Daze?"

"Oh, because it was all a big misunderstanding, of course. I was confused. I needed attention." I recite my parents' words verbatim.

A part of me died that day.

And each time my parents pulled further away from me, refusing to believe their only daughter, another tiny part of me died too.

I don't tell August that, though.

"Where is he?" August's voice is cold.

"If you're also wishing he was dead, unfortunately, cockroaches can withstand even global apocalypses. Charges were dropped and everything was swept under the rug. I saw Dr. Saltore three times a week for a year. Then we moved it down to once. Then the sessions dropped altogether when my mom got pregnant with the boys."

I finally remove the blanket that's covering us. I take a big gulp of fresh air with the intent of finally sitting up on my own, but I slump back into August in the next second.

"I'd kill him, Daze. I need you to know that. I know it's fucked and wrong of me to say, but I wouldn't stop until he was dead."

Logically, I'm aware that should terrify me. I should be high-tailing it the heck out of August's house to safety. This, combined with the incident at that bar, are clear indicators that Gus might not be the most stable when it comes to my well-being.

But this is where I'm safest. With him.

I know it. My body knows it.

"I don't think I'd stop you," I admit, adding my insanity to his.

A long while passes before either of us makes any attempt to move or say anything. It's Gus who finally breaks the silence.

"It's a big deal that you trusted me with this, Daze."

"I know," I agree.

"I don't want to say the wrong thing," he admits.

"You won't," I assure him. And I believe it. Because I know whatever August finds important to tell me right now is coming from that heart of his he normally keeps locked up tight. It's a wide open door for me now, though.

"You're the strongest person I know, and you should have never have had to go through that. Everyone fucking failed you, and yet you're still here. I'm—" His breath becomes shaky. "I'm so proud to know you. Even the shitty parts. Especially those ones."

"August—"

"No, wait. I got something going here. Daze, I never let anyone in. You know how it is. But you poked and prodded until I had no choice but to accept you as a staple in my life. I look back on our time sitting in that stuffy guidance office and realize that was a really important part of my life. It changed me. The domino effect of giving me a place where I was something besides a waste of space."

"We were just a couple of broken kids," I sigh.

"Maybe true. But it was more. I think you know that."

I don't admit I do.

August doesn't try to force it out of me.

"I wish I could wipe this date off the calendar for you. I'll still try, anything you want. But for now, today, we won't leave this bed except for food and bathroom breaks, I guess. And then tomorrow won't be November twenty-eighth."

"That doesn't feel very productive," I say, attempting to swipe away at least some of the wetness drenching my face.

He shrugs, and it's so boyishly cute, a rogue crack of a laugh leaves me.

"Depends on your definition of productive. I'm gonna go raid the snack cabinet and be right back. Holler if you have any requests." August's lips graze the top of my head, and he gently sets my back against the pillows before heading downstairs.

He returns several minutes later with two armfuls of a collection of food that would make most teenage boys salivate. Lucky for me, I have the same taste palette.

We spend the day exactly as August described, in bed with too many snacks, watching nature documentaries narrated by celebrities. My favorite was *Vanishing of the Bees.* I fucking love Elliot Page.

I drift in and out of sleep, and every time I wake, August is there. He never leaves my side.

CHAPTER 24: AUGUST - 0922

While Daisy slept yesterday, I got to work on something I should have done years ago. But if this time with Daisy has taught me anything, it's that maybe there isn't such a thing as too late when it comes to certain areas of my life.

Like fulfilling a lost promise and making someone I care about's dream finally come true.

Daisy needs a break. I'm gonna give her that.

After clearing with Beth that I would be good to take off for a couple of days, I found a hotel with two nights of availability and put together a list of activities I think Daisy would be interested in based on memory. I nailed down the best route for the drive and started packing.

This morning, when I finally saw the sadness leave her eyes, I asked if it was okay to surprise her with something. Yeah, I know. Unconventional to the normal routine of a surprise, but like I always tell her, I'm never not going to give her a choice.

I didn't tell her the whole plan, obviously. But I'm thankful as fuck that I've earned back enough of her trust that she only slightly cautiously said yes.

Our destination is a little under four hours away from Merry-mount, and Daze has been content to sit in suspense beside me for about two hours. She's getting antsy now.

"Let me pick a playlist, *please*," Daisy begs from the passenger seat over the sounds of Post Malone's latest album. She picks my phone up from the center console and taps it to life, stuck on the lockscreen. "What's your passcode?"

"There's nothing wrong with Posty," I say, ignoring her question.

"I never said there was. But this is the third time we've listened through this album, and that's not even counting the other one we played before this. We can change things up. Come on, Gus. Passcode." Her index finger taps on my screen again.

"Just give it to me. I'll do it." I reach my hand out for my phone, keeping my eyes on the road.

Daisy doesn't pass me the phone though. Because why would she make this easy for me? When has she ever made anything easy for me?

"Seriously? I'm not going to snoop while you're right next to me. Scout's honor." Her tone remains playful.

Mine doesn't. "You don't need to know my passcode."

"For fuck's sake, August. This is one of the dumbest hills you could choose to die on. It's four digits. I'll forget them as soon as they're typed in."

"Bet you won't," I try to mutter under my breath.

"What?" she asks.

"Nothing," I huff.

"No, you said something. Say it with your chest."

Up until two minutes ago, I was thinking about how this was probably one of the best stretches of time Daisy and I have spent together in years. I felt like old times, but different too—seeing as we're adults now, with lives that have been lived. We've had time apart to grow as individuals. But then again, some things never change, and as much as I'll lie to your face and say I'd never back down from Daisy Stiles, I'm relenting to her request at the last second.

"It's 0922," I practically bark.

She chuckles as she types in the four numbers. My phone unlocks in her hands instantly. "That's funny, that's my…"

Silence. She hit pause on the song right before realization dawns on her so there isn't a single sound aside from the tires of my truck rolling over the beat-up old highway we're driving down.

A hole the size of fucking Texas opens up in my stomach. My hands are wrapped tightly around the leather steering wheel, to the point of pain.

"August." Her tone is low and slow. "That's my birthday."

I say nothing. I swallow.

"That's my birthday," Daisy repeats, a little louder this time. Like she's making sure I hear her. Like there was even a sliver of a damn chance I missed it the first time.

"I don't know what you want me to say," I finally admit.

"Tell me why," Daisy demands.

Because one time, forever ago, you told me that no one bothered to remember your birthday. You woke up in a house filled with people who didn't give a shit about you, and you waited. You waited all day for someone to acknowledge the day you came into this world, and not a soul in your family did. I never forgot it, and I never forgave them.

"Easy set of numbers to remember." Lie.

"That's fucking bullshit." She sounds almost breathless. I still haven't looked over at her.

Movement in the corner of my eye forces me to see Daisy gently placing my phone back in the cupholder. She pulls her legs up so her socked feet are flat on the seat and wraps her arms around her knees. She kicked her shoes off to get comfy before we even left the Merrymount town limits. She lowers her chin to rest on her knees and blows her bangs out of her face with a huff. We're still driving along in silence. I don't offer to break it.

Minutes—maybe hours with the way it feels—pass before Daisy finally speaks again.

"I just don't get it, Gus. You're supposed to hate me. Did you like, change it as a prank or something? Is this you playing the long game in a big joke?"

Now I'm fucking pissed. That's where her head immediately goes? She can still pretend that I ever hated her?

There doesn't seem to be much of a point in keeping up past appearances now. I shrug my shoulders and finally loosen my grip on the steering wheel.

"I never hated you. I've spent the better part of ten years angry with you, sure. But never hate. I'd never put you in the same category as others."

"What does that even mean?"

"Nothing."

"Don't do that again, Gus."

"You're just…You're Daisy. It's different. It's always been different with us." That barely scratches the surface, but I hope it'll suffice for now.

"Fine. Say I agree with you for the sake of the conversation. We're different. What did you mean by 'same category as others'?" She uses her fingers for air quotes.

"I meant I hate five people in this world, and you've never been one of them."

"But—"

I cut her off, effectively ending any hint of privacy when it comes to my thoughts apparently.

"My mother." I tap the steering wheel with a single digit. "For choosing an abusive piece of shit with money over her own son. My stepfather." Tap two. "For being that abusive piece of shit with money. Your parents." I add fingers three and four. "For everything. For every single thing they've done or said or swept under the rug to save face when all they should have ever done is save *you*." The last part comes out louder than I intended, and I immediately regret it when Daisy jumps in her seat.

I tried harder than I ever have at anything to hide how I truly felt the other day. November twenty-eighth. I wanted to let my vision only see red. I wanted to right every wrong that crossed Daisy's path, not caring where that landed me. But I kept it locked down. I'm mustering up the ability to do that again.

I lower my voice again.

"Number five…" I pause.

"August," Daisy whispers. She's shaking, and as important as I think the truth is for her to hear, I wish I could take it back. But I have to finish this out.

"Number five doesn't deserve to exist." I flick on my blinker, and pull the truck to the side of the road. When I shift into park, I turn my body towards the passenger seat where Daisy sits with her eyes squeezed shut.

"Daisy." I use my gentlest tone. "Can I have your hand?" She wordlessly places her left hand in the middle of the bench seat, and I take it into mine. I rub soft circles in her palm. "I didn't want to make you uncomfortable."

"You didn't," she interjects. Her eyes remain closed. "It's just— We don't—We *haven't*, in a long while anyway, talked like this. With one another. I told myself the other day was a one off. I don't…I don't bring up—"

"I know," I remind her. "I know we don't talk about it. About anything anymore."

"That's starting to feel like it's not true though. And I don't know what to do with that. Feuding with you has been almost like a crutch to me. It was easy and familiar. And now I know."

"Know what, Daze?" I try to not let myself hope. Hope and I have never been friends.

Her eyes burst open, and there are practically flames dancing in her irises.

"Now I know you don't hate me. And maybe you never did.

My fucking birthday is your phone's passcode, for crying out loud! Maybe that's trivial to some, but it's huge to me, August. I'm not remembered or important. But to you? Maybe I am to you? What the hell do I do with that kind of information?"

"You accept it because it's the truth. And if there's anything you hold dearly in this world, it's honesty."

Daisy surprises me by leaning over. I release her hand, in favor of putting my arm around her shoulders, pulling her into my side. I grab hold of her hand again once she's resituated. I feel the rise and fall of her breaths, and we sit without the need for words.

"I missed you," she whispers. The words float like a feather through the charged air of the truck. I hold myself as steady as possible when internally I feel like I'm about to explode.

I think long and hard about how to respond. The wrong thing could spook her right back to where we were. I settle on the simple truth.

"Missed you too, Daze."

"Since we're doing the whole honesty thing…Are you ready to tell me where we're heading?"

"I thought you would have figured it out by now," I say into the top of her head.

"Can't say I've been paying much attention to our surroundings. Which now that I say it out loud, is terrible self-preservation skills on my part." Feeling her laugh against me feels good.

It feels so good, I can't hold out on the surprise any longer. "It's time you got out of Merrymount. I'm taking you to your version of *The Emerald City*."

I let her think it through, see if she can connect the dots of a past promise. She freezes in my arms, whipping her head up in the direction of my face.

"Really? New York?" Her lips are so close to mine. I'd only have to lean down maybe an inch or two, and we'd be connected.

I exhale and nod, snapping myself out of that pesky little

hopeful feeling again. "The very one. Against my better judgment, ignoring the rats and the sheer amount of people, mixed with all that noise, we're spending two nights in the Big Apple. Or whatever the fuck they call it."

Daisy squeals, and my ears start ringing.

"You're kidding! You're *joking!*" she cries, grabbing me by the shoulders and shaking. "Gus—I—I don't know what to say," she breathes.

"No need to say anything. Scoot on over and buckle back up. Let's get a move on, Daisy darling."

I smile bigger than I probably ever have, wishing more than anything that I could crash my mouth into Daisy's with the way she's looking at me right now. There isn't a hint of hatred on that pretty face. For the first time in fucking forever, she's just my Daze, happy to sit beside me in the cab of my truck on the way to wherever.

I'm gonna enjoy the fuck out of the next couple days. I'm not going to entertain how badly this is gonna hurt when it's all over and I lose Daisy Stiles for good.

Because somehow I know I will lose her. She'll leave. She was always supposed to leave.

I think it's always been borrowed time with us.

CHAPTER 25: DAISY - THE GREATEST CITY IN THE WORLD

I'm so fucking done.

No one be surprised when I pack a bag and leave this godforsaken town and never ever come back.

The art department is sponsoring a class trip to New York City, and I can't go.

I could, but my mother refuses to sign the permission slip. She says there's no need for me to go to a rat-filled, crime-ridden city for no good reason. She doesn't care that this has been my biggest dream for as long as I can remember. She doesn't care about me at all.

I watched her rip the paper into shreds and then toss it in the dumpster behind the flower shop.

Bitch.

But...

August told me he'd take me someday.

He promised, actually.

And I trust him.

So, one day I'll go to New York City while holding August Burton's hand. And we'll laugh about how shitty things used to be.

And then we'll smile because when the two of us are together, every-thing's better.

* * *

FOR THE FIRST time in my life, I'm ecstatic to be sitting in bumper-to-bumper traffic.

August is less than thrilled by our current predicament, but he's doing a fabulous job of keeping his frustrations at bay while horns blast around us, and he slams on his breaks for the sixtieth time in the span of about forty-five minutes to avoid a rear-end collision.

"Are we driving to Jersey?" I ask. August hasn't told me a single plan he has in store, including where we're staying.

He doesn't take his eyes off the road, focusing on the dozens of cars ahead and behind us in the rearview mirror. But I see the look of disgust cross his face. "I'm not dealing with all of this to stick us in a hotel not in the city. We're getting the full experience."

I don't want to get my hopes up. This is already more than I could have ever asked for.

"So...we're staying...?" I attempt to pull a solid answer out of him.

August chuckles. "In the heart of it all, Daze. And fucking thankfully, we're almost there. Sit tight." He pats my thigh and leaves his hand resting there. I lean into how good it feels to enjoy casual physical affection with someone.

But it's not just someone. It's August.

August, who holds me while I sob and has my birthday as his phone's passcode. August, who I'm ninety-eight percent positive pretended to hate me for a decade but quietly—*silently*—cheered me on from afar? August, who despite all of the bullshit has remained a constant in my life.

At the next red light, August flicks the blinker on to turn right

221

into a parking garage. We find a spot next to an elevator on the tenth floor, and Gus doesn't let me touch a single one of our bags as we make our way back down to ground level.

We walk two blocks, with August's hand in mine in a vice grip so he "doesn't lose me." I don't know where to look—up, down, *everywhere.* I listen to employees shooting the shit while working in a loading bay and a woman yelling into her phone while she passes us looking like Carrie freaking Bradshaw in a fur coat. I smell boiled peanuts and smile at the man playing the violin on the corner.

Before I have the chance to ask, Gus is pulling a few loose dollars out of his pocket and thrusting them in my free hand to toss in the instrument case propped open for tips.

People weave in and out of the streets, ignoring any signals for stopping or walking. Sounds of construction and continuous traffic fill the air in a way that you just know never silences.

This is it.

The greatest city in the world.

When we turn a corner, I halt, causing August to abruptly stop with me, seeing as he still refuses to let me go.

"*Oh,*" I breathe.

I blink. I blink again to assure myself I'm not dreaming and everything I'm looking at is real. I'm here.

"Woah," August echoes my thoughts.

The vision of everything that is Times Square keeps both of us firmly planted in place. Billboards take up entire skyscrapers. Music pumps through speakers, and people are trying to sell something to every person that passes them. Whistles, horns, steam from manholes, police sirens, and more drown out my ability to think properly.

We can see the air of our breaths with every exhale, and normally I'm the cold's number one hater, but right now I don't care. Right now, I feel like I'm exactly where I'm supposed to be.

It's overwhelming and exhilarating at the same time.

To be one person in a sea of so many is humbling.

I take in the fact that right here, in this moment, I can be anyone. I don't need to be the closed-off girl with a dark past that's not worth reliving. Here, August and I never fell apart. We're just two small fish in the world's biggest pond.

Gus squeezes my hand, pulling me back to reality. "Sure is something, huh?"

"I don't...I mean, this is..." Finding words is proving to be difficult. "Gus, I've dreamed of this for so long."

"I know," he says. "And I know it took me a while to make good on that promise. I'm sorry for that. But, you're here, Daze."

"*We're* here," I correct him.

"We're here," he echoes, and I can barely hear him over all of the other sounds taking over. His smile is so easy when he looks down at me, his top lip kept cozy under his neatly trimmed mustache. He has a navy beanie covering his messy mop of brown hair and a thick brown Carhartt jacket zipped up to his collar. Gus looks so out of place in the city, and yet at the same time, he looks so perfectly *mine.* It's a possessive feeling I lost long ago, now found and wound tightly back up in my heart.

He tugs me forward. "Come on. Let's go get checked into the hotel and warmed up before we venture out."

* * *

MY FEET HURT, and the cold is biting my face in a way I know is going to leave a red burn across the bridge of my nose and cheeks, but I don't care.

I simply could never muster the energy to care about anything negative when the rest of *everything* is so fucking perfect.

My body jerks when August suddenly stops on the sidewalk, pulling me back toward him by our linked hands.

"Hold on, I wanna pop in here," he says, gesturing to the small antique store in front of us.

He's already carrying my regular tote bag, plus a few shopping bags we've picked up along the way of our travels through the city. But hey, what's one more?

"See something you like?" I ask.

"Something like that." And when August looks down with crinkles around his eyes as he smiles at me, I have to blink to save myself from free-falling into the feeling of getting lost in him.

But a tiny, nagging voice in the back of my head tells me I already have.

Once we're inside and faced with rows of shelves that reach up to ceilings, creating a labyrinth of items of the past, Gus informs me he's finding a bathroom and tells me to check the place out.

I don't hesitate. I dash down the first aisle, filled with old books and knick-knacks from my childhood and before. I lose myself in it all, amazed by how each item I pick up feels as though it was chosen with so much care and attention to take up space on the shelf. This isn't a store of old junk. It truly is all beautiful treasure.

I don't know how much time passes, but by the time I find Gus again, he's chatting it up with the cashier in the back of the store.

Maybe it's my baseless assumptions of the inner workings of antique stores, but I never would have pictured the guy manning the place to be someone who looks to be our age, maybe a few years older in his mid-thirties. He pushes large, round, wide-rim glasses up to sit properly on his nose, and he laughs with Gus like they're old friends.

Obviously I'm biased because I'm lucky enough to climb the giant man next to him like a freaking tree on the daily, but if it was anyone but August standing next to this guy, I'd be very into the Jonathan Bailey thing our new city friend here has going on.

"Okay, you had the right idea popping in here. Ohmy*gosh*," I exclaim, unceremoniously dumping my finds onto the counter. "Also, hi!" I greet the cashier.

"Daze, I left you alone for like ten minutes. How much damage did you do?" Gus laughs, and I bump into him with a hip check.

"Hey, I'm Carson. Gus here's told me a lot about you." The cashier—now known as Carson—reaches his hand across the counter.

I meet him in the middle and shake. There's no electric spark or pull like there always is with August, but a warm feeling creeps up my arm. A signal only to me that this is a good and safe kind of man.

I side-eye Gus before flashing another smile at Carson.

"Don't believe anything he says," I joke. "Do your parents own this place? It's magical. I could be lost in here for hours, probably even days."

Carson chuckles and runs his hand through his mahogany colored hair. "My dad's retired, so now I'm the old man running the show."

"Damn, that's cool. How long has this place been in your family? Do you like it? What's the craziest thing you've seen?"

"Hm, uh, okay lemme think," Carson starts. "My dad opened the store in 1989. He took over the lease when it was a laundromat at the end of its life, and transformed it into *Beyond the Closet Door*. I grew up here. I love it more than anything. I'd love to tell you the craziest thing I've seen but…"

He hesitates for dramatic effect, leaning in just a little bit closer to us. Honestly? I'm captivated by the way Carson talks. He wants to lure you into his tales, like a true and practiced story teller.

"Then I'd have to kill you," he finishes, clapping his hands together.

"Daze, you about to ask for a job?" August interjects.

"Maybe I am." I stick my nose up and childishly stick my tongue out.

Carson again laughs us off. I don't blame him. We probably look and sound like silly, small-town characters. He starts ringing up my pile of stuff, and when I look at the total on the screen, I'm shocked by the steep discount Carson very clearly applied. Gus taps his card on the reader before I can object.

"Consider it a *'welcome to New York'* gift," Carson says to me, handing over yet another paper bag to Gus.

"This is, hands down, the best day of my life." I mean every word.

Carson walks around the counter and embraces Gus in one of those typical man-style half hugs. Words are exchanged that I can't make out. He holds out his hand for mine to shake again, and I really appreciate him not pushing me into further physical contact I never asked for. Observant, interesting antique store man.

"It was really nice to meet you, Carson," I say while August wraps his arm around my shoulder to walk us out.

"Can't imagine it'll be the last time we meet, darlings!" he calls.

"I liked him," I tell Gus once we're back on the cold sidewalk.

"I'm not saying he's not a cool guy." Gus pulls me closer into his side and presses his lips to the top of my head. "But I don't need to hear you gawking over other men."

"Territorial brute," I giggle.

"Call me whatever you want," Gus says.

We continue to fight the bite of early winter to squeeze every moment we can into the day, traveling through the streets of New York. I eat a questionable hot dog. I befriend a pigeon. We try to get tickets to a show, and when we're unsuccessful, Gus promises we'll be back.

And for some reason, even though all of this with us is temporary, I believe him.

CHAPTER 26: AUGUST - I WANT TO KISS YOU, DAZE

After however many miles of walking around Central Park, a *can't-miss, must-stop* to a hot dog vendor, countless stores, and at least an hour of standing in Times Square in absolute awe about how small we really are compared to the rest of the world, Daisy and I crashed onto our hotel bed, completely spent.

We haven't moved much since then. We haven't said much either, content in our silent companionship, ignoring the fact that we're practically fused together.

In more than just the physical kind of way, I admit only to myself.

I don't know if I could tell you a single fact about anything we saw today. I paid attention to absolutely nothing except the excitement buzzing around Daisy and the way her eyes lit up at the smallest of things, like the pigeon who followed us around for forty-five minutes before flying off with his flock.

Daisy named him Bart. She definitely thought we were taking Bart back to Merrymount.

I don't know if I would have been able to tell her no, so I'm thankful for ole Bart flying away before she had the chance to ask.

She's in an element of her own that I don't think she knew existed until we arrived.

I'm not too shocked. She's had New York City circled, underlined, and highlighted at the top of every bucket list and plan she's ever made. Daisy was always meant to end up here, one way or another.

I have mixed feelings on being here to witness it all. The selfless half of me is honored to be here and see this kind of dream come true for Daisy. She deserves every bit of happiness that comes her way. If I had control of things, I'd make it my mission to ensure she never has a bad day again.

But the selfish part of me…I have to wonder if this started the clock. The countdown until Daisy leaves Merrymount—*and me*—for bigger and better. Just like she always planned.

Because Hunter and Chase are getting older and won't need her around forever. Because more days spent in that house with her spineless, pathetic parents would kill her.

And I'm too chickenshit to ask her to stay.

Stay and try to make that future she always dreamed of with me. Even if it's not as far as the wind will take her.

Before I let the most painful thoughts—like watching the back of Daisy's head as she leaves for good—consume me, I allow myself one pitiful truth to escape me.

"I wanna kiss you, Daisy." It's the only thing that feels safe enough to admit.

This isn't the first time I've admitted this to her.

Just like with that grainy picture I stumbled upon a few months ago, I'm thrown back into another memory I've suppressed for far too long.

It's late. Too late, actually. I should have had Daisy home hours ago. But we were having so much fun, and she looks too pretty and content gazing up at the thousands of stars over our heads.

We've been parked in this field, laying in the bed of my truck since sunset. Neither of us have moved much since, focusing on constellations and our conversation that feels like it could be never ending. I don't really ever want it to end.

"God, it's beautiful," she sighs.

"Yeah, you are."

Her face whips to mine, her puffy lips parted. "What did you just say?"

I muster up every bit of courage an eighteen-year-old guy like me can find and clear my throat with my fist at my mouth. "I said you're beautiful."

"Oh." Daisy blinks. She blinks again, and I reach out to gently press her chin up, closing that perfect O-shape her mouth formed.

"Just 'oh'?"

She shakes her head while scrunching her nose, and it's the most adorable thing I've ever seen. I find myself thinking that about a lot of the things Daisy does, the moments she doesn't let anyone else see, where she's funny and carefree. For some reason, I get to be the one to witness them.

"I mean, thank you." She's blushing hard, and that hint of confusion on her face has me wondering if I haven't made myself clear with where my head is at.

"Daisy, I—"

"Wait," she steals my next words, the confession a long time in the making. "Don't. Don't say something stupid that'll mess this all up."

"What? No, nothing's gonna get messed up."

"Yes, it is!" Daisy sits up and scoots over to put unnecessary distance between us. She rests her back against the side of the truck bed. "We say it all of the time, August. You're August Burton and I'm Daisy Stiles. We don't need to be anything else."

"Why?" I ask, desperate for a solid reason, knowing she doesn't have one.

"Because I selfishly don't want to lose you. And if we let something silly, like adolescent feelings, get in the way...Well, that's just a setup for disaster."

"Oh," I huff, crossing my arms. "I get it. I'm not good enough."

We might be working with limited lighting, but I watch her roll her eyes. "Give me a break. You know that's not what I'm trying to say."

"Then spell it out for me, Daisy. Because ever since I walked into Merrymount High, I've been pulled in your direction, like you're the center of my fucking gravity or some shit. And I never say anything, because I don't want to make you uncomfortable. But you think I don't see the way you look at me out of the corner of your eye when you're journaling? You think I don't hear your heartbeat kick up to probably dangerous beats per minute when we find ourselves teetering on the edge of something more?"

"I—We—You're my best friend," she says, clinging to that half-truth like a lifeline.

"Never said I wasn't. Doesn't mean I don't want more."

"More how?"

"I want to kiss you, Daze. Let's start there." I lean over, and her breath hitches.

My lips are centimeters from hers. I can smell her cherry lip gloss that she's always losing and I'm always replacing. Before my eyes close, I notice the blues of her eyes get swallowed by her dilating pupils.

"Stop." Daisy presses a soft hand to my chest, and I pull back immediately. "I'm sorry," she whispers.

"Never be sorry. Not for that," I assure her, shaking my head at my stupidity.

I was wrong. This was dumb. I need to accept what I can get with Daisy. I can't lose her.

Even though it feels like it's inevitable.

"Can we..." She hesitates, pausing to collect her thoughts. "Can we wait until graduation? We can figure this all out after finals and diplomas."

"Can I ask why?"

She nods, but doesn't offer more. I sit and wait, wondering if I crossed a line. She agreed I could ask, she never agreed to answer.

Daisy looks up to the stars again, and I follow her line of sight. I focus on a few of the constellations she's pointed out to me over the years.

"I'm asking you to trust me." That's what Daisy settles on, and I accept it with no further question. I'll always trust her. I pull her into my side and point up at our favorite constellation, The Twins. The two brightest stars, Castor and Pollux.

Back in the present day of our high-rise hotel room, I wait for Daisy to turn me down. Again. I'm apparently a sucker for punishment.

"You can't. We have rules," she mutters.

"Doesn't mean I don't wanna break 'em," I mumble into the sensitive skin on her neck.

Daisy sighs. "Drop it. Please."

So I do.

Even though it hurts. Even though the rules don't mean shit to me.

I think I'm in love with her.

I think I always have been.

"I think I'm gonna throw up." Daisy coughs while attempting to shove my weight off her.

I try to untangle myself as fast as possible so she can escape. Daisy sprints to the bathroom, and I hear her slam the toilet seat up just in time to listen to her heave what I'm assuming is every bite of food we consumed over the last several hours.

Shit, did we eat something bad? I do a quick self assessment and determine I feel fine. But Daisy...

"I'm okay!" she calls, and it echoes off the porcelain. I make my way to the bathroom with a glass of water in one hand to see her head still hanging low into the bowl, deep breaths making her back rise.

I crouch down to lay my hand on her back and begin rubbing circles, anything to soothe her as Daisy continues to get sick.

"This is disgusting," she sighs. "Just leave me here to die."

"Shut up," I tell her.

"This is not how I wanted to spend tonight."

"Can't say this is what I had planned," I say, thinking about the dinner reservation I should probably cancel. "But it's okay, we have a nice view and fancy bed to rot in. And when you feel better tomorrow, we can check off a couple of the things on my list."

Daisy groans. "There's *more?* And I'm wasting time puking my brains out? *Ugh—*" She's rightfully frustrated, and I feel awful. But it's out of our control, and I really just need her to feel better. I need Daisy to be okay.

I think I'm learning I don't deal well with the people I care about being sick, not because I'm a germaphobe or anything, but because it kills me to feel so fucking helpless.

"What can I get you right now?" I ask.

Daisy looks up and takes the water, braving a small sip. "This is fine for now, thank you."

Her hand slaps over her mouth barely a minute later, and I watch her turn to gag again. "Okay, so water is also not safe right now. I don't get it…Aren't you supposed to feel better after you puke?"

"Hey, it's gonna be okay," I assure her. Maybe I'm trying to assure myself too. "Listen to your body."

"My body apparently wants to expel everything I've ever put into it."

And it does.

After a couple hours of camping out on the bathroom floor, Daisy lets me carry her to the bed. I line the small hotel trash can with a plastic bag to set beside her. Only when I feel confident Daisy doesn't have anything left in her system to actually throw up, I venture out into the harsh cold to find supplies.

I grab Pedialyte in liquid and popsicle form, along with more water and plain crackers for Daisy to hopefully nibble on. I find some Dramamine to take back too. I stop by a pizza shop to grab myself something to eat and hightail it back to our hotel room.

Daisy's mercifully sleeping when I enter. Her skin is paler than normal and her usually wild curls are weighed down by sweat. Her eyebrows are furrowed like she's annoyed, even in her slumber. And I wouldn't blame her if she was. But God, she's still the most beautiful thing I've ever seen.

I put the drinks in the mini fridge to chill and take a couple minutes to scarf down my food before Daisy wakes. When I see her stir, I quickly grab the pizza box with my discarded napkins and toss it outside the room, hoping by doing so any lingering scent doesn't trigger her to get sick again.

"How're you feeling?" I check in when Daisy's eyes finally flutter open.

"Disgusting. Sad. Mad. Bleh," she lists.

"All warranted given the circumstance," I say, assessing her for any other ailments.

"I could rally so we could go out?" she offers.

"Not happening, darling." I press the back of my hand to her forehead. "No fever, but I'm not taking chances. Sorry."

Any progress Daisy made is erased when she throws herself dramatically back into the pillows. "You can't tell me what to do. I'm—Oh my God, did you have pizza?"

She tosses the sheets and once again sprints to the bathroom to dry heave into the toilet.

"Shit, I'm sorry!" I call, chasing after her. I sink to the floor and gather her hair to hold behind her.

After another hour of hanging out on the bathroom floor, I get Daisy back into bed. We spend the rest of the night making fun of infomercials because neither of us wants to move or look for the remote we lost hours ago.

It's not what I had planned, and I wish more than anything that Daisy didn't feel like she does.

But there's also an indescribable sense of peace settling in this small hotel room, high up in some skyscraper in the loudest city you could imagine. A peace between two people who never gave themselves time to figure it out, and maybe this is the universe's way of doing us a favor and giving a little bit of that precious time back.

Or I'm just deliriously in love with Daisy Stiles, and I'm finally allowing myself the right to admit it.

CHAPTER 27: DAISY - THAT'S ONE DOODLE THAT CAN'T BE UNDID, HOMESKILLET

The Journal of Daisy D. Stiles - Eleven years ago

I told Ms. Riccardine that I'm no longer interested in scholarships or colleges outside of driving distance to Merrymount. When I let her know I was pulling out of early decision in NYU, she didn't even try to hide her disappointment.

I don't blame her. I'm disappointed, too.

I was going to tell August, but I couldn't bear the idea of seeing the disappointment on his face. Aside from Ms. Riccardine, he's been my biggest supporter. He wants me to go. He thinks I'm still going.

* * *

LITTLE RED RIDING HOE

girls night game night at my place tonight. be there or be fucking square

MARGOT

What sort of games are we playing? What should I bring? Is this a sleepover?

LITTLE RED RIDING HOE

i'm supplying the games. bring literally just
yourself. yes plz sleepover

LITTLE RED RIDING HOE

and no more questions

ME

What if I have plans?

LITTLE RED RIDING HOE

cancel them

LITTLE RED RIDING HOE

i'm not kidding

WELL, that's rather aggressive, even for Red. But I respond telling them I'll be at Red's a little after five and decide not to give it much thought beyond that.

I don't really have the mental capacity for much else. I still feel like shit, and I'm so beyond over it. I'm not sure what else to do besides beg urgent care for a high dose of Zofran. I've been avoiding going to the doctor, but Gus's fuse of patience for my refusal to do so shortens by the day.

He barely lets me out of his sight, constantly asking if he can do anything (he can't) or if I feel better (I don't). It's not just the constant nausea either, it's the hot flashes, and vivid nightmares, and fatigue even when I've slept over ten hours.

I'm like ninety-nine percent sure I have, or rather had, some sort of wild food poisoning/flu combo that wiped me out and now my body is trying to recover. My period has been weird too, extremely light where normally I'm bitching about the amount of monthly blood loss.

It's taking a lot longer than I would prefer to get over whatever the hell has infected me.

I was supposed to put together baby shower favors together with Margot, but I canceled in fear of getting her sick. I suggested she leave everything on the porch, and I swing by to scoop and assemble at home—or at August's—but she said there was no need to risk getting my germs on the gifts.

But I can't possibly be contagious anymore, if I ever was.

"I'm going to Red's tonight," I tell Gus, who's busy tinkering away with an old rocking chair he pulled down from the attic.

"Uh huh," he half acknowledges me, lost in his project.

This is a project of his that he hasn't really said much about but which has taken up most of his free time today. When I woke up, August was already out here on the front porch, poor rocking chair taken apart and laid out on the floor for his inspection. I shuffled out here with two hot cups of coffee, a blanket, and my phone to catch up on riverside socials and watch him work.

This is one of my favorite versions of us. Where we can be together but not, letting ourselves be consumed by our individual interests in the comfort of doing them alongside someone else. Where we can just be us. Whatever that is.

Safe.

Because even when I was most angry and the mere thought of Gus made my insides boil, he's always been safe.

At some point, we're going to have to let the dam of our secret break. Before we can do that though, we need to address what's actually going on between us. We're not even having sex. We're like…cohabitating to some degree. There is a laundry list of things we need to go over. I know I don't have a solid answer as to what this all is, so I don't expect August to.

For right now, this safe middle ground is good enough for us.

I stand to head inside and change into something more appropriate than a pair of Gus's sweatpants and one of his sweatshirts, both swallowing me to the point where I look like a walking blanket. It's a standard outfit for following Gus around when he insists on still spending as much time in the frigid outdoor air as he can, not caring that it's officially *cold as shit* season.

"So, just to reiterate, when I leave here in a couple of hours, I'm going to Red's house, and I will be fine at *Red's house*," I emphasize my intended location again so hopefully it sinks into the subconscious part of Gus's brain, and I won't have to repeat myself again when he gets all worried as I'm heading out.

Gus finally lifts his head. "What's going on at Red's?"

"Girls' night. Sorry, you're not invited." I smile, looking at the pink of his cheeks from the chill, another one of his knit beanies pulled down over his ears, the folded piece sitting perfectly on his brows. He looks so cute and cozy right now.

"You're feeling up for that?" Gus places the screwdriver he was using on the wooden floor of the porch, giving his full attention to me.

"*August*," I exasperatedly sigh. "I'm fine," I reiterate for what feels like the five millionth time. Bulldozery, hovering, caring, motherfucker.

I don't pay mind to the way my insides flip at the thought of him doting on me. For one, it'd trigger the nausea. And two, I don't need that—to be waited on. I never wanted that. I just— Fuck it. It's nice, okay? It feels nice to be cared for.

But also, I'm fine. I wish he would accept that I'm okay, so he stops worrying.

"You've been saying you're fine for almost two weeks now, and yet here you are, still looking like shit."

"Real nice," I scoff.

"I think it's time you went to the doctor," Gus says, ignoring my reaction to his insult.

"And I think it's none of your business."

"You're my business." Gus stands, practically puffing out his chest at his full height. He's towering over me in a way that has me sucking in a breath. He presses the back of his hand to my forehead and then my cheek. It's a routine he's adopted that I've grown *very* fond of.

I lean into his touch and bask in the intimacy of his rough

hands on my soft skin. I close my eyes and sigh when his hand creeps around to cup the back of my neck, and he pulls me into him, wrapping his other arm around my back. August rests his head on top of mine, and I swear to God, I melt.

"You're a brute," I say with no bite into Gus's shirt.

"You've called me worse." He chuckles. "Alright, will you at least let me drive you to Red's?"

"Uh, no," I quickly answer as I pull away. "I'm not explaining why you're dropping me off. Besides, I'm not staying over, and I don't need you coming out in the middle of the night to pick me up. I'll be fine to drive myself home."

Gus's gentle smile breaks, replaced by an agitated scowl.

"Right," he huffs. "Forgot about the fucking *rules*," he mumbles, turning away from me.

"We're not doing this right now," I say, marching into the house after Gus.

"'Course we're not!" Gus throws his hands above his head, continuing down the hall into the kitchen.

"What just happened?" I ask, trying to recover.

He whips around to face me, and I practically skid to a stop to avoid crashing into him.

"It's killing me, Daze. Whatever this is—" He gestures between the small distance between us. "I'm going crazy. You're in my house, in my bed, in my *head* all of the time. The boys…I fucking care about Hunter and Chase. I care about you. But we're playing a game, and I'm losing."

"It's not a game!" I argue.

"No, you know what? You're right. I…I'm heated right now. Not at you!" Gus practically shouts. "Just…This is a lot, okay? I can't have this conversation in this state."

I take a deep breath in through my nose. I close my eyes and count to three, then five, then ten.

"Okay." I open my eyes to see Gus, hat ripped off, one hand buried in his hair, face filled with so much emotion. "Let's take the night. I'll be back tomorrow, and we can…We can talk. About all of it."

"You promise?" he asks so goddamn earnestly that I think about throwing caution to the wind for a fraction of a second, lost in August Burton the way I feel like I've always been.

"I promise." And I mean it. Tomorrow, we can lay it all out on the table and see what's left when we're done.

* * *

You know, I'm starting to think Red had an ulterior motive in inviting me and Margot over here tonight. Because hours have passed, food has been had, shit has been talked, and yet—not a single game has been played.

And I don't think it's a coincidence.

"We were promised games, Red," I start. "And before Margot here passes out…"

"Hey!" Margot interjects, failing to stifle a rogue yawn. "Okay, fine. Daisy has a point," she admits. "Sorry! I'm a sleepy girl! It's hard work growing humans!"

"No one's faulting you for that, Margot." I lean over from my spot on the couch and squeeze her knee. "But I think our Red here has something up her sleeve." I turn my gaze to Red who jumps up to run into the kitchen.

She returns fast with a plastic bag from The Store in hand. She holds the bag up dramatically and dumps the contents onto the coffee table.

Three boxes of pregnancy tests.

"Uh…" I start.

"Hate to break it to ya, Red, but I don't think I need to pee on a stick to confirm my hCG levels." Margot giggles.

"No shit, Margot," Red scoffs. "But I wasn't leaving you out of the fun! Pregnancy roulette!"

"What the hell are you going on about?" I ask.

Red looks taken aback. "*You*, Daisy Stiles, queen of the chronically online, haven't heard of this trend?"

Now that I pause for thought, I have. Groups of women all take a test and squeal and flip out over their negative, or sometimes positive, results. It's silly.

What's even sillier is Margot being the first to reach for a box, peeling the cardboard flap back to pull out a stick. "Well, I have to pee anyway. Be right back!" She shimmies herself to the edge of the couch and Red holds out a hand for her to balance. Margot half walks, half waddles to the bathroom down the hall.

Red picks up the other two boxes, handing me one.

"Let's go! You can use Penelope's bathroom. She's sleeping in my bed with Miller."

"This is a waste of money," I say with a laugh as I follow Red up the stairs. But I don't argue my point further because there's no use. This is just a game, and when I get eyes on that negative line, all will be over.

Before I shut the door to Penelope's bathroom, Red's hand lands on the wood. "Don't look at the result! We need to record them all at the same time. Just pee on that end"—she points to the pink capped side—"and shove the stick back in the package and meet us back in the living room."

"Thanks for the detailed instructions, Gwendolyn," I reply sarcastically.

"Whatever. See you in a minute!" Red tiptoes into her dark bedroom.

I hold the stick in my hand to inspect it. In my thirty years of life, I've never actually been subjected to a pregnancy scare of any kind. My period might be a bitch, but she's reliable. So I've never felt the need to actually take a test, aside from the times I've peed in a cup as a part of my routine physical at the doctor.

I shouldn't be nervous. There's nothing to be nervous about. I mean, it's a game, really. I'm just an active participant in the night Red put together for us. For funsies.

So then why is this stupid piece of plastic shaking in my hands?

I dismiss these out-of-character nerves, do my business, recap the stick, and wrap it in a piece of toilet paper. After washing my hands, I exit the bathroom and quietly make my way back downstairs to the kitchen where Red and Margot are already huddled around the island.

"Stick in cup, please!" Red demands, holding out a plastic red cup that's normally reserved for jungle juice or beer from a keg at house parties.

"How long do we wait?" I ask, hopefully not sounding as panicked as I feel.

"Usually, like, two minutes. We should be good to check pretty soon," Margot says, absentmindedly reading the instructions on the back of one of the boxes. "Why?" She looks up with a sly grin. "Worried about the results?"

"I'm not worried," I scoff.

Why would I be worried?

Red positions her phone so the screen is facing us, camera app already pulled up. She sets the cup rattling with our three pee sticks in the frame. She checks the time in the clock above the stove.

"Okay, Margot, you can go first since well…" Red gently urges Margot forward to reach into the cup. "Just tell us what one says!"

Margot pulls out a test and laughs while showing the camera the little pink plus sign. "Pregnant! Shocker! Wonder who this one could belong to!"

"Okay, Red, you go now," I encourage.

Red practically bounces forward, dramatically plucking one of the tests out. She waves it around before letting us and the camera see…

"*What?*" Margot and I screech, forgetting the two sleeping Caswells upstairs.

Another pink plus sign.

But Red's not in the least bit shocked. Nope, Gwendolyn Bozelli is holding that positive pregnancy test high, proudly showing it off with tears streaming down her face.

"*Surprise!*" she yells. "Oh my fucking God, talk about the hardest secret to keep of my damn *life!*"

Margot is blubbering, unable to control a single emotion. Red wraps her up in her arms and signals me to join them.

"You're having a baby?" Margot asks.

"Merrymount's resident café owner officially has a bun in the oven. Confirmed!" Red reaches for the small drawer beside her and pulls out a sheet of ultrasound pictures. We don't break from our group hug while we stare at the little black and white images. A tiny spot in the middle has an arrow pointing to it that says *baby.*

"Not twins, just the one," Red explains. "They're perfectly healthy, whoever they are. On track for a May delivery. You don't think I'm raining on your parade, right?" Red turns her face to Margot.

"Shut the fuck up, Red." Margot laughs in between tears. "Are you kidding me? Not only am I now getting my own two kids, but *another* niece or nephew? And they all get to grow up together? This is like, the best day of my life!"

"Congrats, Red." I kiss her cheek, so unbelievably happy to see one of my oldest friends in the world have one of her biggest dreams come true. I don't know anyone who deserves it more. Penelope and this unborn Caswell hit the jackpot with her as their mother.

The three—six, if you count the fetuses—of us continue to hold each other, still crying, while we look in awe at the ultrasounds. Minutes pass until Red realizes her phone is still recording.

"Oh shit, we have one more test!" Red breaks free from me

and Margot and scoops up her phone. "Hold on, let me stop this video and restart. I'll edit them together later," Red says.

"There's no need. It'd be anticlimactic." I laugh.

"Sorry, Daze. You can't skip out of pregnancy roulette!" Red counters with Margot nodding along next to her.

They don't want me to feel left out, and I want to hug them all over again for how much they love me despite my inability to let anyone truly in.

Except for August, my mind betrays me with an intrusive thought.

"Oh, what the hell, fine. But you better cheer for this negative as loud as you cheered for the positives," I joke, grabbing the remaining test from the cup.

I give it a glance that doesn't really register in my brain before turning the results to face the camera.

Margot and Red both stop their girlish giggling.

I look at the test again.

The plastic bounces off the ceramic tile flooring when I drop it.

"Daisy…" Red whispers, letting a gentle hand rest on my shoulder.

I shake her off immediately. "Give me another test. Your pee must have contaminated it, or something."

"I don't think that's how that works, Daze…" Margot offers quietly.

I whip around. "I need another test. Right now."

Red recovers faster than any of us.

"Yeah, yeah. Of course. Hold on, I have a drawer full in the bathroom down here." She disappears into the small half bath off the hallway and comes back empty handed. "I left two on the counter for you."

"Thanks," I mumble before locking myself in the bathroom.

I hear Margot and Red whispering to each other just outside

the door. Part of me wants them to fuck off. The other part of me is extremely thankful I'm not alone right now.

Memories of the last couple of weeks flash through my mind as I repeat the process of taking these Godforsaken stupid tests.

Nausea. Sore boobs. Fatigue. Mood swings. Nightmares. Hot flashes.

All things that could so easily be chalked up to period symptoms.

All things that sickly and twistedly could also mean fucking *pregnancy.*

This is all one big joke of a misunderstanding. Like I said, their hormones probably rubbed off on my lone baby-free stick.

I lay both tests face down on the counter and set a three-minute timer on my phone. Red said two, but I'll use the extra sixty seconds for good measure. Just to be sure it's done confirming that I am indeed, not pregnant.

Because I can't possibly be pregnant.

A light knock on the door causes me to jump.

"Daze?" Red's hesitant voice travels through. "It's gonna be okay. No matter what. You're okay."

"I'm *fine,*" I say through gritted teeth with my arms braced, hands gripping the porcelain edge of the sink.

"Can you let us in?" Margot asks.

I close my eyes and reach out to unlock the door. One of them turns the knob and lets it fall open, but Margot and Red don't leave the doorway.

"Daisy, look at me," Red coaxes.

"No."

"You're in shock. Totally understand—"

I whip my head to face them and cut Margot off. "I'm not in fucking shock. It was a bullshit, faulty test, okay?"

"*Daisy,*" Red reprimands with a stern voice. A motherly voice. "I'm gonna let you process this however you need to within reason. But you're not lashing out at us. You hear me?"

I nod once, guilt immediately washing over me.

Red steps into the small space to pick up one of the tests. "I'm going to check this one. And then the other. And *then* we'll discuss next steps. Sound good?"

"None of this sounds good," I whine and sink to the floor.

The silence that follows tells me everything I need to hear and exactly what I want to refuse to believe.

"I have to go," I breathe, standing up and snatching the two tests up in my hand.

"Daisy, wait." Red chases after me as I dash into the living room to gather my belongings. I'm at the front door, slipping my boots and jacket on when she finally reaches out and grabs me. "Daisy."

"Please don't," I whisper.

"Don't what?" Red questions.

"Don't say it. Don't say it's okay. Don't say that I'm...That I'm..."

Red shows me mercy, crushing me into a bone tight embrace. "I love you, Daisy Daf."

The old nickname from our childhood hits me like an arrow straight through the heart.

"I love you, too, Gwennie G," I breathe.

When we separate, I make sure to hug Margot before I leave.

She wipes her tears, and I let her assure me that everything in life has a funny way of working out.

A single laugh escapes me hearing how much she truly is Melanie LeClair's daughter.

I clock it as my last laugh of the night once I reach the bitter and painful silence of my car. Being alone with my thoughts feels like the last thing I need, but I can't bring myself to run exactly where I'm supposed to.

Facing August right now, holding this secret, this *thing* that never should have happened, feels impossible. Saying the word, thinking it—I can't handle it. I'm falling apart.

I reach for my phone, and when I see the last text that came through, I officially want to melt into nothing.

AUGUST

I don't like how we left things and I don't like when you're not sleeping in my bed. I don't like a lot of what we're doing…or I guess what we say we're doing, to be honest. Rules be damned. Text me. Call me. Come back to me, Daze.

CHAPTER 28: AUGUST - WHAT THE FUCK'S GOING ON?

J'm so sick of rereading the text Daisy sent two fucking days ago. I pocket my phone after checking it for the twenty-third time and continue painting one of our smaller canoes a bright shade of pink. It's another project for another one of these rugrats I've come to love so much. The rocking chair I just finished restoring to its glory is gonna look mint in the twins' nursery, now that it's almost complete.

Penelope might have mentioned the other day that a pink canoe would be cool. I might have found some paint lying around and had a few minutes of spare time today to see if it was something I could make happen to surprise her with.

And by all that, I mean I marched my ass down to the hardware store, scoured the paint samples until I found the right shade of pink, grabbed some new brushes, and told everyone at the riverside to not fucking bother me for a few hours.

I'm giving Daisy space. I'm being totally fucking cool about the fact that I'm ready to lay it all out there and put my fucking heart on the line, and Daisy's avoiding me like the newest damn plague.

Some would say not enough time has passed to consider her radio silence as avoidant. But I know I'm not wrong.

"What's got you lost in your head, boy?" Beth calls while walking towards me with her breath puffing clouds and her hands stuffed in her front pockets, snapping me back out of my head.

I think about how Beth has let me and Daisy trot through Merrymount for months now, not mentioning a single thing about our current situation, and I realize she's been waiting. Like a fucking lionness in the tall grass, waiting for the best possible second to pounce. This is her time to shine.

And while lying is a viable option, it's not the one I'm taking today.

"I'm gonna tell you that you were right, so we can skip that part," I say, laying the paint brush down.

"Ah," Beth muses. She grabs the folding chair laid against the building and opens it to sit next to the workstation I set up for myself. "So, we're doing this."

"I'm out of options," I admit.

Beth tips her nose up. "I'm always your first call. Don't get it twisted, my boy."

Damn, how'd she know?

"I see and know everything," she says, reading my mind like a wise old owl we all love.

"Then you wanna cut me some slack and tell me what to do?"

"Oh, August," Beth sighs. "You and Daisy have always been one of my most sensitive cases."

"Yeah, yeah. I know. We're trouble. We fuck everything up. Not the first time I've heard it, probably won't be the last."

"If you're asking for my help, you're gonna stand there and listen. I'm not here for a sob story. I can leave."

"Yes, ma'am," I say, lowering my head in shame.

"I'm gonna ask you this once, and I don't want you to get defensive. Hear me?"

I nod.

"Does Daisy know about the night of your arrest?"

Fuck me.

It's the root of every problem Daisy and I have ever had. The running clock on her time in this little town doesn't even hold a candle to how badly I dismantled everything good between us in one single night.

"No," I answer honestly.

"This will never work then." Beth folds her hands on her lap. "You can fuck 'till kingdom come—"

I grimace. "Beth, please."

"Grow up. You can do whatever the hell this is for however long, but it's a bandaid. If you can't address what you did and how Daisy reacted, it'll never be anything more."

My phone lights up with a call coming in. Hunter's name flashes across the screen, and I'm answering it within two seconds. "Hunter?"

"Hey, Gus." Hunter sounds out of breath on the other end of the call. "You know how you gave us your number in case of emergencies? Is there any way you're not busy right now?"

"What the fuck's going on, Hunter?" I ask aggressively. Didn't mean for it to come out like that, but if this kid is calling, something's wrong.

Beth stands abruptly, concerned etched on her face already.

"*Hunter,*" I repeat when he doesn't immediately answer.

"It's…It's our mom. She forgot to pick us up, and I tried to call her. But she sounded funny and told us to just walk home. And we are but—"

"You're *what?*"

"We didn't make it far. Chase stopped walking and refused to move. He's right here. All he does is hold up his phone with your number on the screen. I was going to call Daisy, but she's been sick, and I know she just would have gotten into a fight with Mom. I'm sorry I called."

"Send me your location right now. I'm on my way." I end the call and start quickly gathering up the shit I have laid out.

"Go, Gus." Beth's hand covers my own frantic one. "I'll get this cleaned up."

I'm already hightailing it to my truck when I respond, "Thanks, Beth!"

"Do not under any circumstance start anything with that nasty woman! Don't get into trouble. Just bring the boys here!" she calls.

I don't make any promises I can't keep because if I lay eyes on Mary Jane Stiles at any point in the near future, there's no way I'm holding back.

* * *

HUNTER AND CHASE are both situated in the living room with one of my old gaming systems hooked up, boxes of George's pizza laid out on the coffee table in front of them, when I hear Daisy's car pull up the driveway.

"I'm gonna go meet your sister outside, okay?"

Neither boy takes his face away from the screen, but both nod their acknowledgment.

I calmed myself down before I got to Hunter and Chase sitting on the side of the road, knowing they didn't need any stress added to their already hellish day. But seeing the anguish on Daisy's face when she flies out of her car has all of my pent up anger flooding back in at full force.

She shouldn't be this worked up all of the time. Daisy shouldn't be handling all of this responsibility on her own. She still looks worn down, and I know this situation won't do anything to help that.

"Where are they?" she asks as a greeting when she barrels up the porch steps.

"Inside, perfectly fine. Hold on. Lemme talk to you." I open my arms, and thank fuck, she immediately steps into them so I can wrap myself around her. "I haven't seen you in days."

"I know, I'm sorry. I've just had some stuff going on." There's a shiftiness to her voice that I'm not used to.

"Has anyone ever told you that you don't need to take all of this on on your own?" I ask earnestly.

"No," Daisy answers immediately.

"Why?" *Seriously, why?*

The way Daisy loves these boys is obvious and beautiful and unconditional. But they're her brothers. She should get to love them the way a sister would, not the way someone stepping in as a mother has to. This isn't her job. It's not her responsibility. There are others who could take on some of the burden, *help*.

"Because I've never told anyone," Daisy admits softly.

"But your grandmother...She's still..." I start and hesitate, worried I just put my foot in my mouth.

"In perfect health and still living two towns over, completely oblivious to the failures that are her daughter and son-in-law."

"Why?" I repeat, pulling back to look at her. My hands find hers.

"Because the can of worms that would open if even a hint of the truth of the last eighteen years came out. I'd assume she'd have a freaking heart attack and drop dead on me."

"Daisy, are you telling me she knows nothing?"

She exhales, and it's all the answer I need, but she continues anyway.

"August—" A pause and a fidget of her fingers in mine. She releases my grasp, and I already know her physically pulling back is just as much of a mental one. "I thrive on control. It's obviously borderline unhealthy, and I don't know how to let some of those reins go, but my story is mine to tell. And I'm extremely selective, because well, when I did talk, it landed on deaf ears. My *parents*," Daisy's voice cracks, "didn't believe me. It almost killed me. I love my grandmother. I want to be able to remember her in that light. And as for Mary Jane's drinking and the boys…Well, Gram is older, in her late seventies now. This is something I can handle."

I get it, I really do. All of it. But it's not right, and it's not fair.

"But Daze, you're killing yourself staying in that house. You're letting yourself be a barricade and punching bag."

She twists her head like I just slapped her.

"You don't understand," she accuses, the mean undertone of her voice creeping in.

"Understand what?"

"Sacrifice. Giving up everything for someone else."

"*Don't,*" I snap.

"*No,*" she throws back at me. "At one point in our lives, we were the same. I'm not saying your upbringing wasn't tragic or wrong. It was. But you got out."

I push back. "You don't get to tell me where I've been or what I've done. I'm thankful every fucking day for Sawyer and Beth. They did save me. But I gave up *everything.*"

Fresh tears shine in Daisy's eyes, and I have a feeling we're really starting to cross that invisible line we've created for ourselves.

"What does that even mean?" she asks.

"I let you go," I say those four words so low they're barely audible. "I need—I need a minute."

And then I walk into the woods, not bothering to wait or care if Daisy follows.

Because I've spent over ten years holding back exactly how I feel and have always felt about Daisy Stiles, and I have no plans on letting my admissions go any further.

CHAPTER 29: DAISY - DIAL DRUNK (WITH POST MALONE)

The Journal of Daisy D. Stiles - Ten and a half years ago

This is the last time you'll ever hear about August fucking Burton.

He played me for a fool. Acting as if he was different.

How much time did I waste? Waiting for what?

For him to throw away the past couple years of us in the blink of an eye?

I hope he found what he was looking for at the bottom of that bottle. I hope he's happy sitting in that jail cell. I hope he got a good laugh at my tear-stained face when I watched him get stuffed into the back of the police cruiser.

But what I hope more than anything is that my feelings fade fast, and I don't have to sit in the pain of a heartbreak that never should have belonged to me.

Because as much as I hate August, I still love him.

And that pisses me the fuck off.

* * *

I STAND on August's front porch, completely dumbfounded. He has no fucking clue.

I let you go.

He let me go?

He let me go.

And then he walked away.

Not fucking happening.

I pop my head into the house, getting eyes on my little brothers who deserve so much better.

"Hey, my dudes."

"Daisy!" Hunter greets me, a slice of pizza halfway to his mouth.

"I'm so sorry about Mom. We need to talk about why you didn't call *me,* but I need to talk to Gus first. You good in here?"

"We have three large pizzas and the old version of *Call of Duty.* We good, sis."

Chase smiles and nods in agreement.

Good. They're good.

I drop my bag beside the door and take off towards the walking trail August decided to "take a minute" on.

I march on, chastising myself for the improper footwear and lack of a jacket in the cool air. In my defense, I didn't think I'd be hiking through the wooded area of Merrymount, chasing after a broody August Burton to go tit for tat on a convoluted history that hasn't felt worth rehashing until now.

And unfortunately, we do need to rehash it now, more than he knows.

"I paid the price for this already. I don't deserve to relive it now." He keeps his back to me once I finally catch up to him.

How can he even say that? How can he act like he's the victim in this situation?

"You can't use a cop-out like that. We've been avoiding this for months, Gus. Years, actually."

He twists around, and I realize I'm about to actually get the other side of the story that I wrote off as a mystery for so long.

"Fine. Let's go, then. I spent the night in jail. And I'd do it a million times over. The only thing I'd change is losing you entirely in the end. Do you know it almost killed me? I didn't care when Beth came to bail me out. I didn't care when she told me I could have ruined the rest of my life. All I could picture was your fucking face through the cruiser's window. I knew right there in that moment that I had lost you. Probably forever."

"You did," I lie.

Gus's shoulders droop slightly at those two words. As if he waited over a decade to be proven wrong, and I just ended his quest.

"Beth told me it would come to this. You know what I think?" he asks. I'm terrified to hear what was said with Beth and what comes next so I nod only once.

"I think you were waiting for me to mess up. You've never let anyone in. Not for real, anyway. You keep us all at arm's length to avoid real connections because you don't want to get hurt. I was the one person who could have changed that. You realized it and kicked me to the curb."

"I needed you, and you weren't there!" I practically scream.

"You didn't give me any time to figure it out!" Gus yells back. "I was a fucking kid, Daisy. We both were. We didn't know what we were doing."

"You knew very fucking well what you were doing. You just didn't care about the outcome."

"I got drunk one time. I fought back one fucking time. He deserved it. Don't you *dare* tell me what I was feeling. I was lost and broken. Just like you." Maybe he didn't mean it like an accusation, but it sure feels like one.

"Well, I'm sorry I couldn't be less broken. I didn't ask for anything that happened to me."

Gus's eyes darken. He looks pained and wounded and murderous all in one.

"Don't ever fucking apologize for that again, Daisy. You know I didn't mean it like that."

"It doesn't much matter what you meant when that's what you said."

"God, what the hell are we even arguing about?" He slides his hand down his face.

"We're always arguing. It's what we do," I remind him.

"What if I'm sick of that? What if I'm ready to make this what it was always supposed to be?"

"We can't." My words are weak.

"Why?"

"Because I'm uppity Daisy Stiles, and you're August fucking Burton. We only work well in the dark. It's where we're most comfortable."

"I wanted it to be me and you. There's a part of me that thinks I never stopped wanting that. I still want that." It's the softest I've ever heard Gus's voice. It cracks my black heart in two.

"You think I didn't want that, too?" I yell, not caring who hears at this point. "But even starting whatever you want to call this would require trust and honesty. Are you ready to be honest?"

I hate myself for demanding something like honesty from him, when I'm the one harboring secrets. Or rather, one ridiculously complicated, life-altering, ginormous secret.

"What do you want to know?" Gus asks. His eyes meet mine, and he looks downright terrified.

"Tell me what happened that night. There was no reason for you to get drunk or fly off the handle. You always showed the most restraint. You *promised*." My voice breaks on the word. A tear falls down my cheek against my will.

"Anything else," he pleads.

I wipe my face, straightening my shoulders. "This is it. It's the truth or nothing, August."

Several minutes pass. Each one is more painful than the last. I lose track of the seconds and gather the courage to walk away, once and for all. Because if we can't handle dealing with our troubled past, there's no sense in trying for a future.

A shaky breath from August has my eyes snapping up again.

"I was on my way back to Beth's after the graduation ceremony. I decided to take my truck and drive alone to give myself some time to think. Sawyer rode back with Beth. I knew I had a couple hours before I was supposed to meet everyone for the party at Katie's."

"I remember all of this, Gus. This isn't news."

"Let me tell you the whole story, would you? Context matters. I was in a weird headspace. Thinking about graduating, where I came from, where I was heading. I was lost and the only constant things in my life seemed to be sort of shaky."

"Shaky how?" I interrupt him again. I can't help it. I've been waiting for this for so long it felt like ever getting it was a pipedream.

"It's embarrassing to admit," Gus sighs. "But Sawyer had Katie, and I thought Beth assumed her job was done with me."

"There isn't a world where Beth Rivers—"

Gus's hand reaches out to mine, and I instinctively take it.

"Believe me, I know that now. She drilled that into my head enough for a lifetime. But in *that* moment, that's what I believed to be true. And well, you…Fuck, Daisy. You became my best friend, but you deserved better than anything Merrymount has ever fucking offered you. You wanted to get out. You were going to be free. And I knew I couldn't follow."

"Why?" Another crack of my voice.

"Because as much as you've viewed Merrymount as a prison, it was my escape. If I never moved here, I don't know if I'd still be alive. I understood, I still understand, why you feel how you do—but it was different for me."

God, that feels like a punch to the gut to hear. It's raw and real.

Gus continues, "Anyway, all of this was swirling around up here." He taps his head for emphasis. "I got back to my room at Beth's, changed, told Beth not to wait up for me, and told Sawyer I'd meet him at the party later. I took off to drive around for a while. I don't remember where I went, if I had any destination in mind, but soon enough the sun had set and I was in Katie's backyard, party blasting around me, and an entire fucking handle of shitty tequila deep.

"I couldn't find you. Or rather, I wasn't making it a point to look for you. I knew you'd be disappointed, or more so probably pissed. I found myself walking along the edge of Katie's yard, next to the fence that separated her family's property with the neighbor's when I heard familiar voices."

I feel the color drain from my face. I know whatever comes next in Gus's tale won't be pretty. He might have been right. It's something I wouldn't want to hear. But I need to. For me and the ba—I can't even think the word. I fight the urge to reach for my belly. Gus's grip around my fingers tightens.

"I'm sorry for what you're about to hear, Daze. Say the word, and I stop. Okay?"

"Okay," I mouth. No sound comes out.

"I hadn't seen or heard from my stepdad since the night I was brought to Beth's. But his voice was as clear as the night sky. He was talking up a fucking storm about his latest lay. Disgusting, vulgar shit that made me sick to my stomach. I was ready to turn around. I needed to find you because you were the only person on the planet who could have calmed me down in that moment. But then…"

Again with the hesitation. I want him to continue, but I don't. So, I wait. I let him decide what he and I can both handle.

"He bragged—" Gus looks like he might be sick. "She must have said no. He made that very fucking clear. He's an evil, waste of an excuse of a human, Daisy. He deserved more than anything I did to him. I told you. I don't regret it. Jumping that fence to beat his face in until he was unconscious was a fucking mercy compared to what I could have done in my book."

I don't know when I started shaking, but I am. Gus guides us to sit on a log. Tears are falling down my face, into my lap, in showers. Gus won't use the explicit words, but I know what he couldn't finish saying. His stepdad is a monster who believed he deserved whatever he could take from someone, consent or not.

"Whatever sick fuck he was running his mouth to called 9-1-1. He tried to get the D.A. to charge me with assault and battery. Beth and Mark took care of it. I was never privy to the details." Gus seemingly finishes, pulls me into him, and buries his face in my neck. I'm stiff with too many thoughts and emotions to process much.

"Why didn't you just tell me?"

Gus pulls back. "I saw your face. You hated me as much as you've always hated every other man in your life. I didn't think I could come back from it."

"You didn't even *try*," I argue.

"I didn't deserve your forgiveness. I didn't want it. I wanted it to be easy to hate me so I could..."

Let me go, I finish in my mind.

My whole body aches with the *could-have-beens.* There was a future for me and Gus, and I immediately wrote him off. He might have let me go, but I was the one to firmly shove him away. Past biases and trauma blocked me from any real semblance of a partner in this life. I...I'm everything he said I am over the course of the past decade.

I'm a stuck up bitch with no understanding of a real relationship.

The weight of this new reality could kill me.

Maybe I'll let it.

"So all of this was for nothing?"

"What?" he asks.

I throw my hands up above my head.

"All of this, August. The fighting, the insults, the giant waste of fucking time!" I scream. "I don't think I've ever been more mad, and I don't know if it's at myself or you, or a sick combination of the both of us!"

I'm officially losing it. And I'm digging myself a hole bigger than I could have imagined by not telling August...

Not telling him about...

"I have to—"

I turn and proceed to vomit in a bush.

Gus's hand is on my back in the next second.

"Daisy, I'm taking you to a fucking doctor."

"*No,*" I cough. "I'm fine. I'm okay."

Lie after fucking lie. They're just falling out of me now, I guess.

"Daisy, something's wrong. You've been really sick. Forget all of this, I'm *worried* about you."

"It's none of your goddamn business! None of it!" I yell, wiping my mouth with the back of my hand. "I'm going back, getting the boys, and leaving. Do not follow me. Understand?"

"You're leaving," August repeats, defeated.

"I was always going to leave." My hoarse voice doesn't sound like my own, and the words taste like dirt on my tongue.

"I didn't say it then, and I've regretted it every day since, so I'll say it now. You don't have to leave, Daisy. You could make a home here with me."

I pause my dramatic exit. I tilt my head, giving his words true thought.

"You mean that?"

So many versions of myself would have sprinted for the hills at the offer. Big parts of me wouldn't dream of allowing such a reality to exist.

"Every word."

But I remember that this kind of promise can't be made when so much hangs in the unknown.

And I'm not doing anything to rectify the gap in information that Gus is privy to at this present time.

So I nod and turn once more without further comment. I march the short walk through the trail up to Gus's beautiful house that feels a hell of a lot like more than just four unfamiliar walls to me now. I round up my little brothers who groan and moan at my request to get out of there.

I hold back each tear that threatens to fall with every wobble of my bottom lip.

CHAPTER 30: AUGUST - I'M NOT SUPPOSED TO BE ANYONE'S DAD

*W*here the fuck is Daisy?

I scan the small crowd of guests, searching for that head of pitch black hair and coming up short. I move my way through, excusing myself as I head down the hall, peeking into each room as I go. All of them yield the same result. Missing my girl.

Red's throwing an early Christmas party for just about every resident of Merrymount. She and Miller rented a big ole party tent for the backyard and those flameless space heaters have kept everything nice and toasty. There's a s'mores station, hot chocolate bar, and an ice luge for adults.

The party is bumping inside too, people gathering with drinks in hand while more food than any of us could eat covers every bit of counter space.

Basically, anything you could think of to make winter wonderland come to life, Red made happen.

Including asking me to dress up as Santa Claus for the kids earlier.

I've put on my jolliest smile, and it really has been fun. Don't get me wrong.

But Daisy and me? We're not talking. It's just like old times.

And I've never been so goddamn miserable in my life.

In a week's time, I've typed up and deleted entire novels of texts to Daisy. I've hovered over the call button more times than I can count. And I check the front windows of my house for her car pulling into the driveway at least four times each night before I finally call it quits and fall into bed.

I miss her.

I know she's here somewhere. She wouldn't miss this kind of event. It's just a matter of finding her.

I stop when I hear voices coming from the bathroom to my right. I halt because I've been following those voices for years now. I'd know them anywhere.

The door is cracked open and for some reason, I lean in to listen. I mean to knock, make myself known, but when I go to lightly tap, my knuckles push the door further.

Red's bungalow is older and the door is loose, so it swings open. My eyes lift, and I go to apologize when every word—every fucking *thought*—leaves my body when I see Daisy.

Daisy. Holding a pregnancy test in one hand and Red's hand in the other. Tears in both of their eyes.

My entire world flips upside down. I see so many different flashes. Daisy with a big, round belly and my hand splayed across it. Bottles, diapers, rattles, and more. I picture T-ball tournaments and parent-teacher conferences. I finally see myself in a rocking chair, reading a bedtime story to a faceless toddler, and I shake away the idea that I could ever deserve something so delicate and precious.

"No," my voice booms. I don't mean it.

Daisy's eyes look frightened, and when she breathes *"August,"* it sounds like a plea.

"I'm not doing this," I tell her. Why the fuck did I just say that?

"Doing what?" Daisy asks exasperatedly.

"Gus, what the hell?" Red questions.

I drop my gaze and focus on that fucking stick. It feels like it's taunting me with a future I never tried to picture. Wanted to picture. *Thought* about picturing.

"You can't be pregnant. I told you I wasn't father material. I told you I couldn't have that kind of life. You heard me say it wasn't in the cards for me."

"Now, Gus," Red starts.

But Daisy stops her.

"No. Wait. I'm sorry, Gus. Are you saying that if I was *very accidentally* pregnant right now, it would be a product of immaculate conception and there was no man out there who would also be half accountable for it? Explain it to the class, please. We're hanging onto every word." Her tone drops to a chilling level.

"Daisy, what are you doing? What do you—*Oh my God.*" Red whips her head in my direction, shock painted across her face. "It's yours."

For some reason, instead of being scared like I should be, my brain is on a one-way track to burning every last bit of hope I had in that tiny glimpse of a future I never got to picture for myself, the kind of future I maybe just needed the right person to help me really *see.* Maybe I could have wanted it. If I wasn't busy blowing it to pieces like I am right now.

"I'm saying—" I look Red in the eye, hating myself more than ever imaginable. Realizing since I'm already going to hell, I might as well break another promise along the way, and let everyone know what Daisy and I have been up to for the past half a year. I avert my eyes back down on that test, because looking at Daisy directly isn't an option. I'm a coward. "I'm saying I'm out."

"Out?" Daisy questions, giving me one last chance to act like a decent human being.

I fail, just as everyone would expect.

"I'm not supposed to be anyone's dad."

We're retreating back to the safety of our toxic back-and-forth. The familiarity is too tempting for the both of us.

I feel the hair on my arms rise when Daisy laughs and says, "Thanks. Glad to know everything you said earlier was bullshit. I mean, I expected it. But the confirmation is nice. Good news, or whatever. We don't need to discuss this further. I can leave. You can stay."

That gets me to snap my head up. I watch a single tear fall from Daisy's eye. She doesn't bother to swipe it away, her death glare almost knocking me on my fucking ass.

"What did you just say?" I breathe.

"Do you need me to speak more slowly?"

Red steps in between me and Daisy. "No. No, you are not doing this. Whatever"—she gestures at the both of us—"*this* has turned into clearly still needs a hell of a lot of work. What the fuck is wrong with you two? Gus, it takes two to fucking tango. Daisy, your words are dangerous."

Daisy chooses to ignore Red.

"All *I'm* saying, Gus, is it was just sex. I'll have this taken care of. I can handle it all on my own. Just like I have with everything for my entire life." She flippantly hands the pregnancy test to Red and steps towards me.

"This was all meaningless anyway. I'd never willingly chain myself to someone like you," she whispers with every bit of disdain that I deserve.

I know she's lying, saying that it all was—*is*—meaningless. But I started this, so I guess I have to finish it off.

"Hard to have anything that means something when you don't have a heart." I want to take it back as soon as it's out of my mouth.

Regardless of the bullshit we're both spewing right now, I've gotten to relearn Daisy Stiles over these past months. I recognize her tells and cues. I know she's dying to get the hell out of here. I'm gonna be the bad guy who lets her because I'm fucking hurt too, and I need to cower away from everything just as bad as she does. My head feels like it's filled with wasps.

Daisy straightens her back into prim and proper posture as she juts her chin out and sticks her nose up at me. Her favorite armor.

"Right you are, August. I'll give you that." She turns back to Red. "I love you. I'm going to go say goodbye to everyone else, and then take off."

Red tries to object, but Daisy silences her with a quick hug, and pushes past me until she's out of sight.

Red doesn't even bother looking at me while she shakes her head, passing by.

"That was…" she breathes. She keeps her back to me. "You should be fucking ashamed of yourself. I have spent *years* jumping in the middle. Sawyer has wasted so much fucking time on trying to get you two to at least act like normal people for even just five goddamn minutes. All he *ever* wanted was a big family to love. He found that with all of us. And both you and Daisy are hellbent on letting it go up in flames."

Red finally faces me with tears rimming her eyes, and I have never regretted an argument so fast in my life.

"If she goes, I want you gone, too."

I have nothing to say. There's nothing *to* say. I stand here, still planted in the doorway of the bathroom and watch Red storm out.

I see Sawyer peek through the glass from the back deck, and I don't give him time to address me. I can't talk to him right now. I turn abruptly and head towards the staircase. I just need a couple minutes to pull myself together, and then I'll be out of here.

* * *

"Did you know I'm gonna be a big sister?" Penelope asks absentmindedly. She hasn't looked up from the chapter book she's been trying to sound the words out in for the last ten minutes that I've been seeking refuge in her playroom.

267

This was the first room I poked my head into upstairs, and when I saw P, it felt like the safest place to be.

I must have misheard her. Or she's really confused. Because Red's not—I mean, that doesn't make sense.

"P, you wanna run that by me again?"

She blows her bangs out of her face, already sick of my shit and needing to repeat herself. I don't blame her. The girl knows her worth and demands it out of all of us. As she should.

"I *said*, did you know I'm gonna be a big sister?"

"To who?" I couldn't be more lost if I tried. My head is pounding. The room kind of feels like it's spinning, and I'm straight up terrified this kid is about to drop a bomb on me. The kind of blow that's going to have me hating myself more than I thought possible.

"To the baby that my mom is growing in her belly? Duh, Gus. Don't you know where babies come from? I hope it's a baby sister. But Mom and Daddy say we just have to hope it's healthy."

Uh, I do know where babies come from. And I sure as shit hope seven-year-old Penelope doesn't. "Your mom…as in Red. She has a baby in her belly?" I already know the answer to my stupid question. I just made an absolute ass out of myself in front of a newly-pregnant Red. *Fuck.*

"I *just* said that." Penelope abandons the book on her lap and throws her hands in the air. "Usually you're fun. Today you're not." And with that, Penelope untangles her legs from the pretzel shape she had them in and heaves herself up.

Before she crosses the doorway, she looks back at me with a disappointed look on her face that tells me the list of women I need to apologize to just gained another name.

"I heard you yelling from up here, you know. I don't think it's nice when you talk to Daisy like that. She's family."

"I'm sorry you had to hear that, P." I don't know what else to say, but I already know it wasn't good enough.

"Don't say sorry to me. Say sorry to Daisy!"

"I'm gonna, kid. I know I messed up. More than I thought actually…" I let my sentence trail off. I got nothing.

Fuck.

Suddenly, Penelope darts back across her playroom and plops herself right in my lap. I have to readjust myself to accommodate her so she's comfortable. I came up here for space, but for once, I don't want to be alone. And even if I don't deserve it, I can't think of a better person to sit with.

"Hey, P, you think I can ask you something?" I ask once she's settled.

She ignores my request. "Just so you know, I'm still mad at you. But you also look really sad, and Mom says we shouldn't leave sad people by themselves."

"Your mom is one of the smartest people I know."

"Yeah, I know. What did you wanna ask me?"

"Do you think I could be a good dad?" I can't believe I'm burdening a seven-year-old with my insecurities, but I'm desperate.

"Hmm." Penelope pauses to think. Tapping her little pointer finger on her chin. "Do you care about throw-up?"

"Can't say I'm a *fan*, but I don't think I'd have a problem cleaning it up if needed," I answer, recalling the fact that I haven't had an issue with helping Daisy through what I now know was morning sickness for the past few weeks.

"Will you read a bedtime story every night? And play dress up? And make the French fries that smile up at you?"

"I don't see why I couldn't do any of that."

"Will you always be ready to squash a kid's face in if they're mean to your baby?"

"Damn fucking straight, Penelope. Shit—Sorry," I say, shaking my head. God, I can't even hold a simple conversation without letting expletives fly. How could I ever hack raising a baby? I was never cut out for all of this.

"Then you'd be a good dad, Gus. Because my dad and mom

would give all the same answers, and they're the best of the best." Penelope pats my arm reassuringly.

"Thanks, P. I think you're the best."

"Yeah, I know." She once again hoists herself up to a standing position. "I'm gonna go downstairs now because I'm hungry. You can come if you want, or you can stay here to think some more."

"I think I'll hang here for a little bit longer, if that's okay with you."

Her little arms wrap around my neck and she squeezes. "Love you, Gussy."

"Love you, lil P," I respond, squeezing her back.

When Penelope skips out of the room, I'm left alone with my thoughts. I couldn't tell you why getting P's approval caused a warming sensation to wash over me. I can't really grasp why I suddenly feel like maybe I could have one of these little humans of my own. Someone to tuck into bed and take on vacation. I could be their shoulder to cry on when things go wrong. But I do.

I could be their safe space.

Unfortunately, the fact of the matter is that at the end of the day, the only person I'd want to do all of it alongside is currently downstairs, probably hating me more than ever. And that's a lot given our past.

I don't have a single thing to say that would fix it. Sorry won't cut it. I deserve to sit with every ugly thing I said to Daisy, and she deserves to be free of me, once and for all.

We didn't even talk. We have…No, *she* has decisions to make. She has choices. Daisy needs to know who I just was isn't me. That's not…I'm not that kind of man. At least, I don't want to be.

I replay the scene over and over again. I don't know how much time passes, nor do I care.

If a hole in the earth opened up right now, I probably wouldn't hesitate to jump in and let it swallow me completely. That'd feel better than this sick, empty sense of dread sitting in my fucking stomach.

Daisy's pregnant.

Daisy's pregnant with our child. It's a future neither of us saw for ourselves, but maybe…the one we were supposed to have all along?

Hurried, heavy footsteps clunk up the staircase, and without knowing for sure, I prepare for the blow of Sawyer swinging the door to the playroom wide open. It hits the wall.

"Shit," Sawyer curses.

"What the hell?" I ask, rising to my feet.

Sawyer is breathing heavily, collecting himself when he finally raises his head to face me.

"Is it true?"

I avert my eyes down as shame washes over me.

"Don't do this, Gus. Don't."

"Do what? It's already done. Seems as though you're already aware of the situation. There isn't more to say." I still can't look my best friend in the eyes. I don't know if I'll ever be able to again.

While I might be a year older and a hell of a lot bigger, I've always looked up to Sawyer. No matter what hand he's dealt, he makes the best of it. He *sees* the best in everyone. He always pushes for more, because he knows it's attainable. Sawyer is the kind of man everyone should aspire to be.

I think I'm the opposite.

"Fuck you," he says, stepping towards me. Sawyer crowds my space and pushes with two hands into my chest. I let myself fall back into the wall. "There's a shit-ton more to say. Who the fuck do you think you are?"

"I'm a piece of shit," I murmur. "Just leave it be. I'm gonna be out of your hair."

"I want to fucking throttle you right now, and the only reason I'm not is because of the people downstairs."

"I'd deserve it," I shrug.

"Yeah, you would," Sawyer agrees. "She's pregnant, and you

just…what? You're gonna walk away? You really think Daisy deserves that?"

"*No*," my voice booms again for the second time this evening. I suck in a breath, trying to find the words to describe the pain swirling around in my head. There's no excuse though, nothing can fix the damage I caused by reacting the way I did. "She deserves so much better. She always has. But I…Sawyer, I'm not you."

"No one, not a day on this earth, has anyone asked you to be me. You have shit to work through. I want to help, but right now I'm pissed. I'm disappointed. I'm—It's hard to look at you right now, Gus."

"Heard that. Look, I can't apologize to you. I need to talk to Daisy."

"Not happening." Sawyer widens his stance and crosses his arms over his chest.

"What?" I finally look up and balk.

"She's already gone. You've done enough today. You need to take off."

"You can't keep me from her. You're not my fucking babysitter."

Sawyer doesn't back down. He stays standing in front of me with a scowl that shows he has no issues with letting this play out however I choose if it means he's protecting those he cares about.

Because that's Sawyer fucking Hale.

"Contrary to whatever you're thinking right now, I'm doing this for you, too. Because if you somehow make this worse by trying to force a conversation when you haven't given yourself time to sort out or process, there's no coming back from it. Honestly? Don't even know if there is now. But I'm trying to give you a chance."

"What do I do?" I don't have the right to ask for advice now, but I do it anyway.

"Go home. Figure out if you really want to be another deadbeat dad."

Sawyer turns and leaves. I wait until his stomps down the stairs settle, and then I make my way down too. I don't bother looking down the hall for anyone, instead just using the front door as my escape route.

CHAPTER 31: DAISY - I'LL BE THE MOTHER I NEEDED

I'm not somebody who paces. My nervous energy manifests in different ways, like chewing the inside of my cheek to the point of pain or wringing my hands together until they're a contorted jumble.

Today, though? Today I'm about to wear down a path in the beige carpet in my childhood bedroom with how much I'm pacing back and forth.

I feel funny knowing this will most likely be one of the last times I stand here. I could actually laugh about how I've waited thirty years to get out, and now that it's here, I'm terrified.

This room has always held so much of me—sanctuary in a hellscape—and today I'm saying goodbye.

Because I'm about to tell my mother the good news about our bloodline continuing, and I'm not stupid enough to think I'll be met with anything better than the quick removal of my presence from the residence.

Do I know where I'm going? No.

Am I worried about Chase and Hunter? Yes, obviously.

But, like someone very important to me—even if I am very

angry with them—has said numerous times, I always have a choice.

I choose myself and this baby.

It actually wasn't a hard decision to make once I finally said the hard words out loud.

I'm pregnant.

I love this baby, and somehow, cosmically, this baby already loves me, too.

Nothing else matters.

Well, finding us a stable and safe living situation along with possibly a job to support us after my savings run out are among the list of things that do actually matter. But the foundation of unconditional love is there. And that's propelling me in the right direction of knowing, despite all of the unknown and bad that might be coming our way, that this is going to work out.

Even if the reminder that August is not joining us for the ride is so painful that sometimes I feel like I can't breathe at the thought of it.

I've ignored every call and text. And boy, have there been a lot of them. But he said he was out. I understand it was most likely coming from a place of shock, but it doesn't change the fact that in that moment, I needed any other sort of reaction.

One where he stayed, and I didn't run.

I pick up the ultrasound I got today from the top of one of the suitcases I've packed to look at the blob of cells for the zillionth time. Seeing the factual information laid out in small font on this tiny piece of paper is, for some reason, comforting.

I click play on the short video clip on my phone and close my eyes to listen to the faint thump, thump, thump of the world's littlest heartbeat. My baby's heartbeat. The tech said there was a chance it was too early to hear it, but apparently, luck was on my side today. Hearing it made me feel less alone.

I then side-eye the clear plastic bag that contains my ridiculously pointless IUD they had to remove during my appointment, the one that was sitting perfectly in place within the walls of my uterus. Did you know they can sometimes fail for literally no reason whatsoever? I sure as hell didn't. The doctor joked that it must have been taking PTO the day I conceived.

I didn't laugh.

August would have laughed.

Oh, for fuck's sake, Daisy. Who gives a shit what August would have laughed at?

How long is this internal battle going to rage within my mind?

Forever, the mini-Daisy voice in my head tells me.

Well, forever's a long time, and the voice can wait. I'm about to blow up my life. I'm busy.

A soft knock on my bedroom door startles me. Hunter pokes his head in.

"Hey…Wait, what're those bags for?"

I sneakily tuck the ultrasound into my old journal.

"Hey, dude. I'm uh, actually—I wanted to talk with you. And Chase."

Hunter opens the door further, skepticism painted across his face.

"Why?"

"Can you just bring Chase in here?"

The twins return not even two minutes later, both hopping up on my bed, looking around at the near empty room. I have no time to prepare how I want to do this.

"So, I'm gonna be taking off for a while."

Hunter bounces up, for once looking so much younger than he usually presents himself.

"Where? Why? Is Gus going with you?"

The mention of his name stings.

"No, August is staying here in Merrymount. I have some things to figure out. But I love you guys so much—"

"Why does it feel like you might never come back?" Hunter

asks. Chase whips his head in his brother's direction, shocked to his core. Like he never imagined a day where I wasn't right here in the room across the hall.

"I'll always come back for you. I promise. But I have to go talk to Mom and Dad, and I'll be honest, I don't think the conversation is going to go well."

"We'll come with you." Hunter puffs his chest out defensively. He's changed so much in the months since August was introduced into his life, as if all he needed was that one person to break him out of his angry shell. He's *my* Hunter again, the one who wants to fiercely protect and do the right thing.

I shake my head, willing the waterworks forming to stand firmly behind my lashline.

"This is a fight you do not need to, should not, and will not be a part of."

I vowed to protect them in any way I could. I'm still standing by that.

"That's bullshit," Hunter spits.

"Don't think you can talk to me like that," I throw back at him.

Chase looks from Hunter to me, unspoken thoughts and emotions swirling through his deep blue eyes. He throws himself back, looking up at the ceiling.

I clear my throat.

"There is one more thing. I haven't told anyone. You're actually…" I hesitate. God, why is this so hard? "You're the first people I get to tell, like, for myself."

Chase props himself up on his elbows to look at me. Hunter shifts in his spot.

"I'm having a baby."

Both little twelve-year-old jaws fall open, and I pull the ultrasound out of the worn pages of my high school journal, tossing it in between them on the bed.

"That little white dot is going to become your niece or nephew."

Hunter slowly and carefully picks up the ultrasound to inspect while Chase leans his head over to get a better view. Both remain silent.

"I'm an open book. Anything you want to know, just ask. I know this is a big deal, but you're both my number ones. I love you more than anything, and I don't want you to think that things are going to change with the three of us."

"They're gonna kick you out," Hunter mutters.

I suck in a breath and blow it out.

"Yeah…I'm leaving before they can, but yeah." There's not much else to say.

"You do everything for them. You run the flower shop and take care of us, and they'll still kick you to the curb. With a baby."

I wince. He has a point, but shit. It's harsh.

"You're right. But you're also wrong, Hunter." I take a step towards the two boys who kept me grounded here for so long, my whole fucking world. "I did—*do*—everything for *you*. And this new baby growing inside me." When I place my hand on my belly, both sets of eyes follow my movement. "Mom and Dad…they—"

"Suck," Hunter finishes my train of thought.

"They try," I say with defeat. As much as I tried to shelter and protect them, our parents' true identities slipped through the cracks somewhere along the way, and the facade feels like a moot point now. "They try, and they fail a lot. I wish they made better decisions. I think we all wish that for a lot of people."

My mind travels to August and how we've both handled things so fucking poorly. Everything is a goddamn mess.

The three of us hear the back door open, but not one of us attempts to move even an inch. Chase's wide eyes find mine, and when he reaches out to grab my hand, I take it and squeeze. I hope with everything I am that our tried and true wordless connection is running strong today.

"Boys?" our mother calls up the stairs.

I nod in the direction of the door, silently telling them to go before either of our parents come searching and find a reason to start an argument about three siblings having the audacity to gather and talk.

Hunter doesn't let go of the ultrasound and before he has to ask I say, "Keep it." I push the hand holding the ultrasound toward him. "I'm serious. I have three others. I'll send you updated ones as I get them done, okay?"

When they reach my doorway, both twins turn around to face me and come barreling into me at the same time. I embrace them both, holding them so tight, not knowing the next time I'll get to do this. Wishing more than anything I did this sort of thing more often.

* * *

I TIME EVERYTHING PERFECTLY. Once I hear the shower running downstairs, I get the majority of my bags down from my room, packed into my car undetected.

I'm waiting at the kitchen table by the time my mother emerges from her bedroom in an over-the-top silk nightgown, her nightly cocktail already in hand.

"We need to talk," I say, breaking the silent staredown.

Mary Jane rolls her eyes, and I clench my fists. A battle is already beginning apparently. Lovely.

"Out with it, Daisy."

I toss the ultrasound down on the table between us.

A humorless bark of a laugh escapes my mother's worn face. She places her glass down in favor of picking up the black-and-white picture to inspect.

"Well, well, well. It appears your antics and games have finally caught up to you."

"Excuse me?" I wiped my mind clear of any expectations

279

surrounding this conversation before coming down here, but this isn't a response I could have prepared for.

"You thought you could fuck your way around and not wind up in this sort of predicament?"

"Y-you're…" I sputter. "You're slut-shaming me. I'm telling you, as your daughter, that I'm pregnant—at thirty, mind you, not sixteen—and you throw in my face that I'm some sort of town whore?"

"If it looks like a duck…" Mary Jane makes a tsking sound.

"Oh…my God." I push away from the table to stand. I need to get the fuck out of here *now*. I don't know what to say, what to do…There's no fixing what's broken here.

"Leaving so soon?" Mom asks in a singsong voice that slices right through me, throwing the ultrasound back onto the table. "Aren't celebrations in order? Let's call your father in here. I'm sure he'll be so pleased. *Ron!*" she yells. When she picks her drink back up, she swigs the whole thing back in one go.

I swipe the ultrasound up. If I'm going, I guess I better go out with a bang.

"It really was never me. All this time, I tried to find blame in myself when in reality, you really are just…bad people." I shake my head. "I waited *years* for you to have some come to fucking Jesus moment. I guess a small part of me held onto hope."

My father enters the kitchen, already looking done and over this conversation. It's his usual appearance whenever he has to face me, the daughter he discarded.

"Daisy here has something to share."

"I haven't put much weight in any tale Daisy felt the need to burden us with in years. I don't see how something today could change that."

"You know what? Fuck this. Dad—I actually hate calling you that. Ronald, Mr. Stiles, *whatever.* You're spineless. I hate that I'm related to you, and I hate that we share a name."

His face never changes. It remains cold and emotionless, just like it always does whenever I'm around. Maybe it's always been this way, and I just never noticed until I got older. Until I "ruined" things for him for good. His gaze drifts to the ultrasound.

"The feeling is mutual. You've been my biggest disappointment. I'm not sure why I was bothered with this. Mary Jane, I need a refill whenever she's gone. Good luck." He leaves the room without another word.

Mom's face contorts for a second, as if she's recovering from a slap to the face, possibly a minuscule moment of regret, a sobering blip of time. But when she fixes herself into yet another look of blankness, I accept this ending for what it is.

My hand is on the doorknob when my mother finally speaks.

"Are you keeping it?"

I don't turn around when I answer her, not strong enough to look her in the eyes, but my response is clear and confident.

"Yes."

The sureness of my voice kicks everything else my body was holding back into gear, and I whip my head around.

"And I will love this baby with everything I am. Every day. Unconditionally. And I'll believe them when they tell me something's wrong or someone *hurt* them." I suck in a breath to gather myself. I don't want to fall apart in front of anyone, least of all her. "I'll be the mother I needed."

Everything else can, and most likely will, go to shit, but that fact will remain true forever.

When I slam the door, it feels like the whole house shakes as I walk away. Once I'm at my car, I look up to see Hunter and Chase side by side in the window of their bedroom. I wave and blow a kiss. A promise that I'll be back for them.

CHAPTER 32: AUGUST - HAPPY NEW YEAR

I haven't seen Daisy since the Christmas party. I actually haven't seen anyone.

Well, except Beth who tried to drag me out of my house on Christmas Day to join her, Melanie, Sawyer, and Margot for the ham dinner she cooked. I declined through the door, a coward in every way. She left a plate for me though.

The fact that she's showing me pity by not pounding me in the head for my stupidity is terrifying. I know there's a storm brewing there that I'm gonna have to face eventually.

I spent the holiday in sweats on the couch, rewatching *Forrest Gump* and every other movie Daisy has mentioned either intentionally or in passing ever since I've met her. Anything to feel like she's sitting next to me. Anything to forget how badly I fucked everything up.

But I haven't touched a drop of alcohol. As much as I've wanted to hide in the bottom of a bottle, I've refrained. I hear Daisy's voice in the back of my head every time I look towards the small bar cabinet I have in the living room. Bottles of liquor are collecting dust at this point.

I'm a mess.

Rereading the unanswered texts I've sent to Daisy does nothing but remind me of the pain, but I do it anyway, because I deserve to feel like this.

ME

Daisy, I'm sorry. I'm so sorry. Please come back.

ME

I miss you, I'm sorry.

ME

I'll do anything.

Those are only a few of the dozens. It probably looks stalker-ish. I can't find anything in me to care about that.

Red sent out a very cryptic text earlier this week. It was short and to the point.

RED

i expect you to be at my house on new year's eve at promptly eight p.m. wear something nice.

So I've found myself back under the same party tent in Red and Miller's backyard, even more hopeless and desperate to find Daisy. I won't cause a scene. I won't make it about myself or dig my pathetic hole any deeper. I just want to see her. I just want to know she's okay. As okay as she can be.

There are lights twinkling above and a handful of mismatched chairs that I'm pretty sure are from the café facing a small plat-form. A wooden arch sits on top with purple and pink flowers wrapped around the side posts, all the way down to the ground.

I should have known Red would pull an elopement. I'll never forget how forced her smile was when she married Dean. She deserves the peace she has now.

"She didn't want a big wedding like the last time. But she

wanted to make sure everyone she loved was here for this one. She said it's the one that matters." Miller's voice startles me from behind.

I turn around and see Miller in a sharp black suit with a light purple bow-tie popping out, no doubt picked out by Penelope. His hair is still classically messy, but he looks damn good. And most of all, proud.

"Miller, man. You look great."

"You clean up nice, too," he says, gesturing to the navy suit I found in the back of my closet. I opted for no tie, just a white button up underneath.

"So, you're getting married?" I don't know what to say. I know everyone here has the right to be pissed at me, and I'm grateful to even be given the opportunity to still be included.

Miller shrugs, sticking his hands in his pockets with a smile beaming on his face. "Gwen didn't want to wait any longer, and well…I've been ready since I saw her."

"Where is everyone?" I ask.

"The girls are all upstairs getting ready. I'm not allowed up there. Sawyer's been hanging with me in the kitchen. You coming?" Miller turns to walk towards the back deck that leads to the slider into their kitchen.

"Uh," I start. Facing Sawyer after the last time we spoke feels impossible. I'm so fucking ashamed, and I still don't have anything to say since I still haven't talked to Daisy. I have to live with my mistakes, and I don't think he's gonna let me off easy.

"Hey." Miller pulls me back from my overthinking. "You fucked up. You gotta own it, but that's not for today, okay?"

"I'm not here to start anything. I promise."

Miller gives me another almost pitying smile. "I know, Gus. Red knows it too. No matter how pissed she is at you, she wants you here. We all do, especially Penelope."

"Thanks," I lamely offer, following Miller into the house.

Sawyer is leaning against the kitchen counter, sipping a bottle of beer when I enter. Neither of us says anything when he looks my way and places the bottle down beside him.

Miller coughs, clearly uncomfortable and trying as hard as he can to ease the tension.

I don't want to put pressure on his big day.

"Nice suit," I greet Sawyer, referring to the navy pants and jacket he has on that match mine.

A *humph* leaves him. "Thanks, you too."

I opt for a bottle of water. After cracking it open and taking a sip, I attempt conversation again. "How's Margot?"

"Pregnant and happy. How's Daisy? Oh, that's right. You wouldn't know."

"Saywer…" Miller groans.

"No, it's okay, Miller. I deserve that. You're right, man. I wouldn't know. And it's my fault. But I'm trying here."

"Are you? Because from my perspective, it looks like all you're doing is moping around while the rest of us try to clean up your shit."

Fuck, he's a lot more pissed than I thought he would be by now.

"I'm doing what I can. I call and text every day. I'm not going to just bombard her." My argument is weak, but it's all I got.

"Bombard her where? *Calls and texts?*" he mocks. "Are you aware Daisy is living in the playroom upstairs? Her parents kicked her out."

My head whips to Miller, and when he nods his solemn confirmation that Sawyer is telling the truth, my vision blurs. Wild, hot anger creeps in at the mention of Daisy's parents and what they've done. How could they do this?

Which is a rich thought, coming from the guy who told Daisy he was "out" at the sight of a pregnancy test.

"I need to talk to her." I start moving towards the stairs, but Sawyer's hand claps me in the chest, pushing me back.

"Not fucking happening," Saywer says. "What's done is done.

You *do* need to talk to her, but it's not today. We're here for Miller, Red, and Penelope. Got it?"

Footsteps on the staircase make Sawyer remove his hand from me, backing off. Beth rounds the staircase in a peach colored blazer and pants, holding a binder. "Ah! All of my favorite men in one room."

She enters the kitchen and kisses each of us on the cheek. She lingers on mine to whisper in my ear, "I'm happy you're here, my boy."

Beth claps one hand to the binder. "Let's get this show on the road!"

"Are you officiating?" I ask.

"Psh." Beth waves a hand my way. "Who else?"

* * *

WHILE RED and Miller exchange personal vows that ensure not a single person in this small audience is leaving with a dry eye, my line of vision doesn't leave her.

Daisy.

Her name repeats in my head over and over like the beat of a drum, calling me to her.

I watch her tears fall, and she makes no move to swipe them away, holding my stare while clutching a tissue in her hand.

We're sitting on opposite sides of the makeshift aisle. We're supposed to be facing forward towards the lovely bride and groom in front of us, some of our closest, best friends. But goddamn it, I can't look away from Daisy. And it appears she can't look away from me.

She has her hair done up in this pretty bun, and she's wearing a long black dress that hugs every fucking inch of her perfectly. I can't stop staring at the dark shade of maroon painted on her lips, the lips I still don't know the taste of.

I miss her, and she's only feet away from me.

I don't hear what comes next in the ceremony. I don't focus on anything else until the clapping around me brings me back to the platform where Miller and Red just kissed for the first time as husband and wife.

Music crescendos, and Miller picks Penelope up, hoisting her onto his shoulders, while Red wraps her arm around his torso. The three of them practically bounce back down the aisle together, their smiles as wide as can be.

"Okay, everyone!" Beth calls into her tiny microphone under the arch. "Food is buffet style. Chris will have the tunes cranking. Everyone have their glasses for the toast and lips ready for the midnight smooch in a little over an hour's time!"

I make a beeline for Daisy.

Margot crosses my path, standing in front of Daisy like a scary little protective barrier. "Nuh-uh."

"Yes-huh, Margot. I love you, I really do. But I need to talk to her."

"She can approach you when she's good and ready." Margot's index finger jabs into my chest. I'm pretty positive she picked a button to dig into my skin for maximum punishment.

"Margot, it's okay." Daisy's hand wraps around Margot's bicep from behind, and she steps forward.

All of the air leaves my lungs.

"I'll give you five minutes," Daisy says to me while looking at the ground.

"Thank you," I breathe.

"You're sure?" Margot asks Daisy.

Daisy kisses Margot's cheek, a soft smile on her face. "I'm sure-sure. Thank you."

My hand finds the small of her back, and I quickly pull away when my fingers brush bare skin. I didn't realize this slinky black dress could get any more perfect for Daisy until I discover it has an open back. The swooping of material collects right above the round of her bottom. We walk silently into the house and find ourselves in the same laundry room that started this whole mess all those months ago.

"I mean it, August. Five minutes, not a second more, and then I'm joining the party and putting this behind me." Daisy leans against the washing machine, smoothing her dress nervously.

"How are you feeling?" I ask.

"You have limited time, and you're wasting it with small talk?"

"No. I'm not just asking for the sake of it. I want to know if your nausea has gotten any better, or if you're sleeping without those night terrors that woke you up in cold sweat. I'm asking if you're dizzy or fatigued. I want to know what happened with your parents." I try to get the words out as fast as possible.

Daisy doesn't look up even though I'm desperate to see those baby blues. "You didn't seem to care much about any of that last week."

"There will never be enough ways that I can apologize for that. I was wrong. I'm sorry. I'm so fucking sorry, Daze." I can't control the crack in my voice.

"Sorry doesn't hold its weight when I can't trust you."

"You can," I plead, taking one tentative step towards her. "I swear. I'm standing here telling you that I'm the man for this. I'm scared. I don't know what I'm doing. But if I was ever going to figure it out with anyone, it'd be you."

Time slows and the silence surrounding us practically engulfs me.

Daisy finally looks up. "I'm leaving."

Remember a second ago when I said time slowed? It lurches to a complete fucking stop.

"What do you mean?"

"I need to figure out what I want. For myself. Not for anyone else."

"Where are you going? For how long? What about—"

"Gus," Daisy exhales. "Stop. What we started was dumb. It was a lapse in judgment. Me and you..."

"Daisy, don't. Don't chalk what we have up to nothing, please." This is fucking killing me, and she doesn't even know it.

"Well, what we have and what we should be are two entirely different things now, aren't they?" She huffs a laugh that doesn't feel very funny to me. "I'm having a baby, August."

Goosebumps creep up all over my body. "I know."

"I don't want to argue. I don't even know if I'm so much mad anymore or just...done? Done with people running with assumptions and past biases of me. Done with this town. At least for right now."

"What does this mean for us?"

"I don't have all of the answers right now. Or any of them, for that matter." Daisy shrugs. "I don't want to make decisions based on these emotions. It would be irresponsible. I know I want this baby to have a happy and healthy life. Whether that's with one parent or two."

"I'm not going to be a deadbeat like my dad," I assure her.

"Okay." Daisy doesn't agree or disagree with my statement. She just lets it sit there.

I'm pretty sure we've passed the five-minute allotment she gave me when we entered this room. I'm not making moves to acknowledge that though.

"Can I ask you something?"

"Sure," Daisy says.

"While you're gone...Uh, would it be okay if I checked in on Hunter and Chase? I won't bother them too much, I promise. But they're important to you. To me."

Her walls come crashing down at the mention of her brothers' names.

"Really?" She shakes her head. "I mean, yes. Of course. I wouldn't keep you from them. They love you, Gus. And I'm not keeping this baby from you." My vision blurs when her palm falls to her belly. The belly growing our baby. "I just need...I don't know how to explain it."

"You don't have to."

"No, I do. You're standing here owning your mistakes, and I respect it. I need to know if I have a life outside of this town. Something that's entirely mine."

"I want that for you." I do. I mean it. I want her to be happy and get everything she's ever wanted. I just wish I got to come along for the ride. I wish she wanted me. Here.

"Thanks." A strand of hair from her bangs falls forward, and Daisy tucks it behind her ear before I can make the move myself. She lets her small purse slide off her shoulder, and she begins rummaging through the contents of it. "Do you, umm, want to see the ultrasound? I went to the doctor earlier this week."

I'm by her side in the next second, and my breath shallows when she pulls out the tiny sheet of thin paper.

"Please," I beg, reaching out.

I sink to the floor, and maybe it's showing me mercy, or out of pity, but I don't care either way because Daisy joins me.

We sit together, side by side, shoulders kissing, staring at the small, grainy black-and-white picture of the baby we made. Everything's a fucking mess. Daisy's taking off to who knows where, and I don't know when she'll be back. I have a lifetime of shit to sort out. But this little thing? Whoever they are, busy growing vital organs and limbs? And this small moment of peace? It feels downright fucking perfect.

Time passes, and Daisy lets me listen to the heartbeat from a video on her phone. She explains to me that just over eight weeks have gone by with this little bundle growing and both of them are as healthy as can be.

With heavy eyes fighting sleep, my ears barely register the sounds of everyone counting down to midnight outside. But when the crowd gets to one, and the clock strikes midnight, I can't help myself from leaning over and letting my lips graze the top of her head to whisper, "Happy New Year, darling."

"Happy New Year, August," she breathes. I watch a single teardrop fall onto the top corner of the paper in our hands.

I must drift off to sleep, and I'm ready to burn the fucking world down when I wake because Daisy's gone. The ultrasound we held together is left sitting in her place on the floor beside me.

CHAPTER 33: AUGUST - WHAT, LIKE A SHRINK?

For the first time in my life, I'm standing outside Red's, nervous to walk in.

I bounce on my heels and move to the side each time another customer is attempting to get through the front door, each time offering a grunted apology for being in the way. I watch Margot take orders and handle transactions from a stool behind the register while Red flies around her, slinging cups of coffee and pastries over the counter. Miller's working on his laptop from his normal booth, heart eyes straying to his new wife every so often.

Some regulars dash in and out, while others are sitting at the barstools along the counter or tables in the middle of the café. Everyone's smiling or chatting with each other.

And then there's me. Out here on the sidewalk like a fucking creep.

I gave myself one more day of pitiful solitude and vowed to myself to make it out of the house and into town to face everyone. I have apologies to make and advice to ask for. A shit ton of both, honestly.

The ultrasound Daisy left behind is burning a hole in the back pocket of my jeans. It hasn't left my hands much since I got a hold of it. Feels silly, seeing as there isn't much to look at. Just a tiny speck of a blob. But goddamnit, that blob is half me and more importantly, half of the smartest, most beautiful, *strongest* woman I've ever known. And that's everything to me.

I must zone out longer than I originally intended because next thing I know, the door to Red's flies open, and I have a mad as hell Red standing before me with her hands balled into fists on her hips.

"You're lucky I haven't called the cops on you for loitering."

"I'd understand if you did," I mutter. I kick a pebble with my foot.

Red's face softens. The anger washes away, replaced by an embarrassing amount of pity.

"Shit," she breathes. "You're not okay, are you?"

"No. Not really," I croak.

A gentle hand lands on my arm, and I focus on the gold band with three diamonds on top. The one in the middle is bigger than the ones on either side, but none of them are over the top or clunky. It looks like a ring that was picked out with a lot of care and thought. That's no surprise knowing Miller.

"Congrats on the wedding, by the way."

Red squeezes my bicep. "Thanks. I think I got it right this time."

"You did," I assure her.

"Congrats on the baby, too," I add.

Red's hand flies to her stomach. "The same could be said to you."

I don't have an answer for that.

"Come upstairs. I'm sure Mel would love to chat," Red encourages me.

I follow Red through the café to the door that leads to the small apartment upstairs that Melanie currently occupies. I offer Margot and Miller a small wave as I pass by. Miller smiles back while Margot scowls. It's probably going to take me a while to win her back.

When we knock, Melanie opens the door in a fraction of a second, as if she was waiting there the whole time. I'm immediately hit with the smell of…

"Are you making a blueberry pie?"

"Blueberry *crisp*, actually," she corrects with a smile. "It's Margot's request of the week." Melanie opens her arms for a hug, and I practically fall into her small frame.

She squeezes me tight, and next thing I know, I'm bawling like a fucking baby, shaking both of our bodies as wave after wave of emotion crashes through me.

"Shit, I'm sorry," I sniffle.

Melanie doesn't let me go but guides us to the small green velvet couch. When we both sit, she rubs my back, and Red wordlessly hands me a tissue.

This is embarrassing as fuck.

"I'm sorry," I repeat.

"For what? Having feelings? I promise you're in for one heck of a ride with those now that you're going to be a father," Melanie says.

Red crashes back into the small chair beside the couch. "I mean, hey. At least we know you have emotions now."

I finally lift my head. "Respectfully, Red, you have no idea how I'm feeling."

Any drop of sympathy Red might have had before dissolves.

"*Dis*respectfully, August," Red leans forward. "That's not my doing. *You* blew up your situation with Daisy. *You* decided to sequester yourself after the fact. Honestly, I'm just glad you're torn up about this. You should be gutted over what you did."

"I am!" I don't mean to raise my voice, but it happens anyway.

"Okay, okay. Tensions are high," Melanie interjects to try to diffuse the situation. "Gus, how about you start by telling us how you're really feeling? While Red might have worded it differently than I would have, she has a point. You haven't given any of us the chance to help you."

"I don't deserve your help. I—I never deserved anyone's help. This goes way back too. When Sawyer and Beth took me in, I accepted it. Even though I shouldn't have."

It's a truth I've known from the beginning. I was a selfish teenager who never thought I'd get out of the house of horrors I grew up in. So when Sawyer wouldn't take no for an answer, I decided to take the opportunity.

The only thing I was ever taught was how to throw and dodge a punch. This big, makeshift family was never supposed to be mine. I've always been the interloper.

"Wait, what?" Red asks. "What're you talking about?"

"Look at me, Red. I'm the big fucking idiot who isn't afraid to throw my weight around. I'm a fun time at parties. I'm good for nothing else."

"You're throwing a pity party right now, and frankly, it's fucking embarrassing," Red throws back.

"Hey now," Mel interrupts us again. "August, my goodness. Do you really believe all of that?"

My non-answer is apparently answer enough.

"Have you talked to anyone about this?" Mel asks gently.

I shake my head in shame but don't respond.

"Would you consider it?"

"What, like a shrink? Nah." I wave. "I'm good. I don't have shit to work through. I know where I came from and who I am. I just need to fix shit with Daisy."

I'm more than sure therapy helps people. I saw the work Daisy put in when we were younger. I'm just not one of those people.

"I believe those things go hand in hand, Gus," Melanie whispers. "I know…" She hesitates. "I know I don't know everything about your past, where you grew up. And I wasn't there for your initial reaction to the news of Daisy's pregnancy…"

"Consider yourself lucky," Red spits.

"Gwendolyn, either you're here to help your good friend, or you can see yourself back downstairs to the café. I understand this is a high stake time for everyone involved, but clearly Gus already feels remorse. The jabs are unnecessary."

Red gives a humph and sits back in her chair.

"I don't think negatively about therapy," I address Mel, leaving Red be. "But everyone has had bad shit happen to them. My shit may look worse to others, but it just is what it is to me. So what, my dad took off? So what, my stepdad saw me as just a body to beat on to get his frustrations out, and my mom never gave a fuck? As long as her glass was full," I end with a sick laugh.

"What's a therapist going to tell me that I don't already know?" I continue. "That I have to be careful not to continue the cycle? That it'll be almost impossible, and I'll be defying all of the odds if I manage to not burn everything up in my life? I know my chances. I already blew them. I'm good. What's that saying? 'I've seen what I needed to see.'"

"You're not them," Melanie assures me sternly with a low voice.

"*I told her I was out!*" I shout. I stand and pull at my hair with frustration. After taking a deep breath, I keep going. "Daisy stood there, stronger than I'll ever fucking be, and I let her down. I let that baby down. I failed from the start."

"You can come back from this, August. You were scared, you're still scared. But it doesn't have to mean anything more than that." Melanie stands by my side, and *fucking Christ*, why do I feel like I'm gonna cry again?

"I'll never be good enough."

"You could try," Red offers with sincerity in her voice. "You could decide literally right this very second to just *try* to be the man someone like Daisy deserves. And a good starting point might be sifting through your demons with a professional. I wouldn't be the friend, wife, and mother I get to be today if it wasn't for my therapist, Lisa."

I hold back a scoff. "You see a therapist?"

Red crosses her arms. "Weekly."

Huh. I never would've guessed. Red's always been strong on her own. She's sure of herself and confident and the kind of person who always manages to get the job done, no matter the obstacle. I thought it all came naturally to her.

"I didn't let people see the broken parts of me for a long time, Gus," Red admits. "I hid behind my work in the café, and that was *with* my appointments. I had to want to change. I think you want that, too. You just might not know how. You're not a bad guy. Hell, you're one of my favorite guys. If we all really thought you were a lost cause, we'd forget about you like the rest of them. But you have to tell us what you want out of this."

"I want Daisy to be happy."

"Anything else?" Melanie questions.

I take another deep breath and think on it, and neither Melanie or Red attempt to fill the silence of my thoughts. I sink back into the couch.

"I want…I think I want to be happy, too. I want to be the kind of man Daisy deserves. I want to be the father I never had. I want us to be the parents who do it right. Maybe not always. I'm sure I'll fuck up again at some point. But I never want to walk away, or watch Daisy walk away. I let her go, honestly, in hopes that she'll come back. I want to love her and receive that love back. But if she decides she can't…Well then, I want to be the kind of man who accepts that, and do everything I can to support her."

Even though the thought of losing Daisy and this unborn child I haven't gotten to know yet makes me feel like my heart is being ripped out of my chest and shredded to pieces, I mean every word. I'd do anything to right my wrongs if it meant Daisy and our baby would be okay. If that means sitting in some stuffy office facing bullshit from the past I thought I got over, I'll fucking do it.

Red covers her mouth with her hand.

"I don't think I've ever heard you string so many words together. No offense," she adds, shooting a quick glance at Melanie in apology, who is side-eyeing Red big time. "But listen, Lisa works in a practice doing virtual appointments. The doctors are flexible with your schedule. You can pop inside and have a session in between jobs at the riverside. I can give you a referral."

"I'll take it, thanks." I nod along.

"And August, you don't have to do any of this alone. The brooding can only go on for so long," Melanie advises.

"I know. That's what dragged me here today. I had enough with the isolation."

"An excellent first step," Melanie praises.

Four quick, aggressive knocks on the door startle all three of us.

"Hello?" Melanie calls, getting up.

"Who the hell would even bother to knock?" Red questions, leaning forward.

I move past both of them to get to the door first. When I swing it open, I'm confused because I don't see anyone, or anything.

But then I look down, and I see Chase panting heavily, papers crumbled in his right fist.

"*Hunter...knows...*" Chase's hoarse voice cracks as he stares with wide, nervous eyes lifting the paperwork into my view.

I barely have time to register the fact that Chase just fucking *spoke* when I see I'm face to face with court paperwork dated over eighteen years ago. Horror washes over me. This is Daisy's past, and even though I trust everyone in this room explicitly, it's not my story to tell.

"Is everything okay?" Melanie asks.

"We need a minute," I call back, stepping into the landing and shutting the door behind me.

"Where did you get this?" I ask him.

I watch Chase take a giant gulp of air. I practically see every muscle in his body and gear in his brain working to find words so long tucked away. A wave of astonishment and pride washes over me, leaving goosebumps everywhere in its wake.

"M-mom and Dad started throwing out her things. Her diary…She must have accidentally left it behind. These fell out. Hunter found them."

It's hard to catch a breath reeling from how proud I am of this kid and battling how fucking awful this situation is for everyone involved. How much worse it can get.

"Chase," I sigh after a chill snakes down my spine. "Did *you* know?"

A small, single nod confirms everything. It's a punch to the gut that makes me instantly nauseous.

"How long?"

"Right before our t-tenth birthday. I snooped when I shouldn't have. I'm s-sorry," Chase's voice cracks again, and I'm pretty sure my heart does the same. It's not hard to connect his sudden onset of muteness to his discovery.

"Hey." I rest my hand on his shoulder. "Don't be sorry. You have nothing to be sorry for. You're doing amazing, Chase. I'm so proud of you. Daisy would be so fucking proud." There's time to sort out what this means, and where we go from here, but right now, I think we have more pressing matters.

"Hunter's gonna do something bad. I saw your truck out front. You're the only…Gus, you gotta h-help me."

CHAPTER 34: AUGUST - YOU'RE COMING HOME WITH ME.

*B*efore I can fling the door to the flower shop open, Chase's small hand on my arm stops me in my tracks. I quickly turn, giving him my full attention before I bust into this goddamn store and raise hell.

"What's up, kid?"

"I c-can't t-talk to them," Chase whispers, looking down at his shoes.

"I'm the one doing the talking. You stand behind me. That's your job, okay?"

Chase jumps when we both hear glass shattering inside. I can only assume—*hope*—it's just a vase.

"Behind me, got it?" I confirm.

Chase nods in answer.

I whip the door open and enter, Chase close by on my heels. My eyes search the room, clocking every bit of movement. Hunter stands on the counter, a large green vase raised in his right hand. Mary Jane stands with horror-stricken eyes in the doorway leading to their back room, and Ron is attempting to walk over the broken glass of a different vase towards Hunter with his hands raised in surrender.

"Hunter, please put the vase down. Let's have a conversation," Ron tries to calmly coax Hunter down from his spiral.

"Oh, I'll put it down alright. On your fucking *head*," Hunter snaps, raising the vase just a little higher.

"Hold on a sec, Hunter," I call.

Ron's eyes dart to mine when he notices my presence.

"Long time, no talk, Mr. Stiles."

"This doesn't concern you," Daisy's father responds.

"Seeing as I'm the only thing standing between you and a head full of glass, I'd say it might concern me. Just a little." I pinch my fingers together, mocking Ronald Stiles's current predicament. If it wasn't at the expense of three people I care deeply about, this would be a hell of a lot more fun to mess with him.

"You've done enough!" Mary Jane yells.

"Did you know?" Hunter asks. And even though he hasn't turned to look at me, I know who the question is directed at.

"Yeah," I confirm, and Hunter finally turns his head in my direction. "Believe me, Hunter. I'd love to see what damage you could do right now. And I'd think they'd deserve it. But you don't deserve to live with the consequences of the aftermath. Daisy wouldn't want that for either of you boys. Everything she's ever done is to protect you. Don't let it be for nothing."

"So what?" Hunter scoffs. "I'm just supposed to pretend my parents aren't monsters? Everything was a lie! My whole life! They protected *him!*" His hands start to shake along with his voice.

I chance a step towards him, wanting to find a way to calm him down to get us all out of this with as few issues as possible.

"I don't have the answers." I let myself go tunnel vision, blocking everyone else in the room out when I focus on Hunter. "Don't let them win. Daisy never has."

My hand reaches up, and when I have a good grip, I pull the vase from Hunter's grasp. The room remains silent. I bend over, gently placing the vase on the ground and then hold my hand back up for Hunter to take.

"You can get down now. I'm here. It's okay."

"Don't speak to my son like you know anything about him," Mary Jane spits.

I ignore her. I repeat to myself over and over again that letting this escalate further would help no one. If Daisy were here, she'd know exactly what to do. I'm trying to channel that sureness.

Hunter glances at his mother, and then accepts my hand to jump down. He sprints over to Chase, and I gather my thoughts to get us the *fuck* out of here.

"Listen…" I sigh.

"Leave." Mr. Stiles cuts me off.

"Planning on it, Ron," I say, wagging a finger at him.

"What about us?" Hunter asks. I turn and see him with an arm around his brother's shoulders.

"You're coming home with me." I point to the two of them. I don't miss the wave of relief that washes over the twins.

"Like hell they are," Mrs. Stiles seethes. As expected.

"My patience is running thin, Mary Jane. The only reason I haven't lost my goddamn mind on the both of you is because of those boys. I'm just as sick and angry as they are. More, actually. I hate you. You disgust me. You don't deserve to be parents."

"And you do?" Mary Jane laughs. "You think we don't know? She didn't tell us, of course. Because why would she even need to? It was obvious you'd be her downfall from the start."

"You know, I don't know what I deserve. But I'm gonna work every fucking day to earn what I have. What I've been given. I'll love my baby, just like I love Daisy, just like I love these boys. And it'll always be more than anything you could have ever offered."

"You can't just take them." Mary Jane steps towards her sons with a slight panic in her voice, and they take a step back towards the front door. "They're children."

A kidnapping case probably wouldn't look good when I have

a baby on the way, and I don't trust these motherfuckers to not pull some shit. But I can't leave Hunter and Chase. I just can't.

"Call their grandmother," I offer. "I'll wait."

Ron's head whips to Mary Jane's with wide eyes. He slowly shakes his head.

"We don't want to go to Grandma's," Hunter says. "We want to go to Gus's."

"I'm offering you the chance to make the right choice, for fucking once. Take it, and maybe sort out your shit." I continue to stare at two of the worst people on the planet.

"Chase?" Mary Jane calls with a shaky voice.

Just when I think Chase will ignore her, his voice is heard clear as day through the flower shop.

"No."

Mr. and Mrs. Stiles gasp. Hunter breathes a not-so-subtle *"What the fuck?"*

I look at Chase with nothing but absolute pride in my eyes and then direct my attention back to the losers in front of me.

"They know the truth now. I can't mediate this, though. This situation probably—actually, definitely—requires professional help. And I'm not convinced you'd be willing to do that. I need Hunter and Chase safe. I know they're safe with me. I've never asked you for anything, and I can't imagine a day where I'd need to do it again, but right now, I'm asking you to let them come home with me."

"We're going either way," Hunter adds.

I raise a brow at him. He mouths an apology while Ron and Mary Jane discuss their options in hushed tones.

It feels like hours pass, even though I know it's only been maybe three minutes tops when Ron blows through the back door, leaving Mary Jane standing there with tears in her eyes.

It's a sad sight. Not enough for me to feel bad though. "So, we're good?"

Mary Jane tries to reach out to her sons, and they again back away even further. "Chase…you…you spoke." She's clearly still in shock.

Hunter angles his body in front of his brother.

"You don't get to talk to him. To either of us. Daisy, too."

Mary Jane nods. There's a battle raging inside of her. I don't know what the outcome will be. It's most likely too little, too late. But she'll figure that out either way on her own.

"Be good, boys." She follows in her husband's footsteps out through the back, just as she has for years now.

It's not until we hear the sound of a car starting and driving away that any of us makes a move. Shocker to no one, it's Hunter who breaks the silence.

"Since when can you *talk*?" Hunter looks to Chase, completely taken aback by this new development.

"Y-you wouldn't g-get it." Chase shrugs.

The hurt that flashes across Hunter's face is hard to miss, but he tries to suppress it anyway.

"Well, okay. But could you maybe try to explain it to me?"

I clap a hand on each of their shoulders. "Plenty of time for that, but not right now. Let's go get you some of your stuff packed, and we'll drop it off at my place before heading to Beth's."

"Why are we going to Beth's?" Hunter asks.

"She knows a thing or two about taking misfits like you in." I ruffle the black hair that matches Daisy's on the top of his head. "Let's get a move on."

"I HAD a whole scolding speech planned for you, you know," Beth says over her steaming cup of tea. She's sitting at the table I have tucked against the wall of windows that overlooks the backyard. The last person to occupy that spot was Daisy, and I'd be lying if I said I didn't miss that view.

"By all means, you're more than welcome to still dish it out." I chuckle, leaning against the counter after finishing the dishes.

Hunter and Chase are finally passed out in the spare room upstairs. Tomorrow I have to finagle another bed in there and maybe another dresser. It'll all come together, I'm sure.

"No sense in doing that when you turn your shit around and save the day all on your own. I'm proud of you, my boy. I'm so fucking proud."

"I don't think I'm deserving of that yet," I admit. "If you haven't noticed, I have two of the three Stiles in my care. I'm missing arguably the most important one."

"Baby steps, Gus. Besides, you've never truly lost her. She'll be back."

"She might not be," I argue.

"For you and those boys? Always. It's not really up for debate."

"Have you…talked to her? Is she okay?" I ask hesitantly.

Beth sighs and places her tea cup on the table. "Oh, August. You asked me this once before, and it broke my heart the same way it is now."

My mind pulls the memory from the back of my brain against my will.

The tightness of the handcuffs are pinching the skin of my wrists raw and the air of this little room is so fucking stuffy I feel like I'm choking.

I fucked up big time, and I'm pretty sure there's no one coming to save me.

Not that I'd deserve it.

I'm sure Beth is throwing my shit out on her front lawn right this very moment, happy to have a reason to be rid of me. I'm sure Daisy is thanking every star in the sky she didn't seek me out tonight, looking for romance when all I can offer is destruction.

I'm not sorry though. I'll never be sorry.

They can lock me up for life, take away every good thing I ever had, and I'd still never apologize for beating that piece of shit up. Matter of fact, I don't care if he even pulls through.

My skin heats with refueled rage at the thought of my stepdad and every sick thing he's done in his pathetic life. I wish I hit him harder. I wish I had more time.

"Don't I get a fucking phone call?" I ask the empty room.

Don't even know why I bother. I don't have anyone to call.

Sawyer's probably busy with Katie. I saw the look on Daisy's face.

I'm alone.

I was always supposed to be alone.

The last two years were me playing pretend. A short-lived fantasy of a life that was never meant to be mine.

I have nothing but time to shift through memories and moments that feel like a knife to the chest with every flash while I sit here and wait for whatever comes next.

Family dinners with Beth and Sawyer that end in stomachaches from laughter and a movie on the couch.

Late nights under the stars with Daisy, sharing secrets and stories neither of us would have had the courage to voice in the light of day.

It was simple, but it was everything.

And now it's gone.

The door clicks open, and I whip my head to see Beth Rivers enter. She looks fucking exhausted and she's standing here in sweatpants. Beth hates leaving the house in sweatpants.

"My boy, what did you do?" she asks. Her voice is filled with worry and confusion.

I've done nothing to earn her concern.

I try to stand and quickly remember the cuffs are attached to the metal table in front of me, jerking my body so I'm forced to sit back down.

"Have you talked to her? Is she okay?"

Beth seemingly ignores me, clicking her tongue at the marks the handcuffs are leaving, brushing what I'm assuming is dirt off the back of my shirt, and kissing the top of my head. She sits down at one of the two chairs on the other side of the table, and when she sighs, her shoulders droop.

"I guess I shouldn't be surprised your first concern is Daisy. She's the why behind all of this, isn't she?"

"This isn't her fault," I snap.

"No, my boy. I'm sorry, that's not at all what I meant," Beth assures me gently, a lot more gently than I deserve. "But between the look on your face right now and the sobs the rest of us heard coming out of her when you were driven away...I don't think they're unrelated."

"They're not," I mutter.

"I'll give it to you straight, August. Mark sent me in here to get your side of the story. He's a smart man, guessing you wouldn't be willing to talk to anyone else."

I grunt to acknowledge she's at least mostly right.

"I need you to tell me what happened. Word for word. Anything that can help me help you. Please."

I offer nothing, focusing on a speck of paint on the wall behind Beth.

"August," Beth sighs. "You got away from him. You had everything under control. I can't believe you would decide to throw your future away on that waste of a man for nothing. Not after all of the progress you've made."

"Maybe I did," I grumble.

Beth's smack on the table causes me to jump in my seat. "Don't lie to me."

I don't want to. It's one of the last things I want to do, but I made a promise to Daisy that I'd keep her secrets. I have no intention of breaking it.

Another painful exhale from Beth. "Okay. Let's work around the roadblock. I'm gonna do the talking, and you're gonna nod that thick head of yours, mmkay?"

I solemnly lift my head and do as Beth tells me.

"I know bits and pieces of Daisy's history. You do too?"

Nod. With how much time Daisy and I have spent together, it was impossible not to get an idea of what she's been through, even if she hasn't told me outright. I put the bits and pieces she did give me together some time ago.

"Was something of that regard brought up tonight?"

Minutes pass by and Beth never breaks eye contact with me. I finally dip my head in confirmation.

"I'm sorry," she whispers. "I'm sorry for it all. I think I already know the answer, but I gotta ask, are you willing to—"

"I'm not saying shit, Beth. Everything I needed to say, I did with my fists tonight. I appreciate you coming down here and trying to help me, but I'm a lost cause. I told you that the night Sawyer dragged me to your house."

"Tell me what I do and don't know again, August. Watch where that lands you. You might throw some deadly punches, physically and verbally, but I'm not scared of you. I love you, nothing will change that. So, drop this little woe is me act, sit up straight, and do as I fucking say."

My mouth falls open.

"Roy antagonized you. He baited you into a fight."

"That's not what happened," I try to correct.

"Shut up, Gus."

"Yes, ma'am."

"Roy bit off more than he could chew. Most importantly, he threw the first punch." She emphasizes the last five words pointedly.

"Why are you helping me with this?" I ask. My head is spinning, and it's sure as shit not from Roy punching me. He got one swing in, and if a bruise even forms, it'll be gone in a day or so.

Beth looks at me like I slapped her in the face.

"Because you're my family, August. I protect what's mine. Besides, Roy is very well aware of the damage he has caused over the years, and I will be reminding him of the same when I pay him a visit next. You might be content right now to rot in a jail cell, but I'm not having it."

The chair makes a scraping noise when she pushes back from the table and stands.

"Finish up your pity party, I'm going to handle this with Mark.

Despite the mess you made, and I know I'm not supposed to say this, so if you ever quote me, I'll deny it. But—I'm proud of you."

"You loved her then, and you love her now," present day Beth says, pulling me back to the here and now.

"I don't think I ever stopped," I admit.

"Me either, to be honest. You gave the whole enemy thing a real shot, I'll give ya that." She laughs.

"I thought she deserved better than what she had here. I still kind of think that." I shrug, crossing my arms over my chest.

"That's what love's all about, my boy. You want and hope for more for them. You know there's a chance they might leave searching for it. But you gotta give them your all and the best version of yourself while you have them. Because when it ends, you gotta make sure you did everything in your power to make the time spent together worth it."

While I'm letting Beth's words settle, she continues. "My Dale didn't leave me by choice. I think we all know that. But our time together here did come to an early end. Do you know what got me to accept that?"

"No, not really."

Beth doesn't talk about her late husband often. She's just recently started coming around to casually bringing up her daughter, Nora, Sawyer's mom, and Drew, his dad, in conversation. I think the loss of the love of her life might still be too painful. But maybe she's proving me wrong right now.

"All of the good we packed into the shortened amount of time our paths did cross. The big moments, like when we brought Nora into the world, and her wedding to Drew. Or the day we became grandparents. The small snippets, too. Like when Dale would wink at me across a crowded room, making me feel like we were teenagers smitten with each other all over again. I miss him every damn day. But even if I was given a book on our life, and it ended the same way it did, I wouldn't change a thing.

That's real love, August. I think you have that. Or you could, if you let yourself."

"I don't want to fuck it up."

"Well, you will," Beth counters with a smile. "Fuck-ups are inevitable in all areas of life. But they're not always irreversible. You have a strong woman who has always seen exactly who you are and accepted it. Maybe not kindly." Beth chuckles. "But acceptance without the demand for change, nonetheless. You have a baby on the way that needs the kind of unconditional love only you two can offer. Fight for them."

"I am. Hunter and Chase, too." I stand up straight, letting the after-effects of Beth's confidence in me seep into my bones. "But as much as I want to blow up, find her, and drag her back, I feel like I need to give her this space."

Maybe I don't believe in myself yet, but Beth does. I think she might have always believed in me. I've just been too stubborn to see it. I want to prove her right, not wrong.

"I agree with you, for what it's worth. Lock shit down here. Show her what she has to come home to when she's ready."

"Thanks, Beth."

She shimmies herself to the edge of the bench and stands. She pats her hand on my arm as she passes me to dispose of her cup in the sink. Beth remains silent until she reaches the front door and puts her jacket on.

"I love you, August. Love yourself enough to let everyone see what I see."

CHAPTER 35: AUGUST - I FELT A BABY KICK, AND IT WAS WEIRD AS HELL: A MEMOIR BY GUS

Three weeks later

"She's not coming." Sawyer's voice echoes from behind me.

I heave a sigh, leaning into the brick wall on the side of the building. I had a feeling Daisy wouldn't be back yet. But I held onto the smallest inkling of hope that she'd make an appearance for Margot's baby shower.

It's a small party for our little group in the café. The get-together has been great, but I think everyone feels the Daisy-sized hole in everything we do while she's not here.

"I'm sorry," Sawyer adds, bumping his shoulder into mine when he joins me.

"For what?" I huff. "You didn't blow up my future. I did."

"You're right. But you're wrong too."

I cock my head in his direction. "Wanna elaborate on that?"

"I promised Gran this wouldn't end with broken noses."

"Shitty thing to do, y'know. Make a promise you can't keep."

Sawyer snorts when he hears the humor in my voice, and for

the first time in a long fucking while, I feel like I have my best friend on my side again.

"What the fuck's been going on with us?" he asks after we collect ourselves.

"You're excused, having a fiancée and two kids on the way and all that. I've just been an asshole like usual."

"You have a kid on the way now, too. Remember? And she might not be your fiancée, but you have Daisy."

"Do I?" I laugh. "Doesn't feel like I've ever had her."

"I think you have the whole time. You both just pretend otherwise."

I don't respond, mostly because I'm not sure what to say.

The fact of the matter is, I've realized I was pretending for just about the entire time I've known Daisy Stiles. And when it finally came time to take off the mask, I botched it. I don't really think I deserve more than what I have right now. I'm working on it though.

I have a bed with the left side still made, one of my old T-shirts sitting on top of the comforter waiting for Daisy to throw it on to sleep in. The passenger side of the bench in my truck remains unoccupied, hoping for my girl to prop her socked feet up and sing along to the radio. And there's the ultrasound, the only proof I have of the one good thing I had a hand in creating.

I took some time off riverside work for the first time since I started to get things around the house in order. Beth helped me build a tentative bridge with Daisy's grandmother for the boys, both of us making sure we weren't crossing any lines Daisy wouldn't have been comfortable with. Basically, we explained to Marjorie that things at home have been rocky for the twins, and they're taking an unconventional break from their parents.

With the way she reacted, I have a hard time believing she didn't have an inkling as to what might have been happening behind closed doors. I'm trying to not hold a grudge against the woman for turning a blind eye. She's a great lady. I just find myself protective over Daisy, Hunter, and Chase.

After nailing down a routine and schedule that worked for all parties involved, I realized our living situation was also going to need some work. With my house only being a two-bedroom, my party of one growing to five in the blink of an eye forced me to get creative. I looked to my unfinished basement and committed to the project of giving Hunter and Chase a place to call their own. I built out the framework and set up the drywall in record time, and both of the boys helped me paint after school and on the weekends.

Not to toot my own horn or anything, but it's basically a teenage boy's dream down there now, with the LED lights and gaming systems set up. I found a small couch and coffee table to set up too, along with two full-sized beds.

The spare room is now free to become…Well, it's becoming a nursery. Even if I still have a hard time wrapping my head around it.

I might be making moves here in town based on the off chance Daisy decides she wants to make a home here with me. But I'm not in the business of getting my hopes up yet. I'm focusing on what I can control, right here and right now.

At least, that's the mantra my new therapist Sue ends each of our sessions with.

Because yeah, I'm seeing a therapist.

And maybe she's even helping me.

Okay, she's definitely helping me.

"I'm sorry for being a dick. I could have been there for you more, and I wasn't."

I hang my head. "Sawyer, I mean it. You really don't need to apologize. You were a grumpy sonofabitch before Margot. I'm used to it, in case you forgot."

"So, we're cool?" If you didn't know Sawyer Hale the way I do, you wouldn't pick up on the nerves quietly laced in his words. But the guy's not *like* a brother to me, he is my brother.

"Always, brother. Always." I pull him in for a hug. Sawyer pounds my back with a fist, and I do the same to him.

"How are things with the boys?" Sawyer asks once we're done with our moment.

"We're doing good. They miss Daze, obviously. But that's what the phones are for. They keep in touch, and she lets them know she'll be back soon. Well, Hunter does the talking. We haven't told her about Chase yet."

"She talking to you at all?"

I shake my head. "Nah. I haven't put her in that position. She needs space. I'm happy to give it to her while handling this. As long as she talks to them, her grandmother, and Beth, I'm good with it."

"And how are you doing with the uh, you know..." Sawyer trails off.

"My impending fatherhood?" I suggest with a laugh.

"Yeah," he exhales. "Sorry, is it still a touchy subject?"

"No. I mean, am I still scared shitless? Yep. And I still don't really know a lot. But, and please don't shut me down right now, I kind of have a thing going, I feel like I can do this."

"You can," Sawyer assures me without further thought. "That was never a question, Gus. You're the figure-it-out guy. You're the fixer. Sometimes you just need a kick in the ass."

"Felt that—hard. But hey. My gift is for both of you, obviously. But I kind of wanted you to see it first. Walk around back with me?"

Sawyer follows me down the alley to the back of the buildings on Main Street where my truck is parked. Sawyer's childhood rocking chair I refinished is sitting in the bed with two pink bows tied on top.

"Gus," Sawyer exhales. "Holy shit."

I hoist the chair out of the truck, placing it on the ground in between us.

"There wasn't too much damage when I found it, but I still took it apart and reinforced everything. So, it's nice and sturdy for the late nights. I guess I could have asked you or Margot about a color preference, but all of the pictures I looked at online had this kind of stain and—"

"Gus Burton, you motherfucker," Sawyer says, shaking his head.

"You hate it," I guess. Shit.

"You're dumb as rocks sometimes, you know that, right? Because this—" Sawyer grabs the backrest of the chair. "This is priceless, Gus. You gave me back a piece of my parents. Thank you." Sawyer pulls me back in for a hug without warning.

A wave of relief washes over me. Maybe it's embarrassing how much it means to me to have Sawyer's approval, but I don't care. He's the first person in this world who picked me as his family, unconditionally. He's always wanted better for me with nothing in return. Pushing that kind of bond away isn't an option.

"Yeah, yeah," I choke out, patting him on the back. "You think Margot's gonna like it?"

"This might be your ticket to early forgiveness." He laughs, picking the chair up and tucking it under one arm.

We both re-enter the café through the back door, and when Margot spots what Sawyer's holding, her hands fly to cover her mouth and the room collectively gasps. Sawyer places the rocking chair down in front of us.

"Oh." A strangled sob leaves Beth's mouth, and Melanie reaches out to grab her hand.

I clear my throat. "Happy baby shower? Is that something you're supposed to say?"

No one answers me, so I keep going.

"Anyway, I guess I'm doing a speech. Cool. That's cool." I put my hand on the backrest for something to lean on. "Umm, well, I found this old rocking chair in the attic of my house when I first moved in. Didn't think much of it at the time, but it felt like something worth holding onto and saving. Kind of like another thing—or person—in my life. But you know what? This isn't about me. When Sawyer and Margot told us they were having twins, this chair was the first thing that popped into my head. I knew it had to mean something."

I look around the room to see everyone is focused on me with rapt attention, like I'm a storyteller or some shit. It's fucking terrifying, but I started this. I gotta see it through.

"And sure enough, when I pulled it down from the attic a couple days after the blueberry festival, I found an engraving on the back." I turn the chair around to face the crowd.

I point to the hand carved words etched into the wood.

Sawyer Fern 08.08

"Obviously we don't know when the two newest little girlies will be joining us, but I thought it'd be nice to add their names and birthday whenever they're born. So it's a two-part gift, and the second half is coming. As soon as you get to birthing, Margot." I finish the most long-winded speech known to fucking man (at least to me) with a chuckle and hope to all that's holy or whatever that Margot doesn't punch me in the face like I've been scared of for weeks.

"Hand! Someone give me a hand!" Margot yells while flailing her arms trying to extract herself from the big chair they propped her up in. Sawyer and Red race towards her at the same time and both offer her a hand so she can stand.

Her run is more of a fast-paced waddle across the café, and I clear the remaining feet with a few steps to meet her in the middle. I bend over, enveloping Margot's tiny body with my own as she struggles to wrap her arms around me with her pregnant bump getting in the way.

"Well, I sure as shit can't be mad at you after that," Margot sobs into my shirt.

"That was kind of the whole plan," I admit.

Margot sniffles and pulls back to look up at me. "I'm not apologizing for protecting Daisy. She's family just as much as you are—"

"I know."

"But I *am* sorry you've been hurting," Margot finishes. "I never want that. But things are gonna get better, yeah?"

I practically jump back when I feel something poke into me near my belly button.

"*Oh!*" Margot grabs hold of my wrist, pressing my palm into her stomach. "They're saying hi," she says in a soft voice.

I'm pretty sure my eyes bulge out of my head when the movement happens again.

"That's Drea," Margot tells me. "She's the feisty one."

Oh my God. The babies are moving in there.

"How can you tell?" I ask.

Margot shifts my hand higher, and I feel what I can only assume is another...kick? "That's Nora. She sits higher, and she's generally a lot more chill than her sister."

There are real life human beings growing in Margot's stomach right now, and I can feel them. They have personalities. And like, fingernails.

Daisy has a real life human being growing in her stomach right now. Our human being.

I've said it no less than five hundred times, and I'll probably say it another five hundred more. I miss Daisy more than anything on this planet, and at this moment right now, I'd do anything to be with her.

"Gus?" Margot whispers. I don't know how long I've been standing here with my hand on my best friend's fiancée's belly in a room full of people. But it's probably been long enough where this is considered out of the norm.

"Mhm?" I don't look up.
"I think it's time to bring Daisy home."

CHAPTER 36: DAISY - LONG STORY SHORT

I don't love August Burton.

I've repeated this sentence to myself over and over, too many times to count, in the mirror and not, over the course of the last month.

I can't love him.

But I do.

I've loved him ever since that first day I laid eyes on him.

I was his, and he was mine. That was that.

And I fought like hell for so long to undo it.

But the weaver in the sky did her very best work the day we found each other. She made sure the end of my string found his and tied them together in a knot so tight she knew we'd never be able to fully untangle it.

I place my hand on the lower part of my stomach. While I logically know I won't be able to feel anything happening in there for another several weeks, it brings me peace to know there's a bundle of cells the size of a small lime in there that's made up of me and August.

I hope Gus finds that same sense of peace, if he hasn't already.

Some might say running away was a bitch move, and honestly, I get it. But I needed time to sort through everything, on my terms. I needed to decide if I was going to forgive August, if I believed he was capable of learning and growing with me.

I needed to know for certain that I belonged in Merrymount. I wasted so much time picturing the grass being greener on the other side. And maybe it is. I could see myself here in New York. Or maybe some other big city like Orlando or Los Angeles. I could be happy elsewhere. I can see a life for myself and this baby in so many places.

But is that what I want?

No.

It feels good to know that for sure now.

And *August,* who let me walk away, knowing I might not come back. He somehow understood with almost zero explanation that I needed this. He took my brothers in without a second thought. He's been the lifeline I've always needed.

He doesn't know I've already forgiven him. And now that there's time and space between the memory of when he found out about the baby and now, I can't say I would have handled things any better if the roles were reversed and I was standing there in his shoes.

Old habits die screaming, and we have to relearn handling and tackling the messy stuff together, side by side. We did it before, and I know we can do it again. We've survived worse.

Because long story short, I love August Burton.

And I know he loves me too.

But shit, now I have to find him.

I blow through the small hotel room I've made a home in over the past few weeks, throwing every random article of clothing I can find into my suitcases. I collect makeup and hair products, shoving them into their travel bags. I discard all of the trash I've accumulated, and double-check all of the outlets and drawers for chargers and anything else I might have missed.

When I snatch my phone up, my fingers fly across the touch screen, typing out a frantic text to Red.

ME

Hi. I know I'm the worst. I'm sorry. I love you. Forgive me so we can skip to the part where I ask if you've talked to and/or seen August.

LITTLE RED RIDING HOE

well well well look what the cat dragged in - how're ya feeling my knocked up sister in christ? happy to hear you'll be gracing us with an appearance

ME

I'M FUCKING SERIOUS

LITTLE RED RIDING HOE

idc bitch, you're the one who ran off and acted like you didn't have a whole village to support you and then thought we'd be content with halfass postcard-esque updates

I'm about to hit call when another text chimes in.

MILLER CASWELL

Gwen's holding a grudge. Side effect of pregnancy. She'll get over it by the time you get home, but Gus is on his way to Manhattan. If you're *not* there, it might be best to break no contact and give him a heads up.

"What?" I scream.

August. He's on his way *here.*

But how? I haven't told a single person where I've been, and I turned off my location in fear someone would show up, trying to drag me back before I was ready. There's no way.

Do I call him? And say what? This isn't a conversation to be had over the phone, and once I hear August's voice, there's no telling what will fall out of my mouth.

My stomach grumbles, my little sidekick's not so gentle reminder that if I don't eat *something* at least every two hours, my body revolts.

"Okay, okay, let's get some food. Then we have to find your dad...Huh. That sounds funny. You have a dad. His name's August, and he's on his way here. To us. Can you believe that?" I muse to my temporary uterus inhabitant.

I swipe my jacket off the hook by the door and sling my tote bag over my shoulder before darting out into the hotel hallway, beginning my hunt for something to eat. By the time the elevator brings me to the ground floor, I've argued with myself seven different times about how to get ahold of August without actually...getting ahold of August. Nothing makes sense. I'm a basket case.

"Good afternoon, Ms. Stiles!" Sally, my favorite front desk attendant, greets me when I enter the lobby.

"Hi, Sal!" I call back.

Sally is fucking fantastic. I was obsessed with her as soon as I dragged my broken, pregnant self, along with most of my belongings into this small hole-in-the-wall hotel three weeks ago, and she insisted on helping me bring everything up to my room.

She's tall and lean, surely from her years of dance training, with the longest jet black hair, so dark that it's tinted blue. It's pin straight, and there's never a hair out of place. She's in her early thirties, working two jobs while trying to land her breakout role on Broadway. I could listen to her talk for hours with her slight accent I can't quite place, and she thinks it's the funniest thing to refuse to tell me how it came to be.

"I'm a hodge-podge of a person, Daisy. That's all there is to it," is what Sally said to me when I tried to ask her life story over Shirley Temples in the lobby bar after one of her shifts.

I don't know what got me to open up to her. Maybe it was the fact that she knew nothing about me or my family or what happened. But once I was semi-unpacked, I asked if she wanted to get something to eat, and she immediately agreed, telling me she knew the perfect place to go. I think she's been my version of Merrymount since I arrived in New York. We clicked instantly, and I know that saying goodbye to her won't be forever, but it'll be hard.

"You look frazzled, my dear," Sally assesses, putting her book down on the desk and pushing her reading glasses up to perch on her head.

"Bad news, good news. Which am I dishing first?" I ask.

Sally takes a second to ponder her response. She never uses umm's or ah's. She's extremely aware of every word that comes out of her mouth, and she has the patience to ensure it's exactly what she wants to say every time.

What a goddamn talent, I'll tell ya.

"Bad," she finally lands on. "Then heal me with the good."

"I'm going home."

The smile that breaks out across Sally's face almost knocks me down with its brightness.

"Daisy!" Sally rounds the corner of the front desk and holds out her arms, waiting for me to fall into them. I do almost instantly. Because just like August, Sally immediately knew—without words—my need to be held at arm's length (no pun intended) with physical affection.

"I'm so sad for me, but I'm so happy for you," Sally mumbles into the top of my head. "What changed?" she asks when we pull apart.

"August is on his way here. Well, not *here* here, seeing as he has no idea this is where I've been staying. And it's like some weird twist of fate, I swear, because I was planning on going to him anyway!"

"It's not weird or a twist, silly girl. I know I haven't had the pleasure of meeting August—*yet*," Sal adds with a pointed look.

"But this was always just a place for you to rest your head. He is your home."

"I don't suppose you're getting off work soon and could come grab a bite to eat with me?"

Sally's complete and total happiness for me dims only slightly.

"Sorry, I'm pulling a double today because I took two days off for auditions later this week. I need to make up the hours for rent. When are you leaving?"

"Great question. I have no clue. I need to find food, and then I need to find August. In that order, because I'm starving." My hand finds its way to my stomach when a perfectly timed grumble moves through.

"I think a hot dog and a park bench are calling your name."

My mouth waters at the mention of something so simple.

"Yep, you nailed it before I even had time to decide on what I wanted. I won't leave without saying goodbye, I promise. But, Sally, you've—" Shit. I'm already getting choked up. Pregnancy makes me a crier. I hate it. "You've made my time figuring everything out significantly better, and I don't think there will ever be a day I'm not thankful I found a friend in you."

"A friend in me always you will have, Daisy. One day I'll have more than mere hours off in between jobs, and I'll find my way out to that perfect little Merrymount you love so much. I expect the five star treatment when I arrive, too!" She laughs.

I pull her in for another hug and then slip out the revolving door into the harsh January cold. I'm thankful I can still button my coat as I make my way down the street to my favorite cart vendor a couple blocks ahead.

I take in the sights and sounds, knowing it's probably one of the last times I'll have this kind of moment to myself. I'm lost in my head, romanticizing this chaotic period of my life when out of the corner of my eye—

A hulking, brute of a man, standing taller than any of the heads around him on the busy Manhattan sidewalk. An insufferably sexy mustache. A beanie covering dark hair that I love to run my fingers through. Scuffed and worn work boots, one with the laces undone, like he was in a hurry to get here. Jeans that pull tight across thighs that could crush anything. A thin long sleeve shirt hides beautiful, swirling tattoos. He looks a little lost, and a lot confused.

But when his eyes find mine, everything clears.

CHAPTER 37: AUGUST - IS THIS SOME GRAND DECLARATION OF LOVE?

I'm cursing every higher being in the sky that could possibly exist, rethinking every half-ass plan I constructed, and questioning just about all of the decisions I've ever made that led me to pushing my way through millions of people in the fuck show that is New York City.

Again.

But then it all washes away when I see a flash of black curls abruptly stop in the middle of the busiest crosswalk I've found myself in. People crash into my shoulders. I hear muttered words of annoyance at the guy—me—blocking the flow of things. But none of it matters.

Because against all odds, even though it seems virtually impossible, Daisy Stiles, in a puffy yellow coat that I've never seen before, is standing in front of me. Too perfect to be true. But she is. This moment here is real.

"Hi."

"Hi," she greets me back, almost breathless.

"Get out of the *fucking way*," a pedestrian barks, shoulder checking me while blowing by.

"Shit, we should—" I start.

"Get out of the fucking way?" Daisy finishes with a smile on her face that almost knocks me on my ass. I watch fresh tears form on her lash line.

"Come here, darling." I hold out my arms, and when she crashes into them without a second thought, I realize I could be anywhere in the world, anywhere at all, and if I had Daisy in my arms like this, it would feel like home.

Daisy huddles into me as I lead us both out of the middle of the street. She directs me down a block, and then another until we're back in a place I actually recognize.

"I've come back here every day," Daisy tells me, gesturing to a bench in Central Park. I let her sit down, and only when she pats the seat next to her do I join her.

"Looking for your friend Bart?" I guess.

"How'd you know?" Daisy laughs while her eyes scan the area, surely still hoping to spot the pigeon.

God, that laugh. It's been so long since I've gotten to hear my favorite sound in the world.

"Because I know you, Daze. Always have."

"Is that how you knew I was in New York?"

I laugh, because it really is humorous to me that she thought that no matter where she ended up in the world, I wouldn't find her. I've been pulled in Daisy Stiles's direction for as far back as I want to remember.

"Can't explain it. I just had a feeling." I shrug. "Daisy, I just wanna say—"

"I forgive you, you know."

"You shouldn't," I admit.

"That's not your decision to make."

I lean towards Daisy, pressing my forehead to hers. I breathe in my favorite kind of flowers, wild and mine at the same time. Always.

There was never going to be a world where Daisy didn't pull me and I wouldn't be inexplicably drawn to her. We gave it a good fight, both of our stubborn asses prolonging the inevitable defeat. But giving in feels better than any win in the goddamn universe.

My worn hand cups her soft cheek. My thumb grazes where I know there's a cloud of pink that's darkening with every passing second. My pinky rests on the point of her neck where I feel her heart beating a million miles a minute. I finally open my eyes to a sea of blue ocean water, the kind that would shock your whole body upon contact.

Those eyes. Fuck.

"Don't." The word barely reaches a whisper. If my ears weren't somehow programmed to hear and recognize that voice anywhere, I'm not sure I would have caught it.

"Don't?" I breathe. I'm a man of my word. I won't take anything she's not willing to offer, but I'm begging. I'll get on my knees right now to show her how badly I need to kiss her.

I've never been so sure of anything in my fucking life. This is it. This is where things work out for me, for her, for *us*. We finally found ourselves on the same page of this never-ending book. I'm so close to tasting Daisy's lips, over a decade of waiting has built up to this moment.

But, maybe not. Actually, definitely not, seeing as how her single command has halted me.

The loss of her is immediate when she pulls her head away from mine. Some remaining dormant part of my heart cracks when I see the doubt plastered across that perfect face.

"I—" She closes her mouth. When she opens it again, no sound comes out. And then she clamps it shut again. I wait for Daisy to finally find that voice of hers again. "I don't want you to kiss me if you don't mean it. I meant it when I said I forgive you. But I don't want to give you that part of me if you're going to run away with it."

I shake my head in disbelief, giving myself a minute to pull my thoughts together before I say something stupid. Fucking this up isn't an option.

"Daisy." I roughly grab her, pulling her onto my lap to straddle me. Her body doesn't fight me in the least, molding to mine so naturally. Her arms snake around my neck and those dangerous eyes search my face for answers I haven't made clear enough. Yet. "I made a promise to you, and I broke it. Smashed it to pieces, actually. And I broke your heart, along with mine, probably in more ways than one. As much as I want to change that, I can't. I'll never be able to give you that first kiss you deserved all those years ago. But I want to be your last, if you'll have me."

"Is this some grand declaration of love?"

"I don't know what that's supposed to look like, if I'm being honest. But if you need me to stand here or get on my knees and tell you and anyone else who can hear that I promise to love you and this baby with everything I have in this heart that I thought died a long time ago, I'll do it. I'll beg to carry your tote bag around every day until my legs don't hold me up anymore. I'll vow to treat Hunter and Chase like my own, because I love them almost as much as I love you. I'll insist on putting your towel in the dryer every single time I hear the shower running, so it's warm when you get out. I'll coach soccer or man the camera for every dance recital. I'll fight you for the title of our kid's biggest fan in anything they do. I'm promising you everything, Daisy. Forever. And my everything might not be fancy or *grand* but—"

Lips pressing into mine cut off my train of thought. Daisy's lips.

Daisy Stiles is kissing me.

It starts off slow and curious. Unfamiliar territory for the both of us.

I take a second to catch up, and then I'm practically mauling her. I hold her as tight as I can while I take everything I've been missing all this time. She opens for me, and I glide my tongue across hers, desperate to learn and taste every bit of her. My ears are ringing, and my chest is heaving as I moan into her mouth.

She's a Sunday morning with raindrops pitter-pattering against the window and you have absolutely no where else to be.

The last first kiss. A promise is a fucking promise.

"August, oh my God, *August*," Daisy murmurs. Her palms frame my face. "That was…You…Did you practice that?" she asks, and I laugh.

"No, darling. That was all straight off the dome. Doesn't make it any less real, and it doesn't make me unsure in any way. We had time before and we wasted it. I don't—I can't do that anymore."

"You love me?"

My fingers tangle in the curls falling down her back. "I love you. Every damn inch. Love me back, Daze. Can you do that?"

She pinches my cheek. "I've tried for over ten years to pretend that what I felt for you was hate instead of love. I thought if I ever got too close to that flame, it'd burn me to ashes. And maybe if I gave in sooner, it would have. Maybe it was never time wasted, just time spent leading up to this moment, right here, right now. I. Love. You." A pause in between every word for a kiss.

"Oh, thank fuck," I say on an exhale, and Daisy giggles. "What's so funny, Daisy darling?"

"Your mustache tickles." I pull away from her face, but she drags me back to her. "No! I love it."

"I love you," I tell her again.

"You're going soft on me, Gussy."

I'm not gentle when I nip at her neck. She digs her nails into my back in answer. "Teasing me like that only gets me hard, Daze. You know that."

She grinds her hips into me, and I'm sure as shit she's feeling how *not* soft I am right now. God, I've missed her.

"I have to tell you something. It's my last secret," she says into the sensitive crook of my neck.

My world spins, but I don't get dizzy. I know that no matter what she admits right now, nothing will change. I love Daisy for everything she is, flaws and all. Because I know she loves me right fucking back in the same dark and twisted sort of way. I rub her arms up and down.

"Lemme hear it, Daze."

She leans back to be eye-level with me. "You never broke your promise," she says in a hushed tone. She closes her eyes. "That was…I've never been kissed. Until now. Until you."

"But…" I search her face for any hint of a joke I'm missing or a piece to the puzzle I lost somewhere along the way. This doesn't make sense. She hasn't—She couldn't.

"How?"

Those blue eyes slowly open back up for me, and I know to my bones she's giving me a truth in the form of an honor I'll carry for the rest of my life.

"Everything else was taken without my permission."

The blood in my veins turns to ice at the mention of her past. I've never wanted to single-handedly change anything more. But I keep my face neutral. Daisy isn't a victim. She's a survivor, and I'll treat her as such.

"This was my one thing that I got to keep and protect and hold onto. I got to be the one to give it away. I picked you, August. I picked you then, and I pick you now. I'm so fucking glad I waited."

She buries her face in my neck, and I hold her while quiet sobs wrack her body. She's not looking for a response, so I don't offer one, just a place for her to let everything out. I feel tears spilling out of my own eyes. It's a new feeling I'm still getting used to. I never want to let her go, and I wait until she's ready to pull back.

"I'm sorry for crying all over your shirt," she says after sniffling.

"Oh, this?" Without thinking, I reach my right arm over my shoulder and grab at the fabric on my back, swiftly pulling the long sleeve tee over my head, tossing it on the ground.

Passersby whoop around us.

Her palms run up and down my bare chest. Daisy traces a few of my tattoos and then her fingers grasp the hair there and starts kissing a trail all the way up my neck. I moan when her lips meet mine again. This is something I'm going to have a lot of fun and take my time getting used to.

"I take back my apology. I'm glad the shirt's gone," she says in between kisses.

We probably look ridiculous. I don't give a single fuck about any of the people around us. I don't care that it's definitely not warm enough to be without a shirt. The biggest city in the world and it feels like we're the only two who exist.

"Daisy?" I prompt.

"Yeah?"

"So, here's the thing. I didn't know how this was gonna go. You very well could have told me to go fuck myself, and I would have. But I didn't book a hotel in case I had to run back to Merrymount with my tail between my legs. So."

"I've been blowing through my savings staying in a hotel a couple blocks in that direction." She tilts her head. "But the truth is, I don't want to stay in the city another night. I want to go home. I'm sick of looking up at lights."

"Home?" I ask.

"Merrymount. Wherever you and the stars are. That's my home, August."

"Say less. Let's go pack your bags, baby. We're outta here."

"Oh, they're packed and sitting by the door. We're ready to go." Daisy's hand rests on her belly.

I place mine on top of hers, remembering how it felt to feel the twins move inside Margot, now knowing it's my baby inside Daisy.

"It's still pretty early," Daisy whispers. She remains quiet, probably trying to not freak me out.

"I'll feel kicks first from the inside. It hasn't happened yet." My eyes shoot up to meet hers with worry. "Totally normal!" she assures me.

"What have I missed?" I ask.

Daisy leans her head into my chest and I feel her laugh. "Not much, to be honest. A lot of me gagging, but not puking. That would give me some relief. She's not too keen on making things easy for me."

"*She?*" I croak. I'm holding back a wave of tears right now.

"Oh!" Daisy pulls back. "I—We don't know yet. I just…It's dumb, really. I'll be happy with either, obviously I just want them to be healthy and happy but…"

"You're hoping for a girl?" I question, letting a teardrop escape from my eye and slide down my face.

"Yes," she exhales while wiping the tear with her thumb. "I'd love a daughter, August. I can picture her and everything. A part of me wonders if it's intuition, or if I'm just crazy."

"You might be crazy, but you're never wrong. You're growing our daughter in there, Daze?" I press my forehead into hers again. I haven't moved my hand from hers, with no plans to do so.

She nods against me, tears spilling down both of our faces now. "I think so."

"Then I gotta get my girls home."

CHAPTER 38: DAISY - WHAT IS MY LIFE?

I roll the passenger window down, not caring how much the cold bites my face as I breathe in the fresh air of home when we pass the *Welcome to Merrymount* sign.

Gus and I decided to stay one more night in New York to soak up missed time with each other, really connect, and catch up.

I can't believe I've been gone almost a whole month, and it simultaneously feels like everything and nothing has changed in that period of time.

Saying goodbye to Sally was as hard as I had expected it to be, but my promise to see her soon wasn't empty. I'm no longer going to live my life on the outskirts like I had been for so long.

Plus, as much as August loves to bitch and moan about the city, I think he secretly loves it. I know we'll be back for more than one occasion.

Even though I didn't mention wanting to go this way, and there's surely a shorter way to the house, Gus takes us down Main Street. I have a big, goofy grin on my face when we pass George's Pizza, and we see him and his husband John working as a team behind their counter.

The pink and purple balloons flying around outside Red's remind me of the baby shower I missed yesterday, and that pang of sadness only deepens when we pass the flower shop. There's a piece of paper taped to the door that just says *Closed for now.*

Gus's hand squeezing my thigh pulls me out of my funk and I look at him.

"It's okay that it hurts. We'll get through it," he assures me. It's easy for me to believe him.

When we pull up to the house ten minutes later, I'm surprised to see Hunter, Chase, Beth, and Mel sitting on the porch. The empty parking spot where my car usually sits reminds me that at some point I'm going to need to retrieve it from the long-term parking at the train station. Whoops.

"I tried to tell them the welcome brigade wasn't necessary..." Gus groans.

I wrap my arms around his biceps and kiss the top of his shoulder. "No, it's okay. I love it."

The truck's barely in park when I sprint out of the passenger door, not apologizing as Gus tries to yell at me for not letting him open it. Hunter and Chase somehow know to barrel down the porch steps and both of their little bodies crash into me.

"Oh my God, I'm so sorry I was gone for so long. I'm never leaving you like that again," I say while kissing both of their heads and breathing them in.

"Daisy, it's okay. Gus has been taking care of us," Hunter tries to assure me with a chuckle to calm me down.

"Yeah, did you know he can cook?" Chase asks me.

Chase.

Asks.

Me.

I go still. I look from one twin to the other, trying to see if Hunter threw his voice or something to mess with me. Chase stands there, looking at me. Waiting for an answer?

Because Chase asked me a question.

"What was that?" I breathe.

"Did you know Gus can cook?" Chase repeats slowly with a sly smile on his face.

"Chase Anthony Stiles…did you? *What?*"

"God, Daisy, don't make him feel weird," Hunter mocks.

"She's gonna lose it when she gets inside," Chase whispers to Hunter at a level that makes it obvious he wanted me to hear.

I close my eyes and put my hands on my hips, trying to get my bearings on what I just came home to. My little brother is talking for the first time in two years, and he's razzing on me with his twin. While living with my…boyfriend? Baby daddy?

"What is my life?" I look up and ask the sky.

"Yours," Beth says while approaching us. "Your life is wholly yours now, Daisy."

"Beth," I choke and easily fall into her arms next.

Mel is on her heels, reaching around to rub my back.

"You came home, we're so proud of you."

"How're ya feeling, mama-to-be?" Beth asks while assessing me. "You been eating enough in that big city?"

"Yes," I assure her with confidence. "I feel great. Better than ever, actually."

"It's good to see your face." Beth kisses me on the cheek. "Well, Mel and I just needed to get eyes on ya. We'll be leaving you to your new digs. Get settled and all of that."

"Thank you," I whisper as I hug Beth one more time. "For taking care of me and my boys. All of them."

* * *

IT'S BEEN some time since Gus last threw wood on the fire out back, and the flames are starting to die down. Hunter and Chase went to bed at least an hour ago, but it doesn't seem like me or August are itching to leave our spot out here anytime soon.

"I dreamed about this," August says from where he lounges

under me, a hand lazily drawing patterns on the top of my thigh. I plopped myself down on his lap with a blanket when I came back from saying goodnight to the boys.

"Which part?" I ask, urging him to keep talking. The deep rumble of his voice soothes me in a way I'll never be able to articulate.

"You won't believe me if I tell you."

"I promise I will. Please, August," I beg.

I look up with pouty lips, and I'm immensely pleased when August dips his head to meet me in the middle for a kiss. It starts slow, our lips learning each other at a languid pace. The tip of August's tongue teases my bottom lip, and I sigh, opening for him to take over without a second thought.

My brain turns to mush, and I melt further into him when August's hand snakes to bury his fingers in the hair at the nape of my neck. He deepens the kiss, and I try to hold back a moan into his mouth with no success. It's not exactly a failure though when August practically growls back at me in answer.

I spent years wondering what it would feel like to kiss August Burton. If someone was to ever get ahold of my journal and read the pages and pages of entries dedicated to how badly I wanted to experience this very moment right now, I'd have to die of embarrassment.

But instead, I get to be held in August Burton's big tree-chopping arms, growing our surprise baby, and getting tickled by that sexy and timeless mustache while he kisses me to his heart's content.

To my heart's content too, because I think falling in love when we were teenagers molded our souls together in a way that I just know is permanent, despite our many attempts to slice at the tethers.

August finally pulls his face from mine, and we spend the next however many minutes staring at each other. The flames swish and flick in the deep pools of honey in his eyes. Warmth and the feeling of home ebb and flow throughout my body, locking in a sense of peace I don't think I could find anywhere else in the world, except August's embrace.

He blows out a breath. "Back in high school, I used to picture us sitting just like this one day. I used to hope for there to be a time where I could touch you freely, not needing to hide behind an excuse of swiping something off your face or being too close in small quarters. I've always been drawn to you, Daze. Hell, I even built this fireplace with the thought tucked away in the back of my mind. Not enough to hold out hope or anything like that, but it survived all these years."

"We survived all these years," I add.

"And as much as I want to bask in my version of a dream coming true," Gus starts, leaning forward and pressing a kiss to the side of my head. He tucks one arm under the backs of my knees, and positions the other against my back to lift me up in a cradle. "There's one more thing I gotta show you. Actually, two."

I giggle and kick my legs the entire time it takes Gus to cross the yard up to the house. He doesn't release me from his arms until we enter the kitchen. Still wrapped in the blanket, August sets me down so I'm sitting on top of the kitchen island.

"Close your eyes. Please," he adds with a soft flick on my nose when I stick my tongue out at him. I have a feeling we'll be this immature and playful and snarky to the end. I wouldn't want it any other way though.

"Fine," I concede with a teasing huff.

I hear August open a cabinet or two and the clicking of ceramic while I stay busy staring at the back of my eyelids, resisting the urge to peek.

"Okay, darling." Gus gently cups the side of my face, urging me to open my eyes. When I do, my jaw falls open with them.

Sitting on the counter in front of me on two white shelves with the most adorable scalloped design is the full, twenty-four piece set of the original spice village, the one I scoured every nook and cranny of the flea market for. The one that my mother smashed like it was nothing all those years ago. The one I was certain I told no one about.

I brace my palms on either side to jump down from the counter. I cross the two steps of space to pick up the first house I can get my hands on. I grab the little purple-roofed oregano and run my fingers over each groove. I inspect the little divot chipped on the peak of the turret with a smile, knowing this is the most perfectly imperfect, well-loved set.

"How? Where did you find this?" I whisper, not taking my eyes off each building, picking a different one up to admire every other second.

"I think the better question is where *didn't* I find them. I've been checking off each of these damn houses for years. The last one was a bitch to find. Thankfully I had a friend put tarragon aside so I could pick it up."

"Which friend?" I ask, finally meeting Gus's gaze. He's staring at me so intensely, it almost causes me to lose my balance.

"Carson. In New York," Gus sheepishly admits. "It was no coincidence we found his shop, Daze."

Oh. My. God.

"You're telling me you've been secretly rebuilding this collection for me for over ten years?"

"I'd have searched for another ten years too if it wasn't done."

"And then what?" I probe for more answers.

Gus shakes his head, the smile I gazed at by the fire hasn't faded even a little since. "I would have left them on your doorstep and never said a word about it."

"You read my journal," I guess.

He nods, not a drop of shame on his face. "When I wasn't busy trying to keep my hands to myself, my eyes might have strayed once or twice."

"August—"

"Daisy," Gus effectively cuts off my next words with his own as he grabs hold of my face. "I loved you then. I loved you when I hated you. And I love you even more now. I was serious yesterday, I'll do anything to show you that love. But before you blubber about some knick-knacks, can I show you what I'm proudest of?"

"I don't know if I can handle another surprise of this caliber," I joke.

"Too bad." Gus releases my face and intertwines his fingers with mine, pulling me towards the staircase.

I haven't even been back up there yet because Gus insisted on bringing all of my bags up by himself while Hunter and Chase showed me their new mega room in the basement, the room Gus built for them out of sheer determination and unconditional love.

Anticipation fills my belly when we reach the top landing. Gus stops us when we're standing in front of the closed spare bedroom door.

"Okay, this one comes with some caveats."

"Ooooh, so serious," I mock.

"Daze," Gus groans, and I realize he's actually nervous.

"Okay! Sorry! I'm ready." I square my shoulders and puff out a breath.

"Just know we can change anything you don't like."

It turns out I, in fact, am *not* ready for what lay beyond the door. When Gus turns the knob and the door swings open, I lose just about all ability to function.

The spare room with a bare bones bed and bureau I occupied the first night I stayed at August's ceased to exist.

A big rug in the shape of a rainbow lays over the hardwood floors in front of me. There's a white crib and a matching rocking chair with a blanket strewn across the back, crocheted with pastel pinks, blues, greens, and yellows. It's clearly handmade and all of the furniture looks perfectly second-hand. Speaking of yellow, the wall is freshly painted the lightest shade of buttercup. A dresser matching the chair is pushed against the wall opposite the crib.

There's a single gold eight-by-ten frame hung on the wall above the crib. I take a few tentative steps inside the room to get a closer look and confirm what I'm pretty positive is indeed what I'm actually seeing.

"Is that…" Tears blur my vision of an already low quality picture. One that I haven't seen in years, but there was never a need. It's been seared into my brain for over a decade now.

A young Daisy Stiles and August Burton, sitting side by side—a position you'd be hard-pressed to not find them in on most days of the week—against the wall of their high school on the day before their graduation. The happiness is practically radiating off them. His eyes are twinkling with hope of a bright future filled with fresh starts, and that girl is looking at him like he hung the goddamn moon and stars.

Gus's hands land on my hips, and he urges me forward.

"It's us, Daze. A version of us, at least. And I don't think a single one of our versions isn't important." He removes his hands, but before I can mourn the loss, wraps his arms around me until my back is flush with his front. "I want our kid to know it all. I want them to know we found each other in the middle of a mess, made a mess of our own, and then worked to clean it all up. Together."

"We're gonna tell our kid we were mortal enemies due to some serious miscommunication?" I jokingly offer while willing the tears to stay in my head. They don't listen, of course.

"No." Gus's laughter vibrates through his chest. "We're gonna show 'em." He releases me to walk over to the dresser. He opens the top drawer to pull out another frame. He holds it up, turning to me with a dangerous smile on his face.

I wordlessly accept the frame to inspect it.

"No fucking way," I whisper, pressing my fingertips to the glass. I bite my lip to keep myself from barking out a snort. It's a candid, surely taken by Margot last Thanksgiving. August and I aren't the focal point of the picture, but it's been zoomed in to showcase the fact that we're absolutely death glaring at each other with our arms crossed over our chests, seats turned in the opposite directions of one another. It's fucking ridiculous.

"August!" I practically cry. "We hate each other in this!" I toss the frame on top of the dresser.

"They say there's a fine line between love and hate…" August spins me around and securely lifts me up by my ass. I wrap my legs around his middle and angle my face, searching for a kiss.

"That sounds like something Beth would say." I giggle into him.

August walks out of the nursery and right into his—well, I guess now *our*—bedroom. He gently tosses me onto the bed, and I feel all of me bounce. August's body hovers over my own.

"There are things I want to do to you right now, Daisy darling. And those things require you to not utter Beth's, or anyone else's name, except mine."

"Oh."

"Just oh?" Gus plays with the hem of my hoodie. Technically it's his hoodie.

"I meant…" I drag out the word to stall. I don't even know why I'm stalling. Maybe the last twenty-four hours are catching up to me.

Gus's eyes soften and he caresses my cheek.

"Or we strip out of these clothes, because they reek of smoke, and we change into pajamas to go to bed. We can rain-check everything else."

"Wait, no! No." I snake my hands underneath his shirt, letting them roam across his skin, pulling him closer to me, scrambling to sway the direction Gus is trying to take this night in because he's reading me wrong. "I'm tired, but I'm also beyond fucking horny and seeing you go dad mode on a nursery I didn't think we'd get started on until well into this pregnancy has made me borderline feral. *Please,*" I plead. "Please fuck me, August."

"Oh." His body goes stiff.

"'Just oh?'" I repeat his taunting words back to him.

Gus tumbles our bodies and flips us until I'm straddling him.

"The rest of our lives are gonna be fun, aren't they?"

CHAPTER 39: DAISY - THE MERRYMOUNTAIN MAN

Five months later

I hear the ripping of fabric before I look down. Struggling to see over my growing bump, I find Gus shredding my panties to get them out of his way.

"Those were my favorite," I huff, rubbing the sleepiness out of my eyes.

"I'll buy you another pair. I need you. Please. Say yes and then shut up."

I look at August's messy bedhead and that perfectly rideable mustache, taunting me, begging me, and I forget what I wanted to argue about in the first place.

"Yes," I breathe, throwing my head back into the pillow.

August devours me, just like he starts most mornings. I have not one single complaint.

"Oh, baby, *yesss,*" I hiss as his tongue flicks my clit in a pattern he knows works me right the fuck up.

I try not to wriggle in his grasp, but it doesn't matter when I fail because his grip on my hips holds me in place. I'm at his mercy and honestly, it's one of my favorite places in the world to be.

"God, Daze, I could do this every day," he murmurs into my core.

"You do. You do it so well too, August. So fucking good for me." I grab hold of his hair with one hand, twisting one of my sensitive nipples with the other.

August's moans of satisfaction vibrate through my whole body.

My orgasm crashes through me like a tidal wave. It doesn't take me long to get there. The next thing I know, August's frame is hovering over me, and I'm tasting my release on his tongue as he tangles it with mine in a passionate kiss that feels like it should be reserved for homecomings, but it's just another Tuesday for us.

"I love you," he breathes into my mouth.

"I love *you*," I echo.

August falls onto the bed next to me and gently lifts my leg to accommodate for my ever changing body. When his hard cock lines up with my entrance, and he presses into me, it really does feel like coming home. It always does.

"Oh my God," I sigh.

"Never gets old," August says into my ear. His front presses into my back as he rocks into me from behind.

August's free hand never stops moving, roaming all over my body like a form of worship. Light touches and tight grasps have me coming undone all over again.

"You're fucking perfect," Gus muses in between kisses along my shoulder. My core tightens around his length.

"*Fuck*," he pants. "Squeezing me so tight, Daze."

"I'm gonna come again. Please, I'm right there. *Right—there—*" And I do, August spilling into me at the same time.

August's hand smoothes down the length of my arm until his hand captures mine, both of us breathing heavy. The early rays of light are already casting through the window, and the birds living in a nest on the branch that sometimes taps on our bedroom windows if the wind is strong are singing away.

Another kiss is planted on my temple, and then August is pulling himself out and up. I turn over on my back, and watch him take in the sight of me while I openly gawk at the vision of *him*.

He might have just been the one praising me for being perfect, but—and excuse me for this, truly—*holymotherfuckingshit*. Do you know what it feels like to have an incredibly possessive but patient listener of a man who looks like he could (and would) step in front of any danger for you? And he looks like *this?*

Faded black lines of American traditional tattoos cover most of August's torso. New ink sits right above his hip, my new favorite—a small bouquet of daisies and magnolias.

His eyes linger admiringly on the mess he made between my legs. If I wasn't due to give birth in just a few weeks, and August didn't have a vasectomy a month ago, I would be sure he was picturing knocking me up all over again.

The vasectomy was the right move for us. This baby is about to be the most loved little thing there's ever been, but I just know deep into my bones that she's supposed to be our only. Along with Hunter and Chase, of course.

I didn't want to go back on birth control after pregnancy, neither of us want Gus wearing a condom, and frankly, we both have too high of a sex drive to leave anything to chance.

All of this coupled with the fact that he was approved for the procedure faster than most first-time home buyers looking for a mortgage, and Gus was in and out, ice pack on his balls within fifteen damn minutes, it was an easy decision.

"Earth to August," I tease.

"Let me enjoy my view, woman." Gus leans back over the bed, leaving a soft kiss on my forehead. He then journeys down to my bump and plants a kiss there too. "Come on, up you go." Gus's hand snakes behind to my back, gently lifting me up, helping me ease into a sitting position.

"I know everyone says I'm gonna miss this, and maybe there are parts of pregnancy to reminisce fondly over, but needing help just to get out of bed in the morning is not one of those things," I huff.

Pregnancy is beautiful. Growing life is a miracle, yadda-yadda. But my body is not my own, and it hasn't been for quite some time now. I'm going crazy.

"I don't mind," Gus says, guiding me into our bathroom. He gets the shower running, and only when he tests the temperature to confirm it's both hot enough for me to enjoy it, and cool enough to not burn my skin, does he hold his hand out and step aside to let me enter.

August follows behind me, and we take turns washing each other. I love to soak up these slow, quiet mornings.

"Red and the baby are being discharged today. I want to stop by with flowers and a meal after I wrap up work," I inform August while we get ready for the day side by side in front of the bathroom mirror.

"Way ahead of you, darling." August bumps his hip into me. "Picking up the order from that Italian place Miller mentioned later, *and* a gift card."

"Wow, that was hot." I secure half of my hair up in a claw clip and pull a few pieces out in the front.

With a mouthful of toothpaste and the toothbrush dangling out, August shoots me one hell of a smile.

"Yeah?"

"Planning ahead to help take care of the people we love? Yeah, August, hot as fuck."

Gus spits in the sink, and I'll just go ahead and blame the pregnancy again for how hot and bothered that move makes me.

"You're doing too much. I think you forget you're the one giving birth next. Let me take at least some of the load off."

"You do plenty, babe." I attempt to stand on my toes, and Gus mercifully leans over so I can give him a quick peck on the cheek. "I love you for all of it."

"Daze? Gus?" Chase calls from the bottom of the stairs.

"Be down in a minute!" I yell.

Gus and I want to drive the boys to school, seeing as it's the last day before summer vacation. We thought we'd celebrate by stopping at Red's for bagels before dropping them off and heading to work. Normally they take the bus, but I've been big on new traditions ever since moving out of our parents' house.

While everything over the past few months has been the most unconventional fresh start, it's also somehow been exactly what all of us needed.

With Gus meeting with his therapist weekly, I decided to give Dr. Saltore a call to see if he was still practicing. Thankful to report he is, and I'm a regular bi-weekly patient now. We found a good children's therapist for Hunter and Chase, who agreed to monthly check-ins while we navigate everything.

My brave, incredible Chase is also doing exceptional with his occupational and speech therapy. The leaps and bounds he's made in such a short window of time is the most rewarding thing to witness. I've had to deal with some lingering guilt and anxiety surrounding the newly-discovered reason for him not talking for so long, but I'm managing. It's one of those "out of my control" things I'm working on.

After long nights of back-and-forth discussions, both with the boys and just the two of us, August and I came to the decision to talk to my grandmother. She knows *everything* now.

It was hard getting the truth out about my parents and my past, probably one of the hardest things I ever had to do. Watching my grandmother's heart break is something I wouldn't wish on many people. But it was necessary. As much as I love control and figuring everything out on my own, it would have been a disservice to Hunter and Chase (and myself) to continue living life the way I was.

The boys go to Gram's house at least twice a week, if not more. They love her, and she is not shy about how happy she is to have her grandchildren around. It's brought back a youthfulness to her eyes that is impossible to miss.

Co-guardian-grandparenting for the win?

"You know…" August's hands smooth over my bump from behind, and he leans in to whisper in my ear. "Hunter and Chase are heading to your grandmother's for the next two weeks. It'll just be me and you in this big house all alone."

Goosebumps rise along my neck as I tilt my head to the side to give him more access.

"Mhm," I mumble.

August licks a light trail up and then nips at my earlobe.

"You can make as much noise as you want. I can have you anywhere I want. The kitchen again?" One of his hands starts to roam south, teasing me. "Maybe the couch?" A finger starts to draw slow circles on top of my panties, right where my clit is, and I moan, leaning into August's chest with my back.

"We don't have *time*," I whine. The lethal combination of having a hot partner that knows you better than anyone mixed with pregnancy hormones has made me insatiable. Gus knows this and uses it to his advantage more often than not.

"But we will," Gus assures me with a final pinch on that sensitive spot that causes me to practically squeal.

* * *

RED'S IS a madhouse without the captain herself manning the ship.

Coupled with Margot still being out on maternity leave with Nora and Drea?

I'm just surprised the temporary team of Chris, Melanie, and the fresh-out-of-high-school girl Red found right before she went into labor hasn't blown the café up yet.

Shit. I cannot remember her name for the life of me, and she's standing right here in front of me with a look on her face that says—

"It's Becka," ~~fresh out of high school girl~~ Becka says with a friendly smirk.

"I knew that," I lie. *Fucking pregnancy brain.*

August appears behind me.

"She definitely didn't know that, but don't hold it against her." His hands land on my shoulders with a squeeze.

Becka giggles. "No offense taken. You are definitely preoccupied." As soon as the words are out of her lips, Hunter and Chase crash into the counter on each side of me.

"Hi, Becka!" they both greet the pretty cashier simultaneously. Now that Chase is talking, their identical, synced-up twinness is kind of terrifying.

"Hey, boys," Becka says, offering a wave. "Excited for the last day?"

"One more year of middle school, and then we're high schoolers, baby." Hunter fails at attempting a cool demeanor by pointing a finger gun at Becka. Everyone in the vicinity can tell he has a big crush, and while it's adorable, I'm cringing.

"Anywayyy." I palm my brother's face, lightheartedly pushing him away from the counter. "How are *you* enjoying your summer vacation?"

Becka waves her hand, gesturing to the busy and filled café. "What you see is what you get. I've been practically living here since graduation. I'm saving up as much as I can before the fall semester starts. But, it's awesome."

Chris swoops by behind Becka. "What's not to love? She gets to work with me." A classic, cheesy, overconfident Chris smile plasters across his face.

"And me!" Melanie adds from the espresso machine.

Becka rolls her eyes. "Well, Ms. LeClair is the shit. But I knew that before I started working here."

"Becka, my dear, I told you to please call me Melanie or Mel."

Becka leans across the counter with an exaggerated whisper, "Not happening, that's weird."

When spring rolled around, Merrymount High School just so happened to be in need of a new swim coach. Who better for the job than Melanie LeClair? It was a perfect fit instantly. The students love her, and she gets to do exactly what she loves while being near her family.

"Do you call your mom Mrs. Hayes?" Melanie asks.

Oh, that's right. Becka's mom is an English teacher at the high school.

This earns another eye roll from Becka.

"For one, Madison Hayes is not a mrs. She left my dad when her frontal lobe developed, and realized she played for the other team. And two, that's beside the point."

Mel aggressively coughs. "Oh. I'm sorry, I didn't—"

"She's gay and divorced, not dead." Becka cackles.

"Goddamn, Becs, you fit in here with no issues," Gus says, clearing his throat after a deep belly laugh.

Mel continues to look frazzled beyond belief and turns back around to finish the drinks she was prepping earlier.

We place our orders, pay with Becka, and then move aside to let new customers step up. Hunter and Chase find an empty booth to occupy, and Gus steers me in their direction with his hand on the small of my back.

Bagels are devoured, and Hunter and Chase take turns talking over one another while they plan out how they're spending the next two weeks by the beach with Gram. Gus keeps a hand firmly planted on my stomach to feel each time our daughter graces us with a kick. Or an elbow jab. Or a rogue hiccup. I love each and every form of movement she decides to give me. The proof of life is reassuring for an anal control freak like myself.

She's a little more chaotic than usual in there today, though.

When I check the time and see the boys definitely missed the first bell, we say quick goodbyes to everyone in the café and speed to the middle school. After dropping their tardy asses off at the front office, Gus and I pull up to the riverside to see the parking lot already almost completely full.

Tourist season is starting early this year, and not to toot my own horn or anything, but I might have a teensy bit of an idea as to what sprung it on.

Gus groans from the driver's seat of the new SUV we traded my car in for. While I'll always hold a special place in my heart for that old beater of a truck that's parked up next to the house, it doesn't fit the twins, and I'm sure as hell not bringing a newborn home in a truck with no backseat to rear face the car seat.

I try to stifle my giggles with no luck. "Oh, shit."

When Gus cuts the engine, he shoots me a scowl. "I know you get a kick out of this."

"I don't have the faintest idea of what you could possibly mean," I answer, avoiding eye contact by looking out the passenger window.

"Don't touch the fucking door," he grumbles and exits the SUV. When he rounds the vehicle to open my door, he juts his hand out for me to take. "I used to just show up, do my job, and retreat back to the quiet of my house. Now I'm dodging these piranhas like I'm a piece of meat."

Okay, so yeah. Maybe the uptick in customers has a demographic of early twenty-something-year-old women who might have a little parasocial crush on *the Merrymountain Man*, as they have so lovingly coined him online. And Beth and I are quite possibly using every bit of it to our advantage.

"Is it really so bad?"

With an arm draped around my shoulders, Gus pulls me into his side and kisses the top of my head as we walk towards the main cabin.

"Nah. Not when I get to see the look on their faces after I point in your direction to let them know who my baby mama is."

"I abhor that title," I say, scrunching up my nose in disgust.

"Marry me, then."

I come to a complete stop. "*What?*"

August removes his arm to step in front of me. He grabs my chin gently with his fingers, tilting my face up towards his.

"I love you."

"I love you, too," I breathe.

All six foot, five inches of August Burton sink down to one knee, right in the middle of the dirt parking lot, in front of at least twenty strangers and a hooping and hollering Beth.

"Marry me, Daisy. Grow old with me just like how we grew up together. Be my wife."

"But we—I mean—It's only been so many months and—"

I'm floundering. This isn't a part of the plan. Actually, there is no plan. We're building a life together with kids and a house and a business but…marriage? That's quite the commitment without a conversation.

"And what, Daze? There's no one else for me, never has been. And I'm pretty sure you feel the same way about me. I can't offer you the world, but I can give you our own little version of it here."

"Well, when you put it like that, you're not giving me much of a choice." I shake my head in disbelief, trying to will the tears back into my head even though they're already falling down my face.

"You always have a choice, Daisy darling. I'm just kneeling here, hoping you pick the one in my favor." The wink he offers me melts me dead on the spot.

And even though it's insane, even though I normally crave authority and routine and the expected rather than the unexpected, I'll throw it all to the wind every time for August.

"Yes, you big fucking oaf," I manage to choke out in between sobs.

Gus is on his feet, grabbing each side of my face with his hands and pulling me towards him in the next second. When our lips crash together, I grab hold of his forearms for purchase, and the rest of the world melts away.

All I know is that August is kissing me in a way I dreamed about as a teenager. And if teenage me could see us now?

Wowee. She'd need medical attention.

But when what I can only describe as a feeling of *gush* pulls me out of the love-filled trance the kiss with my newly titled fiancé had me in, I realize that I currently—*not teenage me*—might also need medical attention.

"Uh, August," I pant into his mouth.

"Daze…" Gus says with a shaky voice as he pulls his face from mine and opens his eyes.

"I think my water just broke."

"You think your water just broke," Gus repeats back to me in a robotic voice. *He* might be broken.

A lightning bolt of pain I probably wouldn't wish on my worst enemy slices through my lower back. I wince and jerk at the feeling.

"*Shit.*"

"Oookay," Gus calls out. He gives his head a few quick shakes. "We're doing this. Well, you're doing this. You're already fucking killing it, Daze. Let's get you to sit down for a minute." Gus tries to guide me over to the main building, but I'm rooted in place by another bolt.

"*Fucking Christ,*" I cry out. "No sitting." I think if I tried to bend my body in any way right now it would snap in half. Sitting is not an option.

"No sitting. Got it," Gus confirms with his hands on his hips now assessing me with nervous eyes.

Beth joins him in the next second.

"Oh, we're doing this early. That's okay. Everything is okay. Gus, go pull the car up, drive it on the grass."

"Great idea." Gus turns to walk away and then abruptly stops, turning back to head to me.

"I love you, you're doing amazing. I'll be right back. I'm not going anywhere."

"I know, August," I breathe when another contraction settles. "I love you. But we gotta go."

He sprints to the SUV, and Beth moves to stand in my line of vision.

"Well, shit. The bunch of you move quickly with everything you do. You're giving me whiplash. An engagement and a baby in the same day has to be a new record for us."

"Beth, I don't know what to do," I admit with a whine.

I'm every variation of scared. I thought I had more time. My due date isn't until next month, for fuck's sake. What the hell is she doing coming almost a whole month early? I'm not ready.

"You listen here, Daisy." Beth points a finger at me, and I focus on the movement to ground myself. "You listen to your body. You're the perfect person for this job, okay? You're her mother. You know best."

"But—"

"No buts. You are the strongest woman who has faced much scarier things than this. Childbirth? A cake walk. You know why?"

I shake my head.

"This part of it all ceases to matter the second you lay eyes on her. Think of that moment. Keep it on the forefront of your mind as you breathe through each contraction and push. Let August take care of *you* while you take care of *her*."

When Gus pulls the SUV up, the first thing I notice is the

sense of calm that has taken over his face. Everything about his demeanor is suddenly clear, steady, and strong.

My lifeline. My rock. My person.

I find smiling easy when I look at him.

"Let's go have a baby, baby."

CHAPTER 40: AUGUST - WOAH, BABY

"*P*ush, push, push!" Nurse Paula chants to Daisy while she holds up her right leg.

I'm in charge of the left leg. I swipe the sweat-drenched tendrils of Daisy's bangs out of her face while she continues to defy the odds, pushing through another brutal contraction.

"Daze, you're so close. She's almost here," I repeat for probably the hundredth time.

"She's…getting…on my nerves," Daisy pants, trying to regain control of her breathing. She falls back into the pillows.

"She's stubborn like her mama," I joke, pressing a kiss to her head.

We've been in this room going on eight hours now. Daisy has been, no surprise to me, an absolute fucking rockstar. Knowing that doesn't stop me from being in complete awe of her strength and who she is as a person though.

The doctor has come through a couple times to check her progress. While she's technically early, the baby won't be considered premature because today is the thirty-seventh week of pregnancy exactly. So as long as things look good once she's out, there won't be a need for the NICU.

Daisy refused an epidural even though she's apparently one of the one-in-four women who experience back labor. Contractions. Through your fucking back. It's intense.

The doctor—whose name has left me at the moment—lifts from her crouched position at the end of the bed. "Okay, Daisy. I need you to rally, can you do that?"

Daisy's facial features morph into a serious scowl, a game-day face if I've ever seen one.

"Absolutely."

"Good girl. These are the big ones. The deepest breaths you can muster and then push with everything you've got."

I'm a mere man standing in a room of absolutely legendary women, championing each other to bring actual life into the world. I watch the doctor dish out orders and Nurse Paula continue to cheer Daisy on.

I bring my face to the side of Daisy's after ensuring I have a good grip on her leg. I run my fingers through her hair.

"I love you. You're the strongest person I know. You're going to be the best mother on the fucking planet. I love you, Daze."

"This is it, Daisy! There's the head!"

It's a blur of chants and a guttural scream from Daisy as she heaves one last push.

All of the noise from a second ago gets sucked out of the room like it has a vacuum seal.

And then there's a cry.

The doctor holds up the smallest, crying baby with a head of thick, black hair. She's covered in, well—she's covered in a lot of I don't fucking know what. And she's attached to what I know is the umbilical cord, but it's blue. I really wasn't prepared for that.

I whip my head to Daisy, who's laying with her head back sobbing.

I realize I'm sobbing, too, when I press my lips to the side of her face.

I accept a pair of giant scissors being thrust at me and cut where the doctor is pointing, and then the baby is placed on Daisy's chest.

Burying my head in the crook of Daisy's neck, listening to the sound of our baby cry, I try to articulate the euphoria coursing through my body in this moment.

"Fucking hell, Daisy. I've never been so in love in my life. You did it. You gave us this. She's perfect. You're perfect. I'm—You're—"

"August," Daisy whispers with her eyes closed as the wails start to quiet.

"Yeah, darling?"

"Shh." With one hand on our daughter's back, she brings the other up to cup my face. She opens those bright blue eyes to look at me, the softest smile on her face. One of my favorite versions of home.

"This is nice."

She doesn't need to elaborate. To make a long story short... Everything we survived—the good, bad, messy, chaotic...All of it was worth it for this.

* * *

"I DON'T KNOW what to do," Daisy whines. "I mean, this is a big decision! We can't be expected to just like, *decide right now.*"

"I think we are, Daze," I laugh looking down at the birth certificate paperwork in our laps.

The hospital staff showed me mercy when we showed up, and they realized I was not fitting on the small couch they have in the rooms to normally provide to the birthing partners. I wasn't gonna say anything, I was fine to make do.

But I also didn't turn down the cot that arrived in our room after the baby was born. I slid that thing right up alongside Daisy's bed so we've been able to somewhat lay together while our daughter sleeps safely and soundly in the little clear bucket of a bassinet next to us.

Our daughter, the perfect and the most beautiful, Kit Magnolia was born in the early evening yesterday at 5:08 p.m. on June twelfth. Daisy is ecstatic that we're parents of a Gemini. I don't know what the fuck all that means, but I'm ecstatic right alongside her. Because Kit could be anything: a Gemini, gay, transgender, missing a limb, or growing another head, and I wouldn't care. She's everything.

While the rest of the world argues about their children's first and middle names, Daze and I nailed that portion of things before we left the hotel room in New York however many months ago.

It's that pesky, legally-required last name we're stuck on.

Daisy and I both have our own reasons why neither of our current surnames would ever be good enough for our daughter. And every single one of them is valid. That doesn't help us resolve the issue at hand though.

"Hyphenating isn't an option," Daisy says, tapping the paper with a pen.

"And combining them is still dumb, right?" I double-check.

"That would make her a Buriles or a Stirton. Not happening."

Paula—who is technically a labor and delivery nurse and doesn't need to be checking in on us in postpartum—sticks her head in our doorway.

"You two still going on about the last name?"

"It's impossible, Paula!" Daisy sighs loudly.

Daisy latched onto Paula the second we arrived at the hospital. Daisy saw her soft features and heard her calm voice, and it was an immediate connection. She's the plump and sweet variation of Beth.

"We'll figure it out, Daisy darling. We always do." I try to rub her thigh reassuringly.

Paula steps into the room, leaning against the wall with a quizzical look on her face.

"Hmm," she muses.

"Do you have an idea?" Daisy perks up. "It sounds like she has an idea," Daisy informs me, shaking my arm.

I sure as shit hope she does. We've been going at this for hours with no end in sight because we don't have a single viable option amongst everything we've thrown around.

"Where did the nickname come from?" Paula asks.

"What?" Daisy and I both question at the same time.

"Darling. Is it just a regular ole term of endearment?"

"He's been calling me Daisy darling for…God, I don't even know how long."

"And you two mentioned you're running off and getting married, right?"

Daisy giggles, and I pull her closer to me. We keep forgetting about my impromptu proposal yesterday before Kit decided it was time to make her appearance. I have no regrets, even if it wasn't some big to-do like Daisy probably could have had if she picked anyone else to shackle herself to. But she picked me. And it was classic Gus and Daisy behavior.

I bought a ring back when Daisy was still holed up in the city. It's been tucked away while I've been waiting for the right moment. I guess I didn't plan on the right moment being a time when I wasn't prepared in the slightest. But I looked at her, and I just knew.

I think I've always known.

"Damn straight," I confirm.

"You could be the Darlings," Paula suggests. "There's no rule that says you can't make your own family name. And with everything you've both been through, maybe this is your fresh start."

A fresh start? The last time I was offered one of those, I gained Sawyer and Beth. This feels just as pivotal.

Daisy laughs, but it dies pretty quickly.

"Wait," she says. "Paula, that's—"

"Daisy Darling," I quietly say. "August Darling. The Darlings," I test out.

"I…" Daisy pauses and slowly turns her head towards me. Hope blooms in those perfect blue eyes. "I kind of love it."

Without the need for further discussion, I pluck the pen from Daisy's hand and carefully write out each letter using my very best handwriting. That doesn't mean it's good, just legible.

Daisy leans in, pressing her head into mine, and we stare at the full, official name we picked for our daughter and family.

Kit Magnolia Darling

"Woah," I exhale.

"I'll leave the three of you be. Congrats, Darlings," Paula bids us farewell with a wink.

Kit stirs in the bassinet, and I'm picking her up to cradle in my arms in an instant. This little girl has me wrapped around her finger, and I don't mind in the slightest.

I look at her mom, the center of my fucking universe, just to soak her in with her pretty eyes, untamable hair, and filthy mouth.

There are probably a million and one reasons why I don't deserve this kind of happiness. But I'm trying my best to be the kind of man who earns Daisy and Kit and everyone else I love in Merrymount in my life.

I think I'm finally ready to close the chapter of my life that was dedicated to existing on the outskirts.

CHAPTER 41: DAISY & AUGUST - MERRYMOUNT'S ANNUAL BLUEBERRY FESTIVAL

Five years later

DAISY

"We're late!" I scream up the staircase to my husband and daughter who are taking far too long to pick out a friggin' hair bow. I pivot and walk towards the door leading down to the basement.

"We're late!" I repeat to my brothers who are wasting time doing *God knows what.*

Chaos. I knew today was going to be chaos. But did anyone believe me? No. Of fucking course not.

I recheck the big bag set by the front door, confirming we have everything for the day. Sunscreen? Check. Change of clothes for Kit? Got it. Snacks? Too many, don't care. Water? Bug spray? What am I missing?

"Mama! Mama!" Kit chants as she clobbers down the stairs. "Daddy said I can do the pony ride."

"Did he now?" When Kit reaches the first floor, I adjust the straps of her little striped dress with blueberries embroidered all over, a favorite hand-me-down from Penelope. I ruffle her black hair, adjusting some of the wilder pieces of her curls.

Our Kit Magnolia has my hair and eyes, her daddy's height, and our attitudes mixed together—a lethal combination, if I do say so myself.

"I said I'd have my hand on her the whole time, and I'd threaten Chris's life to keep his four-legged beasts in check while she rode," Gus clarifies while making his way to us from the second floor.

"That sounds more like my man." I lift up onto my tiptoes to kiss him, and he graciously meets me in the middle, like always.

Chris finally figured his shit out. No judgment, we all take our own time. Once Goldie was born, Red realized she was happy to take a step back from the café to focus on her and Penelope. And with Margot dividing her time between Nora and Drea and her photography business, she didn't want to take on more responsibility either. So, Chris quit cashiering at The Store to take on an assistant manager role at Red's.

Then one day about a year ago, Chris saw an ad in the paper for two Shetland ponies for sale.

I don't know who encouraged this plan, but Chris jumped on it. Turns out, he was saving almost every penny he made across all of his jobs to start his own business, he just didn't know what he wanted to do. Twelve months later, he owns two ponies, four bounce houses, a dozen old fashioned popcorn machines, and a photobooth all available to rent for parties and events.

The town hired him this year to run the entertainment portion of the Blueberry Festival. We're all trying to be supportive through the nerves. I'm holding my breath and not letting my daughter become some injury statistic among town fair pony rides.

Hunter and Chase, who both now tower over me, finally

grace us with their presence, slipping their sneakers on at the front door. "Hey," they greet us in unison.

Creepy twin telepathy.

"Uncle Chase," Kit says, pulling on Chase's arm. "Are you gonna ride a pony? Is Brenna gonna ride a pony?"

Chase blushes. Even though the boys are freshly graduated from high school, and I've given a very clear blessing for them to date whenever and whomever, he's still my sweet, shy Chase. His new girlfriend Brenna is a dream, and she absolutely adores Kit.

I know they say teenage love doesn't last, and maybe we're the exception to the rule—or we broke the rules and made up our own–but when I peer over at my husband, who's the same boy I loved at sixteen, and gently trace the black band tattooed around my left ring finger, I have to balk at the idea of the impossibility of it all not working out.

August got down on one knee *again* the day we came home from the hospital with Kit, presenting me with the most gorgeous aquamarine engagement ring. I said yes *again*, obviously. But I've never been one who likes the feeling of something constricting my hands. So my pretty ring sits on a chain around my neck. Gus booked us appointments to get matching ink with his tattoo artist Jessi once I was done breastfeeding to seal the marriage deal.

"Nah, Kitkat. We're too big for the pony. But we can do other stuff together."

"*Best day ever!*" Kit shrieks.

"And what about me?" Hunter asks Kit, a hint of jealousy in his voice.

The twins have been enamored with their niece since the day we brought her home. It's been the complete opposite of what I expected raising teenage boys alongside a baby girl would be—in the best way.

"Yeah, you can come too," Kit answers flippantly, adjusting the flower-shaped sunglasses on her face.

"Alright, time to pack it up. We'll meet you out there. Chase, make sure Kit's straps are good on her car seat for me. We just need to grab one more thing," Gus declares, holding the front door open. The kids file out of the house.

Next thing I know, I'm pressed against the wall, and August has his hand slipped underneath my dress while he starts to kiss, suck, and nip a path up the side of my neck.

"They just kept talking," he breathes into my skin.

"They do that a lot," I say, palming his cock through his shorts.

August kisses me frantically, and I meet him with equal need.

Nighttime is for the slow, drawn out foreplay and sex. Love-making, if you will.

Gus and I have a hard time waiting for the sun to go down most days, so quickies where we can fit them in work just fine for us.

When he plunges a finger inside of me, I gasp. It's an electric current shooting through my body.

"August, we don't have time. I don't want to have to change," I whine. But it's breathy and I know it's only going to drive him crazier.

"Who said anything about changing?" he growls.

His tongue tangles with mine while he fucks me with his fingers. It's fast and dirty as I try to quietly cry out. Thankfully each sound is muffled by August's lips claiming mine.

I greedily ride his hand, letting his praise build up my impending climax.

"So pretty when you're a mess like this, Mrs. Darling."

August's thrusts go shallow, and his thumb toys with my clit.

"Let me come, August. *Please. Please. Please.*"

"So *nice* when you want to come, *Mrs. Darling*," August teases. He mercifully concedes to my demands though, filling me up at a rapid pace.

"*Fuck*," I exhale and my orgasm crashes through me.

August removes his hand from underneath my dress and

brings his fingers to his lips. A shiver races down my spine when he sucks them in his mouth.

"You're foul," I pant, smoothing out my dress.

"I'm just a guy obsessed with his wife. What can I say?"

* * *

AUGUST

"Grabbed you a drink." Sawyer says, handing me a can of seltzer water and taking a seat on the blanket beside mine.

"Thanks," I say before cracking it open and taking a swig.

I haven't had a sip of alcohol in over five years, with no plans to start up again. I wasn't an alcoholic. I might have never become one either, but it was an easy thing to cut out to ensure Daisy always feels safe around me.

It also feels real fucking good to never wake up and nurse a hangover or have to wonder what I did the night before. I'm a better partner, father, and friend because of it.

And hot damn, do I love to be August fucking Darling. A good partner, father, and friend.

I don't know what to call our big, blended bunch, but we're all set up on the grassy hillside next to the high school waiting for the annual fireworks display. There's not really a day that goes by when we don't see one another, but this is one of our favorite traditions.

We wrangle all of the kids after a day of too much sugar and fun, and spend the night laughing and talking on laid-out blankets from everyone's houses with drinks and snacks we all coordinated bringing.

Red and Margot are cackling together, dishing out sparklers to Kit, Goldie, Nora, and Drea, the littles of our crew who we refer to as *The Quad*, seeing as how they were all born within three months of each other.

Miller is doing a less than stellar job of trying to inconspicuously keep an eye on Penelope who's on the brink of adolescence and sure as shit ready for space from her overprotective dad. I spot P's best friend Noah sitting beside her under an oak tree.

Hunter and Chase asked to watch the fireworks with their mom on the other side of the football field, but they'll meet up with us later.

Right after Kit's first birthday, Mary Jane showed up at our doorstep to tell us she left Ron, and she was in the process of finding a rehabilitation program to treat her addiction. They sold the flower shop. It's a dispensary now. Despite everything, she's made significant progress over the last several years. She's put in the effort and dedicated the time to really work through truckloads of trauma.

I can't say I'll ever like the woman. We still barely speak when we're in the same room. My loyalty is to Daisy, and I'll never be able to forgive and forget the way others might. But I'm glad to see her try for the sake of the kids.

Beth is doing what she does best: meddling. I find her down our row of blankets, third-wheeling Melanie and Madison Hayes, the high school English teacher who's most definitely Melanie's not-so-secret girlfriend.

It'll all come out in the wash eventually. It always does here in Merrymount.

Goddamn, the Blueberry Festival makes me nostalgic.

Now where the hell is my wife?

I scan the crowd, looking for my favorite head of black hair, just like I always do. My nerves start to prick at the back of my neck when I can't immediately spot her.

"You seen Daze?" I ask Sawyer.

Sawyer's eyes go wide.

"Daisy Darling?" This motherfucker is playing dumb.

"For fuck's sake." I push myself up and off the ground, pulling my phone out of my pocket. "Whatever she's up to, you're gonna clue me in now." I easily find her contact, press call, and put the phone to my ear.

Sawyer laughs. "I'm more scared of your wife, and she told me to keep my mouth shut. So that's exactly what I'm doing."

The call goes to voicemail.

Small soft hands reach around me from behind. I spin, and sure enough, there she is.

But…there's been an outfit change.

"Daze, what's going on?" I huff, lost in admiration at the short white frilly dress she's got on. It's somehow familiar, but I can't place the recognition.

"Shh," she whispers. "Follow me." She takes my hand in hers, trying to guide me away from this spot on the hill.

"But the fireworks?" I question, gesturing forward.

"We're not missing the fireworks, Gus," Daisy assures me a bit impatiently.

"Kitkat's good here! You kids have fun!" Sawyer calls as we walk away.

"If I ask you to close your eyes and let me lead the way, will you do it?" Daisy asks me.

"Yeah, darling. Always." I nod and let my vision go dark.

Daisy walks us through crowds of people, and I feel my boots hit pavement after a little bit. We finally come to a stop, and she tells me I can open my eyes.

We're standing in front of the brick wall of Merrymount High's gymnasium. One of our blankets from home is laid out on the ground, along with a picnic basket and a disposable camera.

"Surprise," Daisy whispers with both of her arms wrapped around one of mine. "I thought we could watch the fireworks from here."

"This is our spot," I say, pointing out the obvious. The memory of the day before graduation flashes across my mind. Things are so different now.

"One of them, yep," Daisy agrees.

I notice the mural on the wall next. It's been redone, that fresh paint smell still slightly lingers in the air. The piece is crazy good, better than whatever the hell the past students did before.

It's a map of Merrymount's landmarks and each one is labeled. I hold my hand up to rest my fingertips on the part of it that's dedicated to the riverside. The little painted sign reads:

Rivers' River: One Hale of a Darling Time

"What is this?" I breathe.

"Beth and I have been working on some updates at work. The name didn't really reflect everything we have going on anymore. It didn't showcase the two men who kind of make it all happen, y'know?"

"But…this is Sawyer's business. It's his family."

"You're not really still believing those lies, right, brother?" Sawyer's voice comes from my back.

I spin to see him, Margot, Miller, Red, Beth, Mel, and all of the kids staring at me with tears in their eyes.

Beth steps forward. "It's your business, too. It's your family, too, my boy. It always has been. I'm sorry we didn't make it official sooner."

"I don't have words," I say, shaking my head.

"How about, 'Wow, Chase killed that shit!'" Hunter suggests with a laugh, elbowing his brother who stands nervously to the side.

That gets me to turn back around to inspect the signature in the bottom right corner of the mural. Chase's chicken scratch is scrawled there. If there was any air left in my lungs, it dissipates.

"You did this?" I ask Chase directly.

He rolls his eyes. He still hates any amount of attention on him.

"It was my senior project."

"Fuck you guys," I choke out, wiping my eyes. Daisy latches onto me like a spider monkey, and I lift her up into my arms with ease. When Kit sprints over, I scoop her up just the same.

"I know we're all aware I'm not the speech guy," I start.

"Come one, Gussy! Speech!" Red yells.

The rest of the gang starts chanting *Speech!*, egging Red on. Jesus Christ, if we miss the fireworks for this, I'm gonna be pissed.

"Okay, okay. Like I said, this is not my thing. Daze and I got married at the courthouse to avoid this kind of fiasco, in case you all forgot."

"We didn't." Beth narrows her eyes.

"Still sorry about that." I nod. "Anyway, I love you all. I love the life I've been given the opportunity to build here in Merrymount. Sometimes it feels like we live in a place surrounded by magic. I know I've made mistakes, and I know I'll continue to make some more, but every day I wake up trying to be the best version of myself for you guys. So, to make a long story short, thank you. For well—just about everything."

"We love you more than anything, August Darling." Daisy smacks her lips on my cheek. "Forever."

Forever in this town with these people sure sounds like the very best place to be.

EPILOGUE: BETH - A FOUND LETTER ON DALE RIVERS'S TOMBSTONE

Dear Dale,

I miss you, honey. I miss you every day. I hope you've been taking good care of Nora and Drew up there. I promise I've been trying to hold the fort down here.

Although, I do need to admit that over the years our little family has grown so much I don't think I could wrangle this gang if I tried.

It's the big family we always wanted, Dale. I wish you were here to see it, but I'm happy to sit here and tell ya all about it. You don't really have a choice. I'm doing it either way.

Baby Sawyer isn't so much a baby anymore. He has a wife of his own now, Margot. You'd fucking love her. She's a little spitfire who keeps our grandson on his toes while they both chase our beautiful great-granddaughters around day in and day out.

Nora and Drea. Yep, named after them. I'm sure you're not surprised I wailed in the hospital room when I met them. I know in my heart you sent them here. Thank you.

We have a second grandson now too, August. He's a tough one, I'll tell ya. Broody and grumpy, and it took me quite a while to gain his full trust. But I couldn't imagine life without him. He's shaping up to take over the riverside with Sawyer. You'd be so proud.

He went off and had a baby with Mary Jane and Ronald Stiles's little girl, Daisy. And I know what you're thinking. That sounds like trouble. Our Daisy Darling is nothing like 'em. Thankful for that. And their baby girl, Kit, she's magnificent.

Remember little Red? Not so little anymore either and also with a family of her own. She had some shit to go through, but it all worked out in the end. Her husband, Miller, he's Margot's brother. They have two girls, Penelope and Goldie. Oh, and a cat. He's an asshole. You'd love him.

And I can't forget Margot's mom, Melanie. Dale, I promise I've kept my vows. My eyes have never strayed. No need when you know you've got your person waiting for eternity with you up in heaven. But Melanie LeClair is my soulmate. The universe must have known I needed someone like her to live out my days with.

I think she's my last case of meddling, given how I've seen her with the high school's English teacher, Madison. But that's a story for another day.

I love you. I miss you. I say it every day, but I can't wait till I see you again.

Keep my side of the bed warm for me up there.

-Beth

AUTHOR'S NOTE

I hope you notice I didn't type the end.

You'll see those two words at the end of *For The Hope of it All* and *Daylight*, because it felt like something I was supposed to do. All books have an ending, the end. It's the way the world works.

I couldn't bring myself to do it here. Merrymount was always intended to be three books. I saw Margot and Sawyer, Gwendolyn and Miller, and Daisy and August so clearly as my core couples. There wasn't room for more. I thought I'd move out of Merrymount without looking back, finding a new fictional small town to take up residence in. A nomad of an author traveling to cruise ships and cities and maybe even visiting the more magical types of places.

And I guess it's partially true. I do need to journey outside the town lines of Merrymount, much like Daisy did. But also following in Daisy Darling's footsteps, I'll never be able to stay away.

Seeds have been planted. The little moments that make you tilt your head, wondering if *maaaaybe?* Those are intentional.

So, we're saying goodbye for now. A see you later.

I hope until then you're cozy with rereads and bonus scenes I'll be sprinkling throughout various times. I hope you decide to follow along with new characters in new places in the new books I'll be writing. And most importantly, I hope you're always living for the hope of it all.

xo

ila

COMING SOON

Sail La Vie — 2026

ACKNOWLEDGMENTS

The population count of Merrymount grows with every book, and for that I am eternally grateful. Thank you so much, dear reader, for being here and taking a chance on me and my stories. I feel like the luckiest gal in the world to do this.

B—anywhere with you is my home. I love you with everything I am, till death and even after that.

HJ—My girl, my girl. You'll never know how inspiring it is to simply watch you grow and flourish. Being your mom is the honor of a lifetime.

Marissa, thank you never feels like enough. But I hope saying it five hundred million times puts a dent in things. It's a privilege to know you and work with you and love you.

Kim, I'm supposed to eloquently express my gratitude for you here. But I don't think anything I write will actually articulate the magnitude as to how deeply thankful I am that you actively choose to be by my side every day.

Jessi and Mads, you WAGs keep me laughing through life, even when things feel impossible. I'll never get over how lucky I am to be loved so big by you. You're the exception to the don't talk to strangers on the internet rule.

To my beta readers. You saw Gus and Daisy from the messy start and loved them regardless. Thank you, thank you!

All of the thanks to my mom and dad for supporting me through this journey. The shock on peoples' faces when I tell them my dad is always one of my earliest readers will forever be priceless. And thank you to my family and friends; my little brother, aunts, uncles, cousins, and IRL pals. I'm so lucky to have you all in my corner.

It will never be lost on me how kismet it was to move to Orlando the same year Jane opened up The New Romantic's brick and mortar. From meeting as strangers and dropping off 3 copies of FTHOIA in hopes just one would sell, to now feeling like family when I step into the store as a ~bestseller~. Thank you to the entire team—who I love dearly—for making a home for my stories.

Valentina, Amy, Fozi, and Nela—my weird little Orlando family. Thank you for the memes, hype, advice, and podcast level long voice notes.

Kay—thank you for holding my babies and guiding them through editing to make them shine in publishing.

To my Merrymount ARC readers. Whether you signed up to read FTHOIA before I put a single word out into the world, or you joined us for the conclusion here with Long Story Short, thank you.

Thank you, Taylor Swift. Your words are magic and make me feel safe and heard and understood.

Honey Lemon, gawd. I love ya. The books get written because you keep me sane. And while the feelings of unconditional love have not settled in yet for you with him, I have to thank your new little brother, Avocado Toast. You two are the kitties of my dreams.

THE SPICE GUIDE

ABOUT THE AUTHOR

Ila is a hopeless romantic who loves to write small town stories with found family, banter, happy endings, and a dash of spice.

Born and raised in Massachusetts—now calling sunny Orlando, FL home—an overly emotional pisces, she is a girl mom to the coolest kid ever, married to the boy she had a crush on in high school, and completely obsessed with her cats.

When she's not writing, you can find her and the family checking every Disney destination off their bucket list, speaking in song lyrics, binging early 2000s tv shows, reading books that make her cry, and sending ridiculously long voice memos to her friends.

Ila is so excited to be here with you.

Instagram: @authorilasikorski

Threads: @authorilasikorski

ALSO BY ILA SIKORSKI

Merrymount

For The Hope of it All

Daylight